"Speak now."

Brigid told her story. She had been engaged in following a line of inquiry ordered by the Magistrate Division. She had no idea the orders had not been sanctioned by Kane's superior officer.

Golden waves shimmered across the screen. The baron said, "I'm not sentencing you to death for these arbitrary reasons. Even if you are a Preservationist, that's not what brought you here before me."

"What did, then?"

"Knowledge," Baron Cobalt answered. "In this tortured period of humanity's existence on earth, knowledge beyond what's needed must also bring death."

Brigid said nothing. Frozen, she only stared at the shifting pattern of light on the screen.

"The course of execution is set by expedience and custom. You will die quickly and painlessly."

As if responding to an invisible cue, the door opened. The baron said, "The sentence is to be carried out forthwith."

JAMES AXLER

OUTLANDERS™

EXILE TO HELL

A GOLD EAGLE BOOK FROM
WORLDWIDE®

TORONTO • NEW YORK • LONDON
AMSTERDAM • PARIS • SYDNEY • HAMBURG
STOCKHOLM • ATHENS • TOKYO • MILAN
MADRID • WARSAW • BUDAPEST • AUCKLAND

To Melissa and Deirdre—
my favorite blue-eyed Celts

First edition June 1997
ISBN 0-373-63814-0

EXILE TO HELL

Printed in U.S.A.

"Go, bind your sons to exile
To serve your captives' need—
to wait in heavy harness
On fluttered folk and wild—
Your new-caught, sullen peoples,
Half-devil and half-child."
—Rudyard Kipling

"Pigs, geese and cattle,
First find out that they are owned.
Then find out the whyness of it."
—Charles Fort

Prologue

Once called the land of the free, in the aftermath of the Russian-American conflict in that end-of-the-world year 2001, it became the Deathlands. A shockscape of ruined nature, a hell on earth for the few huddled survivors. But life's raw drive made sure that enough endured, and that they carried on.

Even after a full century had passed since the skydark following the nukecaust that devastated the planet, the population was well below the vital level. Infant-mortality rates were staggeringly high, and outside the baronies, life in the Deathlands was cheap, brutal and short.

There were a few who thrived in this new environment. Tribes of American Indians believed the nukecaust was the purification of ancient prophecy, and they reclaimed their ancestral lands.

Others gained power and wealth, digging out Stockpiles, the surviving caches of tools, weapons and predark technology laid down by the government.

And then there were the hidden ones, shadowy, their existence only hinted at during the predark years and dismissed as hoaxes or the imaginings of conspiracy fever and paranoia.

Traces of their existence remained after skydark, but those few people who stumbled across them assumed they were the handiwork of whitecoats—the government scientists working on projects to safeguard America from the very holocaust that had consumed it.

Persisting over the course of postskydark generations,

strange stories, rumors, campfire tales circulated about bizarre places buried deep in the Deathlands.

Barbarism and anarchy lasted 150 years roughly, and then another change came over the irradiated wastelands.

The baronies united, and power spread outward from their fortified villes, a power enforced in the newly christened Outlands, where the exiles roamed, along with the rebels and all the unwanted—the very ruin of humanity's lifeblood. Black-armored Magistrates brought them a taste of the baron's power on punitive expeditions.

Technology made a mysterious and surprising comeback in the villes, along with law and order. It was a technology used to control and punish, and law and order was imposed to banish any vestige of freedom.

All for the people's own good, necessary penance for a better future. That is what Kane, born and bred a Magistrate, had been taught at his father's knee.

Chapter 1

Wings outspread, the Deathbirds swooped out of the setting sun and plunged into the hellzone.

The cliffs on either side of the three choppers were worse than sheer—they tilted crazily above the floor of Mesa Verde canyon, sloping inward, then outward. Crevices beneath the out-thrusting overhangs were in deep shadow and could conceal anything, even alarm devices.

Though the Deathbirds' approach trajectory was too low for a ground-based radar sweep to find them, Intel had indicated vid cameras and motion sensors were planted on any likely area where an aerial incursion might be attempted.

The vanes of the Deathbirds chopped the dry air. The engines and turbines were equipped with noise bafflers, so only the hiss of steel blades slicing through the sky was audible.

All three of the craft were sleek, compact and streamlined, painted a matte-finish, nonreflective black. The curving forward ports were tinted in smoky hues. The metal-sheathed stub wings carried thirty-two 57 mm unguided missiles, two full pods to a wing. Multibarreled .50-caliber miniguns protruded from chin turrets beneath the cockpits.

They flew in a delta formation, and the Deathbird occupying the forepoint of the V flooded the rock-strewn canyon floor with infrared light, the electronic eyes of the craft reaching out to their full five-mile limit. The signal-processing circuitry broadcast the view to monitors aboard all three aircraft.

Seated in the cockpit of the point bird, Kane gazed at

the computer-generated image of the landscape on the overhead tactical display. It was a harsh black-and-white view,
all colors and shadows washed out. Data scrolled down the
side of the screen, reviewing primary areas of interest beyond his line of vision. Each boulder, outcropping and
curve in the canyon showed in detail. A red square of light
suddenly appeared on the screen, superimposed over a
small, grid-enclosed area of the terrain. Simultaneously the
warning chime sounded.

"Registering an anomalous signature," Kane announced,
the voice-activated microphone at his throat transmitting his
words on the scrambled frequency to the crews of the other
Deathbirds. "Looks like part of the ground ahead is made
of plastic."

In the pilot's seat, Grant reached toward the fire-control
console. "Locking a Shrike."

"That's a big neg," snapped Salvo's voice through the
comm link. "We don't want to give Reeth forewarning."

Kane and Grant exchanged puzzled, irritated glances.
"With all due respect, sir," Kane said, trying to smooth
the tone of annoyance from his voice, "he must know
we're here."

"He doesn't know that *we* know," Salvo replied sharply.
"My order stands."

"Yes, sir." Kane's voice was neutral, but his lips were
tight.

He glanced again at Grant, and their eyes met in a silent,
wry acknowledgment of their opinion of the order and the
man who had issued it. Since all three Deathbirds were
communications linked, they couldn't voice their opinions.

They could make faces, though, and Grant's long, heavy-
jawed face momentarily twisted into an imitation of their
superior officer's standard expression—pursed, puritanical
and miserly. Kane smiled wryly in appreciation of the
mockery. He noticed Grant was sweating. Droplets of ten-
sion-induced perspiration reflected the lights of the control

console, causing them to sparkle against his ebony skin like stars in a black sky.

Kane realized he was sweating, too. He could feel the drops forming in the roots of his thick, dark hair, starting to slide down his high forehead from his hairline.

Grant and Kane hated forestalling preemptive action. Like all hard-contact Magistrates, they cursed the long hours of preparation for a mission, the seemingly endless briefings and strategy sessions that burned the details of the operation in their memories. The other four members of the hard-contact team, deployed in the two Deathbirds behind them, were finely honed enforcers, superbly conditioned by a constant regimen of merciless training and even more merciless experience.

But it was the minutes directly preceding a deep penetration into a hellzone that felt like a long chain of interlocking eternities. Those minutes were the hardest to endure. Though the streets and alleys and Pits of Cobaltville were sometimes dangerous, leaving the security of its walls was always a little unnerving. There had been no outward display of fear, or even false bravado about the mission—just a calm, self-confident and professional ease.

Banking the Deathbird slowly around a curve in the canyon wall, Grant kept one gauntleted hand near the fire-control board. The course was narrow, with little room for fancy evasive maneuvering if it was called for.

Kane kept his gray blue eyes fastened on the display monitor and the rapidly changing features of the terrain above, below and all around them. He intoned, "Coming up on the anomaly in thirty seconds—mark."

Grant nodded, glanced at the illuminated compass on the panel and made a three-degree course correction.

From ahead and below, a searchlight came on.

A white funnel of incandescence swept up and across the ramparts of the canyon walls. It struck the Deathbird and stayed there. Despite the tinted Plexiglas canopy, the light was momentarily blinding.

"Well, shit," Grant mumbled mildly, squinting and pulling back on the yoke.

The Deathbird rose swiftly, the rotor blades whining, churning to a blurred, hazy circle. Before Grant was able to correct for attitude, a fireball bloomed portside, barely two yards below the missile-fitted stub wing.

The craft shuddered from the rolling concussion. Kane felt the shock from the deck plates traveling up from his feet to the top of his head, only slightly absorbed by his body armor.

From the bottom of the canyon, a cylindrical tower rose, a hump of textured brown plastic falling away, popping up like a trapdoor, sand and pebbles cascading down.

The tower rotated, and the searchlight mounted on top of it swung up, following the Deathbird's sudden ascent. Protruding from four oblong slits on each side of the ten-foot-tall tower were multiple blaster barrels.

"What the flash-blasted hell?" Grant bellowed, angling the Deathbird away from the questing finger of light.

Kane stared with stunned disbelief at the image of the Vulcan-Phalanx gun housing on his tactical display. The rotating multibarreled weapons fired uranium-tipped explosive shells at 6600 rounds per minute. Only one shell had been fired, either as a feint or as a range-finding tactic.

The Vulcan-Phalanx system was a standard defense at Cobaltville and most of the other network of villes stretching across the length and breadth of the Outlands. The housings were automated, containing tracking and fire-control radars. Finding one of them in a Colorado hellzone was as unprecedented as finding a swamp-mutie in Baron Cobalt's bathtub.

Salvo's voice crashed over the trans-link: "Point Bird! Status!"

"Under fire," Kane responded smoothly. "A Vulcan-Phalanx turret."

No reply filtered over the link. Kane repeated the report and added, "Bird Three, do you copy?"

"Copy," snapped Salvo. His voice was full of strain and even anger. "Take evasive action. We're falling back."

"Complying," Kane replied. "Further orders?"

Once more there was a long, static-filled silence. Then Salvo said, "Point Bird. Take it out."

Grant's and Kane's eyes met briefly, and Grant nodded curtly, fingers tapping the keys to transfer the fire-control system to Kane's console.

The Deathbird began a slow, careful descent, following the canyon floor as it snaked its way between the cliff walls, sliding under the searchlight beam. The gun turret was less than a hundred yards ahead.

Flickering spear points of flame erupted from the slits of the housing. The Deathbird lurched sideways as a piece of the canyon wall exploded in a flaring shower of rock chips. The fragments rattled noisily against the fuselage.

Applying full throttle, Grant pulled into a steep climb, rising so swiftly and sharply that the craft appeared to be standing on its tail. The maneuver created a force equivalent to three times that of gravity, and both of them were slammed into the nylon webbing of their seats.

Grant referred to this maneuver as "peel up, pop down" and it was successful—the radar-controlled searchlight and miniguns couldn't react quickly enough to the abrupt change in the target's altitude and trajectory.

At the apex of the ascent, with the airspeed decreased to thirty knots, Grant pushed the yoke forward and nosed the Deathbird into a steep dive.

Kane swallowed, hoping to keep the contents of his stomach from rising into his throat. The cockpit resonated with the high-pitched whine of stressed engines and the slipstream of air sliding around them.

Struggling against the amplified G-force, Kane reached for the fire-control board. The craft dropped rapidly to an altitude of barely thirty feet while increasing its airspeed to a hundred and twenty knots. Grant leveled the craft off, and the Deathbird hurtled forward, skimming the rocky ground, leaving streams of grit swirling in its wake.

The searchlight was still tracking across the empty sky, swinging to and fro. The thudding hammer of the Vulcan-Phalanx guns continued, pulverizing the walls, starting miniature avalanches, punching the stony ramparts full of gaping cavities.

Kane knew that the few seconds' respite from the radar could be counted on the fingers of one hand. The tracking controls would reestablish their lock at any second. He worked the keyboard of the console, raising the mast-mounted sight over the main rotor assembly. On the display monitor, he adjusted the electronic cross hairs, superimposing them over the image of the gun turret.

He achieved target acquisition just as the cone of the white light dropped straight down out of the sky, washing the interior of the cockpit with a blinding blaze. He pressed a key.

Trailing a short, fluttering flame banner, a Shrike missile burst from the starboard stub wing. The three-foot-long projectile inscribed a fiery, down-plunging arc, like a lazy meteorite.

The Vulcan-Phalanx gun tower was swallowed by a billowing red-orange ball as the high-ex warhead, mixed with an incendiary agent, detonated precisely on target. The seachlight went out with the suddenness of a candle being extinguished. The thudding of the guns ceased abruptly as the delicate circuitry within the turret was smashed, scorched and melted. The roar of the explosion rolled down the canyon, bouncing back and forth off the ramparts.

Grant pulled the Deathbird into a climb and reduced the airspeed to a hover as Kane punched up a status display. The missile had struck at the base of the tower, leaving only a split-open stump of smoldering metal protruding from the ground.

"Target flash-blasted," Kane said calmly. "Zone secured."

"Copy that, Point Bird," came Salvo's reply. "Get dirt-side. We'll join you in a minute."

"Acknowledged."

The aircraft flew a few hundred feet beyond the shattered gun turret, and Grant settled its skids gently onto the ground. Before disembarking, both men methodically inspected their ordnance. Though they had double-checked each other before leaving Cobaltville, their training told them that Magistrates should never assume they were invincible.

Kane ran his gloved fingers over the joints of his black polycarbonate body armor, making certain all the seals were secure. The armor was close fitting, molded to conform to the biceps, triceps, pectorals and abdomen. Even with its Kevlar undersheathing, the armor was lightweight and provided no loose folds to snag on projections. The only spot of color anywhere on it was the small, disk-shaped badge of office emblazoned on the left pectoral. It depicted, in crimson, a stylized, balanced scales of justice, superimposed over a nine-spoked wheel.

Kane knew it was designed to symbolize the Magistrate's oath to keep the wheels of justice turning, but to his mind it was nothing more than a target. To chill-crazy blaster-men, all it said was, "Shoot here."

Raising his right forearm, he inspected the Sin Eater holstered there. It was a big-bore automatic handblaster, less than fourteen inches in length at full extension, the magazine carrying twenty 9 mm rounds. When not in use, the stock folded over the top of the blaster, lying along the frame, reducing its holstered length to ten inches.

When the Sin Eater was needed, Kane would tense his wrist tendons, and sensitive actuators activated a flexible cable in the holster and snapped the weapon smoothly into his waiting hand, the stock unfolding in the same motion. Since the Sin Eater had no trigger guard or safety, the blaster fired immediately upon touching his crooked index finger.

It was a murderous weapon and almost impossible for a novice to manage. Recruits were never allowed live ammunition until a tedious six-month-long training period was successfully completed.

Attached to his belt by a magnetic clip was his close-assault weapon. The Copperhead was a chopped-down autoblaster, gas operated, with a 700-round-per minute rate of fire. The magazine held fifteen rounds of 4.85 mm steel-jacketed bullets. Two feet in length, the grip and trigger unit were placed in front of the breech, allowing for one-handed use. An optical image-intensifier scope was fitted on top, as well as a laser autotargeter. Because of its low recoil, the Copperhead could be fired in a long, devastating full-auto burst.

Kane lowered his right hand to touch the familiar handle of the fourteen-inch-long combat knife scabbarded in his boot. Honed to a razor-keen cutting edge, it was also balanced for throwing, although only a fool would throw a knife in hand-to-hand combat. If a Magistrate was down to his blade, then tossing it made him weaponless and as good as dead.

From a hook on the back of his seat, Kane removed his helmet. Like the armor encasing his body, the helmet was made of black polycarbonate, and fitted over the upper half and back of his head, leaving only a portion of the mouth and chin exposed.

The helmet annoyed him, even though it was lightweight and its polystyrene lining conformed perfectly to the shape of his head, ensuring a snug and comfortable fit.

The slightly concave, red-tinted visor served several functions: it protected the eyes from foreign particles, and the electro-chemical polymer was connected to a passive night sight that intensified ambient light to permit one-color night vision.

The tiny image-enhancer sensor mounted on the forehead of the helmet did not emit detectable rays, though its range was only twenty-five feet, even on a fairly clear night with strong moonlight.

Kane slipped the helmet on just as Grant did, both of them snapping the underjaw lock guards simultaneously. Glancing at Grant, Kane realized again that the design of the Magistrate armor served something beyond functional, practical reasons. His partner was now a symbol of awe, of fear. He looked bigger somehow. Strong, fierce, implacable.

When a man concealed his face and body beneath the black armor and the red visor, he became a fearsome figure, the anonymity adding to the mystique. There was another reason for the helmet and the exoskeleton, and it was a reason all Magistrates were aware of but never spoke about openly. When a man put on the armor, he was symbolically surrendering his identity to serve a cause of greater import than a mere individual life.

Kane's father had chosen to smother his identity, as had his father before him. For that matter, all current Magistrates, the third generation, had exchanged personal hopes, dreams and desires for a life of service. It had been the only way to bring a degree of order to the anarchy of post-nukecaust America.

Removing the throat-mike hookup, Kane stepped out of the Deathbird, ducking his head beneath the vanes, striding through the dust devils the rotorwash had created. The other two choppers were alighting behind him, but not as expertly as Grant had maneuvered theirs.

The craft were not easy to control. Grant, who was rated the best Bird jockey in the Cobaltville Division, had experienced his fair share of close calls over the years. Though it wasn't common knowledge except among the handful of techs and mechanics, the Deathbirds were very old, dating back to the days right before skydark. They were modified AH-64 Apache attack gunships, and most of the fleet had been reengineered and retrofitted dozens of times.

For that matter, every piece of Magistrate hardware was based on predark designs and materials—the body armor was the same polycarbonate substance used by twentieth-century riot-control police officers, the Copperheads were SA80 submachine guns, issued in the 1980s, and the Sin Eaters were customized, reframed Spectre autoblasters.

Kane had never asked where all the ordnance had come from. He was familiar with enough postnukecaust history to know that Stockpiles, caches of material and technology, had been laid down by the predark government just in case of a national emergency. He also knew that many of the original barons had built their power bases with the Stockpiles, but all of that was a long time ago, nearly a century before the Program of Unification.

The rest of the hard-contact team tumbled out of the Deathbirds. Unlimbering their Copperheads, the six men fanned out in the standard deployment of firepower. They spread out with about twenty yards between them. Backlit by the burning Vulcan-Phalanx gun tower, they cast long shadows over the canyon walls and floor.

Carefully the squad worked its way forward. No one spoke over the helmet transceivers. They were all experienced fighters and needed no last-minute warnings or pep talks.

They searched the rocks for snipers, scanned the ground for trip wires or motion-activated blasters. They gripped their Copperheads in gloved hands, selectors switched to full-auto. All of them knew the remote uplands of the Colorado hellzones had claimed their fair share of Magistrates, so anything moving in the shadows would have been decimated by six streams of continuous fire.

"Where the fuck are they?" Pollard whispered over the helmet link. "They know we're here."

"Cut the backchat," snapped Salvo.

They moved on slowly through the canyon, every man watching the man ahead of him, glancing back at the one behind, peering into the dark depths at something that might have stirred, avoiding small mounds of sand that might conceal an antipersonnel mine.

Kane snatched a backward glance. The gun turret continued to belch plumes of dark smoke, curling and twisting into the sky, visible to anyone for miles around. He wondered where Reeth, a small-time slagger specializing in the smuggling of outlanders into the villes, had gotten his hands on such tech and firepower.

According to doctrine, all the Stockpiles had been discovered and secured decades ago, so it didn't seem reasonable the smuggler had stumbled across one overlooked in the program.

Salvo's voice rasped in his ear. "Halt."

Obediently the squad stopped.

Over the helmet link, he said tersely, "Kane. Take the point."

Kane had expected the order. For the past few years, he had always been assigned the position of pointman. He was never quite sure why, except that his superiors knew he was very good at it. When stealth was required, most men moved uncertainly, even clumsily in the armor, but Kane could be a silent, almost graceful wraith.

He had never led a contact team into an ambush and, in fact, had prevented an entire squad from being ambushed during a Pit sweep the year before. Kane no longer bothered to question why Salvo always chose him to be the advance scout. If he hadn't, he would have volunteered. When he acted as pointman, he felt electrically alive, sharply tuned to every nuance of what he was doing. Only when performing his duties as pointman did all doubts about his choices in life vanish, and he knew that this was the work he had been born to do.

Kane moved quickly, heel to toe, his image enhancer bringing into sharp relief everything around him. He moved instinctively from cover to cover, from shadow patch to shadow patch, automatically placing his feet so they raised a minimum of dust and didn't dislodge loose stones. He

studied places where sentries and blastermen might be lurk
ing.

Thunder boomed in the distance, accompanying a purpl
flash of heat lightning. A storm was approaching, bringin
not fresh, clean rain, but the acid-tainted rain of the hell
zones. His armor was treated to withstand exposure to tox
ins, but a shower of acid rain, even if only a drizzle, wasn'
something to take lightly. This region of Colorado had re
covered only minimally from the nukecaust, and its peculia
geothermals attracted chem storms. Almost all hellzone
did. Though fewer hellzones existed now compared to those
many decades when much of the entire continent was the
Deathlands, there were still a number of places where the
geological or meteorological effects of the nuking prevented a reasonable recovery.

The west coast of the United States was one such hellzone, where most of California was under water. The best
known zone was the long D.C.—New Jersey—New York
Corridor, a vast stretch of abandoned factory complexes,
warehouses and overgrown ruins. D.C., otherwise known
as Washington Hole, was still the most active hot spot in
the country. Fortunately this region of Colorado was only
warm, not hot, but it still attracted its share of chem storms.

Seven hundred yards past the Vulcan-Phalanx gun tower,
the canyon twisted in a curve, then cut straight south. It
yawned open into a wide, stony expanse, half encircled by
the overhanging rim of a cliff. Thousands of years had
eroded the rim down to a series of stairlike ridges.

Below the jutting ridges of rock was a vast, sprawling
complex of ruins—interlocked buildings of mud and stone,
abandoned, rebuilt, expanded and abandoned again over the
long track of time. Looming above an open courtyard was
a massive structure cut into the rock of the canyon, protected by the overhanging cliff shelf.

The Cliff Palace fortress was a monument to the highly
evolved Pueblo Indian culture many thousands of years
ago. According to the briefing, the ruins had fascinated pre-

dark archaeologists and tourists. Once, the complex had been a maze of hundreds of rooms, hundreds of kivas and a labyrinth of twisting passageways.

The last people to reign over the Cliff Palace were long, long dead. What remained was still grimly formidable. But the thick adobe walls had gaping holes, and many of the interior buildings were half-collapsed. Most of the structures were without roofs.

Kane felt a distant wonder that even a fraction of the Cliff Palace was still standing. The savage earthquakes birthed by the nukecaust hadn't dropped the sheltering cliff rim atop it, nor even shaken many of the ancient dwellings to their foundations. Acid rainstorms had bleached out much of the stonework but not seriously corroded it.

His lips quirked a mirthless smile. The holocaust had virtually vaporized cities barely a hundred years old, but had spared settlements that had watched inestimable centuries crawl by.

Creeping to a heap of broken shale, Kane hunkered down behind it. Ahead of him was a short open space, then a shallow drop into an old drainage ditch. The far bank of the ditch butted up against the base of the outer wall. It was a yard thick but barely seven feet tall.

A sentry walked the wall. He was only a hundred feet away, shouldering a sniper rifle. Though the light of the rising moon was uncertain, Kane identified it as a Dragunov SVD, outfitted with a telescopic sight. Though the blaster was old, it looked to be in pristine condition.

Salvo's voice was harsh in his ear. "Kane. Report."

Not daring even to speak, Kane used one finger to tap a brief coded signal into the microphone mounted in the helmet's jaw guard. The taps were transmitted back to the squad, telling them to hang back.

Salvo didn't speak again. One oversight or distraction on the part of the pointman could cost the lives of the entire team. The only reason Kane was alive and able to tap out a code signal was that he weighed all options before choosing one, and paused for a moment to reconsider before implementing any decision in a hellzone.

Carefully he drew the combat knife from its sheath. The heavy tungsten-steel blade was blued, muting all reflective highlights. Transferring the Copperhead to his left hand, Kane gripped the knife in his right, waiting and watching the sentry.

The man wasn't looking in his direction at the moment, but he would eventually. The pile of shale would conceal Kane as long as he remained motionless, but he had to cross that open space and get into the ditch if he wanted to take the sentry down without blasterfire.

The sentry turned in Kane's direction, his eyes shifting slowly past the heap of broken rock and sweeping beyond it. He turned to look in another direction. Like a coiled spring, Kane rushed from around the rock pile, crossed the open space and down into the shadows of the ditch.

It was only four feet deep, and he went down flat on the bottom of it. He belly-crawled forward, along the base of the wall. When the sentry started to turn in his direction again, he froze. He had learned long ago that at a distance, especially at night, what did not move merged into the terrain. The sentry's eyes passed over him again. The man was looking for invaders in obvious hiding places, not in places with no apparent concealment within spitting distance of his position.

The sentry turned away again, and Kane rose from the depression and climbed up the opposite bank. His back pressed against the wall, he slid carefully along until he was directly beneath the sentry. He waited in the night shadows until he heard the grate of shoe leather against stone, then his left arm snapped up, slapping the barrel of the Copperhead against the man's ankles.

In midstep, the sentry stumbled and lost his balance as his legs entangled. He fell right into Kane's waiting arms. The rifle clattered and slid into the ditch. The man groped for it, but he didn't have time to reach it or cry out before

Kane pressed the barrel of the Copperhead against his throat.

His polycarbonate-shod knee slammed into the small of the sentry's back and arched him forward against the pressure of the blaster barrel. The point of the razor-keen, double-edged knife in Kane's right fist plunged between two ribs, sinking deep.

Kane maintained the pressure on the knife. The man clawed at the barrel of the Copperhead. From writhing lips, he husked out three half-gagged words, "Sec man! Sec!"

The sentry's body convulsed briefly, then went limp, and Kane slowly lowered the deadweight to the ground, pulling the knife free. Gingerly, with the metal-reinforced toe of a boot, Kane prodded the man over onto his back. Blood, black in the wavering light of the night sight, flowed over the edge of the ditch. The man was scrawny, sharp featured, lank of hair and limb. His hands were callused, the fingers blunt and short nailed. He looked around forty years of age, which probably made him closer to twenty-five.

All in all, he looked like typical outlander trash. His use of the archaic "sec man" label marked his origins in the wild hinterlands beyond the villes. Only people raised far from the influence of the secure cities still applied that obsolete term to the Magistrates.

Kane started to push the body down into the ditch, then he froze and leaned forward, staring at the outlander's face. His hair covered a transceiver plug in his right ear, and his shirt collar had concealed the miniature microphone affixed to his throat. His hissed "sec man" hadn't been an insult but a warning.

Dropping back into the ditch, Kane pulled the corpse with him, then climbed out on the opposite side, taking cover again behind the pile of shale. He heard nothing from the other side of the wall. Resheathing the knife, he waited for the count of sixty, then tapped out the move-up-carefully signal on the microphone.

It occurred to him that Reeth may have abandoned the

Cliff Palace either when an alarm was activated or the Vul can-Phalanx gun was triggered, and he had left a single guard behind to alert him to the identity of the intruders Kane was able to half convince himself that was Reeth's strategy.

Turning, he looked across the canyon. The figures of the team moved shadowlike around the bend in the wall, pressed against the darkness. Kane tapped the all-clear code, and the five men eased forward. When they were crouched down around the heap of shale, Kane pointed to the wall and indicated they should go over it rather than walk around looking for a gap.

Salvo nodded brusquely, and the team slid down into the ditch, then climbed up on the opposite side. MacMurphy and Pollard made stirrups out of their hands and heaved Kane high enough so he could see what lay on the other side of the wall. He investigated the top with his fingertips, searching for alarm wires. Then he slowly chinned himself upward.

There was nothing to see but walls and a maze of passageways. There was no one in sight, which meant, he hoped, no one could spot him. Cacti grew out of the packed earth at the ends of the once-solid wall on either side of him. The windows of the caved-in towers were black.

Lithely Kane pushed off from the hands of his comrades, bringing one leg up to one side, and crawled atop the wall. It was nearly three feet wide, and he stretched out flat along it. For a moment he didn't move, just listened and looked. Hands hooked on the edge, he lowered himself noiselessly inside the compound. He dropped to one knee, Copperhead at the ready, waiting for the team to scale the wall and join him.

When everyone was up and over, they moved through the complex toward the Cliff Palace itself. Because of the narrow footpaths, they weren't able to assume the standard deployment. Kane once again took point, leading the team through deep shadow between roofless walls that had once enclosed living quarters. They passed doorways leading into nothing but darkness. The footpath took a sharp turn, and the team spread out across the courtyard, watching the dark windows above them.

A sudden flash of brilliant light flooded the courtyard, instantly turning the deep twilight into high noon.

Chapter 2

Kane froze for an instant before reacting instinctively and lunging into a narrow corridor of semidarkness between two crumbling walls. The ground was slippery with pebbles and littered with fallen roof beams. Through his helmet transceiver, he heard his team cursing in surprise and anger. He knew the others would be diving for any available cover.

The glare of the floodlights concealed their source—somewhere on one of the ridges below the cliff overhang, about a hundred feet up. But the voice, amplified by a loud-hailer that split the silence, left no doubt that the Magistrates had strolled into an ambush. The words were harsh, muffled by his helmet, but still easily understood.

"You trespass!" the high-pitched, nasal voice declared. "Lay down your weapons and return to your machines."

Cursing under his breath, Kane peered around the edge of the doorway and scanned the towering ramparts. Though his visor reduced the glare, he still had to squint. The lights were arranged in double rows, a half a dozen atop another, spaced twenty feet apart. Blastermen were probably behind the lights, provided with clear views and fields of fire.

Salvo's voice shouted into his ear. "Milton Reeth! You are obstructing the duty of authorized enforcers of Cobaltville law. By Code 7b of the Territorial Jurisdiction Act, you must surrender yourself to our custody."

After a moment of echoing silence came a loud, contemptuous laugh. "Salvo, you rad-gelded backstabber! I knew you were behind this! Too late for you to crawfish on me now, you—"

The rest of Reeth's words were swallowed up by the deep hammering of a Copperhead. Salvo raked the ledges in sweeping, left-to-right arcs of gunfire. Three of the spotlights shattered in eye-searing blazes of blue sparks. From behind the lights, blastermen opened up with full-auto fire. Spear points of flame flickered from the darkness.

The Cliff Palace complex filled with the staccato stuttering of autofire as a chain reaction from the pinned-down Magistrates sent a steady steel-jacketed rain storming up toward the ridges. Small fountains of dirt and rock sprouted from the ground. Kane heard two distinct cries of pain.

"I'm hit!" Pollard bellowed.

"Shit!" screamed Carthew. "*Shit!* I can't see!"

The Magistrates knew better than to dig in and return double streams of autofire. Bullets knocked up great gouts of earth from the courtyard, chewed off chunks from the half-demolished buildings all around them. Hanging out of his sheltering doorway, Kane extended his Copperhead and directed short bursts at the floodlights above him. Two of them flared up in brief novas of yellow and blue.

His teammates were trying to find their way back toward the ruins, and he continued to fire upward, covering their retreat. Pollard limped badly as he ran, and Grant and Mac-Murphy's progress was slowed as they dragged Carthew along the ground. Salvo brought up the rear, firing in sweeps at the light array, hosing bullets indiscriminately and hitting only stone.

Even with the illumination from the ridge dimmed somewhat, the men were clearly visible targets for the barrage of slugs punching cross-stitch patterns in the ground all around them. Shifting position, Kane transferred the Copperhead to his left hand and stretched out his right, tensing the tendons. The Sin Eater sprang from its holster, the butt snapping down and slapping securely against his palm. At the same time, he leaped out from the doorway and corridor, both blaster barrels up and smearing the darkness with flame.

Heavy-caliber bullets pounded into the cliff rim, fragments of rock flying in all directions. Ricochets buzzed and whined through the air. Spent, smoking casings spewed from the ejector ports of both blasters in counterpoint to ripping reports of the Sin Eater and Copperhead. Sustained bursts of full-auto only wasted ammunition, but his focus was on creating a diversion, not scoring hits.

As he hoped, the blastermen behind the lights centered their sights on him. Bullets exploded dirt all around his black-sheathed figure, striking sparks from stone. Kane wasn't really aiming, but he felt a surge of savage satisfaction when a shadowy shape pitched out of a cleft behind a floodlight to fall headlong to the courtyard.

The volume of fire from the cliff decreased in response to words shouted over the loud-hailer. Kane couldn't make them out, but it sounded like Reeth, very upset, very angry.

The momentary lull was all the team needed to squirm past Kane into the doorway and into the roofless corridor. He joined them just as the barrage began again. A three-foot-high plume of grit erupted right where he had been standing. He recognized the rattling roar of a .50-caliber machine gun, probably bipod mounted. The steady hammering suddenly stopped.

Panting, Salvo came to his side. "Good work, Kane."

Whirling toward him, Kane stopped short of delivering a leopard's-paw strike to the man's windpipe. "You bastard," he snarled. "What the hell are we up against here?"

"You forget yourself," Salvo snapped, shoulders stiffening. "Weren't you paying attention at the briefing?"

"I was," replied Kane grimly. "Milton Reeth, a small-time slagger. He's been smuggling outlanders into the ville for the past year, providing them with forged ID chips and work orders. Shut down his operation, you said. A simple, no-muss, no-fuss serving of a termination warrant. Strictly small-time—you said."

Kane thrust an angry hand toward the spotlight array. "Does *this* look small-time to you?"

Salvo didn't answer for a long moment. His lips worked. Kane kept his visored eyes on the man's half-concealed face. He knew the rest of the team was looking on, waiting for and gauging their commander's reaction.

In a low, deadly monotone, Salvo said, "This is a hell-zone. One of the first lessons you learn is to expect the unexpected in a hellzone. Now, suck it up or I'll relieve you of your badge. Hellzone or no hellzone."

Kane broke eye contact first, dropping his gaze and turning to look at the team. Pollard rubbed his right knee and cursed softly between clenched teeth. A ricochet had smacked him between the leg joints of his armor, and he'd incurred a painful injury but not an incapacitating one.

Carthew had been seriously stung by a steel-jacketed wasp, directly in the visor. Though the bullet had been partially deflected, the plastic had shattered, driving splinters into his eyes. His face was a wet, red smear. He was semiconscious, faint moans bubbling from his lips.

Grant unsnapped a pouch on his belt and took from it a small squeeze hypodermic. It contained a pain reliever and metabolic stabilizer developed by the division medics. He undid the seals on Carthew's right gauntlet, tugged it off and injected the ampoule's liquid contents into the vein of the upper wrist.

Kane fought to control his rage, to keep from either striking out at Salvo or mounting a suicide charge at Reeth's blastermen. Two men who had been his comrades, as well as his teammates, were wounded, and now all of them were pinned down, waiting for the jaws of the trap to snap shut. For nothing. From the ridge overhang came a cacophony of taunting hoots and catcalls.

Taking a deep breath, Kane realized that their own arrogance had blinded them from covering all angles, examining all possibilities, no matter how remote. Salvo's words about expecting the unexpected were true enough, but only rarely had Magistrates ever confronted adversaries as well-armed as they were, at least in living memory. The majority of hard contacts went smoothly due to the advance fear created by their reputations, the fearsome images the Magistrates went to great effort to maintain. It simply hadn't occurred to Kane that they might encounter serious opposition from outlanders who weren't terrified of them.

Reeth's voice shouting over the ruins snapped him to full attention again. "Salvo, you hear me? I don't want this! The baron doesn't want this!"

Grant's head swiveled toward Salvo. "How does he know, sir? The baron authorized this mission. Didn't he?"

Salvo gestured for him to be quiet. Reeth's words boomed out into the night, bouncing from the canyon walls.

"Drop your weapons and leave! My people will box you in, and you'll have no way to escape unless I allow it. But I don't want to chill you, and you don't want to be chilled. So give me your answer!"

Salvo, without hesitation, cupped his hands around his mouth and shouted, "Milton Reeth! You are obstructing the duty of authorized enforcers of Cobaltville law. By Code 7b of the Territorial Jurisdiction Act, you must surrender yourself to our custody."

The .50-caliber stammered from overhead, the slugs chopping clay dust out of the doorway on both sides of Salvo. He dropped flat, turning a bleat of terror into a strangled curse.

The roar of the weapon ceased, and Reeth shrieked, "Then stay there, you treacherous *shit!* Stay there and starve!"

Pushing himself to a sitting position, Salvo spit out a mouthful of grit. He said nothing and avoided looking in the direction of the team. Grant and Kane shared a brief glance, then Kane said quietly, "Sir, if I was Reeth, I'd be packing up and moving out while he keeps us pinned down here."

As if on cue, Grant added, "If that fortress is where he's processing the outlanders and the ID chips, then there must be a way up there from down here."

Still not making eye contact, Salvo asked, "And how do you propose to find that way up there from down here?"

Ignoring the note of sarcasm, Kane declared matter-of-factly, "We look for it."

Salvo pursed his thin lips but didn't respond. Kane's anger flared again as the image of the Vulcan-Phalanx gun tower flashed in his mind. He wanted to put his Sin Eater to Salvo's head and ask why there hadn't been a reccee of the area before the mission had been ordered.

Instead, he sat and watched Salvo silently assess the situation. Perspiration flowed down his sallow cheeks. Finally the man bit out one short word, "Go."

Kane and Grant inserted full magazines into both of their blasters. From their belts, they removed black, six-inch-long cylinders and screwed them into the barrels of the Copperheads. They were two-stage sound suppressors, absorbing muzzle-flash and gases. The sound of the shots was reduced to no more than a rustle of cloth. The selector switches were adjusted to fire 3-round bursts.

There was no discussion of tactics, no time to devote to a reccee. They were entering dark territory, and from now on, everything depended on improvisation and reaction.

GRANT AND KANE duck-walked through the ruins of the building, found a break in a wall and squeezed through it. They kept to wedges of shadow, angling toward the dark areas not touched by the floodlights. Both men threaded their way through the crumbling structures as swiftly as they could, not penetrating a new area of the labyrinth without checking it out first.

The Cliff Palace complex was utterly silent below the long black clouds racing across the face of the rising moon. Grant was fast and agile for a big man, darting quickly in and out of doorways, striding to the spots affording best cover.

A wide passageway led straight ahead, with a break in the walls on the left. The two men took positions on either side of the gap and scanned the area beyond it. A cloud whipped past the moon, and its lambent glow shone on the many-windowed fortress built into the canyon wall. The flat bottom was only a few dozen yards away, and they could see the many fissures in the stonework below it.

Studying it intently, they saw a narrow opening in the embrasure, a little less than fifteen feet above the floor of the courtyard. Hand- and footholds had been chipped into the rock, making a crude, almost invisible ladder. Because of a puddle of illumination splashed by one of the flood-lights, they couldn't risk a frontal approach. Kane and Grant crept away at an oblique angle, staying close to the shadow of the wall.

Kane knew the blastermen would concentrate their atten-tion only on the terrain lit up by the floodlights, not in the murk beyond. They were confident they had the Magistrates outnumbered, outgunned and outfoxed. They were content to play a waiting game, for a few hours at least. Kane's instincts and experience told him that he and Grant could slip past their defenses and end the game.

Their progress was achingly slow, since the alteration of moon glow and the edges of the floodlights spilled puddles of light in their path. They followed the wall into another roofless building. One entire side of it was a mess of broken masonry and clay. The pile of rubble spread outside, most of it butting up against the cliff wall.

The two men stopped to catch their breath, collect their thoughts and scan the terrain. Then carefully they moved forward, picking their way across the sea of rubble.

The crunch of a shard of adobe under Grant's boot raised the hair on the back of Kane's neck and sent a jolt of adrenaline surging through his body. He froze in midstep, weapon at the ready. Grant followed his lead, coming to a complete halt.

After a few moments, they moved again, not pausing

until they were safe in the darkness beneath the overhanging bottom of the fortress. With infinite caution, they crept sideways, crouched to listen but heard nothing.

They reached the junction of the courtyard floor and the cliff face. Looking up along the embrasure, they saw the stone niches leading up to a hole. A light flickered feebly past the rim of the portal. Kane wasn't sure, but he figured it to be lamplight. That seemed odd, since the fortress was obviously equipped with electrical generators.

Suddenly there was a faint sound from overhead, and a shadow shifted across the lamplight. Kane and Grant stepped back quickly, easing into a wedge of pitch-blackness. An armed man appeared at the portal, then began climbing down, the scuffed toes of his boots digging into the notches carved in the wall. He had a revolver strapped to his hip.

The guard dropped the last few feet and gazed slowly around. By the shape of his skull, the sloping forehead, the apparent lack of ears and the suction pads on his fingertips, Kane recognized him as a stickie, one of the most common of the mutant strains spawned by the nukecaust, though they had changed over the past century. No one really knew where they first appeared, nor was it certain what monstrous combination of genetic malfunctions had created them in the first place.

Supposedly none had been seen until the first couple of years of the twenty-first century. Then, like floodgates opening, sightings were reported from all over. He had heard that the first generation of stickies didn't even possess mouths, much less ears, but that could have only been overblown fable.

Kane had only seen a few in his life, since they tended to give the villes wide berths. At one time, the stickies had been terrors of the Deathlands because of their psychotic love of mutilating norms and torching settlements. But the days of the great stickie clans were long over.

The stickie stood, giving the darkness around him an unblinking stare with his huge eyes. They held a contemplative expression that chilled Kane's blood. One malformed finger touched the microphone affixed to the base of his throat, and the stickie spoke. Kane expected to hear sounds as repulsive as his appearance, but his words were in flawless English. "Timoto reporting. All clear."

As soon as he dropped his hand from the microphone, Kane shot him three times from a range of eight feet. The suppressor made whispery sounds as the subsonic rounds took the stickie in the face, the heart and the throat. The final bullet stifled his death cry to a husky rattle that couldn't carry up through the thick rock embrasure.

The stickie jerked backward, started to fall, but Kane bounded forward and grabbed him by the collar of his tunic, pulling him into the shadows. He lowered the limp body quietly, grateful for his gloves. The thought of touching that slick, rubbery flesh made his bowels loosen.

The guard had given Reeth an all-clear report, so there was no better time to breach the fortress. He and Grant couldn't wait for the rest of the team to join them, since the stickie was probably under orders to supply status reports at regular intervals. At best, they had five minutes to get inside—at worst, one. Regardless, there wasn't sufficient time for Salvo and the others to reach their position before the guard was missed.

Kane planted his feet firmly in the first niche and began an awkward, turtlelike climb, not using his hands. When his eyes were above the edge of the opening, he stopped.

Illuminated by an old, flare-topped oil lamp on a table was a narrow landing of stone and timber. Directly opposite him was an open doorway and a flight of stone steps leading up into gloom. Kane climbed through the portal and moved aside as Grant's head and broad shoulders emerged. It was a tight squeeze, but Kane didn't help him—he kept the bore of the Copperhead trained on the dark doorway.

When Grant was standing beside him, Kane moved through the door, starting up the steps. The stairway was too narrow for them to walk abreast, so Grant gave Kane a six-foot lead.

They went up three complete windings of the corkscrew staircase before coming out onto a broader landing. A steel slab of a door was jammed firmly in the stone. A wheel-lock jutted from the cross-braced, rivet-studded metal mass. A naked lightbulb shone from a socket in the roof.

Kane and Grant eyed the door, looking for trip wires, photoelectric sensors or vid cameras. They saw nothing but stone and steel. Smiling wryly, Kane whispered, "I think it's safe to talk now."

"Kane!" Salvo's voice issued into his helmet, tight with tension, urgent with anxiety. "Location!"

"Inside the fortress," Kane replied softly. "Preparing for penetration."

"That's a big neg. Wait till we get there."

"*That's* a big neg," whispered Kane fiercely. "No time. You'll have to wait until we fuse out the power system, kill the spots."

Grimly, as though he resented each word passing his lips, Salvo said, "Affirm, then. If and when you see Reeth, serve the termination warrant. On sight. Understood?"

"Understood."

Kane gestured toward the door, and Grant stepped to it, putting his hands on the wheel-lock, letting the Copperhead dangle from his belt. Taking and holding a deep breath, the big man gave the wheel a counterclockwise twist. The door swung inward silently on recently lubricated hinges.

Beyond it was a tunnel, with neon light strips stretching along the ceiling. The tunnel was fairly long and had been hacked out of the rock. It obviously ran deep into the bowels of the cliff. A faint murmur of voices and a mechanical hum like a power generator reached them.

"After you," murmured Grant. "Pointman."

Kane took a tentative step forward. "One day some
thing'll happen to tarnish this rep of mine."

"Like what?"

"Like getting myself chilled." He didn't smile when he
said it.

Chapter 3

The absence of guards was suspicious, but they were in too deep to backtrack. Kane stalked along the tunnel, comforted by the faint sounds of Grant's footfalls six feet behind him.

Kane kept close to the right-hand wall, and Grant walked down the center so he would have a clear field of fire. The tunnel opened onto a scaffoldlike assembly made of pipes and heavy wooden planks. A staircase of two-by-fours extended down into the room twenty feet below. The scaffold was built at an angle to the tunnel mouth, so Kane had to creep forward to get an unobstructed view.

The room was square, maybe fifty feet wide, the walls reinforced by heavy timbers and sheet metal. The walls climbed to a ceiling of chiseled rock that was part of the cliff itself. Ten light fixtures attached to wall stanchions provided weak illumination. Taking a wary reccee of the room, Kane understood the absence of guards in the tunnel.

Only four people were down in the room, all very busy packing reams of paper and odds and ends of electronic equipment into crates. Obviously most of their force was outside, watching the Cliff Palace complex, making sure the Magistrates weren't moving in on them.

Milton Reeth supervised the packing. Kane recognized him from the pix he had seen during the briefing. He was a tall, dark-skinned man, the sides and top of his head clean shaved, but a clump of dreadlocks dangled from the back of his skull, falling down the center of his back like a quartet of greasy black snakes. He wore a puffy-sleeved, powder blue bodysuit with a touch of green lace at the collar. A red, yellow and blue snake tattoo coiled across the right side of his face, its fanged jaws gaping open as though it were preparing to devour his eye.

Beside him stood his strong-arm. She had an identical tattoo on the left side of her high-planed face. She wore a brass-studded, red-leather harness that left her heavily muscled arms bare. Her lank hair was styled like Reeth's. She was a stickie, and Kane realized the guard he had killed was probably one of her kin, either a brother or a cousin, or maybe even a son.

Slaggers like Reeth never went anywhere without a strong-arm, but rarely were the combinations of bodyguards and jolt-brained coldhearts women. Kane had never heard of a norm placing any kind of trust in a mutie, especially a stickie. Obviously Reeth was more than a slagger. He was something of a dev, as well.

On the far side of the room was a tangle of electronic and computer equipment, a nest of wires and keyboards and monitor screens that took up almost the entire wall with shelves and worktables. Kane saw a whining, gasoline-fueled electric generator with dozens of feed conduits sprouting from it.

The black-and-white images flickering across the four monitor screens showed different perspectives of the complex, including a rear view of the blastermen posted behind the floodlights on the ledges outside.

Light also flashed from a large tabletop console computer screen. Numbers and words scrolled across it with a dizzying rapidity. On the same wall as the tech nest gaped an open doorway.

One of the men packing a crate asked Reeth a question, his voice muted by the rumbling whine of the generator. Reeth responded petulantly, his sharp, high-pitched voice carrying easily to Kane.

"We've got to wait until all the files are downloaded, don't we, Neal? We can't just cut and run and leave everything, can we, Neal? That would be foolish, wouldn't it, Neal?"

Neal mumbled something and returned to his packing.

Kane gestured for Grant to join him on the scaffold. The big man stepped forward and gazed down into the room without expression. When he saw the female strong-arm stroke Reeth's snake-adorned face with suction-pad-tipped fingers, he drew in a quick breath of revulsion. His Copperhead rose. Kane laid the noise suppressor of his blaster over the barrel of Grant's gun and pushed it down. Grant stared at Kane, mouth opening in surprise.

Shaking his head vigorously, Kane touched a finger to his lips and stepped back into the mouth of the tunnel. Reluctantly Grant moved beside him. Kane covered the transceiver grid of his helmet with a finger, and Grant hesitantly did the same.

"I want him alive," Kane whispered.

"You heard the order," Grant responded in the same low voice. "Serve the termination warrant on sight."

"If we do that, we'll never learn what's going on here."

"We know what's going on here," Grant growled. "A smuggling operation."

"How many smugglers have a setup like this?" Kane demanded. "Where'd a slagger like Reeth get his hands on all this tech, how'd he manage to build such a processing center all by himself?"

Grant's lips twitched, but he said nothing.

"How come Reeth called Salvo a backstabber?" Kane pressed on with his questions, his voice a harsh whisper. "Who's paying the bills on this place?"

Slowly Grant muttered, "I don't know."

"Exactly. Salvo knows, but we won't get any answers from him. He told all of us just enough to put us on the knee of Father Death." After a moment, Kane added, "This is my instinct talking."

Though Grant didn't reply, Kane knew the kind of thoughts spinning through his mind. Magistrates were a highly conservative, duty-bound group. The customs of enforcing the law and obeying orders were ingrained almost from birth. The Magistrates submitted themselves to a grim and unyielding discipline because they believed it was necessary to reverse the floodtide of chaos and restore order to postholocaust America.

By nature, Magistrates were proud that each of them accepted the discipline voluntarily, and doubly proud that neither temptation nor jeopardy ever shook their obedience to the oath they swore. But Kane knew, on some deep, visceral level, that an oath was only as inviolate as the men who put its tenets into practice.

On that same deep level, Kane knew Salvo was playing fast and loose with the oath, superficially abiding by the words while disregarding the spirit behind them. His commanding officer hoped the team was so conditioned that they would respond like automatons in any situation, without suspicion and certainly without question. Kane was gambling that his friendship with Grant would supersede the conditioning to obey, at least for a few minutes.

Finally Grant released his breath in a sigh of resignation. "All right," he whispered. "I'll listen to your instinct—but only up to a certain point. What do you want me to do?"

"What you always do, what you do best," Kane replied. "Back me up."

"If you're wrong about this, you'll find my boot backing up your ass."

After a quick, whispered conference, they settled on tactics. Grant gave Kane a skeptical look but didn't put words to it. The two men returned to the scaffold and took careful aim at the light fixtures around the room.

Quietly Kane said, "Now."

They squeezed the triggers of the Copperheads, shifting the barrels from left to right. Six bullets shattered six light fixtures, leaving only the farthermost pair intact. Glass sprinkled down on the people in the room, and they cried out in alarm. The area around the scaffold was instantly plunged into dark gray murk. The whine of the generator masked the small sounds of the silenced shots, and for several moments, those below were confused as to what had caused the lights to go out. Kane and Grant took swift advantage of those moments.

They leaped from the scaffold, allowing their thick boot soles and reinforced ankle braces to cushion the shock of dropping nearly twenty feet. The light-enhancer units on their helmets allowed them clear vision in the dim light. Though it would have been easier to take out the generator, to kill the floods outside and allow the team to move in, Kane wanted the power to stay on.

He ran on the balls of his feet, the Copperhead trained on Neal. The man squinted in his direction, glimpsed the dark figure looming out of the gloom, and his face contorted in shock and fear. He gasped wordlessly, right hand fumbling at his waistband.

"Freeze!" Kane roared, using his command voice.

Neal froze, but only for a fraction of an instant. His hand whipped up from his waistband, a long-barreled handblaster filling it. Kane squeezed the trigger of the Copperhead. Three 4.85 mm rounds struck Neal in the face and neck. His features dissolved in a wet blur, blood spraying out of his throat like a fountain. He jerked backward, the blaster flying from his hand, arms and legs flopping like a disjointed puppet's.

Kane heard Reeth and his strong-arm shrieking, and the third man in the room yelled. From behind him came the faint triple crack of Grant's Copperhead.

Kane caught only fragments of one-color images. At the same time he heard the suppressed sounds of the Copperhead, something struck him high on the left shoulder. He heard an explosive report and saw a spurt of flame.

Staggering from the impact, the air kicked from his lungs and out his nostrils and mouth, Kane flailed to one side, feet scrabbling for purchase on the stone floor. Though his armor had absorbed and distributed most of the high-caliber bullet's kinetic energy, he was numbed by the shock.

He glimpsed Reeth's strong-arm rushing in his direction, gripping an Astra .45-caliber revolver in her right hand. It was a big gun, with a heavy six-inch barrel. It was far too big, far too powerful a pistol to fire accurately with only one hand, no matter how well muscled she was. She fired again. The gun kicked in her hand, pulling up toward the ceiling as the shot boomed and echoed in the enclosed room. The bullet cleaved air a foot over Kane's head, and he heard it clang against the metal framework of the scaffolding.

Reeth screamed a few unintelligible words at her and turned to flee. The other man in the room started to run after him, leaving the female to cover their retreat. Kane was still a little stunned by taking the .45-caliber round on the shoulder, and all actions seemed to slow down, as though he were stuck in a slo-mo vid loop.

His peripheral vision showed him Grant, centering his Copperhead on the strong-arm, his aim spoiled because he was trying to keep out of the sights of the Astra. He glimpsed Reeth and his subordinate dashing madly toward the open dark doorway.

The Astra revolver vomited thunder and fire for a third time, a wad of lead tearing through the air toward Grant. The bullet missed, punching a hole in a sheet-metal-covered wall.

Kane tossed his Copperhead into his left hand. Before his fingers closed around it, he tensed the tendons in his right wrist. The Sin Eater filled his hand, rounds blasting from the bore immediately.

The stream of slugs plugged a series of dark periods in the back of the man dogging Reeth's heels. His arms flung wide, his back arched in a grotesquely graceful posture and he hurtled forward into Reeth. Both men went down in a tangle of arms and legs.

The strong-arm's thick lips writhed, peeling back from broken, discolored teeth. She adjusted her aim with the Astra revolver, wrapping both hands around the butt, swinging the bore back toward Kane, shrieking, "Fuckin' sec men—!"

Grant's Copperhead snapped. The three bullets caught the strong-arm dead center. She didn't cry out. She just left her feet, flying backward into the worktable behind her, bouncing off it, then slumping forward over a packing crate. The rounds crushed the stickie's chest, smashing ribs and clavicle, ripping both lungs apart and probably perforating her heart. As her body settled, a thin, aspirated scream of anger and hatred floated from her lips.

Kane's and Grant's fingers relaxed on the triggers of their blasters. Taking a shuddery breath, wincing at the ache in his shoulder, Kane stepped forward. He felt a remote surprise that he was moving at normal speed again. Pins and needles burned up and down his left arm. He knew he had gotten off lucky—the strong-arm could have fired armor-piercing rounds, and his arm would do more than burn.

The entire firefight, from the moment Neal had drawn his blaster, had lasted less than fifteen seconds. The peculiar time-distortion of combat never failed to surprise Kane.

Reeth elbowed aside the corpse of the man sprawled over him and tried to climb to his knees. Grant reached him first, gathering a handful of greasy dreadlocks in his left fist and yanking the slagger to his feet.

Howling, Reeth clawed at Grant's fingers. Terror and rage battled for dominance in his eyes. "You stupid bastard! You don't know what you're doing!"

Spittle sprayed from his lips onto Grant's visor. Grant jammed the bore of the Copperhead's noise suppressor against the hinge of Reeth's jaw. Flesh sizzled as the heated metal raised a perfectly round, leaking blister on the flesh. Reeth howled again, the sound trailing off to a despairing croak.

Kane saw Grant's intent to serve the termination warrant. Despite his promise, his Magistrate's pride was wounded. Kane quickly pushed himself in front of Grant. Sliding the Sin Eater back into its holster, he placed one finger over his helmet transceiver and asked, "How many blastermen outside?"

"Seven," Reeth answered in a voice tight with pain. "Not counting the one that got chilled. That's all. I swear."

Reeth's threat to outflank the Magistrates in the courtyard had been an empty bluff. Kane wasn't too surprised. Gathering a handful of lace collar, Kane pulled Reeth away from Grant. He dragged him toward the collection of electronic equipment.

"Call them off. Tell them to throw their guns down into the canyon." He had removed his finger from the transceiver.

As he expected, Salvo's voice crackled immediately inside his helmet. "Kane? Kane! Who are you talking to? Report!"

Reeth's trembling hands fumbled among the collection of gear on the table and came up with an old hand-held microphone, connected by a curling cord to a public-address system. He said shakily into it, "Lay down your weapons. Throw them over the ledge."

On the vid screen, Kane watched the blastermen stare disconcertedly at each other, hefting their guns. They hesitated. He planted the bore of his Copperhead against the side of Reeth's head.

"Do it!" yelled Reeth wildly.

His order also carried to the Magistrates down below. Salvo's voice demanded angrily, "Kane! Report!"

Kane didn't reply until he saw the blastermen begin pitching their guns over the lip of the ledge. He said crisply, "Zone secured. Move the team in."

"You've got Reeth." Salvo made it sound like an accusation. "Serve the warrant."

"Walk along the bottom edge of the palace," Kane said. "You'll find an entrance on the right."

"Kane! Follow your orders!"

Lips compressed in a tight white line, Kane unsnapped the chin lock and pulled his helmet off. By his reckoning, it would take Salvo and the team about fifteen minutes to reach them. He didn't want the man to hear what he had to say, nor did he want to be distracted by orders shouted in his ear. Grant could tolerate their commander's voice easier than he could.

Without the aid of his light enhancer, the room was very dim. The glow from the computer screen cast wavering, eerie shadows across Reeth's face. Kane gestured to the worktable and said casually, "Impressive setup, Milt. Gun turrets, comps, electricity. All the comforts. Only one thing is missing."

Reeth's response was a gravelly whisper. "What's that?"

"The equipment to forge ID chips."

"Why would I want one of those?"

"Word has it you're smuggling outlanders into Cobaltville. Can't smuggle without providing the outlanders with ID chips. You should know that."

Reeth tried to smile, lips twisting. "If you don't see a forger, then I guess I'm not smuggling outies. Simple enough conclusion to reach."

"Your blastermen are all outlanders," Grant said. "Except for the ones who are muties." The last word dripped with contempt, with revulsion.

"So? We're in a hellzone. Who else would work in a hellzone but outlanders? 'Sides, you got no jurisdiction here."

Both Kane and Grant laughed mirthlessly. "It's part of Baron Cobalt's legally ceded territory, from the old Nelson hierarchy," Kane replied. "You should know that, too."

An electronic beep came from the computer console. Kane eyed it appraisingly. The machines in the ville, in the Enclaves, were restricted to a very few. Even Kane didn't have unsupervised access to the computers employed by the Magistrate Division. Archivists enjoyed fairly unlimited use of them, primarily to keep the historical data bases current.

Though he was vaguely aware that Beforetimers had in the three decades preceding skydark relied heavily on the machines, the barons had long ago agreed to prevent a repetition of such technological dependence. Still, Kane recognized the computer as a current DDC type, the same direct-digital-control model as those in the Intel section of his division. As such, it was impossible for private citizens, even the ultraelite of the Enclavers to own one.

"Where did you get this?" he asked. Data still scrolled across the monitor. He poked at the stack of slip-sleeved CD disks on the table.

"I'm not saying shit," grated Reeth. "Not till Salvo gets here."

Grant suddenly stiffened, head cocked slightly to one side. He put a finger over the transceiver on his helmet and said, "Speaking of him, Salvo just ordered me to chill your slagging ass."

Reeth's lips curled in an attempt at a go-to-hell smirk. "Not my ass, sec boy. It's sanctified."

"Who sanctified it?" Kane demanded.

"Maybe old Salvo will let you know."

The machine beeped. The screen went dark and the words "Downloading complete" glowed against the background. A symbol appeared on the screen, a red triangle bisected by three black vertical lines. The lines somewhat resembled stylized, round-hilted daggers. From the drive port popped a gleaming compact disk. Kane reached for it with his right hand.

"Don't touch that!" Reeth shrieked.

Casually, not bothering to look at him, Kane raked the noise suppressor of the Copperhead across Reeth's face. Blood sprang from a laceration above the bridge of his nose, nicking the blunt snout of the snake tattoo. Reeth squawked in stunned pain, clapping both hands to his face.

He staggered on rubbery legs. Grant shoved one boot behind the man's ankles and kicked his feet out from under him. Reeth sat down heavily, grunting, fingers trying to catch the rivulets of blood streaming down his face.

During that brief diversion, Kane slipped the compact disk from the hard drive and stowed it in a compartment in his belt. He was sure Grant hadn't seen him do it.

Chapter 4

"On your feet," Kane commanded.

Groaning, Reeth stiffly climbed to his feet. He pressed a hand against his forehead, trying to staunch the flow of blood. With a fist against his back, Kane shoved the man toward the dark doorway.

"Prove to me there are no outlanders in here. Not that it'll make any difference."

With Reeth in front, they entered a narrow corridor. The stonework and metal girders were pocked and corroded with age. It was lit by a naked bulb shining from a ceiling fixture. It branched into a short T. On the left, the passageway ended at the base of a rock stairway.

Clumping down the stairs came the blastermen, lean and wiry outlanders. Their faces were tight masks of anger and resentment—not an anger at being bested, but a resentment of ville authority that extended deep into past generations.

"Go to the control room," Reeth said to them. "Wait for the sec men. Don't resist. I'll take care of you."

Turning to the right, Reeth strode a few feet and stopped before a heavy wooden door on the left-hand wall. A few yards past it, the corridor debouched to the right. Behind the door, Kane heard the murmuring of voices and shuffling of feet.

He knew the voices and anxious feet belonged to outlanders, wanderers desperate to enter a ville, regardless of the risk or the price. Despite the fact they could aspire only to the Pits, there was electricity, real buildings for shelter, real food, even if it was the recycled and reconstituted scraps from the Enclaves. With forged ID chips, silicon granules injected subcutaneously in their forearms, they could receive regular immunity boosters to combat the insidious infections to which all outlanders seemed peculiarly susceptible.

Of course, they would be barred from the towers of the Enclaves, forced to perform slagwork in return for credit chips, but it was better than nomading across the Outlands. Their existences in the Pits would be marginal, but there was always the distant hope, the dream, that they could someday buy into citizenship.

Now that they were discovered, their dreams would be dashed and their fates infinitely worse. The best they could hope for was a Magistrate's mercy, and that meant nothing more kind than being turned loose in this hellzone.

Kane pointed to the door. "Open it."

Reeth fumbled with the metal locking bar. "Listen," he said in a wheedling tone, "you got me good, okay? No need to go any further with this."

"I'm curious about the quality of your merchandise, Milt," Kane said gently. "As one connoisseur of outlanders to another. Extend me a professional courtesy."

Taking a deep breath, Reeth lifted the bar from its braces. While he did so, Kane slipped his helmet back over his head, assuming the cell wasn't lighted. Though he heard the comm-chat of the team approaching the Cliff Palace, Salvo wasn't shouting at him to report or to follow orders.

Pushing Reeth aside, he carefully toed the door open. It swung inward on squealing, rust-eaten hinges. His Copperhead held at waist level, Kane took a cautious step over the threshold and into the holding cell. Initially he saw only shapes shifting in the shadows. Then the outlanders moved toward the light of the corridor.

First one, then another shuffled from the dark corner of the cell. Without ville immunity boosters, the elements of the hellzone had ravaged their limbs and features. Their skin was scabbed and peeling, with many open, running sores. Kane saw women with patchy bald spots in their lank hair, men with eyes covered by milky cataracts, children with stick-thin limbs and bellies swollen from malnutrition. The stink of their unwashed bodies clogged his nostrils. He recoiled from the contact of their touch, even against his armor.

These were the Dregs, the outlanders who were shunned even by other outlanders. The legacy of the nukecaust and the doctrines of the villes had bred an absolute horror of deviates. Those with severe birth defects were terminated as soon as they were found. Muties, once very numerous, had been eradicated from most of the ville territories. But the Dregs weren't muties. In some ways, they were worse. They were diseased, genetically ruined from generations of exposure to toxic environments and radioactive hot spots, eking out hellish existences as scavengers.

Before they got too close, Kane stepped hastily back into the corridor, pulling the door shut, dropping the locking bar back into place with a thud. Whirling on Reeth, he snarled between bared teeth, "You sick bastard! These are Dregs! You had no intention of smuggling them into the ville. What were you going to do with them?"

"I have buyers in other places," Reeth replied, voice quavering.

"Other villes?" Grant rumbled.

"No, not exactly."

"How do you transport the merchandise to these 'other buyers'?" Kane demanded.

Reeth shook his head and droplets of blood mixed with sweat flew from his face. "Don't ask me that, sec man. You really don't want to know."

Kane's hand darted for Reeth's throat, closed around it and he shoved the man against the wall, bouncing the back of his skull against the stone.

"I'm sick of this," he hissed. "I'm under orders to serve a termination warrant on you, and you've given me no reason to delay it another second—"

"No, wait!" Reeth lifted a pair of trembling, conciliatory hands. "Listen to me, goddamn it!"

Reeth's words tripped over each other in their haste to leave his lips. "I'm talking with a straight tongue now. You *don't* want to know! You find out, and one night you'll have termination warrant served on *you!*"

"You forget who we are," Kane said in a low, deadly monotone.

"You're a Mag, just another of the baron's sec men. There are forces a lot more powerful than you."

"Show us."

Snatching a gloveful of dreadlocks, Kane wrenched Reeth away from the wall and down the corridor. The man dug in his heels and tried to resist, but Kane jammed the bore of the Copperhead into his kidneys to turn him down the bend in the passageway.

The corridor ended abruptly at a barrier. Kane, using the dreadlocks like reins, yanked Reeth to a jolting halt. They faced a door made of what looked like silvery smoked glass. There was a square panel beside the door with several rows of numbered and lettered buttons, some glowing brightly. A metal handle was affixed to the center of the door.

Kane recognized the composition of the door panel as armaglass, a predark invention sharing the properties of both normal glass and steel. It was rare but not unknown. He prodded Reeth with the Copperhead.

"Open it."

Reeth groaned, put both hands on the handle, gave it an upward pull and the door swung outward. Kane peered around Reeth, looking into the chamber. It was circular, perhaps ten feet in diameter, with an eight-foot-high ceiling. He and Grant stared. It took him a silent, confused moment to realize he had no idea what he was looking at.

The chamber was six sided, all the walls featuring the same smoke-tinted armaglass. The floor was patterned with interlocking, hexagonal, raised metallic disks. The pattern was repeated in the ceiling. A few of the disks shimmered faintly, a silvery, moonlight hue. Kane heard the most distant of electronic humming sounds, like a buried generator.

"What the hell is this?" Grant growled.

"Kane! Grant! Report!" Not only did they hear Salvo's imperious tone in their helmets, but they heard it echoing down the corridor.

Reeth heard it, too, and his shoulders slumped in relief. "Listen," he said in a pleading whisper, "if you value your lives, don't tell Salvo I led you to the gateway."

Kane's head swung toward him. "The what?"

Reeth opened his mouth, then shut it again. His lips tightened, and his expression showed that he would say no more despite what was done to him.

"Let's go," Grant urged gruffly, tugging at Kane's elbow.

Reluctantly Kane allowed himself to be drawn away from the chamber. He, Grant and Reeth walked quickly along the passageway, through the doorway and into the big room that had served as Reeth's control center. He saw Salvo standing like a red-faced statue beside the electronics console, and tension cut at him like a knife. His heart jumped, picking up a faster rhythm and holding on to it. Pollard and MacMurphy were fanned out across the room, patting down the blastermen, who stood grimly, hands laced behind their heads.

Pointing to Reeth, Salvo said, "Let him go."

Kane released his grip on the dreadlocks, and Reeth stumbled slightly. He rushed toward Salvo, hands wide. Angrily, petulantly he said, "I don't know what's going on, what put the bug up your ass, but we can work this out before the baron gets wind of—"

The Sin Eater slid into Salvo's palm, and two shots roared, sending out almost tangible waves of sound. Reeth kicked backward from the floor, as though performing an acrobatic trick. It was no trick. A huge crimson blotch appeared on the front of his bodysuit.

The two rounds smashed Milton Reeth's heart, turning it into pulverized meat. He slapped down onto the floor with a mushy thud. Blood from hemorrhaging lungs bubbled from his nose and mouth. He made a very small gurgling noise, like a baby waking from a nap. Then he died, lying on his back, eyes open and bright as marbles. An angry grumble went up from the blastermen, but Pollard and MacMurphy had them covered.

Pushing the Sin Eater back into its forearm holster, Salvo announced, "Termination warrant served."

Staring at Kane, he said loudly, "Flash-blast this slaghole."

Kane said, "There are more outlanders in a cell back there—"

He stopped speaking when he saw the cold smile play over Salvo's face. He knew what the bastard intended.

"I repeat—flash-blast this slaghole." Salvo's voice was sharp, slicing through the air like a steel whip. "Do we understand each other?"

Seconds of silence hung in the air. Kane realized Salvo was challenging him, letting him know that there was a line he dared not cross. Salvo had led the team into a trap, but Kane and Grant had disobeyed orders, and the superior officer was again in charge and letting everyone know it.

Kane inclined his head in a slight nod. "Sir."

Salvo nodded in return, so slight a motion it was almost invisible. He had scored a minor victory. "You and Grant wait for us in the tunnel while we mop up in here."

Crossing the room, Kane and Grant walked up the staircase to the scaffold and along the tunnel. Blocking the transceiver grid with a finger, Grant put the edge of his hand against the base of his neck. "I figure we're up to here in it. What do you think?"

Kane smiled distractedly, then placed a finger over the grid on his helmet. "What did Reeth call that room? A gateway?"

"Yeah. Whatever the hell that means."

"Remember the old stories? About predark experiments in matter transmission? Called them gateways, right?"

"Folklore," Grant replied stiffly. "Legends."

"Could be. Or could be there's a basis in reality for the legends."

Grant tapped his chin with the edge of his hand. "You mention that to Salvo, and we'll be up to *here*."

Kane chuckled uneasily. "Don't worry. I've already had my shit requirement for the day."

From behind them erupted the ripping rasps of three Sin Eaters. The sound rolled down the tunnel, carrying with it faint cries and bleats of terror and pain. The outcries stopped, but the Sin Eaters continued to blast. They heard the clatter of spent casings falling to the floor, the shattering of glass, the clanging of metal. There was the pop of sparks as the generator was cored by armor-piercing rounds, and the neon light strip overhead flickered and went out. The snarl of the Sin Eaters stopped.

Even with only the one-color night vision supplied by his helmet, Grant saw Kane's jaw muscles knot and bunch. "Forget it," he said quietly. "They're only outlanders, most of 'em Dregs and slaggers. They're better off."

Bitterly Kane intoned, "The Magistrate's mercy."

Within a couple of minutes, Salvo, MacMurphy and Pollard emerged from below and into the tunnel. All of them reeked with the sharp tang of cordite. Salvo stalked past Grant and Kane without a word or a glance. They fell into step behind him.

Salvo issued no orders, and no one asked him any questions. They left the ancient fortress by the same way they had entered it, cutting across the courtyard to where they had left Carthew. He was groggy from the drugs, but the pain of his injury was under control. Led by Grant, he was able to walk out of the dark ruins.

As the team entered the canyon, Kane automatically checked the chron inside the wrist of his left gauntlet. Over three hours had elapsed since they left the ville. As far as he knew, Salvo hadn't transmitted a status report back to the division, so if the mission had been strictly by the book, a backup Bird squadron should be arriving at that very moment.

Kane wasn't surprised to see only three choppers still squatting on their skids. A backup was nowhere in sight, either overhead or on the ground.

The team climbed back into their respective Deathbirds. Grant powered up the engine. It whined, coughed and caught. The vanes spun, agitating the dust of the canyon floor into swirling eddies.

Slowly the craft lifted off, rising vertically until it topped the uppermost rim of the ramparts of Mesa Verde canyon. Grant's practiced hand rotated it gracefully, and then sent it winging through the night. This time Salvo's Deathbird took the point of the delta formation.

It was only fitting, Kane reflected acidly. Old Salvo was returning from commanding another successful foray against the legions of chaos, of anarchy, of the sick and victimized. He thought about spitting, but he knew it would irritate the pilot, and he had made enough enemies for one evening.

Chapter 5

Kane looked down at the hellzone, gleaming a dull gray white in the moonlight. It was like looking upon Earth's bare bones, scoured and bleached by nearly two centuries of chem storms and lingering radioactivity.

On the border of the zone, soil, humus and desiccated vegetation still clung obstinately to an imitation of life. People, more than likely Dregs, still toiled and tilled down there, while the others, only a hundred miles away, enjoyed the cake distributed to them by the ville and the benevolent Baron Cobalt.

Things had been different in antiquity, Kane knew. He couldn't be sure how different or exactly in what way. The history he had been taught mostly covered events following the nukecaust, and before that, before skydark, it was dim and inexact. It was said in the texts that people had taken a savage joy in raping and ravaging the world, deaf to the entreaties of more-enlightened minds.

The population had been staggering in number, billions supposedly. Then came the nukecaust, which had fried eighty percent of them, and the subsequent horrors of geological catastrophes, fallout and a horrific retribution for the sins of humanity.

The world had suffered a dark age, though in actual chronological terms, the age had lasted only 115-plus years before the Program of Unification had been put into practice. With the cooperation of the nine most powerful barons, the program had reached a success point in a little less than a decade. Unity Through Action had been the rallying cry.

Part of the program had been education. People were taught that to be alive, to be a human, wasn't a special privilege, since humanity had brought about an apocalypse and its near extinction. The hierarchy of barons was dedicated to preventing another such holocaust.

Their role as guides and protectors for humankind revolved around the same theme—people must never again be allowed to choose their own destinies, since invariably those choices led to disaster.

Kane swallowed a sigh. He didn't understand why he should want things that were dead and buried and gone. The predark, Beforetime world had festered with hate and suspicion and pollution and war. It had taken the barons to clean it up the only way it could be cleaned up—by stamping out any deviation from the standard, forbidding all technology except to the very few elite who defined and maintained obedience to that standard.

Like me, Kane thought.

Within an hour, the black sky mellowed to a pale indigo at the horizon. The comforting lights of Cobaltville beckoned, and he couldn't help but be glad of his return. He desperately wanted to shuck off his armor and wash away the bitter stink of the hellzone.

The Deathbirds soared steadily over the irrigated greenness of cultivated fields and over the silvery windings of the Kanab River, a tributary of the Colorado.

Kane looked down at the city spread below. Cobaltville was built on the bluffs overlooking the river. Towers and walls perched on the hills, looking like a gargantuan battleship somehow beached there. The stone walls rose fifty feet high, and at each intersecting corner protruded a Vulcan-Phalanx gun tower. Powerful spotlights washed the immediate area outside the walls, leaving nothing hidden from the glare. The bluffs surrounding the walls were kept cleared of vegetation except grass, a precaution against a surprise attack. One of the official reasons for fortifying the villes was a century-old fear—or paranoid delusion—of a foreign invasion from other nuke-scarred nations. It had never happened, and Kane had always wondered how the barons figured any country could mount a large enough army to establish anything other than a remote beachhead.

Then there had been the threat of mutant clans, like the vicious stickies, unifying and sweeping across the country. Legend spoke of a charismatic leader who had united the mutie marauders to wage a holy war against the norms. As far as Kane recollected, the war hadn't quite come off, but the memory of the threat was burned deep in the collective minds of the baronial hierarchies. It had burned so brightly that a major early aspect of the Program of Unification had been a campaign of genocide against mutie settlements in ville territories.

Inside the walls stretched the complex of spired Enclaves. Each of the four towers was joined to the others by pedestrian bridges. Few of the windows in the towers showed any light, so there was little to indicate that the interconnecting network of stone columns, enclosed walkways, shops and promenades was where nearly four thousand people made their homes.

In the Enclaves, the people who worked for the ville administrators enjoyed lavish apartments. Every comfort was built into them—plumbing, artificial lighting, refrigeration, air-conditioning—all the bounty of those favored by the baron. Kane and a few other Magistrates lived in the upper levels of the Enclaves.

Far below the Enclaves, on a sublevel beneath the bluffs, light peeped up from dark streets of the Tartarus Pits. Though it was very late, the Pits were awake and seething. The narrow, twisting streets were crowded, neon light flashed luridly, making blacker the shadows of the alleys and lanes. These sectors of the villes were melting pots, where outlanders and slaggers lived. They swarmed with the cheap labor, and random movement between the Enclaves and Pits was tightly controlled—only a Magistrate on official business could enter the Pits, and only a Pit dweller with a legitimate work order could even approach the cellar of an Enclave tower. However, Kane knew of at least one undetected route into the Enclaves.

The population of the Pits was as strictly and even more ruthlessly controlled than the traffic. The barons had decreed that the villes could support no more than five thousand residents, and the number of Pit dwellers could not exceed one thousand.

Kane retained vivid memories of making Pit sweeps, seeking out unauthorized outlanders, infants and even pregnant women. He did not relish those memories.

Seen from above, the Enclave towers formed a latticework of intersected circles, all connected to the center of the circle, from which rose the Administrative Monolith. The massive, round column of white rockcrete jutted three hundred feet into the sky. Light poured out of the slit-shaped windows on each level.

Every level of the tower was designed to fulfill a specific capacity: E, or Epsilon, Level was a general construction and manufacturing facility; D, or Delta, Level was devoted to the preservation, preparation and distribution of food; and C, or Cappa, from an American version of the Greek Kappa, Level held the Magistrate Division. On B, or Beta, Level was the historical archives, a combination of library, museum and computer center. The level was stocked with almost five hundred thousand books, discovered and restored over the past ninety years, not to mention an incredibly varied array of predark artifacts.

The work of the administrators was conducted on the highest level, Alpha Level. Up there, in the top spire, far above even the Enclaves, the baron reigned alone, unapproachable, invisible.

Kane had no clear idea what went on in A Level. The secrecy surrounding the baron and the administrators' activities was deliberate and jealously guarded. Almost everybody in all the other divisions was kept in ignorance about the actual number and identities of the administrators.

Fraternization between division personnel was strongly discouraged, presumably so no one would know anything that the administrators didn't want them to know.

Midway on the side of the monolith, a flat, massive slab began extending like a monstrous, squared-off tongue. A circle of fluorescent light blinked rhythmically on the exact center of the slab. Grant angled the Deathbird down toward the landing pad projecting from the level housing the Magistrate Division and its dozen subsections.

Mechs scurried out of the cavernous opening on the side of the tower, securing the landing skids with cables attached to eyebolts sunk in the rockcrete. Medics rushed out and put Carthew on a wheeled stretcher, quickly rolling him inside. Kane and the team walked inside the monolith as giant groaning gears and squealing pulleys withdrew the landing pad.

The Magistrate Division level was huge, containing classrooms, a weapons range, a vast armory, wardrooms, a cafeteria, a gymnasium and a computerized Intel center. It also held dormitories for recruits.

Kane thought of his first morning at the division—when he was twelve—and how he awakened on his bunk before dawn, cold, frightened, yet strangely eager for the day to begin. Nineteen years had conditioned all childish fears and frailties from his mind and body. He remembered his final examination when he was sixteen, a day that marked his last day as a recruit and his first day as a badge-carrying Magistrate. There was no such thing as failure of the examination—those who survived it were the ones who didn't fail.

Following the standard procedure after a foray into a hellzone, the team filed into a cubicle and removed their armor, handing the pieces to techs who stood by for that purpose. Then, naked, each man waited his turn to enter the Medisterile Unit.

Kane was the first to step inside the man-size, bullet-shaped chamber. Dozens of nozzles studded the tiled walls.

When the door sealed behind him, high-pressure jets of warm disinfectant sprayed from the nozzles. The streams of fluid covered him from the top of his head to the soles of his feet. Kane worked the decontamination spray into his body to help penetration into every pore. The monthly immunity boosters all legal ville residents received weren't powerful enough to protect them from long exposure to hellzone levels of ambient radiation.

Outside, in another cubicle, the techs were washing down his armor and ordnance with a similar decontaminate. He wasn't worried about one of them rifling through the compartments of his belt and finding the compact disk. They were Pit dwellers, outlanders hoping for citizenship, and such a brazen act of disrespect would never occur to them.

The spray ceased, warm air whipped around him and dried him completely. When he stepped through the far door of the chamber, into the ready room, his decontaminated armor and weapons were neatly stacked in his locker.

Kane removed his duty uniform from where it hung and quickly slipped into the pearl gray, high-collared bodysuit. He was tugging on his black calf-high boots when Grant emerged from the Medisterile Unit.

"Just heard," he said, hooking a thumb over his shoulder. "We can go off duty."

"What do you mean? When's the debrief?"

Shrugging his broad shoulders, Grant opened his locker and took out his own bodysuit. "Don't know, but it's not scheduled for tonight."

"Why not?"

"How do I know?" he asked peevishly. "I'm just glad to go home. I'm beat down to my arches."

Kane frowned. A debrief was SOP, especially after a deep penetration. Even after completing a routine Pit sweep, a debrief was always required.

He opened his mouth to mention it, but Pollard and MacMurphy entered the ready room. Pollard was about Kane's age, MacMurphy a little older. Of all the men on the team, Grant was the oldest, a year away from a mandatory administrative transfer.

"How's Carthew?" Kane asked.

"Blind in one eye and can't see shit out of the other," Pollard replied in his booming voice. A black-and-purple bruise showed on the side of his right knee.

"The medics have him in surgery already," MacMurphy offered. "They can maybe save one of his eyes."

Kane grimaced in sympathy, but it wasn't as if the man had a family to support. Magistrates were allowed to marry and produce legitimate offspring only when they held an administrative post. For Carthew, even if he made a full recovery, such a transfer was at least two decades away.

Becoming an administrator in the division wasn't a promotion exactly, nor was it completely based on age, though that was certainly a factor. The quality of service was the most important consideration—supposedly.

However, in the past fourteen years of his active duty, Kane had seen a number of men, admittedly only a few, with less experience and younger than he, assume administrative posts. He wasn't annoyed by it, only vaguely curious.

While the other men were busy dressing themselves, Kane quickly removed the compact disk from his belt and slipped it inside the pocket of his black, ankle-length, Kevlar-weave overcoat. He shouldered into it, a little uncomfortable as always with its weight. The right sleeve was just a bit larger than the left to accommodate the Sin Eater and holster he strapped to his forearm. After attaching his red badge to the coat's lapel, tugging the fingerless black glove over his right hand and slipping on the prerequisite dark glasses, he was ready to go off duty, though he didn't look like it. Even without the body armor and visored helmet, the Magistrate mystique, foreboding and not a little sinister, had to be maintained, especially during his downtime.

It wasn't all for show. The lenses of the glasses allowed him to see clearly in deep shadow, and the overcoat could turn anything from a knife to a .38-caliber round. The glove allowed a secure grip on the butt of the Sin Eater.

A shrill whistle cut through the ready room. Salvo's voice, filtered over the com, said, "Kane. Report to my office."

"My, don't he sound happy," commented Pollard. "I expect he wants to discuss that comment you made back in the zone."

"What comment?" Kane asked.

"You remember, when you made a passing reference to his canine lineage?"

Kane sighed. "Oh. That."

Grant said, "No matter what he says, keep your fuse unsparked."

That was Grant's way of warning Kane to watch his temper. Kane appreciated the sentiment behind it, though he didn't need the reminder. He walked past the rows of lockers, through a swing set of double doors and into the communal day room. People hustled around him, most of them wearing the gray bodysuits. They were arguing about duty rosters, scanning hard copies of daily reports, forcing down steaming cups of coffee sub. There were no women, not even filling support positions. He stayed only long enough to swallow a cup of straight sub. He desperately wished something stronger was available.

Out in the corridor, he strode quickly toward the office suites. Taking disciplinary action against a ville enforcer was a rare occurrence, since a man had to be supremely disciplined to be awarded a duty badge. Generally the worst penalty for an infraction was to be assigned a guard station at the bottom level of an Enclave tower, in the Pits.

The most severe punishment, outside of termination, was to be stripped of citizenship, barred from all the villes, reclassified as an outlander. It had never happened in Kane's lifetime, and even before he was born, barely a handful of citizens were reclassified. It only required a few examples to make everyone else tread the ace on the line.

Salvo's office was shaped like a small oval with one end chopped off. He sat behind a desk, likewise an oval. At his back was a broad window framing the moonlit towers of the Enclaves. He was thumbing through a sheaf of papers and didn't bother to look up when Kane entered.

"You may sit, Kane."

He gestured to a chair on the opposite side of his desk. "Take off the shades."

Kane restrained a sneer. Salvo wanted to assess his every eye flick. Doing as he was told, he sat down in the hard wooden chair, crossing one leg over the other, resting his left ankle on his right knee.

Salvo continued to consult the papers. "Yes. Your behavior tonight is compatible with your bloodline."

Something like anger and shame rushed heat prickles to the back of his neck. "What do you mean? Sir."

"Your father and grandfather occasionally pushed the envelope of discipline. Your grandfather in particular, but then he was a first-generation Magistrate, and all the parameters of duty had yet to be established."

A haunting of secondhand, misted memories of his grandfather drifted through Kane's mind. "He was highly decorated. His service record is still held up as an inspiration to recruits. Sir."

Salvo stopped leafing through the stack of papers, lifted his head and stared unblinkingly. Kane met that stare. Salvo was six or seven years older than himself. He had a flat, sallow face that was almost round, and his eyes were a deep, dark brown like swirling pools of muddy water. His gray-threaded hair was cut very short, and in places, the scalp showed through. He wasn't very big, but he was big enough.

"I don't want to discuss your family tree or its accomplishments," he said dryly. "You and I had problems in the zone tonight. Why?"

Kane shifted in the chair. "Permission to speak freely?"

Salvo shrugged. "This is liberty hall."

Kane pushed out a deep breath. "It was a triple-stupe mission. No preliminary recce, no adequate Intel. The team was undermanned, underprepared. It should not have gone down the way it did. We were lucky to have gotten out with only one casualty."

Salvo's thin lips pursed. "I see. And you hold me responsible."

"As commander," Kane said tightly, "it doesn't matter if *I* hold you responsible or not. You *are* responsible."

Linking his fingers together, Salvo said genially, "Indeed. Why do you think I kept the team to a bare minimum, chose the men I chose and didn't hold a debrief? Simply a whim on my part?"

Kane frowned. "I'm sure you have your reasons."

"Are you interested in hearing them?"

Kane moved uncomfortably in his seat. "I am. Sir."

"Would you agree that the welfare of the villes is entrusted to our care? That we have dedicated our lives to check the spread of poison?"

"Poison?"

Salvo nodded. "Poison like slaggers, jolt-walkers, roamers. By and large, we've been successful. Now, though, the poison is growing in virulence and spreading from the Outlands, tainting the ville territories. Do you understand me?"

"You're talking about another rebellion?" Kane's tone of voice was skeptical. Every so often, rumors would float from the Outlands about the formation of an army of the disenfranchised, preparing to stage a revolt against the ville's cushioned tyranny.

Nine times out of ten, the rumors were simply that. And in the vanishingly small percentage of instances when there was a germ of truth to the rumors, the rebel militia turned out to be a ragbag gang of roamers, outlaw wanderers of the outlands, justifying their robberies and murders by paying lip service to a political cause.

"It isn't a rebellion, not precisely," Salvo replied. "It's something bigger and nastier than that. The baron himself doesn't know exactly what's going on. You know what the outland settlements are like, especially the ones near hell-zones—no 'forcer or ville spy can last a minute in them. So all we get are the rumors.''

"Rumors of what?"

Salvo shook his head. "Fantastic stuff about a self-styled warlord holding ancient predark tech secrets. Military materiel, supposedly. Nerve gas, maybe. Possibly even a nuke warhead. Or even more advanced than that."

Kane gave a slight start. Salvo noticed and smiled. "See anything like that in Reeth's place?"

Kane managed to keep his face impassive. "Beyond the computers, the gun turret and the electrical generator, no. Damn hard stuff to get, but nothing unusual or predark about it."

Pausing meaningfully, he added, "Of course, there's still no explanation how Reeth got the stuff or how he seemed to know you. Sir."

Salvo's response was smooth and relaxed. "And you wanted that explanation and so you disobeyed my order to serve an on-sight termination warrant. You questioned him, I assume. What did he tell you?"

"Very little," Kane admitted. "He refused to speak unless you were present. Of course, when you *were* present, you didn't allow him to speak."

"True enough. I was following orders, as you should have done." Salvo lifted a hand as if to wave away an objection that wasn't forthcoming. "Don't worry. I'm not contemplating disciplinary action against you."

"May I ask why?"

"Tonight's circumstances were unique, but I chose you, Grant, Pollard, MacMurphy and young Carthew because all of you have special qualities. You think fast, you move fast and, though there's a downside to it, you also can be independent. And all of you can be trusted to keep secrets."

Kane smiled wryly. "What kind of secrets?"

"That's still classified, but if the information will ease

your mind, I'll tell you this much—tonight's penetration was part of an ongoing covert op, so covert it won't even show up on the reports. Only the baron and his immediate staff will know about it.''

Kane's mind wheeled and extrapolated. It was possible Baron Cobalt had authorized a black penetration, and it was also possible that Milton Reeth had been part of some type of sting, a link to the warlord rumors. All of it was possible, Kane conceded, but damn little of it was very likely, for a variety of reasons. The chain of command protocols was always observed and respected in the division. By invoking the baron, Salvo didn't have to justify why he broke the chain, and that seemed very convenient.

''I still find these rumors a little hard to swallow,'' Kane said noncommittally. ''I mean, how many times over the years have we heard similar ones? The outlanders are too divided, too concerned with survival, to ever make a concerted effort to overthrow the villes.''

''Think of it this way, Kane,'' Salvo declared. ''A long time ago, fearful of atomic war, the major governments played a stupe game called the 'balance of terror.' It should have been obvious, even to the most idiotic of them, that it was a matter of playing the odds, that sooner or later the balance would be tipped in the wrong direction. It finally happened, and we had a planet that came very close to being destroyed. What we have now is a complete about-face from the predark lunacy. There can never be another balance of terror, with two or more factions holding blasters to each other's head, while everybody else sits on their thumbs, wondering who'll be the first to pull the trigger. We've got to make goddamn sure only one faction has a blaster. We can't afford to ignore any hint that somebody else is trying to achieve another balance. Even if it turns out to be only another wild outland rumor. Do you understand?''

Kane said quietly, ''Yes, sir.''

"Excellent. I hope I've alleviated some of the doubts from your mind. And that's it for now."

Kane rose and started for the door.

"Kane?"

He paused, half turning. "Sir?"

Salvo held a short stack of slip-sleeved computer disks between his hands. Idly he fanned them out on the desktop, like a pack of cards. "You didn't happen to pick up anything from Reeth's place tonight, did you?"

"Like what?"

"Oh, like anything."

Kane slipped his dark glasses on over his eyes. "No. Why do you ask?"

Salvo clucked his tongue against the inside of his cheek. "Just routine. I'll be asking the same question of every member of the team."

"I see." Kane turned back to the doorway. "Good night. Sir."

Chapter 6

As he walked past the armory, Salvo's stomach muscles clenched tightly. They always did when he approached the huge storage facility that occupied nearly a quarter of C Level.

A pair of gray-clad men, eyes masked by dark glasses, stood guard before the recessed, massive vanadium-alloy sec door. They held full-auto Commando Arms carbines across their chests and they didn't acknowledge Salvo's approach or passing with so much as a nod, even though technically he was their superior officer. The protocol of armory sentries was very simple—chill anyone who tried to gain entrance, regardless of rank or social standing. Only a direct voice authorization from the baron was good for admittance.

The knowledge that even he was a legitimate target when around the arsenal always turned the pomp of Salvo's high rank to tinsel. It seemed disrespectful. Oh, he understood the reasons for the strict regulations—the walls of the huge chamber were lined with rack after rack of assorted weaponry, everything from rifles and shotguns to pistols, mortars and rocket launchers. Crates of ammunition were stacked up to the ceiling. Armored assault vehicles were also parked there, the Hussar Hotspurs and the AMACs, not to mention disassembled Deathbirds.

Almost all of it was original issue, dating from right before skydark. The planners of the old COG, or Continuity of Government, programs had prudently recognized that unlike food, medicine and clothing, technology—particularly weapons—if kept sheltered could endure the test of time and last generation after generation. Arms and equipment of every sort had been stockpiled in underground locations all over the United States.

Unfortunately the COG planners hadn't foreseen the nukecaust would be such a colossal overkill that the very people the Stockpiles had been intended for mostly perished, like the rest of the population. Some survivors of the nuking and their descendants carved out lucrative careers looting and trading the contents of the Stockpiles. Hordes of exceptionally well-armed people once rampaged across the length and breadth of the Deathlands.

When the Program of Unification was instituted during the Council of Front Royal, one of the fundamental agreements was that the people must be disarmed and the remaining Stockpiles secured. Of course, to institute this action, the barons and their security forces not only had to be better armed than the Deathland hordes, but they also had to know the locations of the Stockpiles. The barons were provided with both of these requisites, and far more.

The early years of the program had been very violent and bloody, and Salvo missed those glory days as though he had participated in them. When he was young, he had met a few doddering oldsters who claimed to have been in the thick of things, sweeping across the continent, driving the anarchist scum and so-called baron blasters into the sea.

There had been one group of baron blasters who had escaped the deadly sweeps, and in some parts of the Outlands, they were still revered as folk heroes, the subject of ballads and tall tales. The band led by the legendary Cawdor was long gone, but their exploits, if believed, were clearly a lesson for posterity.

Salvo shook his head to clear it of mental meanderings. Now that he was well past the armory, he relaxed a bit. He didn't want to appear tense or distracted during his audience with Baron Cobalt.

A dozen yards beyond the guards and the sec door, he turned to the right, down a tight, windowless passage. The passage dead-ended at a service accessway, a locked door that supposedly led down to a generator room. Salvo inserted a key into the lock and clicked it open.

Inside the door was an elevator shaft, just large enough to accommodate two men. He stepped onto the pancake-shaped disk and pulled the door shut behind him. Automatic lock solenoids snapped into place, and the disk on which he stood shot upward.

Up. Way up, far above all the other levels.

The disk hissed to a pneumatic stop, and Salvo opened the door, striding quickly across the ramp and down into the baron's suite. All the strings of power in the ville extended down from this level.

The foyer was magnificent, as was every room in the suite that Salvo had ever visited. Glittering light cast from many crystal chandeliers flooded every corner of the entrance hall.

He couldn't help but smile wryly at the lavish evidence of power, especially when he occasionally received memos that the Intel section was fast using up its allotted monthly quota of electricity.

At the far end of the foyer, flanking huge, ivory-and-gold-inlaid double doors, were two members of the elite Baronial Guard. Their polished black boots had walked no other surface than these equally polished floors; their white uniform jackets and red trousers had never been exposed to the elements of the outlands, let alone a hellzone. They gazed at him impassively, in his drab gray bodysuit, and inwardly he cursed them and Baron Cobalt for contriving such a situation to instill a sense of uncertainty and inferiority.

The guards opened the doors, and as Salvo walked between them he saw their faces twist, for the merest fraction of an instant, into sardonic smiles of superiority. Salvo ignored them. He had long ago filed their likenesses in the termination-pending section of his memory. If there should ever come a day when they found themselves within reach of his power, he would take great satisfaction in stripping them of their immaculate uniforms and dropping them naked from a Deathbird into a hellzone.

The doors shut behind him, and as he expected, he saw nothing but a deep, almost primal dark. Not black, because he could still make out dim shapes, but a dark that seemed soul deep, extending into an infinite void. Salvo kept walking forward, knowing where he was going. The baron's level was the only one in the monolith without windows, and though he burned a great deal of electricity in the foyer, he always kept his living quarters a few shades lighter than obsidian.

One room led to another, through a wide, low arch. The succession of rooms went on, and Salvo always started to feel as though the rooms would never end, with yet one more lying beyond, then another, all illuminated by the gray glow from an unseen light source. But in the fifth and final room, Salvo stopped.

Eight men stood in a formal semicircle in the center of the enormous Persian carpet that covered the floor. Several of the group were administrative members of the Magistrate Division, one was a high-ranking archivist and four were of Baron Cobalt's personal staff. Though he knew all of their names, he didn't know them personally.

Salvo managed to keep the surprise he felt from showing on his face. At most, he had expected two, maybe three of the baron's staff to be present. He had no idea that the entire membership of the Trust had been summoned. Suddenly the reason for his audience with the baron was much more important than simply delivering a report about the Mesa Verde penetration.

None of the men spoke to him, nor did he speak to them. A meeting of the Trust was neither the time nor the place for social niceties. Every ville had its own version of the Trust. The organization, if it could be called that, was the only face-to-face contact allowed with the barons, and the barons were the only contacts permitted by the Archon Directorate.

The mission of the Trust revolved around a single theme—the presence of the Directorate must not be revealed to humanity. If their presence became known, if the technological marvels they had designed became accessible, if the Directorate's history filtered down to the people, then potentially the Directorate would be forced to visit another holocaust upon the face of the earth, simply as a measure of self-preservation.

And that capability was there, Salvo had been told upon his induction into the Trust. To prevent another apocalypse, maintaining the secrecy of the Directorate and their work was a sacred trust. It was a sworn and solemn duty, offered to very few.

Unfortunately, no secret as complex and as wide-ranging as this one could be completely hidden. Rumors abounded about the Directorate and the Totality Concept even before the nukecaust, though they were relegated to the status of urban legends or contagious paranoia. During the century and a half following the skydark, some of the secrets were discovered. Humanity, what was left of it, was too scattered even for the Directorate to control. The near annihilation of the race hadn't diminished the race's inborn sense of curiosity, the drive to search in strange places for strange things.

Many of those strange places were penetrated, the strange things uncovered, but humankind was too concerned with day-to-day survival to reason out the why's and wherefore's behind them. It required only a generation to reduce the knowledge of strange places and things to mere rumors, and another generation to fanciful legends.

Salvo recalled that some thirty years before, a junior archivist in Ragnarville had found an old computer disk purporting to contain the journal of one Mildred Wyeth, a scientist. According to the journal, she had been in suspended animation during the nuking and she had survived the skydark and the long nuclear winter to be revived a century later.

Sometime during her wanderings, she recorded her thoughts, observations and speculations regarding the post-nukecaust world, the redoubts and the wonders they contained.

Although she had no inkling of the true nature of the redoubts or even the presence of the Directorate, a number of her extrapolations came too close to the truth.

The Trust suspected the *Wyeth Codex* had been downloaded, copied and disseminated like a virus through the Historical Divisions of the entire ville network. There was no solid proof of this, of course—only anxieties that gave rise to the fear that an elite group of historians/insurgents, labelled Preservationists by the Intel section, might know far more than the Trust or even the barons themselves.

At the measured tones of a gong Salvo cleared his mind of thoughts as all the men turned as one to face a patch of murk. In the gloom, a door slowly opened. Behind a filmy gauze curtain, a golden light, suffused in pastel hues, slanted down from above. The gong struck thirteen jubilant strokes, and the shaft of muted golden light became a glare. Right before the glare faded to its previous soft hue, a dark figure appeared within it.

The baron had arrived.

Salvo, in twenty-three years as a Magistrate and his five years as a member of the Trust, had never gotten a clear, unobstructed view of Baron Cobalt. With his eyes still recovering from the sudden glare, and with the figure drifting, always in nervous motion, pacing back and forth behind the golden filter, he received the same impression as always—a gaunt man under six feet tall, head bowed as if in intense concentration, one hand under the chin, the other behind his back. He appeared to be wearing a flesh-colored bodysuit with a short cape drifting from the shoulders.

The baron's face was in dark shadow, but Salvo was able to glimpse a long, narrow visage and a round, hairless skull

hat seemed just a bit too large. He had no idea of the color
or shape of the baron's eyes.

"Milton Reeth." The voice was pitched to a pleasant,
musical contralto. It was Baron Cobalt himself who spoke.

Salvo didn't respond for a moment, and inwardly he
cursed his hesitation as he stepped forward. "The termination warrant was served. By my own hand. I collected
all the evidence of the arrangement."

The slim figure of the Baron paced into the murk, a flit-
ing shadow, then it returned to be silhouetted by the golden
light. "Regrettable. His merchandise was excellent in the
beginning. Why he thought he could continue supplying
such execrable, substandard substitutes remains a puzzle."

"Greed," said Abrams, the Magistrate administrator.
"He was offered a unique opportunity, we set him up to
take full advantage of it, yet he desired more and he desired
it more rapidly."

"Yes," Salvo declared a bit too loudly. He wanted to
keep the Baron's attention focused primarily on himself.
"He found it easier to attract Dregs with his promises of
smuggling them into the ville. Healthy outlanders were
skeptical of him, and the Dregs had nothing to lose."

"Yes," agreed Baron Cobalt contemplatively. "Greed.
It's a kind of sickness, a compulsion, isn't it?"

No one answered.

"What of the men you chose to implement the termination? Did they see or hear anything that would arouse
suspicion?"

"No, Baron," replied Salvo stolidly. "Reeth was too
afraid to reveal anything to them. He evidently thought a
mistake had been made in administration, and it could be
rectified if he spoke with me."

"He was correct in a way, wasn't he?" The baron's
laugh was the trilling of a bird.

Lakesh, the wizened senior archivist, asked gruffly,
"What about that loose blaster of yours whom you took
along?"

Salvo didn't hide the irritation in his tone. "I have no such men under my command."

"Come now, Salvo," said Baron Cobalt. "Lakesh is being annoyingly oblique, but you know to whom he refers."

Taking a breath, Salvo declared, "Kane saw nothing of importance. If he did, it was beyond his understanding. I spoke with him privately only a few minutes ago, and he accepted the cover story. If he is curious, I kept it in check."

"Superficially, perhaps," Abrams argued. "Curiosity runs very strong in the Kane line. We all remember his grandfather and father, possibly two of the best Magistrates in any division in any ville."

"And," intoned Guende, the small-statured staff member, "they suffered the same fate as the fabled cat. At least in the case of your predecessor, Salvo."

The baron moved again, drifting gracefully toward the shadows, then back into the light. "The Dulce operation is a very critical one, as we know. The need for raw materials seems to increase exponentially, the closer the program comes to fruition. Therefore, Salvo, it's been decided by the Trust, after a consultation with the Directorate, that you are instructed to take charge of the accruing, processing and transportation of the merchandise to Dulce."

Salvo couldn't help but smile. He had always hoped, ever since being inducted into the Trust, that his efforts on its behalf would be rewarded with a position of authority.

"Thank you, Lord Baron, I will faithfully—"

Baron Cobalt cut him off with a gently admonishing hiss. "This is a particularly delicate operation, even in these late stages. The nukecaust prevented it from achieving completion, and now finally it is within sight. It is a matter requiring careful planning and, therefore, absolutely no unforeseen variables to contend with. You must use your position in the Magistrate Division to carry out the edicts, and that means you will need help."

"I'm sure the Trust is more than able to provide me with all the support I could possibly need—"

The baron interrupted him again. "No, Salvo. You misunderstand. You need a confidant, a pawn. With all the men under your command, surely there is one who would be of service to you in this undertaking."

Salvo was silent a moment, then smiled coldly. "Only one, Lord Baron."

"Yes."

"Kane."

A shocked murmur rippled among the members of the Trust. Abrams gave a stallion snort of derision. "Are you mad?" he demanded. "His father—"

"The division is Kane's only father," snapped Salvo. "He has no idea of what actually happened to the man. He probably thinks he's still up here, pushing paper and filling out water-requisition reports. No, Kane is as hard and as bright as a blade. He has no use for slaggers or outlanders. With the proper inducement, I'm sure he would find my offer a very unique opportunity."

"And so do you," Lakesh said mockingly. "For cruel irony."

"That has nothing to do with it," Salvo replied stiffly, "Kane is like his father only in his devotion to serving the ville."

Abrams snorted again to indicate his disapproval. "Yes, we believed the same of his father. To our sorrow. And your gain."

Baron Cobalt laughed, a soft, lilting sound. "The proposal has merit, on a number of points. If Kane refuses your offer, Salvo, an accident on duty can be easily arranged. Or like his father, he can be appointed to an administrative position and never be seen again. Yes, Salvo, I approve."

Salvo nodded formally. "Thank you. You will find your confidence well placed."

He was careful to strike the correct balance between expressing his gratitude and a deserved pride.

The golden light flickered, dimmed, and Baron Cobalt stepped back beneath the arch. The audience was over as quickly as it had begun.

The pudgy man named Horan wasted no time whirling on Salvo. "This is a dangerous game you're playing."

Salvo smiled cheerfully. "Consider, then, that the advantage far outweighs the risk."

"How can you possibly *trust* Kane?" Guende asked incredulously. "His father, his grandfather—"

"He's a Magistrate first," Salvo announced. "A Kane second."

He left the other members of the Trust standing on the Persian carpet. Abrams caught up with him before he passed through the final arch. "A word, if you will."

Abrams's carriage was ramrod straight, despite his deeply seamed face, the iron gray in his hair and square-cut beard. Salvo nodded to him respectfully. Abrams was one of the old guard of the division, entering it at the very end of the first generation. Despite the fact he had served as an administrator longer than he had as a Magistrate, Salvo had to admit that Abrams's performance in both positions was outstanding.

"Your plan seems ill conceived," said Abrams softly, grimly. "Almost perverse."

"It is not, Administrator, I assure you." The deference in Salvo's tone was genuine. "Why do you think so?"

"Because Kane has options. He is not alone, he is not isolated. He has a friend, and therefore an emotional center. A grounding in an identity."

Salvo nodded. "You mean Grant."

"Grant. Though fraternization between Magistrates is discouraged, you have allowed those two to forge a bond."

"Grant is due for administrative transfer. That will break the bond."

Abrams shook his head. "It will weaken it, not shatter

it. The bond must be broken as dramatically and traumatically as possible, so Kane will seek a substitute to fill the void.''

Abrams's voice was like his hair—all iron. He took a deep breath and said, ''As was done to me.''

Salvo suddenly understood. Abrams's lover had been chilled by a self-styled Pit boss decades ago. He'd become cynical and morose, and therefore an excellent candidate for the Trust. Salvo also understood Abrams had accepted the likelihood that the murder had been ordered by the baron, not the Pit boss.

''Yes, Administrator,'' Salvo said softly. ''As was done to you.''

He turned and left the chambers. As he entered the brilliantly lit hall, he paused long enough to stare contemplatively at the two guards. They met his gaze impassively.

''Soon,'' he said, and went on his way. His thoughts swarmed with speculations. He would make his new responsibility a spectacular success, and then neither the Baron nor the Directorate could deny him anything, even a whim. Nothing else mattered. Instant termination would be the immediate fate of anyone who opposed or even postponed that success.

Including, even if circumstances didn't warrant it, the third Magistrate to bear the loathsome name of Kane.

Chapter 7

Kane didn't go home. He hung out in the dayroom, taking a corner table away from the door, blocked from the glances of passersby in the corridor by people coming and going. The table was also out of the range of the vid spy-eye attached to the ceiling. He sipped at a cup of sub, and read over the daily Intel report transmitted along the ville network.

Intel Level. Copies All Mag Divs

Ragnarville, MN—After several incursions in the territory, a band of roamers was apprehended and terminated. Sympathizers within ville also terminated.
Mandeville, KS—Measures taken to degrade fighting ability among hostile Lakota group include introduction of nerve toxins into hunting grounds.
    Snakefishville, CA—Report of stickie clan settlement on Western Island investigated, no foundation for report.

The reports from the other five villes comprising the network were similar. Even by reading between the lines, there wasn't even the vaguest hint of a rebellion brewing anywhere, much less the appearance of a charismatic warlord.
    The territories controlled by the villes were vast. Cobaltville itself had absorbed several Colorado baronies, including Vistaville and Hightower. The other ville territories were arranged similarly, so if anything as big and nasty as

Salvo had described was brewing, some crumb of Intel should appear on the reports.

Though it was heresy to even think of it, Kane was certain Salvo was lying. The barbs about his father and grandfather had been aimed to prick his pride, make him question his doubts.

Kane held his two namesakes in high regard, and he felt that he, the third Kane to serve as a Magistrate, had to measure up to a level of duty established decades before.

The use of first names in the division had been taboo for three generations. The original drafters of the Program of Unification had believed that only surnames, family names, engendered a sense of obligation to the duties of their ancestors' office, ensuring that subsequent generations never lost touch with their hereditary roles as enforcers. Last names became badges of social distinction, almost titles.

If nothing else, Kane thought a little sourly, it kept every man toeing the line so he wouldn't tarnish the honor of his antecedents.

Kane had never met his grandfather. He had been chilled fifteen years before he was born in the retaking of the Pits from insurgents who believed ville authority was completely arbitrary. That had been a bloodbath. Many Magistrates had been literally torn limb from limb by the rioting Pit dwellers.

As for his father, Kane had seen him only rarely after he had joined the division. Though they were never close, his relationship with his father had turned stiff and coldly formal, as if the man were disappointed in him. Or afraid of him. His father had virtually disappeared from his life once he assumed the mandatory administrator's post. For all Kane knew, he could have died three years ago, shortly after the last time he had spoken to him.

He lingered for an hour in the dayroom, then went out into the broad, brightly lighted main corridor. He headed toward the elevator tube that would deposit him at his Enclave. He passed Salvo's office. The door was open, but the desk was vacant. Kane kept walking, then turned sharply into the Intel section. Two steps inside, he paused and looked around. His arrival was unnoticed, except by the spy-eye rotating slowly on the ceiling.

The room was spacious, with vaulted walls. More than a dozen people were sitting before banks of computers with flashing readouts and indicators. Vid monitor screens displayed incomprehensible images, probably from the alleys of the Pits. The cool semidarkness of the whole place hummed with the subdued beeping of machines and the quiet murmur of comm-techs communicating with other villes and Magistrates out in the field.

Kane's gaze shifted to the left, and he spotted the man he was looking for. He waited until the vid spy-eye lens was no longer focused on the door, then he strode over to Morales and clapped him on the shoulder. "How are you?"

Morales looked up from his deck of computers, hard drives and monitor screens and forced a smile, trying to wipe away the look of boredom on his swart face.

"Fine," he said. "Working late, are you?"

"Just a little. I wonder if you would like doing a little favor for me."

Morales suddenly sat up straighter in his chair. When a hard-contact Magistrate asked a support tech for a favor, there was no option but to grant it. No matter how it was worded, a request from a Magistrate was always a command. Kane knew that and how to exploit it.

Turning his back to the vid camera on the ceiling, he fished the compact disk from his pocket and handed it to Morales. "Put this through a read program, please."

Morales eyed the disk warily. Normally computer-time demands came through the duty officer, but the likelihood was that the tech wasn't inclined to point this out. He inserted the disk into the input port and tapped a few keys on the board. The triangle-and-lines symbol flashed onto the screen, accompanied by the legend, "Disk is locked. Access denied. Encryption key required."

Morales frowned. "Do you have the key?"

"No," Kane replied casually. "Just run it through the Syne, why don't you?"

Nodding, Morales popped out the disk and plucked a small metal device from a hook beneath his desk. The Mnemosyne, or Syne as commonly called, was a lock decrypter, shaped like an elongated circle divided down the center by a thread-thin slit. He placed the edge of the disk into the slit and thumbed a stud on the instrument's surface. It produced a faint, very high-pitched whine.

After ten seconds, the noise ceased, Morales removed the disk from the decryption device and pushed the disk back into the hard drive. His fingers danced over the keyboard. The monitor screen lit up with the red triangle again, as well as with the words, "Disk is locked. Access denied. Encryption key required."

Both Kane and Morales made sounds of surprise. Morales muttered, "What the fuck? This shouldn't happen— the encryption lock should have been overridden."

Kane was only moderately familiar with computers. To him, they were simply sometimes useful machines, and their more arcane workings held little interest for him. However, he knew the Syne was designed to perform only one function—to sidestep security lockouts and make digital memory accessible and available.

Morales worked the keys again, but the image and the words on the screen remained unchanged.

"This is something you don't see every day," he said, irritated and enthralled at the same time. "Whoever wrote the program knew how to safeguard it against the Syne."

"Who would have that knowledge?"

Morales shrugged. "Nobody I know or ever heard of, that's for sure." He paused, chewing on his lower lip. "Want my best guess? Whoever wrote the program either helped to engineer the Syne or had access to the specs."

He slid out the disk and handed it back to Kane. "The thing's useless unless you stumble onto the encryption key.

I suggest you take it up to archives. Somebody there might have an idea of how to unlock it.''

Pocketing the disk, still sounding casual, Kane said, "Thanks. By the way—"

"Yeah?"

"This never happened. You never saw me. We never had this conversation." Kane folded his arms over his chest, allowing Morales the briefest of glimpses of the Sin Eater under his right sleeve.

The tech's expression didn't alter. "I don't know what you're talking about. I don't know anything about encryption codes. I'm just a key-tapper."

"I know," said Kane with a friendly smile. "That's why I came to you."

He returned to the main hallway and went directly to the elevator. Pushing the appropriate button, he realized there was no point in putting off the inevitable. He had to go home sometime.

The shaft doors opened upon his Enclave living level. Just outside the shaft was a wrought-iron gate, tall and heavy, with metal hinges that looked like tarnished brass. Kane placed his right hand flat on the small iridescent panel on the front of the gate, where the keyhole should have been. Within the panel, the sensor grid read his handprint, decided he was not a slagger thief or a roamer, and the gate swung open noiselessly.

The promenade was virtually deserted at this hour. The broad pedestrian avenue was lined with evergreen saplings, giving the recycled air a pleasant fragrance. The trees were illuminated by lamps hung from the lower branches.

Kane passed rockcrete stoops leading up to single-dwelling apartments. Each facade looked the same, with one window facing out on the promenade. In the half-dozen lit windows he glanced into, he saw the same furnishings, the same color schemes.

Conformity, standardization, whatever the euphemism, the four-room apartments were essentially interchangeable.

He often wondered wryly why outlanders and Pit dwellers viewed the Enclaves as some sort of enchanted land, heaven on earth. He supposed they were, if your idea of heaven on earth was a cell block.

Kane went up the stoop to his flat and opened the door. It was unlocked. None of the doors on any Enclave level had locks. It was a carryover from the Program of Unification, when the Council of Front Royal had decided that privacy bred conspiracy. The council had further decreed that since everyone had the same possessions as everyone else, there was no need to steal, especially among the elite. The desire for privacy was viewed not just as gauche, but as an expression of deviant thinking. Kane was pretty sure, though, that the Pit residents had locks on their doors.

Once inside, Kane went to his cabinet and found his bottle of vintage wine. He uncapped it and took a long swallow. Grant, who had found it during a Pit sweep the year before, had given it to him as a gift. He would be annoyed with him for treating the rare liquor like common trash-hatch hootch. It was curious that the predark delicacy had survived so many years and still retained its full-bodied flavor. The Beforetime vintners had certainly known their craft.

He carried it over to his sagging couch and flopped down, looking out through the three tall windows on the far wall at the lights glittering on the surface of the Administrative Monolith. From his pocket, he took out the compact disk and held it in his palm. Morales had suggested he take it to the Historical Division, but since this wasn't an official line of inquiry, he would be risking having his request channeled to Salvo for confirmation.

He tipped the bottle up and took a pull, felt the thick, fruity liquid scorch a path into his stomach. He considered swallowing a sedative capsule along with it so he could reverse his anxiety and get some sleep. But the tranquilizers often made him feel as if he were walking underwater, and such sluggishness of mind and reflexes was anathema to a Magistrate.

Glancing around at his few paltry personal possessions, he realized that he had absolutely nothing anyone would want, except maybe the bottle of wine. It wasn't much, but it was all he was ever likely to have. Most of his property had been inherited from his grandfather and father. Since his apartment was more or less the Kane ancestral home, it should have been filled with relics of earlier generations.

But it wasn't. A couple of lamps, a chair, a table, a sofa, the futon in the bedroom, a few antique books wrapped in plastic, a couple of ancient muzzle loaders confiscated from traders nearly thirty years ago, and a pix of himself standing between his father and mother.

He looked at the image of the cocky, eager kid he used to be. He was smiling in the picture. His father and mother weren't. His dad had the same dark hair and high-planed features, but he looked brooding and unhappy. His mother looked the same.

Kane hadn't seen either of his parents in years. His mother had vanished from his life right after he entered the division. Her disappearance wasn't unusual. Though matrimony and child producing were considered the supreme social responsibility by the barons, it was also considered only a temporary arrangement.

Children were a necessity for the continuation of society, but only those passing stringent tests were allowed to bear them. Genetics, moral values and social standing were the most important criteria. Generally a man and a woman were bound together for a length of time stipulated in a contract. Once the child entered a training regimen of one of the ville divisions, the parents were required to separate, particularly in the case of male children recruited by the Magistrates. So his mother had removed herself. She probably realized there was a limit to the pointlessness she could endure of being a parent in absentia.

It was *all* pointless, really.

Who was she? Was the entire purpose of her life to give birth to him? After he entered the division, her duties discharged, the rest of her life must have been one long, total anticlimax.

God knew he tried to see a point and adjust his life in its direction. During his first, formative years at the division, he believed in the Unity through Action doctrine, believed that humans were too intrinsically destructive to be allowed free will and free rein.

The ruined planet was mute testimony to that philosophy, and he hadn't argued with it. Who in his right mind could?

He agreed that the wicked old Beforetime of smoldering desperation and unchecked chaos was inferior in every way to the ville societies. Medical advances kept people from dying early from nukecaust-induced toxins, but the world was still underpopulated. Babies needed to be born, but only the *right* kind of babies. Like him and everybody else in the Enclaves.

That was the theory. Deep inside of himself, nearly buried by the strictures of duty, was the notion that there was something very wrong with the theory, at least in practice.

The contradiction in the theory was that all of the predark advances in science, all of the achievements, meant absolutely nothing. They were worthless. Yet those same predark achievements had been the building blocks of the Program of Unification. All that Unity through Action had accomplished was simple control—establishing a status, then a quo, and then a method of maintaining it.

He put the bottle on the floor, noting absently it showed more clear glass than dark wine. Balancing the disk on his fist, he tried flipping it with his thumb, as if it were a coin. Instead, it clattered to the floor and rolled across it on its edge. When he sat up to retrieve it, he felt a not unpleasant wave of dizziness. He plucked the disk from the floor. The mystery it represented gnawed at his peace of mind, like the wine gnawed at his equilibrium. He wondered how many minds throughout history had been unbalanced by drinking the stuff.

When he thought of history, he thought of the archives. And he thought of a woman he had seen several months before on the promenade. He had learned she was a high-ranking archivist and she lived on this Enclave level. He couldn't be sure, but he thought her name was Baptist or something.

Kane unsuccessfully swallowed a belch and eyed the disk, held between thumb and forefinger.

Yeah, Baptist or something.

Chapter 8

Brigid Baptiste stepped out of the tiny shower stall and used a towel to dry her mounds of red-gold hair. There was nothing she could do to keep it from reverting to its naturally curly state. Wearing it pinned up all day tended to give her a headache, and once a co-worker had suggested she cut it short.

She had pretended to consider the notion, while privately scoffing at the unimaginative suggestion. Her hair, as thick and as heavy as it might be, was her only legacy from her mother.

Rather than don the bodysuit with the small rainbow-striped insignia of the Historical Division on its breast, she walked naked into her private cubicle adjoining the bedroom. The cubicle had once been a closet, but she had converted it into a crowded, miniature version of her work area in the division. There was just enough space in the small box of a room for her desk, desktop display and a chair.

The computer was a cast-off DDC model, one that had been remanufactured several times. The older the DDCs became, the less able they were to sustain their workloads. Brigid had picked this one up out of a trash hatch and spent weeks repairing it.

Technically what she'd done was illegal, but archivists were allowed a certain leeway in the pursuit of their professions. Besides, she was fairly certain the machine had been planted deliberately by a Preservationist for her to find and salvage.

She sat down at the machine, turned it on and put on her

badge of office, a pair of wire-framed, rectangular-lensed spectacles. Unlike many archivists, the eyeglasses were not of historical importance to her, but were a necessity. Years of inputting predark data and documents, reading screens and staring at columns of tiny type had resulted in a minor vision problem.

Ville manufacturing hadn't gotten around to mass-producing contact lenses, and she doubted they ever would. The barons frowned on them as expressions of human vanity, and therefore considered them superfluous.

While the machine ticked through its warm-up sequence, Brigid closed her eyes and regulated her breathing, focusing her mind on the documents she had seen that day.

Almost everyone who worked in one of the divisions kept secrets, whether they were infractions of the law, unrealized ambitions or deviant sexual predilections. Brigid Baptiste's secret was more arcane than petty crimes or manipulating the system for personal aggrandizement.

Her secret was the ability to produce eidetic images. Centuries ago, it had been called a photographic memory. She could, after viewing an object or scanning a document, retain exceptionally vivid and detailed visual memories.

When she was growing up, she feared she was a psi-mutie, but she later learned that the ability was relatively common among children and usually disappeared by adolescence. It was supposedly very rare among adults.

Brigid was one of the exceptions, and she often suspected her eidetic memory was the primary reason she had been covertly contacted by the Preservationists. But there was no way they could have known of her ability, except through information provided by her mother. Brigid hadn't seen her in thirteen years, yet she found comforting the possibility that her mother was somehow associated with the Preservationists.

Now twenty-seven, Brigid had trained for ten years to be an archivist, and for the past six had worked as one. Despite the common misconception, archivists were not bookish, bespectacled pedants. They were primarily data-entry techs, albeit ones with high-security clearances. Midgrade senior archivists like herself were editors.

A vast amount of predark historical information had survived the nukecaust, particularly documents stored in underground vaults. Tons of it, in fact, everything from novels to encyclopedias, to magazines printed on coated stock that survived just about anything. Much more data was digitized, stored on computer diskettes, usually government documents.

Even though she was a fairly senior archivist, she wasn't among the highest. Those in the upper echelons, holding ''X'' clearances, were responsible for viewing, editing or suppressing the most-sensitive material. Still, she had glimpsed enough to know there were bits and bytes of information that were still classified, even all this time after the nuking.

Her primary duty wasn't to record predark history, but to revise, rewrite and often times completely disguise it. The political causes leading to the nukecaust were well-known. They were major parts of the dogma, the doctrine, the articles of faith, and they had to be accurately recorded for posterity.

Scheming, wicked Russkies had detonated a nuclear warhead in the basement of their embassy in Washington, D.C., even while they negotiated for peace. American retaliation had been swift and total. The world came very close to transforming into a smoldering, lifeless cinder spinning darkly in space.

People were responsible. Russians, Americans, Asians. People had put irresponsible individuals into positions of responsibility, so ergo, the responsibility for the nukecaust was the responsibility of people. Humanity as a whole.

Brigid had believed that, of course. For many years, she had never questioned it. Humankind had been judged guilty, and the sentence carried out forthwith.

As she rose up the ranks, promoted mainly through attrition, she was allowed greater access to secret records. Though these were heavily edited, she came across references to something called the Totality Concept, to devices called gateways, to a place called the Anthill Complex and to projects bearing the code names of Chronos and Whisper, which hinted at phenomena termed "probability wave dysfunctions" and "alternate event horizons."

She wasn't foolish or disturbed enough to voice her growing skepticism of the accepted dogma. She realized something more was there. But archivists were always watched, probably more than anyone else working in the other divisions. She had worked hard at perfecting a poker face. She wondered if some of the material handed to her was a test to gauge her reaction. Because of that suspicion, she had gained a reputation of cool calm, unflappable and immutable.

The only time that composure nearly cracked was one morning a year before, at the beginning of her shift. She had inserted a computer disk into her machine and opened it up. She had selected the disk at random, and so the message flashing onto the monitor screen had stunned her into momentary immobility. In that numbed moment, she read:

Greetings, fellow scholar. We are the Preservationists. You have distinguished yourself as a seeker and collector of knowledge. Only those deemed most worthy of preserving the hidden history of humanity are selected to join us. We will contact you again very soon.

Then the message faded from the screen, as if it had a programmed time limit.

Brigid never mentioned the message. She was terrified by it, yet enthralled at the same time. Weeks passed before she was contacted a second time, and she supposed the gap between communiqués had been deliberate, a way of finding out if she would report the incident.

She also suspected a trap, something devised by the Magistrates. Only someone in her own division could have planted the disk. God only knew how long it had been on her desk before she had chosen to open it up.

The second message was just as brief, promising to contact her again in the near future. In the weeks that followed, more messages appeared on her screen. She slowly understood that the Preservationists were archivists like herself, scattered thoughout the villes. They were devoted to preserving past knowledge, to piecing together the unrevised history of not only the predark, but also the postholocaust world.

Whoever the Preservationists were, they had anticipated her initial skepticism and apprehension. To show their good faith, she found an unfamiliar disk in her work area one morning. When she opened it, the message said simply, "Read only in private."

Shortly thereafter, she had found, retrieved and repaired the cast-off DDC. Though her curiosity was almost an agony, she kept it in control until the computer was operational. Then she slid in the disk and read the data it contained. Brigid was never the same again, even though she still sometimes suspected she was the victim of an intricate hoax.

On the disk was the journal of a woman called Mildred Winona Wyeth. A medical doctor, a specialist in cryogenics, she had entered a hospital in late 2000 for minor surgery. An idiosyncratic reaction to the anesthetic left her in a coma, with her vital signs sinking fast. To save her life, the predark whitecoats had her cryonically frozen.

She was revived over a century later, by Ryan Cawdor, about whom many tales still circulated. It was startling to read that Cawdor was indeed a real person, not a fabled folk hero, and she joined his band of warrior survivalists.

Though the journal contained recollections of adventures and wanderings, it dealt in the main with Dr. Wyeth's observations, speculations and theories about the environmental conditions of postnukecaust America.

Her journal also delved into the history of one Dr. Theophilus Algernon Tanner, who'd been a test subject for a project called Operation Chronos.

Brigid hadn't known how much of the *Wyeth Codex* to believe. Worse, she hadn't known how much to disbelieve, or who her mysterious contact might be. But the *Wyeth Codex* began her secret association with the Preservationists. Her assignment was to memorize any documents at variance with ville doctrine, put them in cogent form and use the trash hatch where she had found the DDC as a dead drop. She cooperated with the instructions, only to learn more.

She often suspected Lakesh was the Preservationist intermediary, but a year had passed with no overt or even oblique inference on his part, so she had dismissed him as a candidate.

The computer warmed up, and Brigid began tapping the keys. Her machine at the division was voice activated, and a manual keyboard seemed slow and clumsy. She entered the data she had glimpsed on a Department of Defense document, bearing the date of April 30, 1994.

Since she had merely glanced at it, no one would suspect her memory retained almost every word and punctuation mark. She did not input the document verbatim, since the Preservationists encouraged extrapolation.

Possible Origin of Magistrate Division—Source:
DoD Document, Dated 4/30/94

The concept of a one-world government was known in predark vernacular as the "New World Order." The globalist view was opposed by many American citizens as a conspiracy to remove legal and civil rights granted to them by the Constitution (re. file #01405).

The conspiracy theories were given a degree of

plausibility by the so-called Black Helicopter Phenomenon, circa 1970 through 1997. Black and silent, these helicopters were unmarked and therefore unidentifiable. At first reported in remote areas, the aircraft seemed to be engaged in clandestine missions. They were repeatedly seen in conjunction with what was known as Unidentified Flying Objects (Re. file #65391). Contemporaneous with these sightings of both black helicopters and UFOs was the mystery of mutilated farm animals and, occasionally, human beings.

Self-professed UFO investigators speculated that the helicopters were part of a covert military force, working in tandem with extraterrestrials. The extraterrestrials allegedly required animal tissue and blood for sustenance, or for the genetic process of creating alien-human hybrids (re. file #89003).

Though the DoD document does not directly address this possibility, it does refer to the Archon Directive as the project overseeing the animal mutilations. The document also states quite clearly that one aspect of the mutilations dealt with the secret testing of bio-warfare agents, including viruses specifically targeting certain ethnic groups, as part of the Human Genome Project.

The document also makes reference to urban-warfare training programs wherein house-to-house searches for illegal firearms were conducted in major cities during the early 1990s. Men in black armor, disgorged from black helicopters, conducted these searches.

In 1992, Alaska hosted an event referred to as Police 2000, with participating military and police personnel from America, Russia and Canada all merging to form a transnational police organization, designed to "protect the coming global village."

Obviously, by the time of the nukecaust, the creation of an international police force was well under way. The DoD document mentions PPD-25, a presidential directive signed in 1994 that opened the door to direct intervention in domestic affairs by officers of this international police agency. The document defines quite frankly the broad powers granted to this "supranational authority to enforce the edicts of the New World Order."

Therefore, it is reasonable to assume that the formation of what evolved into the Magistrate Division was already under way. The document makes this statement: "Their authority will be based on internal disruption of current societal norms."

Brigid took a breath and raised her arms above her head, arching her back to work out the kinks in her shoulder muscles. She tried to keep her mind empty, visualizing nothing but the rest of the document.

The bedroom door swung open, and her head swiveled toward it so quickly she felt a twinge of tendon pain. Immediately, almost instinctively, she swept her hand across the keyboard, hitting the Escape button, clearing the screen of its data.

She stared at a dark-haired, clean-shaven man in a long black overcoat. Though she couldn't see it, she almost felt the bore of the Sin Eater trained on her naked body.

Nothing had been true.

It had all been a trap after all.

The Magistrates had found her.

Chapter 9

For the second time that night, Kane wasn't quite sure of what he was looking at. This time, at least, despite his alcohol-impaired reactions, he was able to quickly identify and catalog what his vision transmitted to his brain.

He looked at the naked figure leaping to her feet, and he recognized a truly beautiful woman. Her hair was wild and wavy and thick, falling artlessly over her bare shoulders. Her features were delicate, striking. A blush crept from the base of her slim neck and moved up across her face, finally becoming lost in her red-gold mane. Her complexion, fair and lightly dusted with freckles across her nose and cheeks, was left a rosy pink in its wake. Her bespectacled eyes weren't just green; they were a deep, clear emerald, glittering now in sudden fright.

Her body was slender but rounded, long in the leg, the breasts full yet taut, her belly hard and flat above a soft, honey blond triangle at the juncture of her thighs.

The woman put her back to the wall of the little cubicle and stared at him unblinkingly.

Kane could think of only one thing to say, so he asked, "Are you Baptist?"

Some of the terror dimmed in the woman's eyes. "Are you asking my name or my religion?" Her voice was melodically husky.

Kane swallowed the hard lump that swelled in his throat, and he felt a sudden sharp sense of embarrassment. "What?"

"The way things are," the woman continued, her tone growing more confident with every word, "I presume you're asking my name. It's pronounced Bap-*teest*. Brigid Baptiste. Why didn't you knock?''

''I'm Magistrate Kane—''

''And Magistrate Kane doesn't have to knock?''

Embarrassment slowly gave way to ego-induced irritation. ''That's right, Baptiste. Magistrate Kane doesn't have to knock.''

The woman squinted at him carefully over the rims of her glasses. She seemed infuriatingly at ease with her nudity. Her nose wrinkled slightly.

''Magistrate Kane doesn't have to be sober, either. Right?''

The absurdity of the situation finally penetrated Kane's befogged mind, and he surprised the woman and himself. He laughed.

''Magistrates *do* have to be sober,'' he said, ''and archivists do have to wear clothes. At least when they're on duty.''

A bit of the tense wariness left Brigid Baptiste's posture. ''This isn't an official visit?''

''No,'' Kane answered. ''Yes. Hell, I don't know. Why don't you put something on? I'm distracted enough as it is.''

Brigid obligingly turned her back and took a robe hanging from a clothes hook on the wall of her improvised office. Kane watched her slip it on and tie the sash, aware of a strange yearning growing within him. It wasn't lust. It felt like melancholy, as if he had glimpsed something wonderful he'd never see again. He knew Brigid Baptiste was afraid of him, but she controlled it admirably. No, correction—she wasn't afraid of him as a person, but of the office he represented. He experienced a flash of irrational resentment and anger at his Magistrate persona.

Brigid stepped in front of the desktop console, as if trying to shield it from his view. Calmly she said, ''If this isn't an official visit, you should have knocked or transcommed me.''

He waved away her comment. "We're beyond my bad manners, Baptiste. However, if it will make you feel better, I'll apologize." He paused, then added, "I am sorry."

A faint smile touched her full lips. Kane thought, *she never expected to hear a Magistrate apologize about anything. For that matter, I never expected it, either.*

"What can I do for you?" she asked crisply, sitting down before the computer console.

Kane had almost forgotten the disk in his pocket. Making a wordless utterance of self-annoyance, he fished it out of his coat pocket and extended the gleaming circle toward her. She didn't take it. Instead, she eyed it as though he were trying to hand her a venomous snake.

"What is it?"

"A CD-ROM," he answered. "I want you to try to open the encryption lock so I can read it. I see you have a computer here."

"Why me?" she asked suspiciously. "Your Intel section has comps, doesn't it?"

"Humor me, Baptiste."

She didn't move. "Is this some kind of a trap, to get my prints on that so you can charge me with a crime?"

Kane smiled ruefully. "If I wanted to charge you with a crime, I don't need to go to all this trouble."

She returned the smile, though wanly, and took the disk from his outstretched hand. As she slid it into the port, Kane commented, "An old manual DDC model. Thought most of them had been retired."

"Yes," she stated matter-of-factly as she worked the keyboard. "Found it in a trash hatch. The housing is somewhat battered—see the fine cracks on the left of the screen? But that's just a small external flaw. I reconditioned it, but it's not tied into a data feed from the mainframes, of course."

"Of course." Kane realized he should have lectured her about appropriating division property, even that slated for disposal, but it didn't seem pertinent. He knew that some archivists were permitted to bend the rules, just like some Magistrates.

Flashing on the screen now was the maddeningly persistent red-triangle symbol and the glowing message.

"It's locked," she announced.

"I know that."

"Why don't you run it through the Syne?"

"I did. Didn't take."

She cast him a surprised over-the-shoulder glance. "Really?"

"Really. I was told the disk was specifically designed to circumvent the Syne."

She tapped her chin contemplatively. "That's unusual."

"Unprecedented," Kane declared. He managed to turn a hiccup into a throat-clearing sound.

"That, too. Where did it come from?"

"I can't tell you that."

Brigid shot him a sharp, narrow-eyed glare. "I have a 'Q' clearance, you know."

"And I have a 'Q Ultra.' For all I know, the data on the disk may require an 'X' clearance."

"Which neither of us have," she argued. "And if you take it to someone who does, you'll be asked the same question. Where did it come from?"

"I found it in a smuggler's den, a slaghole out in a hell-zone. He had a DDC system, too. A current one."

Her emerald eyes widened. "In a slaghole? Where'd he get it?"

"That," Kane replied grimly, "is something I intend to find out. And the only clue is that damn disk."

Nodding, Brigid said cryptically, "If you read it, it may contain something you'll wish you'd never laid your eyes on."

Kane considered that for a silent moment. "Maybe," he admitted. "But I'm willing to take that chance."

Brigid's mouth twitched in a wry smile, and she returned

her attention to the console. "That symbol rings a faint bell. Something very old. I'll try some random pass codes."

Her fingers played over the keyboard. Looking over her shoulder, Kane saw she had typed "Air Force."

The "Access denied" message continued to glow, unchanged, so she kept trying again and again. Kane stood beside her, hands in his pockets. Her fingers flew over the keys, making a constant clatter. She punctuated each failure with under-the-breath mutters and groans. Some of the key codes she input were unfamiliar and strange, words like "Totality Concept," "Cerberus" and "Wyeth."

"Where are you coming up with those words?" he asked. "They're pretty obscure."

"That's why I'm the archivist and you're the Magistrate who doesn't have to knock."

As Kane stood by and watched, he suddenly realized with a start that he was enjoying himself immensely. He wasn't sure why, except he felt curiously comfortable with Brigid Baptiste, at ease with her in a way that was similar, yet also markedly different than his relationship with Grant. He found her intelligence, her apparent professionalism and the way she had refused to be intimidated by him bizarrely entertaining. Perhaps it was the shared act of flouting authority, like a pair of naughty children, that forged the bond. He felt rebellious, and he liked it. He knew Brigid did, too.

It was crazy, he argued with himself. The woman was a total stranger, and for all he knew, she was pretending to cooperate because she was scared, or she was part of a complex sting set up by Salvo, and he had walked right into it. Hell, as soon as he left, she could call Salvo and report everything he said or did.

Then he realized something else.

He really didn't give a shit.

Suddenly Brigid uttered an exclamation of triumph. Kane bent down to peer at the screen. Instead of the "Access denied" message, two words glowed against the dark background. The words were "Dulce" and "Accessing."

"Dulce?" he muttered. "What the hell is a Dulce?"

"Not a what," she replied. "A where. A town in predark New Mexico. Not even that, exactly—an old military testing facility, where a lot of scientific experiments were being conducted—"

She clamped her lips tight, biting back her words. Her shoulders stiffened in fear. Kane said, "It's okay, Baptiste. You're a 'Q-clearance' archivist. You'd have access to that sort of information."

The soothing, reassuring tone of his voice surprised even him.

She threw him a grateful smile and said, "That triangle symbol was the insignia of the Dulce-base personnel."

Poking a key, she declared, "Let's see what we have here."

Words and numbers scrolled down and across the screen with a dizzying rapidity. Brigid gazed at them unblinkingly, occasionally moving her lips.

"How can you read anything at that speed?" Kane demanded.

"Well, this *is* an old system," she replied distractedly. "I never got around to upgrading the access and scroll time."

It took a moment for the meaning of Brigid's response to register with Kane. When it did, he opened his mouth to ask if she expected him to believe she actually absorbed the speeding jumble of characters. But she brought the data stream to an abrupt halt.

Tapping the screen with a forefinger, she said, "This appears to be a recent file of bills of lading and transfer of goods. The last scheduled delivery is listed as today. However, there isn't an entry of the receipt of the goods."

Kane leaned closer, squinting at the words and numbers. "Dulce delivery," he read aloud. "Eighteen units."

"Units of what?"

Kane did a quick mental calculation. Though he couldn't

be certain, he recollected at least that many people in the Mesa Verde holding cell.

"Units of what?" repeated Brigid.

Kane let out his breath in a slow sigh, and saw the woman avert her face as alcohol fumes washed over her. "People. Sort of. Outlanders."

Her brow furrowed. "A smuggler, you said?"

"Yes."

"Don't they usually smuggle outlanders into villes?"

"Usually."

"There are no villes in New Mexico. That would be under the jurisdiction of Cobaltville, wouldn't it?"

"Yes."

"Unless," she continued, "something is going on in Dulce that requires outlanders for cheap labor. Where was the slaghole?"

"Mesa Verde canyon. He had it in the Cliff Palace." Kane smiled mirthlessly. "I shouldn't be telling you this. It was a black op, a deep penetration."

"And you don't know why."

"What makes you say that?"

Brigid glanced up at him. "You wouldn't be so curious if you knew why the op was black coded. You just went along with the order. You want to know how the smuggler was delivering his units to Dulce. That's a long journey overland, even in a war wag."

"It gets worse," Kane replied. "How did Reeth—that was the slagger's name—bring ville tech into a hellzone?"

"Why didn't you ask him?"

"I did. Before he could answer, a termination warrant was served."

"Oh. Well, maybe he moved the tech through the Pits. Using noncitizens to shift the stuff through the lower squats."

"He still would have needed a flyer to get it into the canyon. There's no road into the hellzone that I know of."

Brigid massaged her temples. "This makes my head

hurt. You can maybe find a wag in the Pits, but the only place you can find a flyer, even a disabled one is—''

"Let's not go there," Kane interrupted sharply.

Brigid fixed a penetrating green gaze on his face. "You brought all this up. Curiosity always has its price, you know."

Kane couldn't deny that she spoke the truth, and he knew the only place a flyer could be found was the armory, on C Level of the Administrative Monolith. The information on the disk was now unsecured, and as a Magistrate, it was his duty to report it, since he couldn't resecure it. Protocol didn't work that way. There was nothing on the disk indicating a brewing revolution or a planned overthrow of the barons.

His first impulse was to destroy the disk and walk away from the mysteries it posed. But now he had involved someone outside of his division, and his options were limited. Closure was required. His judgment had been clouded by liquor, and that error had to be concealed at all costs, by any measures necessary.

The Sin Eater holstered at his forearm suddenly seemed to increase in weight. It almost dragged his arm down, and his palm itched with the insistent urgency to fill it with the butt—

Kane straightened up quickly, unsteadily. Brigid's eyes flickered in surprise, in apprehension. Kane allowed his right arm to dangle at his side, and he squeezed his eyes shut against the painful throbbing inside the walls of his skull. By any measures necessary. He heard the woman's rich voice, calm and clear through the pounding in his ears.

"Tomorrow I'll scan the data base, run a correlation search, see what we have about Dulce. Okay?"

The drumming in his head receded, the pain faded and Kane opened his eyes. He locked gazes with Brigid. The room seemed to tilt around him, his fingers flexed, the tendons in his wrist tightened—

She smiled at him, and it transformed her face. It wasn't

an empty smile, forced there by fear or tension. It was a smile of openness and honesty, of happiness at finding someone who shared her innate curiosity, of taking a delight in uncovering the unknown, of finding someone with whom she could be herself.

His thoughts fought through the fog of alcohol and paranoia and focused on one fact: you brought her into this, you drunken lout. You take responsibility for bringing her out.

As if from far away, he heard himself say, "Okay. Fine."

Numbly he took the disk from her hand. Their fingers brushed momentarily, her touch a soft caress, yet electric at the same time.

"If I find anything important," she went on, "I'll let you know."

"Okay. Fine."

With the bitter certainty that he would probably live just long enough to regret saying "Okay, fine", he turned and left her apartment. The promenade was empty, and for some reason, it seemed much smaller, much more confining than it had an hour before.

Magistrate Psychometric Report G-1268, Code. Grant, born 2160, Cobaltville. Awarded Active Badge of Duty, 2177. Cited 2178, 2186, 2194, meritorious service.

Courageous but not reckless. Has strong curb on emotions. Suggestibility low. Attitude scales show high stability. Strong candidate for administrative transfer. Action pending.

SALVO LEANED BACK in his chair and tapped his fingers on the open file. The Intel section was very quiet, and its dim lighting always helped him to relax and concentrate. Morales and the rest of the duty staff studiously avoided looking in his direction.

Salvo glanced down at the file again. The psychometric report supplied only the public image. There wasn't even a passing reference to Grant's capacity for friendship and loyalty, and that was the crucial element. There was no point in cross-indexing the material with Kane's own file. Salvo already knew Kane was at the extreme limit of the permitted range in a number of behavioral areas. The psychometric reading didn't fully reveal these.

Suggestibility low.

If that was the case, then Kane would have never been able to persuade Grant to forestall serving the termination warrant on Milton Reeth. Obviously Grant trusted Kane. More importantly, Kane trusted Grant, and very deeply.

Morales announced, "Here you are, sir."

Salvo got up and padded quietly to the vid monitor Morales indicated. On the screen, he watched Kane walk down the stoop of an apartment and, hands in his pocket, shuffle along the promenade. He moved slowly, not with his characteristic catlike stride.

"Who lives there?" he asked.

Morales consulted a sheet of printout. "A midgrade senior archivist. Brigid Baptiste. She has a 'Q' clearance."

Salvo's lips pursed. "Never heard of the bitch."

Morales shrugged, as if to say "Me, either."

"Why was he there?" Salvo muttered. "If he wanted her to take a look at the disk, then he should have ordered her to examine it during the duty shift. That way his ass was covered. Hers, too. This is very uncharacteristic of Kane. Sloppy."

Morales coughed discreetly. "Shall we put her under surveillance, as well, sir?"

"Of course," Salvo snapped. "And tomorrow, while she's at her post, I want you to search her home."

"Me, sir?"

"Yes, you sir."

"Search her home for what?"

"For anything," Salvo growled.

The corners of Morales's eyes crinkled in puzzlement. "What if I can't find anything?"

Salvo fixed his dark liquid stare on the man. He said nothing.

Morales ducked his head quickly. "I'll find something."

Chapter 10

Kane dreamed in choppy fragments, none of which made any sense. A humid darkness swathed most of his mind in sweaty, ebony folds. Only infrequently came brief flares of light and cogent thought. The lights took on the appearance of faces—faces that somehow resembled his mother, his grandfather and father all at the same time. He had an inchoate, faraway awareness that he'd promised to do something for those faces—or was it one face?—but he couldn't remember what.

He felt an insistent, jiggling pressure, as though he were riding on the back of a wag. He tried to roll with it, but he couldn't seem to move. Finally he realized a hard object was prodding his right thigh. He managed to reach down, and his fingers closed on something that felt like the toe of a boot.

"Up and at 'em. Salvo and slaggers wait for no one."

Kane struggled and managed to peel back one eyelid. Grant's scowling ebony face filled his field of vision. He looked curiously distorted, resembling a frog under a magnifying glass.

Clearing a dry-as-dust throat, he massaged his eyeballs with the heels of his hands. They felt as if they had been filled with broken glass.

"You have a good time?"

Removing his hands from his face, Kane saw a foggy Grant examining an equally foggy yet very empty wine bottle.

"No," Kane croaked. He realized he was lying on his sofa, still wearing his bodysuit, though at some point during the night he'd taken off his coat, boots and Sin Eater. They lay in a disordered heap on the floor.

Grant sighed unhappily. "This was rare stuff. You have any idea how hard it is to find?"

"You've told me often enough."

"And you knocked it off in one night, like a goddamn methanol swill-pig. And you didn't save me so much as a sip."

Kane frowned at him. "You don't drink."

"It's the thought that counts."

"Yeah. It's the thought that gets me. What time is it?"

"Twenty minutes till shift change. You've got till ten to pull your sodden ass together."

"Why'd you come by?"

"Because you didn't answer my comm calls."

"You were worried."

"Not particularly."

"Were, too."

"Okay, I were. Wondered what happened with Salvo last night."

"Nothing."

"Bullshit."

"Just an ass-chewing. Not even that. More like an ass-gumming. Gave me a line of hoohah about some roamer warlord with predark weaponry."

Grant grunted. "That old saw."

Kane got his arms under him and heaved his body off the sofa, not even trying to stifle his groans. Pain, like a clawed animal, tore at the inside of his skull. He was grateful that Grant postponed further questions until he was able to function again. He stumbled into the tiny bath nook and doused his face with cold water. He plunged his head repeatedly into the sink, blowing like a whale.

Grant watched him from the doorway. "Want some food?"

At the mention of it, Kane's stomach boiled like a percolator. Face submerged, he mumbled incoherently.

After the pain receded a bit, he straightened up and caught a glimpse of himself in the mirror above the sink. He winced at the sight. His eyes were dark rimmed and netted with red. His color was like mildewed drywall. He felt a small twinge of satisfaction. He looked exactly as he felt.

In a low tone, hardly above a whisper, Grant asked, "What did you do with the disk?"

Memories of his midnight visit to Brigid Baptiste returned in a swirling rush. He remembered everything, and a groan escaped between suddenly clenched teeth.

"Ah, shit," he said softly. "Shit. *Shit.*"

"That bad?" Grant's tone of voice wasn't amused.

Stumbling out of the bathroom, shouldering Grant aside, he pawed through his wadded-up coat. The good thing about Kevlar was that it wouldn't hold a wrinkle, no matter how much it was abused. The disk was still snug in an inner pocket, and he collapsed onto the sofa, not knowing if he felt relieved or anxious. Then Grant's question finally penetrated. Directing a steady glare at him, he demanded, "How did you know about it?"

"Salvo called me this morning," he answered quietly. "Said he was asking every member of our team if we'd boosted anything from the slaghole last night. Said he'd already asked you."

"He did. Didn't tell me what, if anything, was missing."

"That's because you didn't ask him. I did. Doesn't take a psi-mutie to guess who palmed it and when."

Leaning his throbbing head against a coverless cushion, he asked, "You going to tell him?"

"Kiss my ass. Salvo asked me if *I* was the one who took it, not if I knew who did."

Kane nodded, intoning, "'A Magistrate is virtuous in the performance of his duty.'"

Grant grunted. "'You find out, and one night you'll have a termination warrant served on you.'"

"What?"

"That's what Reeth said to us, remember? My philosophy is simple—what Salvo doesn't know won't hurt *us*."

Smiling bleakly, Kane asked, "So you're beginning to think there was something a little plastic about last night's op?"

"It doesn't matter what I think, doesn't matter what you think." Grant pinged a fingernail against the empty bottle. "Tell me the truth. Why'd you knock this off in one sitting?"

Kane dry-scrubbed his hair with his hands. "Do you think I'm going soft?"

"Not physically. Emotionally is another matter. You're breaking old, ingrained habits and acting out of character. That can be deadly."

Kane eyed the big man and chose his words with care. "Our whole lives don't have be part of a predetermined pattern, you know."

"I don't follow."

"You can think, can't you, even if it doesn't matter?"

"Think about what?"

"About that Gateway, for instance, or whatever Reeth showed us. That matters."

Grant shook his head vigorously. "That's where you're mistaken. Even it was one of those things, so the fuck what? It's not within our parameters of duty. Now, get up and let's go. Drop that disk in a trash hatch on the way. Follow the two *F*'s."

Kane slowly arose. "Right. 'File and forget.'"

With Grant's help, he managed to put on his boots, Sin Eater and coat without fainting, but he still felt extremely unwell.

It was the time for many duties to begin, and the promenade was thronged with movement, with people heading to their duty stations in the Administrative Monolith. Even though they were of the Cobaltville elite, the people were subdued, many of them wearing self-conscious expressions of carefully calculated neutrality. Necessarily so, since frank self-expression could catch a Magistrate's attention, and that could lead to any number of unpleasant consequences.

Though he looked for her, Kane didn't see Brigid Baptiste.

The only trash hatch they saw was being serviced by a sullen-faced outlander girl, hardly more than twelve years old, so Kane kept the disk in his coat pocket and he and Grant took the elevator to C Level. Despite the fact that time was growing short, Kane stopped off in the dayroom to wolf down a few sesame-seed biscuits and swig a cup of sub. That made him feel more as if he'd achieved near-human status again.

They walked into the briefing room to find Salvo already standing at the lectern. He was reading shift assignments in a droning monotone. Two dozen Magistrates sat on the rows of hard benches, listening with impassive faces.

Salvo glanced up when Kane and Grant dropped onto one of the benches, but since he didn't pause or even raise an eyebrow, Kane figured he hadn't reached his or Grant's orders for the day.

"Banyon and Colemund, Intel section, collating Outlands reports. Leduc, Jessup and Kovacs, agricultural-section security. Orris, Fielding and Newson, manufacturing-section security. Boon, Grant and Kane, PPP duty."

Salvo continued to read off the duty roster, but neither Kane nor Grant heard him. They were too occupied with exchanging surprised glances, then shifting their stares to Salvo. PPP duty—Pedestrian Pit Patrol—was a first-year-Mag assignment. All newly badged enforcers were required to patrol the Pits as part of their first-year duties. Generally the patrol consisted of nothing more than checking ID chips, making sure they were ville approved and not bogus.

Pit dwellers were stopped at random, ordered to present their left forearms for inspection and a hand scanner would react positively if the subcutaneous chip was legit.

PPP duty was supervised by one senior Magistrate, never

a pair of them. Pits could be dangerous places, especially for rookie enforcers with no real combat experience, but there hadn't been a major outbreak of anti-Mag violence in the Cobaltville Pit in a generation. Even the latest in a long line of self-proclaimed Pit bosses, a border runner named Guana Teague, kept an exceptionally low profile. And though it was true Boon had been recently awarded his badge, and therefore was required to take patrol, assigning two veteran Mags to nursemaid him seemed ridiculous and a waste of resources.

When Salvo completed reading off the assignments and the rest of the shift filed out, Kane approached the lectern. "Tell me why."

Salvo didn't so much as glance up at him. "Why what?"

"Pit patrol."

"It's a standard duty assignment. You should know that by now."

"Why the two of us?"

Salvo collected his papers and pushed past him. "Why not? Where is it written that two senior Magistrates can't be assigned to supervise a PPP?"

Without another word, he turned and strode out of the briefing room. Kane turned toward his friend, raising his hands in a gesture of exasperation.

Glowering, Grant said, "This is your fault, you know."

A young, slender man of Asian extraction moved toward Kane. Falteringly he said, "I'm Boon. It's an honor to be working with you."

Grant sighed and stood up. "Let's get this honor over with."

They marched out into the corridor, Boon a bit behind, trying to match their impatient, long-legged stride. They stopped briefly at the tech desk so Boon could pick up a scanner. It was a small, cylindrical gadget, not more than four inches long with a two-pronged sensor probe at one end.

At the private elevator, they showed the sentry on duty

their badges. The sentry punched in the numbers on a miniature three-digit keypad, and the door panel rolled aside. The elevator was one of six shafts on C Level that dropped directly to the Pits. The largest of the shafts was positioned in the armory and could accommodate an armored wag filled with a Magistrate squad, just in case a Pit outbreak had to be quelled.

After they stepped into the car, the sentry, with studied casualness, pressed a control toggle and set the lift for a fast descent. As the platform seemed to drop from beneath their feet, Boon reacted to the sudden sensation of free fall with a startled murmur. Grant and Kane affected not to notice the feeling of their stomachs forcibly climbing into their throats.

Conversationally Kane said, "Remember the last PPP we worked?"

Grant replied flatly, "You mean when old Guana was paying hard jack for Mag body parts?"

"What?" Boon asked faintly.

"A weird fad," said Kane. "Pit dwellers tend to bore easy, need their diversions. What was it—six gold creds for a Mag nose, eight for a tongue?"

"Twenty for a set of balls," remarked Grant calmly. "Getting those was a real bitch."

"What?" asked Boon again. "When was this?"

Kane gravely glanced over at Grant. "Last year, right?"

"I never heard of that fad before," said Boon.

"No wonder," Grant replied. "Triple bad for morale. Salvo did his best to cover it up, but—"

The platform bumped to a stop. Boon stumbled forward, his face almost slamming against the door panel. It slid aside, and he froze as the air of the Tartarus Pits filtered into his nostrils. Kane and Grant exchanged grins. With a hearty backslap that pushed the young man out of the car, Kane announced, "Let's be careful out there. The price of balls may have gone up."

The base of the Administrative Monolith was completely

enclosed by a walled compound made of six feet of rock-crete. The twenty-foot-high walls were rigged with proximity alarms. The sun, at its zenith, glinted from the sharp points of the coils of razor wire stretched out over the tops of the walls. The massive sec door was made of vanadium alloy and powered by a buried hydraulic system.

The impregnable perimeter hadn't been built simply to protect the tower from invasion by outraged Pit dwellers. Far below, in a sublevel, rested the primary output station that supplied the ville's electricity. Supposedly an underground artery of the Kanab River generated the power, but there were stories that indicated old atomic engines were the true source of Cobaltville's electricity.

A Magistrate guard, in full body armor, stood beside the sec-door controls, lovingly cradling his Copperhead in his arms. When he saw them approach, he keyed in the code numbers and pulled up the control lever. The gate rumbled and squeaked, opening like an accordion, folding to one side. It was so heavy it took nearly a minute for the sec door to open just enough to allow them to step outside of the compound.

"Now," declared Grant, "the fun begins."

"Oh, man, does it ever," Kane said in a monotone.

Chapter 11

Guana Teague held the weekly auction in the deepest part of the Pits, in a warehouse that backed into the foot of the ville wall. Not only was it hidden from casual Mag glances, but theoretically lay very close to the Outlands. At least, that was the way Teague had it figured, even if technically the nearest Outland border was thirty miles away.

In his middle fifties, Guana Teague was an enormous man with the physique of a very plush, fleshy grizzly bear. His massive belly bulged out and down in folds. His hair was still black, as was the small goatee embracing his triple chins. A greenish cast to his pale skin made it look as if it were faintly scaled, though it wasn't. It was an odd epidermal pattern, similar to freckles, but coupled with heavy brows jutting over dark-rimmed eyes, it lent him a reptilian appearance—and the derivation of his nickname from the lizard iguana.

Teague knew a lot of Pitters suspected he was a scalie, a mutie, but he didn't give a damn about their suspicions. He was the Pit boss, and anyone who thought he was a scalie didn't dare voice that opinion within his range of hearing.

Being a Pit boss didn't mean much to the high-towers or the Mags or the admins, but to Teague it meant carrying on a family tradition. His great-grandfather had been the half-legendary Jordan Teague, once the preeminent power in the Deathlands, or at least in the part he had claimed as his own. He hadn't been a part of the baronial hierarchy, though he referred to himself as one, and he had intended his town of Mocsin to become the center of an empire.

Unfortunately he had been chilled before those intentions had borne any fruit, and his descendants hadn't inherited anything much beyond lives as roamers and outlanders. Guana Teague had a mind to change all of that. Early in his life, he discovered he possessed a gift for ingratiating himself with others, particularly those in positions of authority. Despite his appearance, or maybe because of it, Teague rapidly climbed the short success ladder of the Cobaltville Pit. He'd been pit boss longer than anyone else, primarily because he provided unique items and services both to those above and below him. One of those services was the weekly auction.

The items he sold to the highest—and sometimes the lowest—bidder were salvaged from trash hatches or smuggled in from the Outlands. Everything from scrap metal to machine parts to farm implements filled packing crates on the crude podium on which he stood. Most of the stuff was utterly worthless to the high-towers—otherwise they wouldn't have discarded it—but a few Pit dwellers had the facility to jury-rig some useful tech. They in turn sold their creations to others or used them to make their bleak lives a little easier to endure.

Though most of the Pits had electrical power, it was limited to fourteen hours a day out of twenty-four. Only a few places had running water, and folks had to queue up with buckets and containers in order to receive their daily requirement. Therefore, leak-proof containers were always at a premium and the most popular pieces at the auctions.

Teague was careful to never start the bidding at exorbitant prices for necessities. Though the presence of his strong-arms, Uno and Dos, kept his customers from objecting too strenuously to his prices, he had come close to sparking more than one miniriot.

Very few Pit dwellers possessed hard jack to pay for the items, except those who worked in the towers as custodians or cooks. Almost everything was taken out in trade, either with other pieces or terms of service. The service could be anything from a week's worth of slagwork, or in the instance of fairly young, fairly attractive females, sex slavery.

Holding up a corroded circuit board, he announced, "Open bidding, folks. Place 'em."

"On what?" demanded a man in the crowd. "It's just another piece of shit."

Teague did his best to smile. "A gifted somebody could build themselves a right nice data-infeed circuit with this. Tap into the comp bank."

"And bring the Mags down us," somebody else shouted. "You gotta do better than that."

Teague spread his hands. "What can I say? Times are hard."

"Times are always hard," said a small woman standing at the front of the podium. "They ain't likely to get any better, neither. But hard times or good times, a piece of shit is still a piece of shit."

A wave of appreciative laughter rippled through the crowd.

Teague wasn't offended, but he behaved as if he were. He tossed the circuit board back into the crate and announced petulantly, "*Ho*-kay, you ungrateful sobs. Auction is over."

A few people clapped and whistled in sarcastic appreciation as the obese Pit boss lumbered off the podium, followed by Uno and Dos. His quarters were attached to the warehouse, a boxlike structure made of plyboard, corrugated metal and walls of rockcrete. It had no windows, and his strong-arms took up position outside the closed door.

Uno and Dos looked very much alike, twins almost, though neither claimed to be related to the other. They were tall, rangy men, born and bred in the Pits. They were dressed identically in baggy bodysuits, scuffed combat boots and pseudoleather brown jackets a size too small to accentuate the length of their arms. Sheathed at their hips were foot-long knives. Their dark blond hair was swept and greased back with the same homemade pomade. Since its primary ingredient was lard, a cloud of gnats was their constant companions.

Inside his one-room home, Teague turned on the overhead light, and its naked blaze fell on a flagstone floor, four whitewashed walls, a table, two chairs and a daybed. The girl stretched out on the daybed looked up quickly, shielding her eyes from the sudden glare.

She wore a pair of bright red stockings on her long legs and nothing else. Her hips were generously proportioned, her breasts perky, and her bone white hair was cropped very short. Contrasting sharply with her white skin was a pair of upslanting crimson eyes, as red as cut rubies. Those eyes, adjusting to the light, gave Teague a glance edged with resentment and fear.

Pleasantly he said, "How very decorative you look, Domi."

"Fuck off," replied Domi sulkily. "You paid off already. I want to leave."

Teague wagged his head from side to side and eased his bulk into a chair. It creaked beneath his ponderous weight. "No, sweetheart, I don't think so. I'm not tired of you yet."

One of the genetic quirks of the nukecaust aftermath was a rise in the albino population, particularly down south in bayou country. Albinos weren't exactly rare anywhere else, but they were hardly commonplace. Teague found Domi particularly unique and enchanting, though her personality fell somewhat short of inviting.

She was a relative newcomer to the ville. He'd spotted her during one of his periodic forays into the Outlands and smuggled her into the Pits with a forged ID chip. In exchange, she'd been called on to give him six months of personal service. Now seven months had passed.

"Your main function," continued the Pit boss, "is to please me. You haven't always pleased me, so as I told you before, I've extended your term until I'm completely pleased."

Red rage flared in her eyes, and she sprang to her feet. "I run away!"

"To where and to what, sweetheart?" He still maintained his pleasant, reasonable tone. "The Pits are not that large. You may hide, but you can't run. And your striking appearance will prevent you from blending in even in the deep squats. Besides, isn't this place better than wandering the Outlands?"

Domi nibbled her lower lip. "Turn you in, I could. Turn you in to Mags."

Teague chuckled. "You, with a bogus ID chip in your arm? I don't think even you are that impulsive—or foolish."

He sighed wearily. "Haven't I been kind to you? Haven't I provided for your every comfort?"

Domi's face twisted in angry contempt. "You disgusting. Green skin, scales. Body like smelly sack. Lizard tail between your legs. Make me sick."

"No abuse, please, my darling. It causes hot blood to rise in me, and you are aware of what happens then."

It was impossible for Domi to turn pale, but she cast her eyes downward.

"Besides," the big man went on smoothly, "since we are of a kind—epidermally unique—one would think you'd be only too glad to enjoy the company of someone who is a kindred spirit."

Domi sank back to the edge of the daybed, hands pressed together in her lap, shoulders slumping in despair.

"So, is that settled, then?"

She didn't respond.

Teague raised his voice and repeated the question.

Domi inclined her head a fraction of an inch in a nod, then slid off the daybed. On all fours, back arched in the way Teague had instructed her, she slowly crawled across the floor. The Pit boss smiled tolerantly and spread his legs, lifting a slab of flab so he could loosen the drawstring that held up his pants.

Then he heard a sound, a rapid electronic trilling. He had heard that rising and falling tone only three times during his stint as Pit boss. Adrenaline rushed through him, speeding up his heartbeat, even causing the short hairs on his scalp to tingle. He bounded to his feet so quickly the chair fell over backward and he nearly trod on one of Domi's hands. She scuttled sideways out of his path as he made a shambling rush for the far wall.

His fingers scrabbled over the whitewashed surface, nails digging into a thread-thin crack where a piece of board joined with a rockcrete block. He pulled the small wooden panel aside. Behind it, resting in a shallow niche, was a small square box made of molded plastic and pressed metal.

Hurriedly he plucked the trilling trans-comm from the niche and put on the headset, struggling to align the mouthpiece properly and plug the receiver into his ear. He paid no attention to Domi, gazing up at him from the floor.

Thumbing a stud on the side of the trans-comm, he opened the channel and waited through the squawks and crackles of the unscrambling circuit. Then a voice whispered in his ear, a man's voice he had heard three times before.

"Mags on their way. A PPP."

"Who?"

"Two you know, Kane and Grant. A cherry named Boon. Chill Grant, and chill Boon if you have to. Leave Kane. Chill Grant. Acknowledge."

"Acknowledged."

"Repeat—chill Grant. Make it messy. Make it ugly. Do it in front of Kane. Very important. Again, chill Grant in front of Kane. Acknowledge."

"Acknowledged."

His ear filled with a hash of static. With trembling hands, Teague stripped off the headset and replaced the trans-comm unit in the niche. His bowels felt loose, and his heart hammered painfully within his chest.

Five years ago, he had been hauled in for questioning.

He'd been detained for days, or at least it felt like it. He wasn't given food or water, nor had there been any light in his detention cell. Then a Mag in full armor had opened the door. He had expected to be chilled on the spot. Instead of pulling a Sin Eater, the Mag had pulled the trans-comm unit, shoved it in his hands and told him he was free to go.

That very night, Teague had received the first signal, and he heard that cold voice, sounding as if it were whispering across the dark gulfs of space. The voice had curtly told him that if he wished to continue as Pit boss, if he wished to continue to live, he would do what he was ordered. Guana Teague had obeyed and he had continued to live as the Pit boss.

He had no idea whom the voice belonged to, and he was afraid to even speculate. Whoever he was, Teague was allowed to operate without serious Mag interference in his business—as long as he did as he was commanded.

The three prior assignments had been simple and easy to perform—provide the names of jolt-walkers, alert the Mags if unusually advanced tech came in from the Outlands and supply the name of the best smuggler.

The last had been the easiest, requiring no research or expenditure of energy. Milton Reeth was the best, the most resourceful, the most clever. He had reported Reeth's name more than a year ago, and had heard nothing of the man since.

And now he was ordered to arrange a murder, and not just any murder, but a veteran Magistrate's. Grant was known and feared in the Pits, as well as in the Outlands. Kane's rep was just as fearsome. Only last year, a gaggle of triple-stupe jolt-walkers had tried to pull an ambush on a Mag squad led by Kane and Grant.

Teague shut the panel, muttering, "Oh, fuck me, fuck me" like a litany. Sweat slid down his face as he lumbered to the east corner of the room. He suddenly exuded a raw, animal stench of fear. From her place on the floor, Domi watched him with wide eyes, wrinkling her nose at the odor.

Grunting, the Pit boss squatted down and levered up a loose flagstone. From a recess dug into the dirt and reinforced with strips of tin, he pulled out a flat black case. Straightening up, he carried it over to the tabletop. Undoing the latches, he opened the top of the case. Resting within hollowed-out foam cushions was a pair of automatic handblasters.

He had found the matched set of mint-condition mini-Uzi submachine guns waiting for him in his quarters one night last year. He assumed his faceless benefactor/commander had arranged the delivery. Strapped on the underside of the lid were four full-capacity box magazines. Each magazine held twenty-five 9 mm parabellum rounds.

The blasters were worth a fortune, especially to roamers, but Teague knew better than to sell them or think seriously about it. Gun possession in the Pits was a mandatory death sentence, even crappy home-forged muzzle loaders.

Domi laughed from behind him, a musical sound of wicked delight. He turned slightly. She had climbed to her feet and stood there with her hands on her flaring hips, red-sheathed legs wide apart. Mildly he asked, "What do you find funny, sweetheart?"

"You," she said. "Turn me in, huh? Me with bogus chip, you with high-tower tech and blasters. Mags finds out, you get big-time dead, Pit finds out, even bigger-time dead. You're Mag spy first, I betcha. Pit boss second. Term of my service *over,* lizard dick! Term of *your* service starts now!"

Teague put his hand over one of the Uzis. "This isn't the time to renegotiate our agreement, Domi."

She laughed again scornfully. "Time is right. So pucker up and kiss my lily-white ass."

Teague moved. He whipped the frame of the blaster across the side of Domi's head. She didn't cry out, but she careened across the room, slammed into the wall, bounced from it and fell to the floor in a flailing tangle of arms and legs. She managed to catch herself with her hands, but she hung her head, blood streaming from a laceration in her scalp. The crimson flow stood out starkly against her white skin.

Stepping over to her, the Pit boss gripped her by the hair and hauled her to her knees, yanking her head back at a painful angle. She was dazed but still conscious, and she didn't resist when he inserted the short barrel of the Uzi into her mouth.

"Do you want to end your service right now?" he hissed. Spittle strings drooled from his lips. "Tell me, you goddamn bleached-out gaudy slut. Tell me!"

Domi shook her head—at least as much as his cruel grip allowed.

"Then you'll do what I tell you to, won't you?"

Domi tried to nod, her front teeth clinking on the metal of the blaster's barrel.

Teague abruptly released her, and she sagged to the floor, hand pressing against the wound on her head. Blood oozed slowly between her fingers.

Teague wiped his wet mouth with the back of his hand, then realized his pants were about to slip down his hips. He had forgotten that he'd untied the drawstring. Holding them up with one hand, he gestured with the mini-Uzi in the other. "Get up. Clean yourself up." He paused and whispered, "Sweetheart."

Chapter 12

Kane exhaled a wreath of smoke. "They used to call places like this 'pestholes.'"

"What do they call them now?" Boon was eager to know.

"Pestholes," answered Grant, allowing the smoke to dribble out of his nostrils in fitful spurts.

One of the first things Kane and Grant had done upon leaving the walled perimeter was to seek out a wandering tobacconist and buy several cigars. *Buy* wasn't accurate, since the merchant hadn't requested jack. Nor had the Magistrates offered it.

Hardly anyone but outlanders had used tobacco in any form for a long time. There were mild drugs available that were much safer, less offensive to others and with just as much power to even out moods or focus the mind. Smoking was certainly forbidden in the monolith and the Enclaves, but in the Pits, the use of anything that might lower life expectancy was encouraged.

Both Kane and Grant had learned to appreciate a good cigar during their many Pit patrols, and having the opportunity to puff on a few was the only bright spot in an otherwise drab tour of duty.

Kane, Grant and Boon picked their way through the muddy streets, among the narrow, twisting alleys between ramshackle buildings, past hovel and shack and tent. There were no main avenues, only lanes that zagged in one direction, then zigged in the other. The damp breeze had the smell of smoke and spice and old blood in it.

The Pits always stunk of the past. Cobaltville had been

built on the foundation of Vistaville, once the domain of Baron Alfred Nelson. He was a very long time moldering in an unmarked grave, but the Pits still seemed haunted by the memories of his bloody deeds.

Leaning over the narrow lanes, the top stories of buildings pushed out their rickety wooden loggias and duraplast balconies. Almost every structure in the Pits dated back to Nelson's day. The few that did not were not much past that vintage, since they had been built to serve as laborers' quarters when the Enclaves, the Administrative Monolith and the walls were erected. Cobaltville and the Pits had pretty much stayed the same for the past seventy-odd years.

The streets were crowded with people, lean, hard-eyed, hard-faced people—outlanders who gave way when they saw the approach of the Magistrates. Most of them were courteous and deferential. They had to be.

It was Boon's first visit to the Pits, so Kane and Grant conducted something of a walking tour, allowing him to absorb its peculiar, alien flavor. They pointed out the spy-eye stations, which transmitted video images of Pit activities to Intel. Boon acted distracted, nervous and jumpy until Grant relented and told him that Guana Teague was a powerless, fat fool who on his bravest day wouldn't dare make eye contact with a Magistrate.

"Thought so," said Boon, relief evident in his voice. "I didn't really believe that body-parts story."

"Yeah," Kane said dryly. "We could tell you were only playing along with us."

The narrow streets were of hard brown earth, guttered down the center for drainage. A few were cobbled, and all were thick with mud and the droppings of mules, horses and cattle. However, those pedestrian hazards didn't prevent people from running, skipping or dancing. They passed a blind girl who danced in the muck, to the music of harp, fife and drum, her feet shod in filthy slippers.

They saw an elderly man wearing a dented stovepipe hat and threadbare frock coat selling what looked like mum-

mified human hands from an open box. The placard around
his neck read Hands Of Glory Special. Ward Off Rad Cancer, Control Stress, Nourishing For The Weak Spirit.

It occurred to Kane again that there was more difference
than he had been taught between the high-towers and the
Pit dwellers. True, the people in the Enclaves were superior
to those down below, but it was an artificially imposed
superiority. He, Grant and even Boon were trained to serve
an arbitrary order, given direction and set upon an unwav-
ering path in life. The people in the Pits simply existed
moment to moment, quarreling, loving, laughing, crying
and being completely human.

From the open door of a saloon, they smelled wine and
burning incense, and Kane swallowed the bile that rose in
his throat. Beyond the louvered, bat-winged doors, a piano
banged out a tinny, unfamiliar tune, and he saw the gaming
tables inside.

Suddenly an astonishingly short man, barely three feet
tall, came flying out between the doors. He was followed
an instant later by a begrimed outlander who gripped the
short man by the collar and the seat of his pants.

"Don't come back in here no more, mutie whoreson,"
the man said, his words slurred as he catapulted the dwarf
through the air. He landed face-first in a puddle, splashing
Grant's boots and the hem of his coat.

The outlander's stumpy teeth were bared in a ferocious
grimace. Then, as his eyes lifted from the street and took
in the sight of the three black-and-gray-clad men standing
there, the grimace turned into an openmouthed expression
of terror. He mumbled incoherently and stepped back, trying to sidle back into the saloon.

"*Freeze!*" roared Grant, using the well-practiced tone of
intimidation and power. Smoke poured out of his mouth,
giving him the aspect of an enraged ebony dragon.

The outlander froze, his feet rooted to the spot.

To Boon, Grant directed, "Check him."

Boon moved forward, but Kane restrained him with a hand. "No. Make him come to you."

Taking the scanner from his pocket, the young man shrilled, "Get your slagging ass over here, slagger!"

The outlander weaved down the steps of the saloon, peeling back the cuff of his shirtsleeve. At the same moment, the mud-covered dwarf, looking like a beetle fished out of a cesspool, launched himself from the puddle, voicing a bass howl of rage. The bristly crown of his head barely topped the outlander's groin, and that's where he sank his teeth.

Screaming, the outlander whirled in a semicircle, and the dwarf whirled with him, his tiny feet completely leaving the ground. His face was pressed tightly against the man's pelvis.

The dwarf's feet slapped the scanner out of Boon's hand, and he shouted angrily, wordlessly. His right hand tensed reflexively, but the edge of Kane's hand chopped down hard against the Kevlar sleeve just as the Sin Eater filled Boon's hand.

The gun roared, spit flame, and three rounds plowed into the street, sending up geysers of watery muck. Instantly, as if a giant bell jar had been dropped over the area, all sound and movement halted. The dwarf's jaws opened, and he alighted silently on the street. The piano stopped tinkling, and the murmur of laughing voices fell still.

Boon glanced first at the dwarf, then at the outlander, then at Kane.

"Leather it," Kane said, the cigar in one corner of his mouth.

"He assaulted a Magistrate." The outraged words tumbled so fast from Boon's lips they were almost incomprehensible. "Fucking outlander and mutie *interfered* with a Magistrate, and they got to pay the fucking price!"

In a low, calm tone, Kane repeated, "Leather it."

Slowly, reluctantly Boon shoved the Sin Eater back into its spring-loaded holster.

"Pick up the scanner," Kane said quietly. "Check 'em."

Face flushed with rage and shame, Boon plucked the device from the mud and, without wiping it off, grabbed the outlander roughly by his proffered right arm. He stood motionless as Boon ran the sensor prongs over the flesh of his forearm, right below the elbow joint. The scanner emitted a clear, chiming signal, indicating a positive registration.

Boon flung the man's arm away as though it exuded a noxious odor. He fixed his dark-lensed eyes on the muddy dwarf. "No need to scan this little mutie bastard. Know his chip is bogus."

"Check him." Kane bit out the words.

The small man extended his bared arm, and Boon waved the scanner over it. When he heard the positive tone, he repeated the process, with the same result. His face locked in a tight, hard mask of disappointment.

Removing the cigar from his mouth, Kane gestured toward the two Pit dwellers. "Go."

The tall outlander and the little man obediently backed up, then pushed their way back into the saloon. Kane and Grant turned away and began walking. After a moment's hesitation, Boon caught up with them.

"I could have sworn that little—"

Grant cut him off. "It's a condition called achondroplasia. Some kind of congenital trait common among outlanders born near hellzones. He's a dwarf, not a mutie."

"But that guy called him—"

It was Kane's turn to interrupt. "An insult made in the heat of anger. Like a predark racial slur. Both of them were drunk and both of them are probably apologizing to each other right now."

Grimly Boon declared, "Dwarf, mutie, drunk or sober, he assaulted a Magistrate."

"An accident," said Grant. "You'll see and hear a lot of things in the Pits. Ninety-nine percent of the time, none of it means anything."

"What about that other one percent?" Boon was a little calmer now.

"You'll learn to recognize the one-percents," replied Kane. "If you don't, you're dead."

Boon shook his head. "Seems safer just to flash-blast this whole fucking place, send 'em back where they came from."

"Ah," said Grant, trying unsuccessfully to blow a smoke ring, "then who'll clean the floors, fix the sewers, till the fields and wipe the collective asses of all of us in the high-towers?"

Boon didn't answer.

For the remainder of the afternoon, they continued on Pit patrol. Boon decided to make something of a game out of it. At first, he checked the ID chips of every third person he saw, then of every man over the age of fifty, then of every female over puberty. Kane and Grant picked up food from street vendors, ate and drank and smoked their cigars and watched him. They figured that sooner or later, Boon would sicken of it and quit. He didn't. The sun began sinking behind the walls, washing the streets in a purple gray dusk.

"This is ridiculous," snapped Kane as Boon made another female inspection. "He's checked at least a hundred people so far and come up blank each time."

"Maybe he's on the prowl for that one percent you told him about," Grant replied. "The law of averages. There's got to be *one* bogus chip out of a couple of hundred."

"And he's likely to flash-blast the poor bastard on the spot."

"Yeah, like you never itched for the opportunity to sling around lead. Like the time when you thought you had a roamer cornered in a gully and blew the head off a cactus. Spent a week picking needles out of your face."

"That was twelve years ago. Why do you keep reminding me of those things?"

"I'm your partner and your elder. I'm supposed to remind you of those things."

Kane checked his wrist chron. "About two hours till shift change. A half an hour to get back to the division, a half to fill out the reports and another half for busywork. Then we can go home."

"You're half an hour short," observed Grant.

"Okay, half an hour to walk back to the compound." Kane took the cigar out of his mouth and shouted, "Boon! Enough for the day!"

Boon didn't look up from the arm he was inspecting. The arm was attached to a girl who might have been sixteen years old or twenty-six. It was hard to tell in the shifting light. But her eyes gleamed like polished rubies. Her white hair was ragged and short, held away from her angular, hollow-cheeked face by a length of satiny cloth. She wore a T-shirt and a pair of red, high-cut shorts that showed off her pale, gamin-slim legs.

Kane had seen albino women before in the Outlands, but never one so young and pretty. She looked as if she were crafted from flawless porcelain. The treated lenses of his glasses picked out a detail he had missed on first glance. The girl's headgear wasn't decorative; it was functional. Blood seeped slowly from the bottom edge of the bandage wrapped around her head.

Injured people were part and parcel of life in the Tartarus Pits. Some days it seemed as if every street were clogged with the walking wounded. But this girl didn't seem in pain. She seemed terrified. Her eyes darted back and forth like a panicked animal's. Her delicate pale lips parted, and though he was too far away to hear what she said, Kane was able to read the words formed by them.

She said, "Please. Danger."

Boon didn't hear her. At the precise moment she spoke, he whooped in triumph, his hand tightening around her wrist. Grinning, he turned to Kane and Grant and shouted, "I got me a bogie! I got one!"

Grant took the cigar out of his mouth and spit. "Ah, shit. I was afraid of this. Now we've got to handle an ejection. Or if Boon has his way, probably an on-the-spot termination."

He and Kane strode across the lane. The girl shot them a look of crimson terror, then her long left leg arced up, the foot landing solidly between Boon's legs. He choked out a curse and jackknifed at the waist, dropping the scanner. The girl wrested away from his grasp, spun and loped down the street, running in a graceful, ground-eating stride.

Boon struggled to straighten up, leaning against the wall of a building, clutching at his crotch. His "That bitch!" was a strangled gasp.

Kane found himself angrier with Boon than with the girl. Instead of going off shift, they now had to engage in a probably pointless pursuit through a maze of back alleys and dead-ends. As he ran past Boon, he said tersely, "Catch up when you're able."

Tails of their coats flying behind them, Grant and Kane sprinted after the white, flitting shape of the girl. She had a head start, was much younger and could run encumbered by Kevlar coats or blasters.

Grant spit the cigar from his mouth. Kane kept his clenched tightly between his teeth. It was his last one, and he didn't want to throw it away until it was a smoked-out stub. Legs pumping, boots squashing mud, the two men dashed down the lane. Smoke kept curling into Kane's nostrils, and he constantly fought the urge to sneeze.

Since it was close to dinnertime, the crowds were thinning out and many of the street vendors were closing up their stalls. They didn't have to dodge many obstacles or push more than three people out of their path. They turned a corner and sprinted between the shells of old duraplast buildings that had formerly housed laborers but now served as squats. This part of the Pits wasn't wired for electricity, and only the most hopeless and helpless lived here. The girl was leading them through the darkest section of the

Pits, and Kane remembered that since it wasn't equipped for electricity, then it wasn't equipped with spy-eyes, either.

Kane's thigh muscles felt as if they were seizing and locking up, his chest was caught in an ever-tightening vise and his vision was shot through with gray spots. Because of that, it took him a moment or two to realize their quarry was nowhere in sight.

He stopped running and lurched over to a heap of broken masonry. Grant was a score of yards ahead, still trying to run full out, but his stride was faltering.

Cupping his hands around his mouth, Kane shouted, "Forget it! We've lost her!"

His cigar fell to the base of the rock pile, and he stooped over to pick it up. Then he heard the crackle of blasterfire.

Chapter 13

Grant concentrated on running, praying he wouldn't stumble on the rocky, uneven ground, hoping the nagging pull in his groin wouldn't get any worse. He didn't see the girl, only half-tumbled walls overgrown with scraggly vegetation and a pair of dome-roofed duraplast buildings on either side of him.

When he heard Kane shout from behind him, he slowed down in midstride, grateful for the chance to stop. His lungs felt as if they were on fire, and he drank in great gasps of air through his open mouth. He cursed the tobacconist, then himself.

As he stopped running, despising the ache in his knees, a cold knot of warning inched up his spine to settle at the nape of his neck. His scalp felt as if it were pulling taut. Something was wrong. He could sense it the way a seasoned wolf senses a trap. He took a few more steps before coming to a complete halt. There was no sign of danger. The sky was a crimson-and-orange wash, the duraplast structures gleamed in the setting sun. Everything seemed in order.

"KEEP COMIN', you black bastich," Uno crooned quietly. He lay prone beneath a windowsill, the mini-Uzi resting on the decaying wooden sash. He gripped the butt tighter and squinted down its short length. Grant was about five yards below and twenty away. It was fairly long range for such a small gun, but he didn't have to be precise. The effective range was about 150 yards, and the trajectory was just a slight downward angle and there was no wind to worry about.

In the building facing him, he assumed Dos was bringing the big man into his sights, as well.

"Beautiful…keep on comin', just keep on."

Kane had lagged behind, and that made the order so much easier to complete. Guana Teague had been very clear about keeping Kane alive. There was no sign of the third Mag. It was almost as if some divine providence had arranged the chill to be quick, clean and simple.

If only Dos kept his head and waited until the target was in the exact position for a short, effective cross fire. Then Uno heard the stutter from across the alley and he groaned.

IT TOOK GRANT a split second to associate the drumming sound with an autoblaster. As a general rule, it wasn't a noise common to the Pits. The walls of the buildings amplified the sound and sent it booming back from all points of the compass. Pebbles and stone fragments exploded right in front of him, scouring his face with grit.

He went to one knee, the Sin Eater slapping into his hand, and he automatically braced the blaster with the other. He knew Kane was somewhere behind him, but he didn't waste any time looking for him. He swung the barrel of his blaster up, toward the second floor of the building on his right. He saw nothing but dark windows.

"Kane," he shouted. "Spot it!"

"Hit the ground!" Kane's tense voice floated from behind a pile of rubble.

Grant did as he said, hitting the ground full length and pressing his face into the sharp-edged gravel. Several slugs whistled through the air inches above his head, then the sounds of the shots followed them. Spouts of dirt sprang up no more than a foot from his right leg.

"Damn it, Kane!" he bellowed. *"Spot it!"*

CROUCHED DOWN behind the heap of broken brick and masonry, Kane spotted it. Two blasters were speaking from second-floor windows on the facing squats. He gripped the Sin Eater in two hands. There were many things about his life that he hated, but being caught in a cross fire topped the list.

He didn't expend any mental energy wondering why the girl had led them into the trap or if she had tried to warn Boon about it. This was the second time in twenty-four hours he'd been pinned down by autofire, and that was two times too many.

He kept his eyes on the window to his right and saw a twinkle of orange flame stab out of the shadows. A divot of dirt flew up between Grant's splayed legs. One part of his mind identified the reports as belonging to an Uzi or mini-Uzi.

The other part of his mind locked on to the window. He leveled the Sin Eater and squeezed off three rounds. He saw duraplast dust explode in miniature mushroom clouds all around the window.

"Move!" he roared. "To your left!"

DOS WRENCHED HIS BODY aside as a sleet storm of duraplast chips and powder swept over him. He hefted the blaster in both hands and fired what was left in the clip toward the black-coated man rolling diagonally over the ground. Eight brass casings rattled down on the wooden floor. The bullets stitched a path across the ground. He hadn't come close to the target, but he figured Uno could nail him. He watched the man vault to his feet and start running.

Angrily Dos ejected the spent clip and fumbled to insert another one. He'd get the son of a bitch—he'd get the fucking Mag. Or Uno would.

GRANT RAN, shielding his eyes from the spraying columns of dirt and rock fountaining up all around him. Though his eyes were protected by his dark glasses, a shard of stone could shatter a lens and blind him, like poor Carthew. He pointed the Sin Eater over his left shoulder and pressed the trigger. He had no idea if he hit anything.

Dust and pulverized rock danced in fountains around him. Two subguns had opened up in full-auto bursts, trying to chop him to pieces in a cross fire. Bullets snapped the air all around, sounding like steel whips. Ricochets whined and whistled.

He felt two bullets skid along the Kevlar covering his hip, and he staggered. Something tugged at his collar, bit the heel of his right boot, but he kept running, waiting for either deliverance or death.

KANE FELT a twinge of guilt. It appeared as if the pair of blastermen was ignoring him completely and concentrating their pattern of fire on Grant. So far, not a single slug had buzzed his way.

Taking and holding a deep breath, Kane jammed the cigar between his teeth and rose up from behind his stone barrier. He pointed the Sin Eater in the general direction of the two buildings and held down the trigger, firing a continuous left-to-right burst. Grant was lurching toward him, running in a crouch.

"Move!" Kane yelled.

"What the hell do you think I'm doing!" Grant screamed, twisting his body from one side to the other, running broken-field style.

Smoke drifted in flat planes between the two structures. Kane doubted he would score any hits, but his fire spoiled the aims of the blastermen in the squats. The autofire from the windows stopped just as Grant angled his body in a dive that brought him up and over the top of the rock heap. Kane obligingly sidestepped. Grant hit the ground with a grunting curse, rolled to one knee and aimed his Sin Eater first at one window, then the other. His face glistened with perspiration, and he was panting.

"Where are they?" Grant demanded breathlessly. "Who are they?"

They heard the rapid crunch-crunch-crunch of boots on gravel behind them and whirled simultaneously. Boon was racing toward them, coattails flapping, Sin Eater in hand.

"Get down!" Grant shouted, waving at him.

The bullets caught Boon high up on the left side of the throat, just below the hinge of his jaw, spinning him around on his toes like a dancer. Fistfuls of flesh and bone sheared away in a semiliquid spray, and the severed carotid artery pumped out a bright jet of blood. Boon fell backward, and the bullets followed him down, kicking his body from side to side. The autofire ceased.

"Fireblast!" Grant bellowed, pounding a fist against the ground. "They were after *me!*"

Then his lips tightened in a thin line, allowing no more words to escape. Anger was unprofessional and dangerous.

"Yeah," Kane grated, back against the rock pile. "They're after you, not me. But why?"

"How the hell do I know?" Grant's voice was pitched low to disguise the quaver of fury and grief.

"Then let's by God find out."

Nodding tersely, Grant reached inside his coat for the trans-comm unit, pulling the pin mike from his lapel. "I'll call for backup."

"Don't. Not yet," Kane said.

Grant stared at him incredulously. "Not yet? Then when? When all the jolt-walkers, blastermen and chop-mongers in the Pits decide they want to buy into a piece of this action?"

"We'll call for backup *after* we nail these bastards. Not before."

"Another one of your *instincts?*"

"That's right," Kane replied. "This doesn't add up, makes no sense at all. We've walked the Pits for years, on sweeps and on patrols. How many times have we been bushwhacked or shot at, let alone with autoblasters?''

Grant exhaled grimly. "Hardly ever."

"Whoever these blastermen are, why choose you as the target?"

"I've made enemies down here, I guess."

"No more than I have. This a contract chill—on you, and if he got in the way, on Boon. For some reason, my ass is sanctified."

"That's just what Reeth said. Remember what happened to him?"

"Very clearly. But I have a plan."

They shared a hasty, whispered conference, then Kane slowly stood up. He made a careful visual survey of the zone and deliberately walked around the pile of broken stones and into the open, hands at his sides.

DOS STARED in gape-mouthed astonishment as the Mag sauntered casually in his direction. The dumb bastard had his Sin Eater in hand, but he held it against his leg.

Reflexively his finger tightened on the trigger of the mini-Uzi, and it required a conscious effort to relax it. His target was hunkered down behind the heap of masonry and brick, safely sheltered from his and Uno's fire. The man they had been ordered to spare strode single-mindedly forward, as if he were strolling along the promenade of a high-tower, still puffing on a cigar.

Dos bit back a groan of despair. What the fuck was he expected to do now?

THE FURIOUS HAMMERING of the autoblaster echoed from the window ahead of Kane and above him. Dirt divots jumped into the air directly in front of him. His measured stride didn't falter, but he repressed a smile of relief. He had gambled correctly. For whatever reason, the chill team was under orders to spare his life, though the blastermen weren't above trying to scare him off.

Casting a glance over his shoulder, he saw Grant peering anxiously around the base of the masonry mound. Kane saluted him with two fingers to the nose and stepped across the threshold into the squat.

As he expected, the interior was a gutted shell. The air was stagnant, and he detected the smell of old cook fires. The walls of the individual rooms had long ago been demolished. The light was dim but modified by the indirect illumination of the setting sun, peeping through a ragged gap in the domed roof.

The second floor was not much more than a rickety platform supported by a pair of square wooden pillars. A crude homemade ladder stretched from the ground to a square opening eight feet above.

Calmly Kane said, "Throw down your blaster and come down, hands behind your head."

There was no reply, but he heard the creak and squeak of floorboards.

"Look," Kane said reasonably, "I'm not coming up there, so you're going to have to come down here. I promise not to shoot you. Magistrate's mercy."

He thought he heard a nervous intake of breath, then another creak of wood. Kane counted silently to thirty, figuring half a minute was sufficient time for the man to review his situation and reach a logical decision.

At thirty, he announced, "All right, then. This way is more fun, anyhow."

Stepping deeper into the gloomy interior, Kane leveled the Sin Eater and pressed the trigger. The high-velocity, heavy-caliber rounds tore across the room and ripped savagely into the support posts right where the areas of dry rot were the most evident. The building filled with thunder and the sharp sweet smell of cordite. Spent shell casings arced up and clattered down. Sections of the posts dissolved in sprays of splinters.

Kane played the bullet stream over the pair of wooden pillars as if he were washing them down with a water hose. Amid mushy cracks and snaps, the entire second-floor platform tilted down at a forty-five-degree angle, then cascaded down entirely. The whole building trembled with the violence of the crash.

Kane glimpsed a man frantically scrabbling to maintain his balance, feet kicking wildly as if he were running in place. He uttered a hoarse cry as the floor collapsed beneath him. Kane stepped aside as the man struck the floor gracelessly and with breath-robbing force. He tumbled head over heels, the mini-Uzi spinning away and disappearing into a puffing cloud of duraplast dust and rotted-wood particles.

The fall had slammed all the air out of the man's lungs, and his mouth opened and closed in shuddery silent gasps, like a fish stranded on dry land. Glazed eyes took in the dark figure of Kane looming out of the gloom, and his hand streaked for the long knife scabbarded at his waist.

Kane stomped down hard on the hand, breaking and grinding the delicate metacarpal bones beneath his heel. The blasterman tried to scream, but he didn't have the breath for it. All that issued from his mouth was a high-pitched, aspirated gargle.

Then Grant's voice reached him from outside. "Kane! What's going on in there?"

"A little renovating," Kane called. "Just stay there."

He reached down and hauled the blasterman to his feet by gripping the collar of his jacket. The lenses of his glasses easily penetrated the dust-clogged murk, and he recognized the man, or least what he was, if not who.

"You're one of old Guana Teague's strong-arms," Kane said. "Which one are you—Uno or Dos?"

The strong-arm's lips writhed, and he dragged oxygen into his lungs. Cradling his broken hand, he managed to husk out, "Dos."

"Who's in the other building?"

"Uno."

"Talkative as all hell, aren't we?"

"Huh?"

Kane pulled the strong-arm in front of him, stepping back half a pace. He trained the Sin Eater on the small of the man's back, but he didn't touch him with it. He had been taught never to get that close with a blaster, only with a knife. A professional could easily stamp down hard on his instep and pivot around to whop his gun aside.

"We're moving out," Kane said. "Slow. You stop when I tell you to, or I'll stop you. Permanently."

Raising his voice, he called, "Grant! We're coming out! Don't shoot me by accident."

Grant shouted back, voice full of impatience, "After what you've put me through, it wouldn't be any damn accident!"

Kane and Dos edged out of the squat, facing the opposite building.

"Hey, Uno," Kane said loudly, "I've got your brother here, so why don't you come down and talk this over?"

Dos mumbled something in a peevish tone.

"What?" Kane inquired.

"I said he's not my fuckin' brother." He was breathing easier now.

"Dos says you're not his fucking brother," Kane called. "Even without that familial connection, I'm presuming you don't want me to chill him. Right?"

After a long moment, an uncertain voice wafted from the window. "Right. Guess so."

"Can I come out now?" demanded Grant.

Raising his voice, Kane shouted, "Hey, Uno! Grant wants to know if he can come out now."

There was another long moment of silence from the second floor. "Yeah. Sure. Guess so."

Cautiously Grant straightened up from behind his stone-littered shelter, Sin Eater aimed at the window. He began a careful crab-walk toward Kane and the strong-arm, eyes and blaster not wavering from the second floor of the squat.

From Dos, Kane asked, "Why did Guana order this chill? And why Grant?"

The strong-arm shrugged. "I just follow orders."

"As do we all. Where'd you get the blasters?"

Dos shrugged again.

"Who's the girl?"

"Girl?"

"The *albino* girl."

"That's Domi."

"She work for Guana, too?"

Dos hesitated. "Sort of."

"Well, you sort of chilled a Magistrate, so maybe I'll just sort of chill you—unless you and Uno start singing without me having to prompt you."

Grant stopped his advance and shouted angrily up at the window. "Better come down, you rad-blasted mongrel! You don't want me to come in after you!"

The darkness beyond the window snapped flame and noise. Slugs rippled across the ground, and Grant, roaring a curse, hurled his body backward and down. As he fell, he worked the trigger of the Sin Eater, snap-shooting at the muzzle-flash. He missed.

Uno didn't. The bullets from the mini-Uzi stitched a straight line across the ground, chewing up the turf, spitting up gravel, tracking and intersecting with Dos.

The strong-arm screamed and toppled backward, arms windmilling. Staggering under his weight, Kane felt a storm of bullets striking Dos's body, as if a work gang were pounding his torso with sledgehammers.

With slugs kicking up dirt all around him, Kane tried to fling the inert body aside and raise the Sin Eater. Something hard and hot smashed across his forehead and sent him flailing back. He felt himself falling, suddenly blinded by a fiery wetness. Dos fell on top of him, pinning him to the ground.

The stutter of the autoblaster ceased, but the trip-hammer

roar of Grant's Sin Eater continued for a few seconds, then there was silence.

Kane lay beneath the bullet-riddled body, not moving, not even breathing. He was astounded that he was breathing and not thoroughly dead. He heard the rapid scutter of running feet, and then Grant was leaning over him. He heaved Dos's body up and rolled it aside.

"Hell, Kane, don't you be dead—"

Kane lurched into a sitting position, swiping at the scarlet liquid streaming warmly down his face. "I'm not. Let's get him."

Spitting the squashed ruin of the cigar from his mouth, Kane came to his feet in an enraged rush, and nearly fell as a wave of dizziness swept over him. His head began to throb in agonizing cadence with his pulse. Grant caught him and manhandled him down behind the masonry pile.

"Bastard's gone by now," Grant rasped, probing at the wound on Kane's forehead with his fingers. "We'll get him. A graze, that's all. Probably caught one that went through Dos's shit-for-brains, so it was already partly deflected."

"Oh, that makes me feel a whole lot better." Kane pushed Grant's hand away and sluiced the flow of blood from his eyes.

"So much for your guess they were after me and that your overconfident ass was sacrosanct."

Kane started to shake his head, then thought better of it. "I was still right. Uno wasn't aiming at me. He was trying to silence Dos."

Grant glanced over at the strong-arm's bullet-smashed head. "He did more than try."

He glanced behind him at Boon's body, lying spread-eagled and motionless, bled almost white. A ribbon of blood, black in the fading light, had meandered several feet from his neck, gleaming dully on the ground.

Grant sighed heavily. "Can I call for backup now?"

Chapter 14

The red sun of the dying workday washed the promenade with the color of old blood. People still crowded the walkway, going to the elevators to begin late shifts, coming through the entrance gate, heading to their homes.

Morales had been waiting for nearly half an hour. Following Salvo's order, he wore a dark green, untailored bodysuit and was fiddling with the lamps in the evergreen trees, trying to look as if he knew what he was doing. He was faintly insulted that Salvo had instructed him to dress as a custodian. Sure, he was of dark olive complexion with a square, stump-legged mesomorphic physique, but in his opinion he looked nothing like a typical outlander.

He couldn't deny that his great-grandparents had been outlanders, from one of the Western Islands, but inasmuch as his great-grandfather was an accomplished stonemason and was instrumental in erecting the Administrative Monolith, his family had been granted citizenship. Of course, that was before the entrance requirements had tightened.

So, now Morales stood in the decorative tree line and did his best to look like an outlander custodian and not a Mag Intel officer. He was annoyed that none of the passing people spared him so much as a second glance. He refused to admit that he fit the profile.

He grew more impatient, more irritated the longer he waited. Then, finally, he saw the woman. The pix he had called up from a personnel file hadn't really done her justice.

There was no denying Brigid Baptiste's striking appearance, and it went well with her brisk, almost manly stride.

Her blue bodysuit conformed to every curve of her tall, willowy body. Even with her hair pinned up in a constraining bun and the quaint eyeglasses perched on the bridge of her nose, Morales could understand why Kane had made a midnight visit to her apartment. Evidently Salvo did not.

Morales waited until she passed through the gate, on her way to the elevator, before he climbed out from the tree line. He walked casually along the promenade toward the apartment blocks. He had memorized the woman's number and found her place easily. Of course, the door was unlocked.

Brigid Baptiste's apartment was as simple and utilitarian as his own, except his was substantially smaller. He lived three levels below, so the size difference was understandable. But it was still irritating.

The curtains were drawn across the three back windows, so only a dim light filled the place. He groped his way to the bedroom, found the bedside lamp and switched it on. There was nothing out of the ordinary to see, much less the "anything" Salvo had commanded him to find. The room smelled of aromatic soap, with a faint whiff of roses.

Morales made a quick circuit of the apartment, opening and closing drawers, peeking into food canisters, even inspecting the contents of the small refrigerator in the kitchenette. The place was very clean, almost compulsively tidy. That certainly wasn't out of the ordinary, since archivists possessed rigidly regimented personalities.

Careful not to leave anything out of place, he returned to the bedroom. On the bedside table was a framed photo, which at first he assumed was a pix of Baptiste herself. Then he realized the woman in the photograph was a bit older, but the resemblance was startling. She was beaming at the camera, with a wide, pearly smile. Morales wondered if Baptiste looked that heart-achingly beautiful when—or if—she smiled.

He opened the closet door and gave the clothes hanging there a cursory, disinterested inspection. As he was sliding the door shut, a faint gleam caught his eye. He parted a pair of hanging bodysuits, realizing the closet was deeper than standard, and saw the little desktop work area the woman had made for herself. The comp console was an obsolete DDC manual model. He looked at it, turned away, then looked at it again and thought it over.

It was fairly common—if unspoken—knowledge that some archivists were allowed a wide latitude in the performance of their duties. Owning a cast-off comp wasn't a capital crime. It was against the rules, but anyone who ranked high in any of the divisions bent them to some degree or another.

Morales himself had acted on scraps of Intel that came his way from time to time. It was a quick and subtle way to requisition more personal goods before they became generally available or to apply for an upgrade in housing.

Reporting the comp to Salvo might result in a reprimand for Brigid Baptiste, or at worst a lowering of her seniority. Of course, that action might leave her apartment vacant. He brightened at the possibility, though he knew Salvo would hardly be satisfied with a comp-possession charge. He'd need more to obtain a reward.

Sitting down in the chair in front of the machine, Morales turned it on, waited until it had warmed up and the monitor flashed the request for the password. He tried several, hoping the DDC wasn't equipped with an automatic lockout after a certain number of failed attempts.

After the third try, he paused, reviewing the little he knew of the woman, of the sparse clues to character he might have seen in his search of her apartment. A notion registered and he pecked out "Mom."

He couldn't help but chuckle when the screen flashed and displayed the files. There was only one available on the desktop, so he tapped the keys to open it. Text appeared on the monitor, and he began to read. He only scanned a couple of paragraphs before his breath caught in his throat.

Possible Origin of Magistrate Division—Source:
DoD Document, Dated 4/30/94

The concept of a one-world government was known in predark vernacular as the "New World Order." The globalist view was opposed by many American citizens as a conspiracy to remove legal and civil rights granted to them by the Constitution (re. file #01405).

The conspiracy theories were given a degree of plausibility by the so-called Black Helicopter Phenomenon, circa 1970 through 1997. Black and silent, these helicopters were unmarked and therefore unidentifiable. At first reported in remote areas, the aircraft seemed to be engaged in clandestine missions....

Morales muttered, "Well, bitch, you just bought yourself a one-way ticket to Shit City."

The contents of the file fit perfectly within the parameters of "anything." There was only one explanation.

Brigid Baptiste was a Preservationist.

Chapter 15

She stepped out of the elevator, through the archway and into the Historical Division. She passed other archivists going off shift, and most of their facial expressions mirrored her own—somber and serenely detached, with perhaps a touch of cold intellectual resolve. The primary difference between her and the other historians was the awareness that her center of interest had changed completely in the past sixteen hours. Brigid Baptiste was increasingly thinking of a place called Dulce and a man named Kane.

The man had presented her with a mystery to solve, but she wasn't sure if that prospect stimulated her as much as Kane himself. Even though she had never exchanged words with a Magistrate before last night, she doubted Kane was typical of the breed. She had seen plenty of Mags stalking the promenade in search of laws to enforce, and they had always reminded her of tigers on loose leashes.

She was pretty sure Kane possessed a set of fangs, but he hadn't bared them at her. Instead, he displayed a wry humor and even exuded an almost reluctant kindness, touched as it was with reserve and introspection. She hadn't expected that.

Of course, she chided herself, you hadn't expected him to be shit-faced, either.

Though she was anxious to begin work, Brigid maintained a steady pace. She walked through the long, broad corridors of the division, past scores of sealed doorways that led into hundreds of chambers and antechambers. All of them were filled with the relics of vanished cities and long-dead people. The quiet air smelled of dust and time—time past, time present, time future and time wasted.

Many of the rooms were strictly off limits to anyone not holding a "Q" clearance. When she had been granted her Quatro designation, Lakesh himself had taken her on a guided tour of a few of the storerooms. Most were crammed to the ceiling with shelves upon shelves of a vast number of books and bound volumes of magazines and technical manuals that had been printed on nonbiodegradable stock. There were trunks of clothing, crates of paintings, pieces of statuary and sculpture—in short, anything and everything that had survived the nukecaust more or less intact. As far as Brigid was concerned, a lot of it had little or no historical value. In her unvoiced opinion, an item that was junk two hundred years ago was still junk, even if it had weathered the nuking and the skydark.

There had been too much to absorb, so after a while, Brigid stopped trying. Lakesh had told her, voice full of pride, that the Cobaltville archives contained a greater volume of predark artifacts than any other ville in the network.

One room had remained frozen in her memory, however—a dark, musty room with disembodied heads glaring down from the walls. African elephants, African buffalo and rhinoceros, wolf, bison, lion, tiger and bear. They were specimens of animals killed and preserved by so-called predark sportsmen. Many of the species were extinct, and had been endangered even before the first mushroom cloud had billowed up from embassy row in Washington, D.C.

Some of the animals that survived the slaughter of hunters and freezing temperatures of skydark had mutated into grotesque imitations of their progenitors. Of those, the first two or three generations of mutant animals had run toward polyploidism, a doubling or tripling of the chromosome complement. For a time, gargantuan buffalo and panthers and even snakes had roamed the Deathlands, but their increased size had greatly reduced their lifespans. Only a few of the giant varieties existed any longer, or so she had been told. Since she had never been more than ten miles away from the ville, she had no idea if that was a scientific fact or merely wishful thinking.

Brigid entered her work area, the chemically treated rainbow insignia on her bodysuit allowing her to pass through the invisible photoelectric field without activating alarms. There was a long row of computer stations, half-enclosed by partitions, all facing a long, blank wall. Hidden behind the stone-and-steel-reinforced wall was a bank of sophisticated mainframe computers, the heart and brains of the division's data base. Lakesh was waiting, standing by her workstation, holding her day's work in one liver-spotted hand.

"How are you today, Brigid?" he asked.

Brigid forced a smile. "Fine, sir," she said, and reached for the bulging file folder in his hand.

Lakesh was a long-nosed, wizened cadaver of a man. He wore thick-lensed glasses with a hearing aid attached to the right earpiece. No one knew his actual age, but he was old, old, old. He was the oldest man Brigid had ever known or even seen.

He also made her extremely nervous on some days. He purposely made their hands touch when she took the file from him. His skin was cold, clammy, almost as if ice water flowed through him. Brigid sat down before her console. Lakesh lingered, as he usually did, behind her chair.

"Nothing too complicated today," he said. His voice was thin, reedy, as though instead of a larynx, he had a pair of roots rubbing together inside his throat. "Editing down and consolidating a series of reports on the causes of the Bosnian war."

"Simple, is it?" she replied, still forcing her smile. The instant she said it, she regretted it.

Lakesh was utterly, absolutely and thoroughly devoted to his art. History was his obsession, his reason for breathing, and he lived only to record it for posterity. His rheumy blue eyes widened, and she knew she had inadvertently pressed his lecture-mode button.

"Simple? Did the Bosnians, the Serbs, the Croats, the Muslims—indeed, the citizens of the entire predark world—have the future they wanted? Hardly." He pronounced the last word as if it tasted exceptionally unpleasant.

"The causes of war are never simply based on territorial struggle, economic conflict, or religious or ethnic differences. If we don't come to terms with that, the cycle repeats itself, doesn't it? The whole of history all over again."

Brigid had heard variations of Lakesh's pet theories, about time cycles, about one event impacting on another, continents, even centuries apart. Sometimes it was a bit too metaphysical for Brigid to comprehend.

"The future...if we still have one...could have been changed in the past, you know." Lakesh's voice had dropped to a musing whisper, then trailed away.

Suddenly he glanced around him in momentary confusion, as if he expected to see something—or some place—else. He blinked, and his bloodless lips creased in a shamed smile.

"I'm ranting again, aren't I? And you're too well-bred to ignore or interrupt me."

Patting her shoulder encouragingly, he shuffled away. "Get to it."

Brigid gazed after his age-stooped form for a moment. For a ville official, in any division, Lakesh was a definite anomaly. The most-productive years of his service were long behind him, and why he hadn't received an administrative transfer decades ago was baffling.

Exhaling a long breath, Brigid flipped open the cover of the file and began working. She expected the documents to be dry packing, and she wasn't disappointed. But as she always did, she kept her expression and mind neutral as she read the copies of the two-hundred-year-old reports. There were pages upon pages of it, culled from various and sundry predark governmental bodies—CIA, NSA, UNSC, DIA and something called Amnesty International.

Though several pages were already censored, blacked out with ink, she was able to patch together a fairly reasonable account of the causes behind the horrific, genocidal conflict in old Europe.

People were at the heart of it, of course. Disobedient, unevolved, unregenerately selfish humanity who surrendered to their baser natures and slaughtered and massacred and tortured on very flimsy pretexts. The core of the fault lay not with governments, which after all were vast extrapolations of the private citizen's selfish, sinful urges, or with socioeconomic hardships, but only with vicious humankind, who thirsted for the blood of their neighbors.

Despite what Lakesh had said, reading through and collating all the data to conform with the standard point of view was simplicity itself.

Brigid copied the final version onto disk, output it, placed it in her completed tray and indulged in a stretch. Three hours remained on her shift, so she allowed a bit of the professional distance to fade from her mind. Unsurprisingly she found the recollection of Kane's visit occupy her thoughts.

She shook her head impatiently. There had been other men in her life, a few fellow historians, but none she had ever truly connected with. She was ville bred, just like the men she had involved herself with, so she never quite grasped why the emotional spark couldn't bridge the gap. They had been raised much like herself—ordered, fed, clothed, educated and protected from all extremes. And their narrow, limited perspectives, their solemn pronouncements regarding their ambitions, had bored her into a coma.

Of course, she couldn't be certain, but she doubted Kane would have the same effect.

Without appearing to do so, Brigid made sure none of her co-workers was paying attention to her, then she selected a blank disk and inserted it into her machine's hard

drive. Carefully she overrode the voice control and transferred it to the keyboard. She typed in the proper numerical
sequence to access the main data base, then input the word
"Dulce." As she had anticipated, the programmed safeguard kicked in, and the legend on the screen asked for her
access authorization. She tapped in "Baptiste, gr. 6 arch.,
clearance Quatro."

The data infeed digested the identification, and transmitted the message to her console: "Authorization denied."

Brigid tensed. If she tried again and was denied again,
she would trip a security relay and alert a monitoring official. She thought it out dispassionately for half a minute
before she cleared the screen and typed in Lakesh, gr. 12
arch., clearance Xeno."

The words "Authorization granted" flashed on the
screen, disappeared and an instant later were replaced by a
red triangle bisected by three black vertical lines. Glowing
beneath the symbol was a list of available historical files
dealing with Dulce, arranged by date. She chose the one
dated 12/20/2000, highlighted it and opened it up.

Her face remained a detached mask, but her heartbeat
sped up and she had a difficult time discreetly swallowing
the lump forming in her throat. The report had been prepared for the Joint Chiefs of Staff, the Defense Intelligence
Agency, the Defense Advanced Research Programs
Agency—all predark institutions with a monomania about
secrecy—and presumably the incoming Commander in
Chief, since it was dated only thirty days before the presi-
dential-inauguration ceremony—and the nukecaust. Brigid
scrolled down to an index.

I. Totality Concept Progression
II. Redoubt Construction
III. Archon Directive Perspective
IV. Appendix

She read each entry carefully, mentally cross-indexing
them with information already secure within her memory.

Emotionally she felt like a bright-eyed child, eager to play with her new toys, while her intellect was coldly aloof, observing, recording, noting everything.

The third entry intrigued her on an emotional level, though intellectually she provided herself with a thumbnail explanation. She knew that *archon* was an ancient Greek term for the magistrates in many city-states. Presumably the Archon Directive Perspective related to the international police force that was being assembled prior to the nuke-caust.

Of course, another and far older definition of *archon* came from an ancient understanding of the world in which the archons were forces lined up on the side of dark against the glory of light. And that was the source for the word *archenemy* also. She recalled that the recurring mythological image of Archons was that of jailers, imprisoning the divine spark in human souls.

However, due to her recollections of the references to it in the *Wyeth Codex,* she decided to heed her intellect and act in a thorough manner. She highlighted the first index entry, opened it and an organizational chart appeared on the screen.

TOTALITY CONCEPT

Overproject Whisper

Project Cerberus_____Operation Chronos

Overproject Excalibur

Genesis Project____Project Invictus____Scenario Joshua

Overproject Majestic

Mission Snowbird (re. Archon Directive)____Project Sigma

Appendix (PTBE)

SHE RECOGNIZED Overproject Whisper, Project Cerberus and Operation Chronos from the *Wyeth Codex,* so she moved the comp's cursor to Project Cerberus and touched a key.

<u>Quantum Interphase Mat-Trans Inducer Operations</u>

1. Subject scan/coordinate lock
2. Autoscanner initiation
3. Interphase matter stream transmission cycle
4. Subject transmission
5. Subject reception/rematerialization

Operational timeline: 6.2 seconds

A diagram appeared, a jumble of geometric cones and ellipses and hexagons. Though she had to stare hard at it, Brigid realized she was looking at a schematic of a gateway mat-trans unit. It was a six-sided chamber, and the cut-away view depicted machinery beneath the platform of the unit. All the pieces of hardware were labeled, with arrow-tipped lines pointing to them: emitter array, interphase transition coils, virtual focus conformals.

Brigid scrolled down to a column of digits, identified as destination-lock codes. Opposite them was a list of redoubt names and locations—three in New Mexico, she noted right away, and number four in Montana.

A brief postscript indicated that construction and gateway installation on redoubts Tango, Victor, Yankee, Zulu, November, Oscar and Golf were expected to be completed by the first of the New Year.

The data permanently impressed itself on the photosensitive plate of her memory. As it did so, a riot of conflicting emotions exploded in her mind—first and foremost was the wild ecstasy of discovery, then her twenty-seven years of conditioning kicked in and brought a bone-chilling terror that dried the saliva in her mouth.

Her eyes were seeing things never meant to be seen. Her

mind did an insane pirouette, and she recalled the ancient myths of the Gorgons, and of Lot's wife in the Bible. She waited to be turned either to stone or to a pillar of salt.

After a few seconds, neither occurred, and her mind stopped twirling. Brigid returned to the index and shifted the cursor from the bottom up, highlighting the Appendix. A page of text appeared:

Para-Terrestrial Biological Entity (re. III, Archon Directive Perspective)

The typical PTBE as represented by participants in the Archon Directive at the Dulce installation can be described as follows:
1. Between three to five feet in height.
2. Erect-standing biped. Short thin legs.
3. Gracile skeletal structure.
4. Cranium larger than normal human proportions.
5. Absence of auditory lobes (external ear apparatus).
6. Absence of body hair.
7. Large, tear-shaped eyes, generally opaque black with vertical slit pupils.
8. Eyes slanted approx. thirty-five degrees.
9. Small straight mouth, thin lips.
10. Disproportionately long arms.
11. Tough gray epidermis.
12. Internal organs similar to humans', but developed and arranged differently.
13. Blood type is RH (re Basque people).
14. Significant secondary findings after permitted study indicates the PTBEs require human blood plasma and other human biological substances to survive. In extreme circumstances, they can subsist on other animal fluids, such as cattle or other domesticated animals.

BRIGID FELT AS IF HER entire mind were immersed in
soggy cotton wadding. Intellectually she could conceive of
extraterrestrial life-forms, but emotionally she felt a visceral, xenophobic cringing. She wanted to blank out the
screen, to convince herself that what she read was part of
an elaborate predark fantasy, or better yet, a hoax. It was
too late for that; the text was imprinted indelibly within her
eidetic memory. For as long as she lived, no matter how
hard she tried, she would never forget it.

A plaintive wail echoed from deep within her mind.
*Kane, what have you stumbled into? What have I stumbled
into?*

She pushed the keys to begin the copying sequence, her
hands moving with a numb slowness that shocked her. And
then as if from far away, she heard someone speak. "There.
There she is."

Brigid gradually turned her head in the direction of the
voice. In the archway stood Lakesh. For a long heartbeat,
she couldn't understand why he looked so sad, so desperately old, so crushed by the weight of his years. Then her
eyes swept over the three black-coated men with him, and
her near paralyzed thought processes identified them. They
were Magistrates, and Lakesh was pointing her out to them.

Fear flowed through her like a floodtide of icy water,
stimulating her frozen reflexes. She quickly broke the data
link, or tried to do so. The incriminating text still glowed
on the screen, white against amber. The copying process
continued without interruption.

Terror was pushed aside by a sudden onslaught of nausea, of the sickening realization she had been found out,
that Kane had used her for the sole purpose of betraying
her. The taste of the realization was so bitter she nearly
gagged. She had been manipulated into breaking the car-
dinal rule of life in the villes: *trust no one.*

A man suddenly loomed over her, a flat-faced, thin-
lipped man with short, thin hair. Brigid looked up at him.

His eyes, masked by dark glasses, were unfathomable, but she saw her own face dimly reflected in the lenses. She smiled at her face, a small smile of resignation and defiance.

The man tilted his head slightly, toward the screen and the information glowing there. He smiled, too.

Then, with a clenched gloved fist, he struck her in the face.

Chapter 16

Two Mags from Intel were sitting in the bare-walled room, saying nothing and trying to keep awake. Kane occupied a chair at a table across from them, waiting for Salvo to arrive to take his statement. He tried to believe that a statement would make a difference. His head wound, treated at the scene by a medic, felt like a wag tire with multiple ruptures. A thin, flesh-colored film covered the bullet graze, adhering tightly to his forehead. The liquid bandage contained nutrients and antibiotics, and since its chemical composition was very similar to real epidermal tissue, his body would absorb it as the injury healed.

Boon would never heal. He was the first Mag in decades to be chilled while on a Pit patrol, and Kane hadn't likewise chilled all the chillers or even called for backup.

It was hours past his off-shift time. Upon returning to the division, Grant and Kane were immediately separated. Since then, he had been sitting, waiting and wondering how long it would take Salvo to arrive and how bad things would become.

On the table lay Dos's mini-Uzi, retrieved from the wreckage of the squat. That and the strong-arm's body were the only pieces of evidence incriminating Guana Teague as the mastermind. Except Kane didn't and couldn't accept the concept of Teague as the master of anything, even his own soul.

Pollard suddenly lumbered into the room. He smiled blandly and said, "Kane."

"Pollard. Where's Salvo?"

"On an op. I'm the watch commander, so you'll have to talk to me."

"And Grant?"

"Got his story already. Let's hear yours and mix and match 'em."

Kane told him what had occurred during the PPP, not leaving out or embellishing a single detail.

"Marvelous," Pollard grunted, his snub-nosed face drawn in a scowl. "There are holes in your story big enough to drive a goddamn Sandcat through. You're about a millimeter from finding your ass in front of a tribunal."

"What are the holes?" challenged Kane. "You talked to Grant already, so he told you the same thing."

"According to him, you believe it was a contract chill and Boon got in the way."

"That's how I read it. Why else did Uno ice Dos?"

"You tell me."

Impatiently Kane snapped, "To keep him from fingering Guana."

Intertwining his blunt fingers on the tabletop, Pollard replied, "Maybe, yes. Maybe no. Grant has some serious problems with your theory."

Kane forced a derisive laugh, part snort, part sigh. "Don't play that moldy old game with me, Polly."

Pollard slammed the flat on his hand down on the table. "Don't call me Polly, you arrogant bastard!"

Kane came up out of his chair so fast that it clattered over backward. Watching the action, unmoved and unmoving, the other two Mags were as quiet as a pair of statues.

Clenching his fists so hard his knuckles began to ache, Kane said in a low, deadly monotone, "You want to make this personal, you overstuffed dipshit? We're both heeled, right?"

Pollard raised his right hand, slightly curling the fingers. His eyes impaled Kane with twin shafts of anger. "Don't be crazy."

"We've worked together for years. If you're such a stupe

you don't remember I have no patience for games, I'll jog your memory. Here and now. Make your move.''

Pollard heaved a gusty sigh and relaxed his fingers. ''Sit down, Kane. Forget it. I didn't mean to lean on you. Boon is dead, and all of us are shook up over it.''

Kane didn't budge. ''You talked to Grant.''

''Yeah. His story was substantially the same as yours.''

''Then why are we sitting here stepping on each other's dicks? Let's assemble a sweep squad and step on Guana's.''

Pollard lifted the broad yoke of his shoulders in a dismissive shrug. ''Like I said, Salvo ain't here. Only he can authorize a Pit sweep.''

He stared at Kane keenly. ''And don't even think of going back down there on your own initiative. Your unilateral decision not to call for backup buried both you and Grant neck deep in shit. You go down to the Pits again, you better just stay there.''

Kane didn't respond to Pollard's words. ''Where's Grant now?''

''Home, probably. I suggest you go to your own and wait for Salvo's call. I've already told Grant this, so now I'm telling you—you're under orders not to contact each other until a final determination about this incident is reached.''

''We're suspended?''

''No, but you're being assigned to work different shifts until further notice.''

''Whatever you say.'' Kane turned toward the door.

''Hey.''

Kane turned back. Pollard nudged the mini-Uzi across the table toward him with a contemptuous flick of his fingers. ''Drop this off in the evidence room on your way out.''

Kane didn't move.

Pollard added lamely, ''Please.''

Kane picked up the blaster and strode out of the room. He debated with himself on whether to slam the door behind him or simply ease it shut. He opted to close it with an easy, relaxed click.

He stalked down the main corridor in such an obvious anger that no one he passed dared speak to him. The evidence room was adjacent to the armory. It was located there for a number of reasons, primarily so if any weapons of value came into Mag hands, they could be simply transferred over to the ville arsenal.

Kane tapped in his badge number on the keypad affixed to the wall beside the door. Lock solenoids snapped aside and allowed him to enter. The windowless room was always dimly lit, a perpetual twilight. Behind a wire-screen enclosure was the storage facility, mainly a double row of tall metal shelves. The air was hot, stale and motionless.

Russo, the attendant, looked up from filling out an invoice and squinted toward him. He was perched on a stool behind the screen, and he exuded a stale, sweaty odor from his sparse blond hair and his wrinkled gray bodysuit. Kane could smell him, and it wasn't pleasant. Neither was Russo's attitude.

"Whatcha got there?"

Kane hefted the mini-Uzi. "A blaster, lifted from the Pits."

Russo peered through the screen. "An Uzi, huh?"

"Close. A mini-Uzi."

"Kind of rare. Had a matched set in here a while back. Pristine condition. Museum quality."

It took a second for Russo's comment to register.

"How long a while back?" Kane asked.

"A year, maybe two. Longer than that, maybe."

"What happened to them?"

"Transferred 'em to the armory, what the hell else?"

Kane stepped closer to the man, extending the blaster for his inspection. "Does this look like one of them?"

Russo eyed it and answered petulantly. "No, the ones I saw were green and had mustaches. Of course it looks like 'em. A mini-Uzi is a mini-Uzi."

Kane's icy eyes bored into his, and Russo added nervously, "Hell, Kane, there's got to be fifty Uzis in the armory. Maybe even half a dozen of those mini jobs."

He pointed with his pencil to Kane's right. "Put it on the table. I'll tag it later."

The table in the corner was cluttered with recent acquisitions, most of it useless salvage, like home-forged single-shot pistols, knives and even a crude crossbow. Kane cleared a space and laid down the blaster. Squatting on one end of the table was a computer console, a DDC. He glanced at it, glanced away, then looked again. It was an old manual model, and he had seen it a little less than twenty-four hours ago. He knew for certain, because of the fine cracks just next to the screen, which were like a stamp of identity.

And he didn't quite know why, but the floor seemed to split under his feet, leaving him hanging on a crumbling edge by his fingernails.

He spun toward Russo, feeling cold perspiration breaking out on his forehead. Forcing a nonchalance he didn't feel, he asked, "When did that comp come in?"

"An hour, hour and a half ago. Why?"

"Who brought it?"

Russo consulted his invoices. "Let's see…that guy from Intel."

"Intel?"

"Yeah, you know…dark-complected guy—"

"Morales."

"That's him. Why, what's up with it?"

Kane didn't answer. Stomach muscles quivering in adrenaline-induced spasms, he whirled and flung open the door.

"Hey! Kane!" Russo shouted after him. "What's up?"

Half jogging, Kane hurried down the corridor and entered Intel. His eyes swept the room, and when they didn't spy Morales, he approached the nearest tech.

"Morales is supposed to be on duty," he said stiffly. "Where is he?"

The tech, a pock-faced, sleepy-eyed man, blinked at him owlishly. "Salvo put him on another detail. Something about historical."

Kane darted back into the corridor and ran full out for the elevator. A clerk stood before the opening door panel, arms laden with file folders. Kane shouldered him roughly aside amid a flurry of paper and savagely punched the button for B Level. The door shut in the tech's angry face.

The ascent took no longer than fifteen seconds, but to Kane it felt like an eternity, stretched out like a rubber band of infinite length. The elevator hissed to a stop, and Kane whipped out of it before the panel had fully rolled aside. He sprinted through the many archways, knowing his badge was attuned to the photoelectric field sensors.

He raced past doorway after doorway, past room after room filled with all the pride and glory and foolishness of the predark dead. Kane had eyes only for the living, and for the quartet of figures coming toward him beneath the final archway. They were Salvo, Morales, Waylon and a female figure. It was Brigid Baptiste.

His shocked eyes registered that her arms were held behind her at unnatural angles, bound with the standard-issue plastic riot cuffs. Her hair was disheveled and her glasses were missing. The only color about her white, stark face was from the crimson threads streaming from her nostrils, over her lips and across her chin.

Waylon, in the lead, saw him first and he increased the length of his stride to intercept him. He held out his left hand, palm up. "Kane! Stop!"

He didn't stop, but he slowed down just enough to slap Waylon's hand aside and deliver an elbow thrust into the interceptor's throat. Shoving the choking man out of his path, he stormed on.

"Kane!" barked Salvo. "I order you to halt."

Kane didn't even look at him. He had eyes only for Baptiste and her pale, blood-streaked face. Distantly he was aware of his lips peeling back from his teeth in a silent snarl.

"I'll shoot if you don't stop, Kane!" There was a click from his sleeve, and the Sin Eater filled his hand.

Kane slowed to a walk. He saw the fear and the anger in Salvo's face, and it required a great effort to keep from filling his own hand.

"What are you doing with that woman?" he demanded, his voice ragged with thinly disguised fury.

Morales sneered. "What's it look like? Placing a Pres-ervationist bitch under arrest. What's it to you?"

Kane's blow landed like a steam-driven piston. Mewling, Morales folded over and clutched his stomach, then was hammered face-first to the floor by a side-handed smash to the back of his exposed neck.

Locking eyes with Salvo, Kane said, "What's it to me? This archivist was following up a legal line of inquiry at my request."

"Who authorized it?" Salvo shot back. Though his blaster was in his hand, he didn't raise it.

"I did."

"Then it wasn't exactly legal, was it?"

Kane's eyes met Baptiste's. Though fear still swam in those clear green depths, relief gleamed there, too.

"Who struck you, Baptiste?"

"She resisted apprehension," Salvo growled. "Only the minimum force required to subdue her was employed. Damn it, have you fused out completely? She's a Preser-vationist. Do you understand that? A fucking *Preservation-ist!*"

Kane took a long, deep breath. By degrees, the flame of fury in his eyes was contained.

Salvo noticed, and some of the tension left his posture, but he didn't holster the Sin Eater. "You've got some ex-plaining to do," he said grimly.

Waylon was back on his feet, still gasping, and he

weaved toward Kane on unsteady legs, clutching his throat with his left hand. His right hand gripped his Sin Eater. He hissed, "You went too far this time—"

Salvo gestured to him. "Stand down."

Baptiste side-kicked at Salvo, but he grabbed her right arm and twisted it up in a painful hammerlock. She cried out. Kane shifted position, but stopped moving when Salvo cast a hard glance in his direction. Kane assessed the situation more coolly now, looking critically at Baptiste, Waylon, Salvo and the pair of blasters. He decided it wasn't worth the risk. If he finished what he had started, both he and Brigid Baptiste would die.

Salvo smiled coldly. "You lifted a comp disk from Reeth's slaghole, didn't you?"

"I did," Kane admitted, his tone cold and hard enough to match Salvo's smile. "The disk had a data lock-out that defied the Syne."

"And that aroused your curiosity."

Kane pointed accusingly at the moaning Morales. "I acted on that pissant's suggestion to consult historical."

"And you blundered into an ongoing op."

Kane quirked an eyebrow. "What kind of op?"

"Remember what I mentioned to you last night?"

"Yes."

"We've suspected this bitch was a spy for quite some time, that she was feeding crucial ville Intel to the warlord's army."

"That's a lie," Baptiste said sternly. "I was following a Magistrate Division request."

"Shut up." Salvo pursed his lips. "This isn't the time or place to discuss it further. Morales and Waylon, escort this traitor to detention now."

Kane stepped closer. "Wait—"

"Face it, Kane. You were used. You fucked up. Fortunately it helped us to nail her, otherwise you wouldn't be standing here—you'd be on your way to a disciplinary tribunal."

Waylon helped Morales to his feet and Salvo pushed Baptiste at them. "Take her. And Kane—you and me are going to have a talk."

Baptiste was led away, looking lost and slender between the black-coated magistrates. She didn't look back, for which Kane was both grateful and sad.

"I heard about the ambush," Salvo said quietly. "About Boon. I'm taking into consideration that's one reason you're behaving like a wired-out jolt-walker."

"Big-hearted of you," Kane replied, with unconcealed contempt. "I want to be in on the woman's interrogation."

"What makes you think there's going to be one?" Salvo made an exaggerated show of leathering his Sin Eater. "Anyway, we'll see. After our talk."

"I thought we just had it. Sir."

"By no means, Kane. By absolutely no bloody means. Follow me."

Kane fell into step, and they walked down the musty-smelling hallway. Just inside the archway stood a very old man, one of the oldest Kane had ever seen outside of the Pits. His blue eyes were so watery, he looked as if he was preparing to weep.

As Salvo came abreast of the man, he said imperiously, "You're in on this, too, Lakesh. Alert the others."

Chapter 17

Kane and Salvo returned to C Level. By the time the elevator deposited them on the division floor, Brigid Baptiste had already been escorted to detention, at the far end of the operation suites.

Kane followed Salvo into his office. "Why are we here?"

Salvo sat down behind his desk. "Where else should we be?"

"Down in Tartarus, putting the arm on Guana Teague. He was behind the ambush, used a little albino tramp with a bogus chip as a lure—"

"Drop it, Kane," Salvo demanded. "Forget Guana."

"He chilled a Magistrate," replied Kane hotly. "And tried to chill another. Once word spreads, not a single Mag will be safe in the Pits."

"I said drop it!" Salvo's angry bark brooked no debate. "The matter will be dealt with on my terms. You've got a very full evening ahead of you."

"I don't get you."

Salvo gestured sharply. "Take off your coat. Remove your side arm."

Kane didn't move. "Are you suspending me?"

Spots of red appeared on Salvo's cheeks. "Do as I say, or you'll be hoping for something as soft as suspension."

Kane hesitated, then with deliberate slowness shrugged out of his coat and draped it over the back of the chair. He unstrapped the Sin Eater from him forearm and dropped it with a provocative clunk on the center of the desk.

Salvo made no move to touch it. Inclining his head toward the chair, he said, "Sit."

Spinning the chair around, Kane thrust it between his legs and straddled it so that he could see the door and Salvo at the same time. "Now what?"

"Now we wait."

"For what—a disciplinary tribunal to convene?"

"Keep your mouth shut and your ears open and you'll find out."

They waited. The minutes dragged by like broken-legged turtles. Salvo said nothing. Kane said nothing. His mind was focused on Baptiste, on whether she had really used him or whether the reverse was true. He desperately wanted to talk to her or Grant. Or anybody else but Salvo.

Silence enfolded the office, and not even the familiar sounds of normal division activity seemed to filter in. When the tans-comm unit on the desk warbled, the sound was so unexpected and startling that Kane nearly jumped out of the chair.

Salvo didn't open the circuit. The unit warbled once more, then fell silent. From the desk drawer, he produced a set of goggles. The plastic lenses were thick and a deep black in color. He stood up. "Let's go."

"Go where?"

"Where I tell you."

Kane rose, reaching for his Sin Eater.

Salvo snapped, "Leave it." When Kane started to pick up his coat, Salvo repeated, "Leave it."

Kane refused to dog Salvo's heels, so he fell into step beside him as they strode down the corridor, past the evidence room and the recessed sec door of the armory. When they passed it, Kane almost slowed his pace. All that lay beyond the armory was the detention area. His lips moved in a thin half smile. If Salvo intended to lead him there and expected him to meekly enter a cell, he would receive one of the most painful surprises of his life.

Instead, they turned right down a narrow passage. It

dead-ended at a locked service access door. Salvo handed him the goggles. "Put these on."

"Why?"

"Consider it an order."

Slipping them over his head and eyes, Kane was rendered almost completely blind. A thread of blurry light peeped through a seal at his cheek. He heard a rustle of cloth, and Salvo adjusted the elastic strap, securing it tightly around his head. The darkness was total and impenetrable.

"Can you see?"

Kane chuckled dryly. "Think I'd tell you?"

"You'd better." Steel slipped into Salvo's voice. "And for your own good."

"No," replied Kane. "I can't see a thing. Satisfied?"

Salvo grunted, and then came a metal-on-metal clicking and clacking, followed by a faint squeal of hinges. He felt Salvo's hand on his elbow, tugging him forward. Kane resisted.

"Relax." Salvo's voice purred with amusement. "If I wanted to chill you, I wouldn't go to all this trouble."

Kane thought the statement over for a moment and agreed with it. He allowed himself to be guided for a few steps, then positioned against a wall.

"Don't move until I tell you."

He heard the squeak of hinges again, the snap of a locking mechanism and then a faint electric hum. He felt a sudden rising sensation in the pit of his stomach. "We're in an elevator."

"Astute."

"And we're going up?"

"Yes."

"To where?"

"To where we get off."

The elevator rose, ascending far above B Level and even A Level. It hissed to a pneumatic stop, and Salvo urged him away from the wall. The floor was slick and smooth beneath his boots, their footsteps echoed hollowly and Kane guessed they were walking across a big, high-ceilinged room.

"From this point on," Salvo whispered to him, "no talking."

Kane only nodded, feeling tension climb up his spine. With a hand on his elbow, Salvo guided him forward. The echoes of footfalls suddenly became muffled, muted. They were now on a thickly carpeted floor. At the same time, he detected the acrid odor of spicy incense, of unfamiliar resins.

Salvo gently tugged him to a stop. The scent of incense was stronger, almost overpowering. Kane reached for the goggles, but Salvo ordered, "Not yet."

The aromatic air shivered with the steady beat of a gong. Kane felt the vibrations against his face. The gong sounded thirteen times. After the final heavy chime, Salvo whispered, "Take them off now."

Carefully Kane lifted the goggles away and off his head. His eyes were narrowed, prepared to be blinded by light. Instead, he saw only a gray gloom, and his eyes quickly adjusted. He stood upon a thick Persian carpet. Figures shifted around him, and although he could see only shadows, he knew they were men.

Then a blade of white light speared down from somewhere above and impaled him. The suddenness of its unmerciful brightness seared his optic nerves, and he blurted out a startled, muffled curse. His hands came up to protect his eyes.

The whirling spectrum of light dimmed, diffused like pale sunlight barely penetrating a great underwater depth. As he stood there, blinking, a voice spoke to him. The voice was silvery, musical, its pitch exactly matching the gong's, which still echoed from the far corners of the room.

"You are Kane, a servant of order, a soldier of the ville, a warrior of the baron."

Kane's vision slowly cleared, and he saw a dim shape standing before him. The shape looked strange, hazy, and he realized he was seeing it through a semitranslucent curtain, like a veil of gauze dusted with iridescent gold particles.

"Answer me," the figure said. "Are you Kane?"

"I am."

"Do you know who I am?"

Heart hammering, throat thick, Kane replied, "You are the baron."

"Do you know why I have had you brought here?"

Kane breathed unsteadily. He wondered insanely if Baron Cobalt was speaking or if he had merely imagined it. He couldn't seem to focus on his figure—he moved, swaying gracefully, almost as though he were performing some bizarrely beautiful dance. There was only a fragment of an impression of pale golden skin, slim arms, a domed head and lean cheeks. Although he couldn't see the eyes, he knew the Baron was looking at him, waiting for an answer. He bowed his head and whispered, "No."

"Because you belong to me. From the day of your birth, you have belonged to me, as did your father and grandfather."

Kane didn't dare look around, but now that he remembered that other people were present, a bit of his fear ebbed. "Who am I to Baron Cobalt?"

"I offer you the chance to be one of my chosen ones."

"Why?" he asked quietly. "Chosen for what?"

"To hear the truth, to serve the truth, to protect the truth. And in doing so, protect all of humanity and what we have managed to build here from the ravaged ruins of the Deathlands."

Kane didn't understand. He just stood there, cringing inwardly, knowing he was the focal point of critical stares from the shadows behind him. He could scarcely believe what he was seeing, and he was afraid to speak. He waited for the baron to explain.

"Do you wish to hear the truth?"

He hesitated only half a heartbeat. "Yes."

"Be warned, then, Kane. Once you hear it, you must swear to serve it and protect it with your life. If you do not, then you die. Do you still wish to hear the truth?"

Even with his reason clouded by fear, Kane knew that he was in too deep to back out. An audience with Baron Cobalt was an event that had swift repercussions—it meant either a swift reward or a swift demise.

Kane lifted his head, cleared his throat and announced, "Yes, Lord Baron. I wish to hear the truth."

And the baron spoke:

"They are here among us. They have always been here, apart and remote, yet guiding us whenever the opportunity arose. Now their numbers have increased in preparation for the final step in the development of our species.

"Though mistaken for gods in many religions, they are not gods but our superiors in every way—spiritually, intellectually, technologically. Records of their presence can be found in the texts of vanished civilizations—in ancient Egypt, Babylon, Mesopotamia, Greece and Sumer. The knowledge of their presence, their goals, their many accomplishments, was preserved by certain secret societies throughout humankind's history.

"We are the latest in a long line of societies entrusted with the knowledge of their intentions and objectives. Therefore, we call ourselves the Trust.

"I see confusion in your eyes, Kane. Who are 'they' the lord baron refers to in such tones of awe and reverence? you wonder.

"To be completely honest, we do not know for certain where they come from or when they first came among us. This event is lost in the mists of antiquity. We call them the Archons, and since they do not object to such an appellation, we continue to use that term. It is appropriate in many ways. In ancient texts, Archons were identified with the Supreme Being and angels and the law of Abraham. We do not know their origins, and in predark days, there was considerable debate whether the Archons were extra-terrestrial, interdimensional or pan-terrestrial.

"Don't look so startled, Kane. Yes, a few predark peoples knew of the Archons. Secret covenants were struck with them by many governments and military bodies.

"Many predarkers saw their advance guard in the skies, flashing through the ether in their traditional disk-shaped vessels. They were called many things—Chariots of the Gods, flying saucers or Unidentified Flying Objects. A minority of our ancestors knew they were the vehicles of the Archons, and knew them as friends. They have constantly aided us in our process of spiritual and scientific development.

"However, when humankind achieved the means to destroy itself, the Archons offered not only a way of preventing the destruction, but also a path to establish an era of enlightenment upon the earth.

"As was their custom, their directive, the Archons contacted a chosen few, endeavoring to pass on their knowledge to save us from ourselves. This is part and parcel of the Archon Directorate—after a period of turmoil, to assist a civilization to recover, then withdraw to see what humanity would do with its newly acquired knowledge.

"The last great period of turmoil before the nukecaust was World War II. The Directorate's primary thrust was to protect the planet from the new threat of nuclear annihilation. Working through their government and scientific intermediaries, the Archons provided the basic data and technology for the undertaking known as the Totality Concept.

"Ah, I see by your reaction, Kane, that the term strikes a responsive chord. A faint chord, I hope, else all the effort of the Unity through Action program to limit the knowledge of it was in vain.

"Simply put, the Totality Concept and the development of its many interconnected and related researches was the most ambitious and secret scientific project in recorded history. The Archons provided the crucial technology to translate and meld quantum and hyperdimensional physics with relativistic physics.

"The aim of the Archon Directorate and their involvement in the Totality Concept was to make nuclear war obsolete. Indeed, aspects of the many subdivisions—Project Cerberus, Operation Chronos, to name only two—should have rendered the threat of atomic warheads as impotent as stone knives and clubs.

"In a sense, the Totality Concept was a stunning success. The Archon Directorate had given humanity the step up it needed to transcend all its petty squabbles and political differences. Unfortunately, in another sense, its failure to do so was just as stunning.

"Our benefactors, the entities who had nurtured us since we first discovered fire, had continually underestimated our instinctive need to wage war on our brother. None of the achievements of the Totality Concept, none of the hopes of the Archons themselves, were of any use whatsoever on that black, black day in January, 2001.

"Humanity spit upon the great gift the Archons had bestowed. We tried to burn it up with the rest of the world. We did not want to heed their wisdom—we wanted to destroy it. And so we turned our faces away from the glory they offered and wallowed in our self-made mire of violence, bloodshed and endless war.

"Although they had every right to do so, the Archons did not abandon humanity. Their Directorate remained intact. They observed and watched as our planet became a wasteland, then helped as we tried to struggle back to our feet and rebuild. The Archons opened communications with the most-powerful baronies and convinced them to unite and impose a new world order on the rampant chaos. With their help, their counsel, those nine barons ensured the old predark days would not return.

"The Archons provided them with the location of government Stockpiles, of the redoubts that once housed the many subdivisions of the Totality Concept. They taught

CASINO JUBILEE
"Scratch 'n Match" Game

**CHECK CLAIM CHART BELOW
FOR YOUR FREE GIFTS!**

YES! I have placed my label from the front cover in the space provided above and scratched off the silver box. Please send me all the gifts for which I qualify. I understand that I am under no obligation to purchase any books, as explained on the back and on the opposite page.

164 CIM A7YW (U-M-B-05/97)

Name: _____

Address: _____ Apt.: _____

City: _____ State: _____ Zip: _____

DETACH AND MAIL CARD TODAY ▶

If offer card is missing, write to: The Gold Eagle Reader Service, 3010 Walden Ave., P.O. Box 1867, Buffalo NY 14240-1867

BUSINESS REPLY MAIL

FIRST-CLASS MAIL   PERMIT NO. 717   BUFFALO, NY

POSTAGE WILL BE PAID BY ADDRESSEE

GOLD EAGLE READER SERVICE
3010 WALDEN AVE
PO BOX 1867
BUFFALO NY 14240-9952

NO POSTAGE
NECESSARY
IF MAILED
IN THE
UNITED STATES

them how to operate and maintain the technology found within, they put the Barons in touch with the few surviving military and scientific installations that had weathered the nuking and the skydark. In short, if not for the Archon Directorate, there would have never been a Program of Unification.

"They forgave us, you see, assuming some of the responsibility for the failure of the Totality Concept. They had been unable to save us from ourselves. Therefore, they judged it best that succeeding generations never knew of their presence or the role they played in the development of the Totality Concept. One of the aims of the Program of Unification was to hide that knowledge or make sure that the few who possessed it would translate the traces of the Archons and the Totality Concept into terms relevant to their own limited experience.

"The goals the Directorate had set for us were delayed by over a century, until humanity had regained some of its strength and creativity. At long last, the time is almost ripe for those goals to be achieved, but as with all ripening things, the process may not be hurried without risk of damage.

"The Archons have offered humankind another chance to evolve from our irresponsible, animal way, and that is a chance we must not, cannot, ignore.

"So, Kane, despite your impressive record, there is only one service you can bring to us, to the Trust, one duty you owe humanity. You must join us so we may fulfill the Archon Directorate's hopes and dreams, and finally rise above the radioactive wasteland we ourselves created.

"Kane, as your father before you, you are now offered the opportunity to serve a greater cause. We must have your decision. Now."

Chapter 18

"My father?" Kane's voice was barely above a shocked whisper.

A hand gave his shoulder a reassuring squeeze, and Salvo's warm, comforting voice said, "Yes, Kane. Your father. And my father, too. As serving as Magistrates is part of both our families' traditions, so is service to the Archon Directorate."

Kane fought down the urge to pinch himself, to reassure himself that this was all real. His legs trembled. It was as if he'd been living inside a giant soap bubble that was smooth and simple and symmetrical, and suddenly the bubble burst. Everything was different. He struggled to grasp the vast implications of the baron's words. His reeling mind formed a mental image of Earth as a tiny speck whirling through an inconceivably vast universe.

"The Archons," he managed to stammer. "What are they? Are they human?"

"The Archons are a race unto themselves," Baron Cobalt declared. "That is all you need to know. You have heard the truth. What is your decision?"

"Where is my father?" He stared directly at the figure of the baron, whose lean body shifted, nearly swallowed by the shadows on the left side of the archway.

"He is still performing the work of the Trust. It is his wish that you be inducted into the society to which he has devoted his life."

"I recommended you, as well," said Salvo from behind him. "I have been charged with a great responsibility, and your help will be immeasurable in discharging it."

Kane shook his head. "I don't quite...are we talking about *aliens?*"

A deep voice echoed from behind him. After a moment, Kane recognized it as that of Abrams, the Mag administrator. "As far as we know, they've been here as long as we have. They are incredibly ancient, and there is no actual historical record of when they first began interacting with humanity."

"Therefore," said another, unfamiliar voice, "they are not, technically speaking, aliens. Just different from us."

"What do they look like?"

"No one here has ever seen an Archon," said the baron. A note of impatience was evident in his musical voice. "Except myself and my fellow barons. But their existence is not illusory."

Kane felt transparent. He knew he was stalling, as did the baron. He also knew if he refused the offer, he would not leave the room—wherever it was—alive. He couldn't help but speculate if the prime purpose of the divisions was to select candidates for the Trust and to initiate them into the deepest mystery of the human race.

Or it could all be bullshit.

He asked, "If the work of the Trust is so important to our future, why is it conducted in secret?"

A quavery, reedy voice responded from the gloom. "The question is as sophomoric as the answer is obvious. Our people do not have the ability to properly evaluate such a revelation. Their reactions would range from disbelief to fear and then to anger. And bloodshed."

Kane nodded in understanding. Inwardly he reflected that the ville-bred had been taught from birth that if they made themselves helpless, believed themselves to be miserable sinners, then the barons would shower them with rewards. Of course the people didn't have the ability to evaluate anything outside of their limited fields of experience. The barons and the laws they enforced saw to that.

Baron Cobalt spoke again, but this time his musical voice

was sibilant, like the hissing of a serpent. "You possess an admirable facility for seeking out answers, Kane. A facility shared by your father. However, there is a time for curiosity and a time for decisions. If you choose correctly, all your questions will be answered—in time."

Kane ducked his head and said with humble reverence, "I choose to accept this honor, my Lord Baron. It is the duty of my family and I vow to continue to faithfully discharge that duty."

His words sounded false to him, almost a parody of the oath he swore when he'd received his duty badge. It was obviously the answer Baron Cobalt wanted, however, because he uttered a short, tinkling laugh.

"Well said, Kane. And well chosen. Salvo is your guide and sponsor. Heed him and help him. He will administer the pledge of eternal fealty."

The golden light flickered, dimmed, shadows suffused the arch and Baron Cobalt stepped back inside them.

"Turn, Kane," commanded Salvo.

Kane did so, finding himself facing men standing in a semicircle around him. He sucked in a sharp breath of recognition. This was no fussy little men's lodge. Represented here were the top administrators of the ville, plus the pinnacle-level inner-staff members. Though he didn't know them all by name, he recognized a couple, including the doddering old man Salvo had addressed as Lakesh on B Level.

He quickly took stock of his surroundings. The room was as large as a courtyard, lit by clusters of tall scented candles in each of the four corners, but the ceiling was so high that no light reached there.

Salvo stepped forward, placed his right hand on Kane's breast, over his heart, and after a moment, Kane followed suit.

In a deep, stentorian tone, Salvo said, "You are about to take the oath of the Trust. You are expected to obey its conditions. There are sound reasons behind the oath, and it is easy to see why it is necessary, but not so easy to see how you can live up to it. But live up to it you must, and that means you must make difficult choices. All former loyalties are superseded, swept aside by the oath. Do you understand?''

Kane said, ''I understand.''

''Repeat after me.'' In ringing tones, Salvo declaimed, '''Resolve is our armor, will is our weapon, faith is our mission. Personal ambition is our scourge.'''

Salvo nodded at him, and Kane repeated the words, adding a fanatic's fevered flair.

'''We solemnly vow that we will face death rather than disclose the secrets we learn here. We sanctify ourselves in the service of humanity. We accept our responsibilities in the world as ministers of the Archon Directorate. We promise to discharge our duties as befits servants of the future and to hold our knowledge sacred and inviolate.'''

There was more. Kane intoned the words, imitating Salvo's cadence and delivery of them. Once the oath was completed, Salvo moved aside and Abrams took his place, intoning the same vow for Kane to repeat back.

Each member of the Trust administered the pledge, and Kane parroted it back to every one of them. It took a dismally long time. When the ceremonial give-and-take was over, Kane had memorized every word, every nuance of the vow. He was tired and thirsty, and it wasn't until the last man stepped away from him that Kane realized what an emotional ordeal he had undergone. He felt wrung out, enervated, numb.

And that, whispered a mocking voice in his head, was the entire point.

The Trust shifted away, a few of them smiling at him. Abrams gave him a direct, iron-grim stare, nodded brusquely and stalked out of the room.

Salvo draped an arm over his shoulders. ''Guess you're feeling pretty limp by now.''

Kane acknowledged the comment with a self-conscious chuckle.

Salvo guided Kane out of the vast room, beneath a wide, low arch. Another room lay beyond, and another, all feebly lit by an unseen light source.

"Go home and get some rest, Kane. Business as usual during your shift, for appearance' sake."

Kane cleared his throat. "Does that business as usual include doing something about Guana Teague?"

As they approached a set of tall, ornately carved double doors, Salvo stopped abruptly. He turned to face Kane. "Is Teague still important to you?"

Kane presented the impression of seriously considering the query. "No," he admitted. "Not now."

"Good," replied Salvo. "What about the Baptiste woman?"

"That depends. Did her arrest have anything to do with the computer disk I found in Reeth's slaghole?"

Earnestly Salvo answered, "Unfortunately yes. The Dulce operation is our mission. Due to you, she found out too much."

"Is she a Preservationist?"

"She is. We have the proof. She used you, Kane."

"What's her relationship with this warlord's army?"

Salvo waved a dismissive hand through the air. "That, admittedly, is a stretch. Frankly the rumors we've received from the field about the warlord are third-hand. The last bit of Intel indicated they were filtering in from overseas, Asia most likely. If that's the case, there is nothing to concern us. But she's a Preservationist nevertheless."

"And Reeth—what connection did he have to the Dulce mission?"

Salvo's response was so smooth and practiced, Kane knew immediately he was lying. "Contract labor. We of the Trust must occasionally use men, and men make mistakes. Reeth made a very big one, a fatal one. He had no idea how crucial the operation is, so he got cute, he got greedy."

"And he learned too much and he got dead."

"Exactly. Just like Brigid Baptiste."

Kane sighed. "And Grant? He was with me in the slag-hole. Did he learn too much?"

"Not unless you got very careless."

"I didn't."

"Good. Then Grant is safe, though it's probably best to expedite his administrative transfer and get him out of the field."

"I agree," said Kane. "He knows me too well."

Salvo smiled broadly. "True. Remember what I said about old loyalties. Now, let's get you home so you can rest and come to terms with the new burdens you have accepted to carry."

"It's a heavy load," replied Kane, matching Salvo's smile. "But I look forward to the challenge. Sir."

BRIGID WAS ESCORTED to C Level, down a series of twisting corridors and then into a large, featureless room. Several metal doors lined the walls on both sides. There, she was stripped of her bodysuit and underclothes and searched. She detached her awareness and endured the humiliation of rough hands pawing her, sliding down her body, cupping her breasts and probing every nook, cranny and orifice.

The cell into which they pushed her measured hardly six paces one way by five the other. There was not a stick of furniture in it to relieve the monotony of the smooth white rockcrete. A dim, wire-encased overhead light cast a pallid illumination.

As soon as the door banged shut behind her, Brigid's submissive attitude vanished. She darted first to one wall and then to another, laying her hands against the cool walls. By touch, she located the miniature spy-eye lens hidden in a mortared seam, complete with a microscopic sound pickup.

She sat cross-legged on the floor, and the rockcrete beneath slowly warmed from her body heat. She regulated her breathing and closed her eyes, as if she were producing eidetic images. Though it required a great deal of mental effort, she refused to think about Kane. She lost herself in the recesses of her mind, studying, examining and weighing everything she had learned in the Dulce file.

Several hours must have passed when she heard the harsh click-clack of the locking mechanism on the door. She repressed a smile. The Mags watching her at the other end of the visual-audio hookup must have grown concerned over her immobility.

The door opened, and Salvo stepped through and shut it behind him. He looked down at her. "We cannot be heard or observed now, so you can drop your act."

Sighing in relief, Brigid stood up, stretching her arms and rubbing her legs to restore circulation. She didn't attempt to conceal her nudity. There seemed little point in it.

Salvo watched her in admiration. "How could you sit like that for so long?"

"Elementary yoga. How long was it?"

"Six hours, I'm told. It's daybreak. Probably the last time the sun will ever rise on you."

"Since I can't see it, it hardly matters, does it?"

Salvo smiled thinly. "You lead rather a double life, don't you? A key-tapping archivist by day, an insurgent by night. Who are the Preservationists?"

Brigid cocked her head at a quizzical angle. "The who?"

Salvo chuckled. "We've known about them for quite some time. Decades. You do know you're officially charged with sedition?"

Brigid's bare shoulders moved in a shrug. "I have my defense ready."

"It will avail you nothing. When treason is the charge, the baron himself acts as the judge and jury, and the trials are conducted in secret."

"And the verdict is already in," she said dryly.

"Of course. However, you may receive a modicum of

leniency if you tell me what you know about the Preservationists."

"I know nothing. I'm a historian."

Salvo's sallow face twisted in a smirk. "And therefore the perfect tool."

"You seem to know more about them than I do."

He laughed sharply. "The Preservationists represent an underground-resistance movement. They follow an idealistic principle of someday freeing humanity from the heel of the barons by forcing the 'truth' down their throats."

He paused to shake his head. "If it were not for the laws of the barons, as manifested in the villes, we would still be barbarians, trying to reconstruct all the horrors of the predark that led to the nukecaust."

"Or," said Brigid, "we would have learned our lesson and built toward a utopia."

"Oh, *please,*" said Salvo in angry exasperation. "You should know better. History has shown that mankind is incapable of that. Humans are intrinsically destructive, unable to control violent impulses or the desire to choose evil over good."

"Humans are not good," Brigid replied calmly. "Nor are they evil."

"But you believe the barons and the villes are."

She shook her head. "Not really. Classifying behaviors or laws as simply good and evil does not even qualify as empty semantics. From your viewpoint, the set of values you espouse is not only necessary but benevolent."

Salvo raised an eyebrow. "You sound like you agree with me."

"No," she answered, "I don't."

"Why?"

"There is no balance, no equilibrium in this society. Historically, civilizations rose, attained high states of technological advancement, then fell into ruin. Then, after a period of recovery, civilizations advanced again. A continuous, natural cycle. Something opposed this cycle, and civilization was pushed back on all fronts. It's an unnatural opposition, a subtle process of preventing the restoration of balance."

Salvo looked intrigued. "Go on," he urged.

"It's been close to two hundred years since the holocaust. With the sheer volume of prenuke tech that survived in this country alone, the rebuilding process should have been relatively swift."

"You're not factoring in all the other variables of environmental and geologic changes."

"Even factoring in all the negatives—rad hot spots, hellzones, high infant-mortality rates—I calculated the world should have reached a level comparable to the 1920s or 1930s at least two generations ago."

"Your point being...?"

Brigid lifted her hands, palm upward. "There can be only one explanation. Someone or something is deliberately preventing our development. Because what we have in the villes is minimal—" she paused "—and it's as though it's not even ours but...something on loan."

Salvo gave her a sharp look. "You seem to have devoted a great deal of thought to this."

Brigid smiled. "Only for the last six hours."

Salvo nodded in understanding. "Ah. How much did you learn from the Dulce file?"

"Not nearly enough. What is the Archon Directive?"

"It's the Directorate now, and has been for a very long time. One hundred and ninety-eight years, to be precise.

"Since January 21, 2001?"

Salvo laughed in genuine enjoyment. "No wonder Kane had the hots for you. Beautiful and very bright. Unfortunately not beautiful enough and *too* goddamn bright."

She coughed, trying to cover the sudden quaver in her voice. "Was Kane involved in my arrest?"

"Knowingly, you mean?"

"Yes."

"Would it make the prospect of your execution easier to endure if you knew Kane had been used?"

"It would."

"Then you may go to your death never knowing if he betrayed you or not. Part of the penalty phase of your sentence."

Wryly Brigid replied, "The sentence is death. Isn't that penalty enough?"

"No," replied Salvo tersely. "I'll offer you a bargain, though. Tell me who your Preservationist cohorts are, and I'll tell you the truth about Kane."

"I'll ask him myself."

"You'll never see him again. He has a new set of priorities now, and you don't even qualify as a footnote."

"You really hate him, don't you?"

Salvo's eyes widened in momentary surprise. "What makes you think that?"

"Body language. The timbre of your voice changes, too, every time you say his name."

For a long moment, Salvo glared darkly at her, his lips working as if he were preparing to spit at her. Then he threw back his head and laughed. "By God, you *are* the prettiest and most perceptive insurgent I've ever arrested. You're right, Baptiste. I hate him."

"Tell me why. I promise it won't make my execution easier to face."

Salvo grinned, folding his arms over his chest and leaning one shoulder against the door. "A lot of reasons, some of which are purely instinctive, I guess. Maybe he's my yin to his yang, or vice versa. A more tangible reason is that my father and his father were enemies."

"Is nursing old grudges a family tradition?"

Gravely, Salvo answered, "If you are a Magistrate, family tradition and family honor is all-important. Our entire discipline is based on it."

"Kane doesn't seem to like you very much, but he

doesn't appear to be carrying an enmity from the last generation."

"That's because he isn't aware of it. I saw to that."

Brigid shook her head in exasperation. "I don't understand. His father did something to your father, and you don't want him to know, yet you still hate him for it?"

"I didn't say it was completely rational."

"The only resemblance to rationality is that you're not babbling incoherently."

"Cute. Well, if I am irrational, I am also a man of pride, and I must exact what all men of pride must exact in order to live with themselves."

"Like what?"

"Vindication. Revenge for the wrongs compounded upon my family name, my family honor." Salvo's face twisted into a contemptuous smile. "But none of this has any bearing on you and your situation, does it?"

"It might make for interesting testimony at my trial."

Salvo chuckled, a sound like the distant rustling of leathery wings. "Your testimony won't be worth shit, Baptiste. That's the beauty of the baron's court."

He turned and rapped sharply on the door with a fist. "I don't mind admitting I'm reinterpreting my standing orders a trifle. I was instructed to obtain as much possible information from you before your execution, but I'd rather not waste my time on torture. You're only a pawn. Whatever you know will die with you."

The door opened. "Your trial is scheduled for 0800. Sentence will be carried out at 0830." Salvo stepped out, and the door banged shut behind him with a ringing finality.

Brigid closed her eyes, struggling to contain the panic swelling within her. She knew the spy-eye was active again, and she refused to allow the terror to consume her, and so provide entertainment for the Mag monitors.

Regulating her breathing, Brigid managed to reduce the trembling of her hands, then she lowered herself to the floor and assumed the cross-legged lotus position. She smiled at the spy-eye lens and said, "Fuck you. Go watch the Mag shower room for a while."

Chapter 19

If he hadn't received the call from Salvo, Grant wouldn't have caught the communication from Kane.

After giving his statement to Pollard, Grant had been directed to go home and not contact his friend until the matter had been thoroughly looked into. Since Salvo was strangely unavailable, he had figured that a deeper investigation of the incident would have to wait until the following day.

Grant hated waiting. Under other circumstances, a Pit sweep would have been under way, with Kane taking the point as always. The murder of a Mag and the attempted murder of another with an autoblaster were grounds for a full-scale assault on the slaggers' dens of Tartarus, turning over every rock in search of Teague, Uno and the albino girl. Last year's failed ambush by poorly armed jolt-walkers had resulted in a month-long Pit lockdown.

It was very odd, but unlike Kane, Grant wasn't inclined to ask questions. Instead, he stood gazing out the window into the deep indigo sky, looking for a sign that a new day was dawning.

A Magistrate is virtuous in the performance of his duty. The deeply ingrained phrase drifted through his mind. The duties and obligations that came with his badge and blaster had been drilled into him these past twenty-plus years. The oath was a part of his every action and reaction—at once a justification and a reason to live, a psychological shield and a sword for the work he performed.

Living only for duty and service was all a matter of how you adjusted to it, Grant thought fleetingly. He had assumed that both he and Kane had adjusted perfectly, but now Kane was displaying signs of strain, of chafing under the strictures. He asked questions, which in itself was irritating enough, but his questions were good ones, which was downright unfortunate.

It was awkward business, being friends with a fellow Mag. Sometimes even Grant was surprised that two such contrasting personalities worked so well as a team. Teamwork was encouraged, but friendship was frowned upon.

Now Grant knew why. It was a hard thing to endure not to be on hand to help Kane deal with whatever he was battling. He tried to tell himself that Kane had brought it all upon himself—from not serving the termination warrant on Reeth, to lifting the comp disk and conducting his own independent investigation, then calling for backup only after Boon had been chilled.

Still, during the span of the twelve years they had partnered together, he had learned to rely on Kane's instincts. As a pointman, his senses were uncannily acute when something nasty was underfoot or lurking just around a corner. Try as he might to dismiss it, Grant was positive Kane's instincts were on the mark this time around, as well.

The warble from the trans-comm unit on his desk was so unexpected, he jumped and swore. A quick glance at his wrist chron told him dawn was only an hour or so away. Only Kane would be so defiant to contact him after he had been ordered not to do so—but then he wasn't stupid. Trans-comm frequencies were public, and he was absolutely sure Intel had a monitor on both his and Kane's units. He let it warble several seconds before he picked it up and opened the circuit.

"Grant?" Salvo's voice filtered from it.

"Yes, sir." Grant sat down at the desk, leaning back against his coat draped over the chair.

"Hope I didn't wake you. If I did, you can go back to sleep in a few minutes. I've gone over your statement. I regret to say I'm putting you on suspension until further notice.''

"Sir?" Grant felt tension coiling in his stomach like a length of slimy rope.

"Confine yourself to quarters. I'll be sending around a couple of men to pick up your equipment. I realize this is a shock to you, especially with your record, but Abrams insisted on it. Protocol and all that, you know.''

Fingers clenching tight around the box of pressed metal and molded plastic in his hand, Grant asked, "What about Kane?''

"He thinks you were the target," Salvo replied, a faint hint of suspicion in his voice. "Not Boon.''

"Yes, I know. I suspect it, too.''

"Then the primary question is why you? Can you offer any clues?''

Grant groped for a response, then said, "No, I can't. Perhaps Guana Teague can.''

"What does the Pit boss have against you personally?''

Grinding his teeth, Grant said, "I have no idea. Sir.''

"I have a few," said Salvo. "The blaster recovered at the scene was one of two that disappeared from the armory.''

"*What?*''

"Mags selling goods to Pit merchants isn't without precedent, you know.''

"Something like that hasn't happened in either of our lifetimes." Grant's voice rose. "Are you accusing—?''

"Not yet, I'm not. Tell me, were you getting impatient for your administrative transfer to come through? Did you decide to cut a little jack on the side?''

Grant said nothing. His hands trembled in fury. He felt as if he were trapped in a burning building with every exit door locked.

"You're not charged with anything," Salvo went on, "and you may never be. But you'll have to pull some pretty impressive moves to redeem yourself in my eyes.''

"Sir—''

"You have your orders. Out."

The circuit closed with an arrogant click. Grant looked at the trans-comm unit in his hand, then hurled it the length of the room. It struck against the far wall, denting the dura-plast.

He sat motionless at the desk, wrestling with his rage, staring out of the window without seeing anything. A pre-dark term floated through his mind, and though old, it was very appropriate—*scapegoated.*

He was being scapegoated over this, while Kane, for whatever reason, was being haloed. He tried to wrap his mind around the possibility that Kane had rolled over on him to save his own ass. He couldn't.

The concept of such a betrayal was too stunning, too nauseating, to dwell upon. The worst part was he couldn't even call Kane to ask him about it.

He was about to get up when he heard the tiny voice of Kane reaching him from what seemed a light-year away.

"Grant?"

Grant shook his head. Terrific. Now he was suffering auditory hallucinations because of his overwrought nerves.

"Grant? Grant!"

Grant stiffened. The faint whisper wasn't emanating from empty air or his brain. He turned and dragged his coat from the back of the chair. He drew out the pin mike from the lapel and brought the receiver button up to his ear.

"Damn it, Grant—"

"What the fuck are you doing?" he whispered fiercely into the mike.

"Don't worry. This is a closed frequency, remember, not like the trans-comms. Listen, I've got something to tell you—"

"I've got something to tell *you*. I just heard from Salvo. He suspended me."

"On what grounds?"

"On the grounds of your statement," Grant hissed furiously.

The receiver button accurately transmitted Kane's half sighed "Shit."

"Yeah, shit is right. He almost accused me of handing the blasters over to Teague. Said they were stolen from the armory."

Kane's response was terse, tense. "There's no way he could have known that unless he was the one who stole them."

"Why would he do that?"

"Listen to me. You've got to get out of there."

"You listen to *me*," Grant growled. "For some reason, Salvo wants my ass on a platter—"

"Shut up! Shut up and listen!" Kane's tone was tight with fear, with worry. "Is someone coming around to collect your equipment?"

"Yeah, that's standard after a suspension."

"Get out of there, Grant! I can't explain further, but I've learned some things."

"What kind of things?"

"The kind of things that are getting people I've been in contact with chilled. So stop asking me questions and go."

Grant scowled at the mike. "Go where?"

"Tartarus. Remember that route we found down into the Pits a few years ago?"

Ransacking his memory, Grant replied, "Yeah, but it's probably blocked off by now."

"It's your only chance to get out of the Enclaves undetected."

"Why would I want to do that?"

Kane's voice became more urgent, escalating in intensity. "Don't you get it? Salvo's sending a chill squad after you! You're on suspension, you're suspected of corruption, you decided to go out in a blaze of glory. That's how the report will read!"

After a stunned moment, Grant asked, "Have you found another bottle of wine or what? Why would he do that? And how would you know that?"

"You stubborn bastard! It's too complicated to explain.

I'm asking you, Grant. I'm *begging* you—trust my instincts again and get the hell out of there. Hit the Pits, grab Guana and squeeze him.''

"And then what am I supposed to do?"

Kane exhaled a long breath. Wearily he said, "I'm working on it. Now, will you *please* get your shit together and get?"

"All right!" Grant snapped. "I'm gettin'."

"Good. I don't want to risk calling you again. I'll meet you at Guana's place as soon as I can."

"You'd fucking well better," Grant snarled, but the circuit was closed.

Grant stared at the pin mike for a moment, then released it, allowing it to zip back to its place in the coat's lapel. Mentally he replayed the conversations of Salvo and Kane. Then he got up, strapped on his Sin Eater, shrugged into his coat and left his flat. His quarters were on the same level as Kane's, but located considerably farther down on the central promenade.

He walked quickly, in the opposite direction from the entrance gate. There was no doubt at all about the way to Tartarus Kane had mentioned. The only problem was how to reach it swiftly without attracting attention. There was nothing he could do to avoid the spy-eye fixtures on the ceiling except to brazen it out. If what Kane said possessed even a gram of truth, leaving his quarters against orders wouldn't be much of an infraction.

The double-facing row of flats ended after a hundred yards, right against a blank wall. Ferns and shrubbery were planted in a wide strip along the width of the wall to give it the illusion of a garden vista. Several years before, he and Kane had discovered that one section of the wall was a false facade, imitation rockcrete covering a service shaft. A maintenance tech on the premises explained that the opening extended down to a ventilation shaft, which then connected to the inner shell of the Administrative Monolith. For the hell of it, Grant and Kane had explored the shaft and discovered it reached far more than a ventilation shaft.

Grant pushed through the shrubbery, inspecting the rear wall. He found the panel easily enough, and the inch-thick, four-foot square of textured duraplast swung outward on hidden hinges. Staggered tie bars were just within reach. He put his feet on the first one, pulled the panel shut and fished his flashlight out of a pocket. He carefully climbed hand over hand, down to a square opening covered by a thick wire grille. That hadn't been there the first time. Placing the flashlight between his teeth, wrapping his left arm around a tie bar, Grant crooked his fingers into the grille and tugged experimentally, then with all his strength. The mesh ripped loose from the metal frame, and he yanked and folded it to one side, letting it dangle by an upper corner. It required a few painful contortions to step from the tie bars into the square ventilation shaft. It wasn't much wider than his shoulders, and he had to lie on his stomach and pull himself along the polished metal.

Fortunately it was easy going, and this particular shaft was only a score of yards long. It ended at a maintenance walkway inside the Administrative Monolith, somewhere between D and E Levels. He pushed open another grille, climbed out and walked along the narrow catwalk until he reached the upper landing of a corkscrew staircase.

As quickly and as quietly as he could manage, he walked down the steps, the beam of his flashlight lighting the way. Pipes, conduits and ventilation ducts ran up and down the shaft all around the staircase. He went down, down, clinging to the handrail. The monolith's levels could only be entered through the four Enclave complexes, and as far as anyone knew, the only way in or out of them was via the bank of public elevators. But his route led to one other exit, providing it hadn't been discovered and sealed.

When he heard the muffled throb of machinery, he knew he was nearing the end of the staircase. The thin beam of his flashlight made a splash of white on a steel-braced lead door. He experienced a momentary disorientation. The door led to the manufacturing facility on E Level, and that appeared to be the only exit.

Recalling the path he and Kane had followed that day, he turned right at the foot of the staircase. He shone his flashlight up and down along the far wall. A gap was visible between a retaining wall and the foundation. It was barely large enough to admit him, and then only if he turned sideways.

He crab-walked into the gap, the beam from his light cutting through a gray mist of dust stirred up by his shuffling feet. Jagged edges caught at his coat and his stomach. He didn't remember that happening the first time, and he realized, with a surge of annoyance, that he had probably become bulkier since then.

The narrow passage curved slightly, following the construction of the outer monolith wall. The ground beneath Grant's feet suddenly fell away, and if he hadn't been so tightly wedged, he would have fallen. His flashlight showed him earth-slanting downward beneath the foundations. Erosion had taken its toll in the years since he had last been here.

He continued inching along, bracing the toes of his boots against the opposing wall. He progressed only a few yards before chunks of rockcrete collapsed under the pressure of his feet.

Grant managed to keep hold of his flashlight when he dropped, thrashing, into darkness. He didn't fall far, nor was it as much a fall as a feet-first slide. Dust and grit rose in choking clouds as his body plowed a trench through the slope of loose, ancient dirt.

Skidding to a slow stop on the seat of his pants, he shone the flashlight beam around, grunting in relief. He had reached his destination sooner than expected and by another method, but he had reached it. Cobaltville had been built upon the foundations of Vistaville, which had been built upon the ruins of an old predark military storage depot. Beneath the Enclave towers lay a chain of fuel cisterns, probably abandoned before the nukecaust. At one time, the ground around the Enclaves had been honeycombed with reinforced-concrete storage tanks. Even now, nearly two hundred years after skydark, the faint, acrid odor of gasoline still clung to the cistern walls.

Grant waited until he got his bearings before moving again. He and Kane had entered the cistern area by another way, and he swept his surroundings with the flashlight until he found what he was looking for, only a few dozen yards away.

A series of staple-shaped ladder rungs was embedded in the curving wall of the cistern, leading up to an overhead metal hatch. The ceiling of the tunnel bore a spiderweb pattern of cracks through which dirt dribbled down. In another few years, the Administrative Monolith would experience serious foundation problems. The notion of the inestimable tons of rockcrete pressing down from above invoked a claustrophobic reaction, and Grant stood up, quickly walking down the center of the cistern.

At the elliptical end of the storage tank, Grant leaned against the wall, looking up at the hatch. It was still sealed by a thick disk of iron. Grant scaled the rungs and pushed up on the metal plate, hoping it hadn't been covered with stone or welded shut. He tried not to shove too hard, because he couldn't guess who or what might lie immediately beyond.

The cover didn't budge, so Grant pushed harder. He could only use one arm, having to keep the other hooked through a rung. Breathing heavily from the exertion, he shoved again, straining, and finally the metal disk shifted. Rust and dirt showered down from the rim. With a screech of iron against stone, he forced the hatch cover up several inches, held it there until he climbed another rung, then shouldered the heavy disk aside. Before he dragged himself up and out, he turned off the flashlight.

He found himself standing in the same alley he and Kane had climbed into years before. A draft carried the strong stench of rubbish and excrement. Looking up, he saw the sky was beginning to lighten with the approach of dawn.

"Tartarus at sunrise," he whispered. "Somebody ought to sell tickets."

Chapter 20

Grant kept to the side lanes, avoiding the main thoroughfare just in case Salvo had indeed ordered a Pit sweep. Even his ingenuity would fail if he were stopped and questioned by a Mag.

It was either too early or too late for most of the Pit dwellers to be up and about. Grant saw only one person, an ancient woman with skin blackened and seamed, eyes perpetually lowered so she wouldn't have to see the Enclaves or the Administrative Monolith. She was pawing through a heap of stinking, fly-infested vegetable matter outside a food shop. Her voice was cracked but passable as she sang a snatch of an old song:

"In a world of chaos, without plan,
came the mighty one-eyed man.
He'd been to places near and distant,
seen wonders thought nonexistent.
When Marie Mandeville spread her pain,
the one-eyed man turned it 'round again."

Grant repressed a smile of amusement at how some folkways survived, along with the need to create heroes. And Ryan Cawdor, the one-eyed man, apparently was one of those who endured—in a time when survival was a heroic act.

He walked along a street that was little more than an alley of abandoned tar-paper shacks and shanties. Though he knew where he was going, he had to approach it by an

unfamiliar route, and it cost him time. Dawn was breaking
up the dark sky with scraps of yellow and orange when he
sighted the corrugated metal warehouse.

It took him something over fifteen minutes to make a
slow, careful circuit of the warehouse and the squat, low-
roofed, windowless building attached to it. At the end of
that time, he had satisfied himself there were no trip wires
or vid cams or even a sentry. It was possible Teague had
pulled up stakes and either ducked into a bolt-hole or struck
out for the Outlands. Neither seemed likely, though it was
common knowledge there were secret ways into and out of
the villes, known to a select few Pit dwellers.

The only way into Teague's home was through the warehouse. Grant walked briskly to the side door. Lifting it
against its hinges by the shank of the handle, he turned the
handle slowly, producing a single, almost inaudible squeak
and faint metallic jingling. The door was held fast on the
other side by a chain. Alert for any sounds from within, he
leaned his entire weight against the door. The bracket holding the chain pulled out of the rotten frame. Wood creaked
and tore, but the sound wasn't loud, at least not loud
enough to wake anyone from slumber.

As he stepped warily into the warehouse, Grant's eyes
swiftly took in the interior. There were boxes and crates
stacked in helter-skelter fashion all over. The only attention
to any kind of precision was a sprawling, tall pyramid of
boxes, wooden pallets and square containers against the far
wall.

The flagstone floor shone with moisture, and the bare
ceiling rafters were festooned with cobwebs. The light il-
luminating the warehouse was daylight—pale, dirty daylight peeping in through a high, grilled window.

Grant sniffed the air experimentally and smelled nothing
but mold, mildew and urine. He waited for some sound,
but there was none. All of his training and hard experience
had instilled in him the ability to read the atmosphere of a

place. There was no mistaking the aura of slaghole that hovered over the warehouse.

He crept to the side of a large wooden packing crate. His eyes settled on a door on the far side of the place. Swiftly, soundlessly he moved through the jumbled maze of boxes. Then the door opened and somebody came out.

What saved Grant from immediate detection was that the man who emerged paused at the threshold to exchange a few words with someone behind him. Grant dropped to his knees behind a stack of cardboard cartons. He stared hard at the tall, spare figure in the doorway. Even in the uncertain light, he saw the resemblance to Dos, and he also saw the mini-Uzi dangling from a strap around his neck.

Uno closed the door behind him, glanced around for a moment, then walked purposefully across the warehouse, straight for Grant's position. Grant didn't want to draw the Sin Eater until the last possible second because the spring-powered cable made a distinctive click.

Uno came on until he was a bare ten feet away. Abruptly he turned aside. His back to Grant, he strode quickly to the pyramid of crates and boxes. Grant watched him carefully.

Uno spread his arms wide, fitting his hands around several containers at the base of the pyramid. He grunted with exertion, and the boxes of the lower tier all lifted away in one piece, attached to one another by glue or some other adhesive.

With the ease of familiarity with the procedure, Uno removed one entire side of the pyramid. Grant crept forward a few feet for a closer look. Inside the shell of containers was a low-slung, treaded vehicle. It bore a likeness to the Sandcats, rough-terrain wags stored in the armory, but though its contours were similar, it looked far older. The front, sides and rear were sheathed by rust-stained armor plates. The windshield glass was streaked with dust and cracked in places.

Grant wasn't terribly surprised. Some outlanders, particularly the roamers, traveled around in retooled predark vehicles. He had seen some of the junkers, rattletrap trucks, tractors and jeeps.

As Pit boss, Guana Teague could have smuggled the Sandcat into the ville in pieces and assembled it here, for the eventuality he ever needed to beat a hasty exit. Teague evidently felt the need now.

Uno opened the driver's door, and the poorly oiled hinges screeched. He leaned inside, fiddling with the instrument panel. Behind him, Grant left the shadows in long strides, moving silently on the balls of his feet. He snatched the leather strap of the autoblaster around the strong-arm's neck and yanked.

Grabbing at empty air, Uno fell backward, right onto Grant's out-thrust knee. He clawed first for the Uzi, but it was beyond his reach, then he clawed at the strap cinched tight around his throat. The only sound he uttered was a gasping grunt.

Grant kept the pressure on Uno's carotid artery until the man's struggles weakened and finally ceased. He eased him down to the damp floor and dragged him to the rear of the pyramid. He quickly detached the strap from the blaster, and by looping and knotting it expertly, he hog-tied the man in a matter of seconds.

Patting him down quickly, he found no other weapons. Uno moaned faintly. Cutting off a man's oxygen and the flow of blood to the brain was usually good for five minutes of unconsciousness. Tucking the mini-Uzi into a coat pocket, Grant returned to the door.

Pressing his ear to the wood, he heard voices. The words were unintelligible, but he picked out a man's grumbling tones and a young woman's softer but petulant-sounding response. The doorknob rattled, turned from the inside, and he had to act now.

He tensed his wrist tendons and the Sin Eater slid into his hand. Setting himself, he raised his right leg and kicked the door. It flew open, the edge clipping Guana Teague and slapping him sideways. He slammed into the wall, bounced off and fell heavily. The entire warehouse seemed to shake with the impact of three-hundred-plus pounds hitting the floor.

Leaping through the doorway, Grant roared, "Freeze!"

The bore of the Sin Eater covered both people in the bare-walled room. Teague remained on the floor, goggle-eyed and gape mouthed with shock. He was uglier and fatter than Grant remembered. He wore a sleeveless shirt that exposed his greenish, flabby arms.

The girl was the same albino whom they had pursued into the ambush. Grant looked hard at her, from her short, untidy white hair bound by a colorful scarf, her piquant face and shapely arrangement of curves beneath a tight T-shirt and very short, very red shorts. A pair of bulging duffel bags lay on the floor, one near where the Pit boss had fallen.

"Taking a trip?" Grant demanded. "Let's see your travel permit."

A torrent of slack-mouthed words spilled from Teague's lips. Grant couldn't understand much of what he said, except for repeated pleas for a Magistrate's mercy.

"Shut up," Grant snarled. He strode over to Teague, who cringed away, scooting on the seat of his baggy pants until his back was pressed against the whitewashed wall. Grant went to one knee beside him and planted the bore of the weapon against his forehead.

"I'm going to ask you a few questions," said Grant quietly. "If you don't answer them, if I think you're lying or if I simply don't like your attitude, I'll blow your head off. You understand?"

Squeezing his eyes shut, Teague nodded several times. "Yes. Yes."

"You tried to have me chilled."

The Pit boss swallowed with difficulty. His voice was a harsh rasp. "Yes."

"Someone hired you."

He hesitated, and Grant dug the bore into his forehead. "No. Yes. I mean—oh, hell, I don't know!"

The girl raised her hand, as if she were in a classroom. "I know, I know!"

Grant glared at her. "What's your name?"

"Domi."

"You're Guana's piece?"

Her face contorted in a mask of scorn and intense loathing. "He forced me. Held me prisoner."

"Right," said Grant dryly. "All right, Domi, what do you know?"

"I show you." She turned and moved toward the wall behind her.

"Freeze, goddamn it!"

Domi froze in midstep. "Have to show."

"Domi," groaned Teague. "Don't."

"Show what?" Grant asked.

The girl met his level stare unblinkingly. "A comm. Hidden in wall."

"Show me, then," Grant replied. "Do it slow, hear me?"

Domi nodded, stepped carefully to the wall, ran her hands over the surface and swung open a square panel. Slowly she picked up an object from the recess and turned, holding it in both hands.

"A trans-comm," said Grant. "Standard Mag issue. Where'd you get it, Guana?"

"From a Mag."

Grant smacked the side of his head with the barrel of the Sin Eater, not hard enough to cause serious injury, but hard enough to cause serious pain. "The truth, you sack of blistered mutie fat!"

Guana clapped a hand to his head. Tears welled in his tiny, flesh-choked eyes. "I swear! A Mag gave it to me!"

"Who?"

"I don't know. I swear! He was in armor. He just handed it to me."

"When?"

"Years ago. I swear! It's an arrangement kind of thing. Every once in a while, I'll get a call on it, and I'm told to arrange things."

"And somebody called you on a Mag trans-comm and told you to arrange my murder?" Grant snarled out the question.

"I swear! Hell, I'm sorry, Grant. I got nothin' against you. It wasn't personal."

"I'm relieved to hear that," replied Grant. "I've got nothing against you, either, Guana—no more than I have against any other swill bucket that decided to get up and walk around." He whacked him again with the blaster, this time on the other side of his head. "Why chill me?"

Voice nasal and snuffling, Guana Teague choked out, "I don't know. I swear! He told me to chill you and the other Mag—"

"Kane?"

"No, not Kane. This whole thing was about Kane. The cherry Mag, Boon, if he got in the way. You were supposed to be blown away in front of Kane, really messy. Traumatic, like? You know?"

"No, I don't. Where'd you get the blasters?"

"Found 'em here one night. About a year ago. I swear."

Grant said, "Knock off the swearing. Have you been contacted since the hit went sour?"

Teague nodded miserably, his triple jowls creasing and uncreasing, like an accordion made of suet. "Yeah, about two hours ago, on the trans-comm. Told me I fucked up royal, but he could fix it, do some damage control. Said for me to sit tight, keep low, not to try and split the ville. Said I was still of use to him."

Eyeing the duffel bags, Grant commented, "You didn't believe him, I guess."

Wagging his head, brushing tears from his cheeks, Teague mumbled, "Would you, in my shoes? I admit it— I was runnin' to the Outlands."

"If a Mag is behind this, they'll just come after you.
With a squadron of Deathbirds—and blow your two-ton ass
to the coast."

Gesturing to Domi, Teague said, "She claims to know a
way overland into the Mesa Verde hellzone. Figured I
could lose any trackers there, then move on. Maybe to one
of the Western Islands, or even the Darks, where there ain't
no barons and no Mags."

Glancing down at his loose pants, Teague moaned at the
sight of the dark stain spread around the crotch. "Oh,
Christ. See what you made me do?"

"You'll be goddamn lucky if that's all the bodily fluids
you lose today. On your feet."

The Pit boss slowly lumbered to his feet. He cast a slit-
eyed stare at Domi, hissing, "You bleached-out little gaudy
slut."

There was a scuffling and the sound of rushing feet behind Grant. He whirled as Uno, the leather strap dangling
from one wrist, bore down on him, a length of nail-studded
wood in his hands. His face was a bare-toothed snarl of
hurt pride and unthinking, murderous fury.

Grant had to give him credit; not only had he come to
sooner than expected, but he'd managed to wriggle free of
his bonds in record time. Not that it made any difference.
He pointed the Sin Eater and let loose with a 3-round burst.
The staccato hammering of the autoblaster filled the warehouse as three holes were stitched across Uno's shirtfront.
The multiple impacts slammed him back and down in a
twisted tangle, blood flying in liquid arcs from his chest.

A tremendous weight slammed into Grant's back with
bone-jarring force, cannonading him out the door. His feet
struck the newly made corpse, and he fell on his face, sliding across the flagstone floor.

Gasping, he levered himself onto his back an instant before Guana Teague hurled his body atop his. The wind was
literally crushed from his lungs, exploding out of his mouth.
He gasped for air as Teague's hand closed tightly over his

right wrist, immobilizing it and keeping the Sin Eater aimed at the ceiling.

The Pit boss not only outweighed him by a minimum of a hundred pounds, but he was far stronger than he looked. He combined over three hundred pounds, strength and years of experience as a Pit fighter with an outpouring of adrenaline-driven energy generated by sheer terror. He tried to gouge Grant's eyes, and the squeezing pressure of his knees was like an iron band tightening around his rib cage.

With his free hand, Grant clawed for his attacker's face, but the fat man twisted aside and locked the fingers of his left hand around the Magistrate's throat, the thumb pressing cruelly into his windpipe.

"Domi!" shrieked Teague. *"Domi!"*

Over the man's shoulder, Grant saw the girl appear, a very long serrated knife gripped in both of her hands. She held it over her head. Her ruby eyes were wild and bright with kill-light.

Grant heaved and bucked, struggling to throw Teague's mammoth bulk aside, if only for a second. But it was like trying to wrestle a mountain. Desperately he flailed with his legs, hoping to kick Domi or her knife before she plunged it into him.

Suddenly, Guana Teague stiffened, head snapping up and back. His eyes widened and bulged, filled with wonder and pain. A liquid gurgling bubbled past his lips, followed immediately by a tendril of bright crimson.

Grant saw Domi withdraw the long blade from Teague's back. Half of its length glistened with blood. With his head up and back, his squat throat presented a vulnerable target. The knife blade slashed once, very expertly, from behind. The flesh beneath his triple chins opened up in a red-rimmed caricature of a smile. Bright arterial blood cascaded from the wound, drenching Grant as though he were standing beneath a waterfall.

Guana Teague shuddered and collapsed, his spasming bulk falling forward and all but smothering him. Grant cursed in disgust, tearing his wrist free of slack fingers. He heaved and elbowed and thrashed to roll the grotesque corpse off himself.

Domi kicked the mound of flesh again and again, grinning in triumph, tears shining on her cheeks. "Got this lizard-dick," she chanted. "He is big-time chilled!"

Swiping at the blood on his face with sleeve, Grant climbed unsteadily to his feet. "Enough, Domi. You chilled him. Big-time."

She stopped kicking, and let the carmined blade dangle from her small fist. When Teague's legs trembled briefly in a postmortem spasm, she whipped up the knife. "I do it again," she cried.

Then she threw herself against Grant, pressing her face to his chest, heedless of the blood. Her slim frame quivered. Automatically he held the girl, cradling her bandaged head. He felt very weary.

The warehouse now reeked with the coppery stench of fresh blood, cordite and body wastes. It looked and smelled like a slaughterhouse. The smells and sights were familiar, but this time something deep inside of him recoiled in utter revulsion.

"I suppose you expect me to thank you," he muttered.

"Yes," she said in a quavery whisper.

"I guess there's a first for everything, outlander girl. I thank you."

With a faraway shock, he realized that he didn't know what to do next, and that was quite a novelty for him. When he heard the faint voice from the transceiver on his lapel, he felt almost absurdly grateful. Kane would no doubt have a list of suggestions, even if most of them made no damn sense. Even refuting them would be a relief at this point.

Domi lifted her head, blinking in puzzlement at the transceiver button. Her face had been pressed against it, muffling the sound. Grant gently pushed her away and drew the pin mike up to his lips. "I'm here."

"Good," said the cold voice. "Stay there until we come for you." And Salvo cut off the transmission.

Chapter 21

Brigid paced her cell, her mind busy battling with her emotions. She knew it was nearing 0800, and she could no longer submit to the relaxation techniques. There was nothing she could do but wait—for the eighth hour. Even with what was ahead of her, she couldn't keep the thought of Kane out of her head.

You'll never see him again. He has a new set of priorities now, and you don't even qualify as a footnote.

She played around with those thoughts, juggling possibilities and examining them from every angle. Either he had been arrested and was awaiting trial, or once he had successfully ensnared her, he had moved on to another assignment.

She was startled as the lock mechanism of the door double-clicked, and the door swung open. A Magistrate in full armor stood there, frowning beneath his red-tinted visor. Behind him, Brigid saw another pair of armored Mags.

The man tossed her a threadbare, faded yellow bodysuit. "Put it on."

She did so, trying not to think of all the condemned prisoners who may have worn it in the past. Boot socks were attached to the legs of the shapeless garment, and she adjusted the Velcro tabs until they fit her feet snugly.

After zipping the suit up, she permitted herself to be led away, flanked by the two Mag guards. Brigid expected to be marched down the chill, sterile corridor to some sort of courtroom. Instead, she was escorted only a dozen yards down the hall and put into a chamber not much larger than her cell.

At least this room had a piece of furniture, a high-backed sturdy wooden chair with the legs bolted to the floor. The chair faced a small monitor screen. It shimmered a dull gold. Brigid sat down before it, bracing herself against the fear, the devastating hopelessness of the situation.

On the screen, a vague, misty outline took shape, like the head and shoulders of a man hidden behind veils of chiffon and backlit by golden sunlamps. The Mag shut the door behind her. None would see or hear what went on within the chamber; none would ever know the testimony she gave—except Baron Cobalt.

Brigid stiffened, cold sweat springing in icy drops at her hairline. She shuddered to the depths of her soul. Part of her mind knew that maintaining the baron's mystique was contrived, an intimidation strategy, an old psychological gambit. It was theater, it was hokum, it was a sham.

But it was effective.

The serene, musical voice wafted from the speaker at the bottom of the screen, sounding as if it were echoing from the black gulfs between the stars. "Citizen Baptiste, you stand accused of dissent, sedition and treason against the ville. You are further accused of illegal possession of ville property. If you have anything to say before sentence is pronounced, speak now."

Forcing herself to stare into the vid lens on the wall beside the screen, Brigid replied, "I am innocent of these charges, Lord Baron. Save that I did have in my possession the said piece of Ville property. Here is my defense—"

Brigid told her story straightforwardly, without faltering or groping for words. She had only been engaged in following a line of inquiry ordered by the Magistrate Division. She had no idea the orders had not been sanctioned by Kane's superior officer.

The baron said, "You were aware the information you accessed was restricted. You used an authorization code that was not your own."

"Curiosity and fear, Lord Baron," Brigid responded

crisply. "Magistrate Kane had piqued my interest, and I feared for my safety if I disobeyed him."

The baron didn't speak. He waited and Brigid was encouraged slightly. So far, Baron Cobalt hadn't mentioned that Kane was acting as an undercover op to expose a suspected Preservationist.

"And to the charges of sedition and treason," Brigid went on, "I plead innocent. As for the computer, I plead guilty and I throw myself on the mercy of the baron. I claim I meant no wrong."

Golden waves shimmered across the screen, and a ripple of genuinely amused laughter came from the speaker. "You are a clever dissembler. Very well, I will dismiss the charges of possessing the computer. I grant you mercy. However, the other charges remain intact and, as you know, are punishable by death."

It was what she expected. Brigid bowed her head.

The baron said, "Brigid—I will call you that since this is such an intimate moment between us—"

"There's nothing I can do about it, is there?" Brigid's voice was dull and flat.

"No, there isn't. You must understand I'm not sentencing you to death for these arbitrary reasons. Even if you are a Preservationist, that's not what brought you here before me."

"What did, then?"

"Knowledge," Baron Cobalt answered. "It can lead to wisdom and thus to humility, true enough. But in this tortured period of humankind's existence on earth, knowledge beyond what is needed must also bring death."

Lifting her head, she asked, "Why is that so?"

The baron's reply was soft, almost regretful. "Humanity stands on the threshold of a new genesis. It cannot pass over that threshold if collective knowledge expands."

"I don't understand."

"That is the entire point. If you understood, if humankind as a whole understood, the mad rush to mass destruction would begin again.'' Baron Cobalt's voice dropped to a half whisper. "Humanity lives inside its head. That is the seat of the soul. This is true subjectively, as well as objectively. If you control the soul, you control humanity."

Brigid said nothing. Frozen, she only stared at the shifting pattern of light on the screen.

"The course of execution is set by expedience and custom," the baron declared. "You will die quickly and painlessly, if that is of any comfort to you."

As if responding to an invisible cue, the door opened. The baron said, "The sentence is to be carried out forthwith."

The monitor screen dimmed immediately. The Magistrate prodded Brigid to her feet and removed her from the room. Only the one Mag accompanied her down the corridor, his Sin Eater drawn and aimed at her head. As she marched, she was desperately contemplating some outburst of violence, some assertion of the will to live, even knowing that it would never succeed.

They entered an elevator, and the car dropped swiftly. She was too numb to count the levels. The descent halted, the door rolled aside and she and her guard were met by three armored Mags. The trio surrounded her and conducted her down a long corridor, toward a square archway covered by a metal slab. One of the four Magistrates increased his pace and reached for a lever jutting out from the frame of the arch. He pulled it up, and the slab hissed upward, operated by a combination of hydraulics and pneumatics.

Beyond the arch, the overhead lights were an eye-searing blaze. Brigid squinted and made out a blank, featureless wall. No, not exactly featureless—it bore deep pockmarks and dark stains. A set of wrist and leg shackles hung from the wall by brackets. She wasn't surprised that the mode of execution was a basic firing squad, but she did wonder what they would do with her body.

Brigid marched onward, forcing her head erect. She had no plan except to die without shaming herself. To weep and beg for mercy would not accomplish anything or delay the inevitable.

The Mag at the lever reached out and took her roughly by the arm, pulling her aside. To his companions, he said tersely, "Take your positions. Make sure your weapons are properly primed. We want no misfires."

The three Magistrates hesitated, but responded to the tone of command. They stepped beneath the arch. Immediately the armored man slapped at the lever, and the heavy metal panel rushed down, hitting the floor with a booming thud. Faintly, on the other side, came cries of astonishment and angry confusion.

"Don't stand there gawking, Baptiste," said Kane. "They're locked in, but they can comm-call for help."

Brigid dared hesitate only a second, then she started running beside Kane, who appeared to have no trouble jogging in the armor. She tried to think of something, anything to say. "I didn't recognize you," she finally said.

"You weren't supposed to. Can you run any faster?"

Instead of increasing her speed, she came to a complete halt. Kane sprinted on for a few yards, realized she wasn't beside him, slowed and whirled around, advancing on her angrily.

"Do you want to die?" he demanded.

"No," she answered. "But I don't want to participate in a Mag scam. How do I know this rescue isn't a farce, a trick to lead you to a Preservationist hideout?"

Kane's lips creased in a frown. "Is there one? Are you really a Preservationist?"

"Not exactly. Somebody claiming to represent them contacted me anonymously last year, but I never spoke to anyone or met anyone. As far as I know, the Preservationists are nothing more than a straw adversary, a front for a Mag op."

"And as far as I know," Kane said grimly, "I'm helping a traitor escape from a deserved death sentence."

The man and woman regarded each other silently. Then

Brigid gave Kane her smile. "Paranoia is such a subtle yet devastating weapon, isn't it?"

"You're not paranoid if they really are after you, Baptiste," Kane shot back.

"There's the conundrum. I don't know if they really *are* after me."

"Trust me on this. They are."

She sighed heavily. "What's the plan?"

"I'm making it up as I go along. For the moment, we're hitting the Pits."

Brigid tried to consider his words dispassionately, realized she couldn't, so she started running again. "Okay."

Kane fell into step beside her. "What convinced you?"

"If this were a trick, you would have described a cunning and devious scheme, full of twistie-turnie strategies."

"Because I'm flying by my ass, you have faith in me?"

"Sure," she panted.

"Oh."

They spoke no more, devoting their breath to running. They sprinted along the corridor, around corners, following bends, keeping close to the walls. Brigid followed Kane's lead. He seemed to know where he was going. When she heard the steady throb of machinery, she realized they were on E Level, the manufacturing facility.

Coming to a stop at an L-junction, Kane gestured for her to keep back, then peered around the left-hand corner. A moment later, he waved her forward.

A long vista of great machines opened up, arrayed in a number of extended lines. Mechs and techs wearing protective goggles and headgear operated the equipment. She saw drill presses, forges, smelters, crucibles. The combined rattles, clanks and roars were nearly deafening. Some of the machines shot sparks, emitting the metallic odor of ozone, while others spit jets of steam. Chain conveyors rattled in jerks and starts. A forest of girders supported a trussed network of overhead catwalks.

She had never been here before, and she understood why.

The teeth-jarring racket, the sparks, the clouds of steam, gave it an aspect of a pocket-size hell on earth, populated by damned souls.

This was the level devoted to feeding comfort to the Enclaves, producing and manufacturing, and in many instances, reproducing and remanufacturing tools, weapons, engine parts and fixtures of all sorts.

Along one wall, protected by a heavy-gauge-wire-screened enclosure, was a line of humped nuclear generators, which provided the power. The wall behind them was studded with meters, dials and glass-encased readouts. She wondered if Kane intended to knock out the energy source, since it was such an obvious target. Instead, he pointed directly ahead.

"See that door on the far wall?" He spoke loudly to be heard over the incessant clanking, rattling roar.

She narrowed her eyes, wishing she had her glasses. She tried to follow his pointing finger, but her view was obscured by billows of steam and spark showers. "No."

"Doesn't matter. Follow me. Don't look around. No matter what happens, just keep going."

Kane started off, walking in brisk, long-legged strides. Brigid followed him. The noise, the smell, the heat—all were a physical assault. She felt her bones vibrating in rhythm with the crashing machinery. The air was stagnant, choked with the thick odors of grease and superheated metal.

She kept her eyes on Kane's black-shelled back, trying to imitate his steady, measured tread. Several times she had to dodge a flurry of sparks and once she barely avoided being scalded by a hissing spurt of steam.

All of this old ironmongery was incongruous, she realized, powered as it was by atomic generators. She knew more-advanced equipment existed before the nukecaust. Then again, she chided herself, the more advanced the equipment, the more educated the people had to be in order to operate it.

But then, she remembered her recent presentencing exchange with the baron, and his views. In this tortured period of humankind's existence on earth, knowledge must also bring death.

The few people in their path barely glanced at them. Once they saw Kane's armored figure looming out of the mist, they immediately directed their attention elsewhere. They probably feared a surprise inspection was under way.

Long before they reached the door, Brigid was perspiring and breathing heavily. The lead-shielded door bore an exclamatory warning in white paint: Absolutely No Admittance Beyond This Point! No Exceptions!

The hasp was secured by a thick padlock, almost the size of her fist. Wiping at the sweat filming her face, she yelled in his ear, "Do you have a key?"

Kane nodded, lifting his right hand. The Sin Eater sprang into it, flame blooming from the barrel. Because of the background roar, the shot sounded no louder than a hand clap. The padlock jumped and broke apart. Kane ripped the shattered mass from the hasp and pushed open the door. It appeared to require quite a bit of effort. He stepped through, looked around and indicated with a gesture that the way was clear.

After Brigid stepped through, he pulled the door closed, and the volume of the racket was reduced by half. The air was much cooler, and she couldn't help but sigh in relief.

They stood in almost complete darkness, at the bottom of a high shaft. She could barely make out the contours of a corkscrew staircase, twisting up into the dimness.

"I can barely see," she said, unconsciously lowering her voice to a whisper.

Kane tapped his visor. "I'll see for both of us."

"Where to now?"

"Like I said. Tartarus."

"Feels like we've already been there," she murmured.

Chapter 22

When the ground collapsed beneath their feet, they tumbled down together. Kane did his best to cushion Brigid's fall. It seemed only polite since he was in the lead and holding her hand. The fall was completely unexpected, and he had to give the archivist credit— she didn't cry out or curse the way he did.

They landed in a pile of soft dirt and half slid, half rolled to its base. Brigid ended up lying atop him. Pushing her hair out of her face, she said, "I thought you'd come this way before."

"Years ago. There's been some changes. Besides, we ended up where we wanted to end up."

By the light enhancer on his helmet, he saw her blink around and wrinkle her nose. "Smells like gasoline or something."

As he looked up at her bright emerald eyes, the thought came to him unbidden that they were on the run, but it was her wild, disheveled hair that looked like a fugitive sunset. He scoffed at himself as something stirred in him, but he found himself reluctant to push her away. "Old storage tanks for a fuel repository. A long, long time ago."

Brigid climbed to her feet, standing ankle deep in dirt, brushing grit from her hair and clothes. Kane stood, scanning the area. He saw places where the soil had been disturbed and he silently heaved a sigh of relief. These were signs that Grant had come this way, and not too long before.

He took her hand and started to lead her, but Brigid dug in her heels, wresting herself away. "Wait."

"Why?"

"Why are you doing this for me? You're risking everything."

Kane replied quietly, "Partly because I'm responsible. You were just doing your job, what a Magistrate told you to do."

"Is that all?" she asked.

"No. I have to know what you learned, why it scared the shit out of Salvo."

"He didn't tell you?"

"All he told me was that this Dulce place figures very prominently in the plans of the Trust."

"The Trust?"

"Tell me what you know, and if we have the time, I'll tell you what I know."

Brigid talked, quickly and quietly. Kane listened without interjecting comments or questions, not even when she mentioned the Archon Directive, the Totality Concept and the description of the PTBE.

"It's obvious that the seeds of the baronies were planted back in the twentieth century, before the nukecaust," Brigid said. "The Totality Concept, the redoubts, even this so-called Archon Directive were components of a far-ranging plan."

"And the nuking interrupted it," Kane said.

"Or was part of it," she retorted.

"I don't understand."

"Think about it. The population was reduced to a manageable level, to a point where concerted resistance against the unification program was utterly futile."

Kane gazed at her, even though she couldn't see him. He didn't know what to say; he wasn't even sure of his feelings. But the one emotion growing within him wasn't fear. It was despair.

"Come on," he said, taking her hand again.

"What about your story?"

"Later. Someone is waiting for us."

He led her down the hollow cylinder of the old fuel cistern. She stumbled over loose stones and chunks of concrete that had fallen from above. He should have been more observant about the obstacles in her way, but he was thinking about his beliefs, or more importantly, his disbeliefs.

After all, Kane hadn't truly accepted what he'd been told by Baron Cobalt, Salvo or the members of the Trust. He swore at himself for his doubts and confusion. But in the final analysis, it really didn't matter if everything or nothing at all he'd been told was true. What mattered was that he'd stayed alive, survived, eagerly eaten the crap he'd been handed and asked for more.

The issues now confronting him were of far greater import than his life or the lives of Brigid, Grant or even his father. He'd allowed primitive fears and angers and worse—curiosity—to motivate him. Baptiste had given him fair warning, though. She had said only two days ago, "You brought all this up. Curiosity always has its price, you know."

He, Grant and Brigid had paid the price, and now all three of them were on their own and on the run. It was far too late to ask for a refund.

He found the rungs leading to the hatch and, bidding Brigid to remain motionless, he clambered up. The heavy iron cover moved fairly easily, which proved Grant had already dislodged it.

Sliding the metal disk to one side, Kane poked his head up and took a quick recce of the foul-smelling alleyway. He saw no one, and he crawled out. Brigid followed a heartbeat later, blinking in the early-morning sunlight, almost overwhelmed by the odors.

"Welcome to the Tartarus Pits," he said, striving for a light tone. "The tour starts immediately."

Brigid didn't reply. She didn't have to, because her face displayed her emotions. Kane checked the mouth of the alley, found the lane clear and gestured for her to join him. They moved only in shadows, working their way toward the east wall. They stepped over dead rats and Pit dwellers sleeping under blankets of garbage.

"Have you come up with a plan yet?" Brigid asked, not trying to disguise the disgust in her tone.

"More or less. I'm taking you to a man who can—if anyone can—smuggle you out of the ville."

"To where?"

"The Outlands, where else?"

"What makes you think I want to leave?" Fright caught at her voice. "I'd prefer the Pits to the Outlands."

Kane stopped, turning to face her. "We're seizing the offensive here, Baptiste. I'm surprised we've gotten this far. But you can't stay in the Pits. It's the first place the Mags will search."

"If I leave the ville, I'll be an—" She bit back the word, unable to utter it.

Kane spoke it for her. "An outlander. It's better than being dead."

"It's not supposed to be." Her lips trembled. "I've thrown my whole life away."

He stroked her tangled, dirty hair clumsily, trying to soothe her. "No, Baptiste. You still have a life. It'll be hard, but it will be life."

"What kind of life can I have in the Outlands?" Her voice was thin and small like a child's. "I'm an archivist, not a survivalist. Where will I go?"

Kane was growing impatient, increasingly aware of the passing of precious minutes. "I don't know. Unless you know of a Preservationist hideout or can find a secret gateway to paradise, you don't have many options. Neither of us do."

Her eyes suddenly flashed brightly, overwhelming the fear in them. "Quantum interphase mat-trans inducers."

"What about these quantum things?"

"They were colloquially known as gateways. I read about them, the redoubts, their locations. If we could find one—"

"What good will that do? Don't you need some kind of accessing or operational code?"

Brigid tapped her forehead with a finger. "The file I found listed the codes. I committed all of them to memory."

Skeptically Kane asked, "All of them?"

"All of them. I have an eidetic memory." Seeing Kane's blank expression, she added, "A photographic memory. I see something once, and I remember everything about it in detail. Even numerical sequences."

A smile creased Kane's lips.

"What?" she asked.

"Later, Baptiste. But keep on surprising me. I may be able to surprise you in return."

They hurried off, darting down, then up muddy back lanes. Kane couldn't keep the smile from returning to his face. An idea had sprung into his mind, full-blown. The plan was impossible, crazy, but it seemed absolutely lucid compared to the hopeless nightmare of the past couple of hours. Now, at least, there was a faint light of hope shining in the darkness of despondency. Of course, they still had to find a way to escape the ville undetected and reach the hellzone, but he was certain Guana Teague could offer up a few suggestions—especially if he believed his life was at stake. Which it certainly was.

The few people they encountered moved aside quickly, keeping their eyes cast down. On top of its other functions, Magistrate armor was an instant crowd-parter.

When Kane finally saw the warehouse looming up against the inner ville wall, the first thing he noticed was the open door. With Brigid behind him, he pushed it open and stepped inside. Immediately he knew something was wrong. He smelled it and he sensed it. His ebullience drained away, as if poured down a hole.

Turning to Brigid, he put his finger to his lips, then filled his hand with the Sin Eater. She leaned into him, and he became acutely aware of her left breast against his arm.

Even through the armor, he could feel her heart pumping hard and fast. Whispering into her ear, he said, "Find some cover. No matter what you see or hear, don't move."

She said nothing, nor did she even nod. The gaze she gave Kane was the same wary look she might cast toward a tiger, if she came across one in her living quarters. It was a look Kane recognized. He had slipped into his Magistrate persona as easily as he had slipped into his armor, and she sensed the change in him.

Brigid followed the line of the wall, found a stack of boxes in a cobwebby corner and crouched down behind them, hands around her knees.

Kane crept deeper into the warehouse, sidling into the shadows cast by stacks of crates. He followed his nose. The stink of blood and cordite was fresh. Peering around the edge of an open box of machine parts, he spied a flat ribbon of scarlet oozing over the flagstone floor. He didn't have to move closer to know what it was. The fat man lying on his side was three hundred pounds of dead weight. Blood continued to sluggishly ooze from the gaping gash in his throat.

The tall, lean man lying on his back, sightless eyes gazing up at the rafters, lay in a pool of blood, too, just not so much of it. The front of his leather jacket was pulled away from his chest, revealing three bloody holes grouped neatly over the heart.

Guana Teague's near decapitation wasn't a standard Mag chill method, but Kane recognized the size of the bullet holes in Uno's torso, as well as the precision with which they'd been placed.

He had to take the chance. He activated his comm link and whispered, "Grant?"

The response was immediate. Grant's voice, full of strain, replied, "Behind you."

The stereophonic reply came from two directions. One, transmitted over his comm link directly into his ear, and the other, as Grant had said, from directly behind. He turned. In the center of the warehouse, before a high pyramid of stacked cartons and crates, in a semi circle, stood eight Magistrates. Six of them were in full armor, their bodies as rigid as stone. The two Mags not in armor were Salvo and Grant, but their Sin Eaters were out and aimed directly at him.

"Leather it, Kane. And come here." Salvo's tone was as cold and hard as the metal of the blaster in his fist.

Kane's visored eyes sought out Grant's. His dark face was drawn, lips tight. "Do as he says, Kane. I know the whole story now."

The world tilted around him, his belly performed a flip-flop and his head went light. "Why should I?" He was surprised at how steady his voice sounded.

"We're not here to chill you," Salvo replied. "We're here to help you."

Kane slowly approached them, the blaster still in hand. Scanning the jawlines of the Mags, he saw none that were familiar. He felt as if he were breasting waves of despair, of anguish and shame. "By chilling me."

"No," said Salvo quietly. "We still want you, Kane. You just had an extreme reaction to what you've been through the last couple of days. It happens to the best of us."

Kane laughed bitterly, mirthlessly. "Do 'the best of us' help a convicted traitor escape her executioners?"

"You'll have to turn Baptiste over to us. She must die and you must accept it."

Kane kept walking. "And Grant?"

Salvo smiled gently. "He wants to help you."

"How are you supposed to help me, Grant?" Kane asked.

Hesitantly Grant said, "You're delusional, Kane. Some sort of stress syndrome. It can happen, like Anson. Remember him?"

Kane remembered. About six years ago, a Mag had fused out after one too many Pit sweeps had resulted in the deaths of pregnant women. He had become a jolt-walker, and then he had disappeared, presumably into the Outlands.

"I'm not fused," he declared calmly. "I'm not a jolt-brain, I'm not delusional. Salvo is. He thinks he's saving the world from itself, and to do that, he schemes, lies, double-crosses and chills anybody who gets in the way of his grand dreams. Including all of us."

Kane slowed to a stop and stood motionless, legs braced and wide apart. He was about twenty feet away from the Mag line. "Did you talk to Guana or Uno?"

Grant shook his head. "No. They attacked me before I could question them."

"You cut Guana's throat?" He saw the blood drying on Grant's coat, even though attempts had been made to sponge it away.

"Uno did. I came in on the middle of a fight between them. He snuffed Guana, and I was forced to put him down."

"Leather your side arm, Kane," Salvo growled.

"Leather your dick," Kane snapped. "And your fucking Archons."

Salvo's lips went white and the barrel of the Sin Eater jerked a trifle in reaction to his words. "Kane—"

"Chill me, Salvo. Like you did Reeth. Before I start talking about Archons, the Trust, mat-trans gateways, about helping you to build a new world order of masters and slaves."

Grant suddenly stepped away from the line, his Sin Eater trained on his friend. "Kane, I'm begging you. As your partner and your friend. Put away the blaster. Salvo told me you wouldn't be harmed, and I believe him. If he meant to hurt us, if he had planned the hit yesterday, I'd be dead by now. Right?"

He walked closer, voice low and beseeching. "He explained all of it to me, how that Preservationist bitch gave you a load of shit about what was on that disk you lifted, fed you a line about aliens—"

Pain slithered through Kane as he watched Grant's approach. "Stop. No closer."

"You won't shoot me, Kane."

Kane raised his blaster, centering the bore on the middle of Grant's forehead. "The hell I won't. They've stolen your mind. Your will. I should have known the division conditioning was too deep. A superior officer tells you to spill a friend's blood and you say, 'How many gallons and in what color would you like it, sir?'"

"You've got it all wrong. Salvo talked and I listened. That's all."

"That's right," spoke up Salvo. "There's no place for you to go. Tell me where you've stashed Baptiste, she'll be taken into custody and I promise you that meaning will be restored to your life."

Grant stopped walking. Barely four feet separated him from Kane. Matter-of-factly, he said, "You've got to make a decision, Kane. Now."

Synchronized with his "Now," Grant pivoted on his heel in a whiplash explosion of perfect coordination of muscle and reflexes. As he whirled, he brought his right hand up and under his left arm. Even before he had completed his turn, the Sin Eater blazed and roared.

Chapter 23

Autofire raked the semicircle of Magistrates in a whipsawing wave. Grant hit a center Magistrate broadside, bowling him off his feet.

The Sin Eater in Kane's hand spit flame and thunder, unleashing round after round of 9 mm slugs. One of the Mags stumbled and fell, and all of them voiced a garbled babble of screams and profanity.

The bullets didn't breach the armor, but the kinetic shock was sufficient to numb them, maybe slam the air out of their lungs. And hurt like hell, too.

Return fire ripped the air around Grant, tearing through it in a frenzy, like a ground-level gale. A bullet snapped past his ear, sounding like the crack of a huge branch. He dived to his left.

Kane held down the trigger of his autoblaster, swinging the flame-belching barrel from left to right. Hot brass spewed from the ejector. He found himself subconsciously aiming for the red badges emblazoned on the left pectorals of the body armor. He glimpsed Grant on his knees a few yards away, a little to the rear of him, blasting away at the Mags still on their feet.

Wild rounds smashed into boxes and crates, filling the air with scraps of floating paper and wood particles. Flagstones shattered, the shards whining and buzzing in all directions. Bullets punched holes through the tin warehouse walls.

Salvo stitched Kane across the midriff with a zipper of slugs. They bruised him, beat him coughing to the floor. He rolled, came to his knees, his Sin Eater blowing a cavity in the floor at Salvo's feet. The exploding, sharp-edged bits of rock slashed his trouser legs, and he tangoed back, trying to shake the pain out of his legs, like a cat with wet paws.

Conditioning was a wondrous thing. Despite the heavy volume of fire erupting from all the blasters, the men were instinctively aiming to disable, not to kill. Mags chilling Mags, even Mags gone bad, was blasphemous, inconceivable.

Salvo hopped crazily around the base of the box pyramid, slapping at his stinging legs, screaming in maddened fury. "Chill them, you stupid bastards! *Chill them!*"

As if to punctuate his shrieked command, he drew a double-handed bead on Grant and held down the trigger. Grant backpedaled and plunged to the floor as flame sputtered from that deadly bore and a stream of 9 mm tumblers smashed up the flagstones around him, showering him with rock chips.

He threw himself forward in a frantic somersault, trying to roll ahead of the deadly lead stream. His body suddenly spun around like a top, flipping him over on his face. As he twirled, he screamed some gibberish, which to Kane sounded like "Domi! Do it!"

Kane stopped dodging and dancing and rushed headlong toward Salvo and the three Mags still on their feet. He stretched out his right arm ahead of him, flame blooming and sharp thunder cracking from his handblaster. One of the Mags fired at him, and he felt a pair of glancing impacts on the top of his left shoulder. He staggered, his aim spoiled. His shots missed Salvo by a whisper but ripped through the Mag standing next to him, turning his cheekbones, nose and mouth into a red jelly smear.

At the same instant the Mag corkscrewed sideways against the base of the box pyramid, an engine roar echoed throughout the warehouse. It was immediately followed by a metal-on-metal grinding and a clashing of gears.

The pyramid of boxes swayed, the lower tiers stretching and then bursting apart. Salvo tried to run, but the pinnacle and its supporting containers toppled. He was buried beneath a crashing avalanche of boxes and crates and pallets.

Kane vaulted to one side, cartwheeling his way out of the careening path of the wag. Its treads rolled over and crushed one of the fallen Mags, his armor cracking and splitting open like the carapace of a beetle.

The two Mags still on their feet backed away from the charging vehicle in a clumsy, shambling run. They fired at it, the rounds clanging and striking sparks from the armor plate.

The cross-braced steel barricade remover slammed into them like a battering ram, flinging them, arms and legs flailing, across the warehouse. One struck the wall, leaving a vague imprint of his head in the tin, and dropped bonelessly to the floor. The other crashed through the side of a large, wood-paneled packing crate.

With a screech of rusty brake shoes catching, the wag shuddered noisily to a halt. Foul smoke belched from the exhaust stacks. Even on Idle, the engine roared like an enraged beast. Kane didn't know where to look or to aim. Peripheral images crowded his vision. In front of him was the armored wag. On his right, Grant was trying to get to his knees. His face was drenched in perspiration, he was gasping in pain, but his teeth flashed in a savage grin. To the left, a dazed Mag dragged himself along the floor.

The driver's door of the vehicle squealed open, and he glimpsed a small white wraith at the wheel. She waved to Grant and shouted, "Come on!"

The firefight was over, ending as suddenly as it began, and Kane was in instant motion, at Grant's side and pulling him to his feet. He hissed through clenched teeth and grabbed at his right thigh. Blood seeped between his fingers.

Kane pushed the coat aside, examining the wound, touching both sides of the thigh. "The slug went clean through, tearing only the layers of skin. It's the proverbial flesh wound. The muscles are probably bruised, though. You're lucky. Can you stand on it?''

Grant's leg wobbled, but it supported him. Voice tight with suppressed pain, he said, "Let me shoot you in the leg and you can tell me how lucky you feel."

"Since you're bitching already, I guess you'll make a full recovery. Wish we had a medikit, though."

"There's one in the Sandcat. Whatever else you can say about Guana, the fat bastard was always prepared. Except for when Domi chilled him."

Kane nodded toward the girl in the Sandcat. "Domi. Isn't she the same gaudy slut who nearly chilled you?"

"Yeah, but so did you, so I'm not holding any grudges. She's not a gaudy. She saved my life." Grant released his pent-up breath in a gusty sigh, his eyes surveying the carnage. "We've overstayed."

Kane turned and began walking toward the door.

Grant called after him. "I had you going, didn't I?"

Kane paused, a smart-ass remark on his lips. He bit it back and said simply, "Yeah."

Grant grinned. "Bet you feel like the most triple-stupe asshole in the world right now."

Kane shook his head. "No. I feel like the most triple-lucky asshole in world."

He found Brigid where he had stowed her. She had armed herself with a splinter pried from a wooden pallet, holding it like a dagger, one end of it wrapped with a length of fabric ripped from the sleeve of her bodysuit.

Anxiously she asked, "Is it over?"

"It's just beginning," he replied grimly, helping her to her feet.

She followed him back to the center of the warehouse. She averted her eyes, and Kane didn't blame her. The scene was not for the sensitive. Grant stood beside the open door of the Sandcat, his right leg propped up on the running board. The albino girl, Domi, was expertly knotting a tourniquet made of a Mag's belt around his thigh.

"Something tells me you developed a plan," Kane said.

"Of sorts. I'll fill you in on the hoof. Climb aboard."

Kane sent Brigid on ahead. He pushed through the scattering of fallen boxes, kicking them aside. Most of them were empty, but several of the wooden crates were quite sturdy, and therefore quite heavy. He found Salvo beneath one.

His right arm was trapped beneath the crate, but he held the pin mike clumsily between the thumb and forefinger of his left hand. Kane reached down, snatched it away and tore it loose from his coat's lapel. Salvo's normally sallow complexion was ashen. Blood glistened from a shallow gash on the crown of his head, and he appeared to breathe with difficulty.

He had enough breath to bare blood-filmed teeth and gasp out, "Should have known. Like father, like son."

"What do you mean?" Kane snarled. "Where's my father?"

The injured man shook his head, attempting to curl his lips in a sneer. Kane leaned his weight against the side of the crate. Salvo cried out, and a fine spray of bright crimson froth burst from his mouth.

"A punctured lung, looks like," Kane said. "Survivable, if I allow it. How much of this Archon shit is true?"

Salvo's reply was an aspirated wheeze. "All of it. None of it. Only as much as you can authenticate. Which is very little."

"Where's my father?"

"Like the baron said...still performing the work of the Trust."

Kane leaned on the crate again. "I asked *where!*"

"You know already. You just don't know that you know."

"Kane!" Grant's shout was galvanizing. "Let's go!"

Salvo's glazed eyes fluttered. "You think you and Grant are the first Mags to cut and run? You're not. You probably won't be the last, either. Once you run, you've got to keep running. That's the life of an outlander, an outrunner.''

"You're wrong," Kane said quietly. He aimed the Sin Eater at an invisible point on Salvo's broad forehead. "I'm done with running. And you're done with everything."

"Chill me and be damned."

The muzzle of the Sin Eater didn't move and didn't spout fire or noise.

Salvo eyed it. In a gravelly whisper, he said, "Don't tell me pity stays your hand."

"Yeah," said Kane, mocking the whisper. "It's pity. It's a pity I've run out of bullets."

He heaved the packing crate aside. "On your feet."

Salvo clumsily flopped over on his left side, his right hand folded loosely around the butt of his Sin Eater. "I think my arm is broken."

"I'm not asking you to walk on your hands. On your feet—slagger."

Wheezing through his teeth, Salvo made a show of controlling his pain, trying to force himself awkwardly to his feet with his left arm. When he achieved a half-crouching posture, his right hand tightened around the Sin Eater and whipped the muzzle up.

Kane had been waiting for that. He delivered the toe of his left boot full into Salvo's mouth. Salvo went over on his back, spitting blood and bone splinters. He flopped and thrashed, using his heels to kick himself into a sitting position, bringing his blaster to bear. Through pulped lips, he was snarling with rage.

Kane slashed the barrel of the Sin Eater across the side of his head, splitting open the scalp. Blood pouring down his face, Salvo fell heavily onto his back, his skull striking the flagstone floor with a cruel crack. He made no movement after that.

Kane unstrapped the Sin Eater from his forearm, took the two extra clips of ammo from Salvo's belt and left him where he lay.

Grant crooked a quizzical eyebrow when he approached. "You didn't chill him."

Kane shook his head. "If we're leaving, let's leave. A squad could be on its way, and I don't want another firefight before breakfast."

"Why didn't you?"

With a certain amount of bitterness in his tone, Kane replied, "One of the few old, ingrained habits I can't bring myself to break. He's a Mag, and I can't murder a Mag in cold blood."

Grant grunted, looked around and said, "Little late for that." He said nothing more.

There wasn't time for more than cursory introductions all around. They all scrambled into the armored box. Kane took the seat next to Domi, who still held the wheel. There was just enough room for Grant and Brigid to sit in the back. Cartons of survival equipment, food and containers of water were stored there.

Eyeing the girl, Kane saw for the first time the mini-Uzi tucked between her thighs and the seat. Turning toward Grant, he asked, "Does she know where she's going?"

Domi reached for the instrument panel, saying, "Ask me. I talk."

"Do you know where you're going?"

She pulled down a couple of switches, worked the shift lever and put the machine into gear. The engine beat faster as the Sandcat lurched forward. "Watch and learn, sec man."

The armored wag rolled across the warehouse, the treads flattening boxes and crushing cartons. Steered by Domi, the machine rolled steadily toward the rear wall. The barricade remover struck it with a loud banging of metal. A section of tin, just wide enough and high enough to admit the Sandcat, folded inward, a reinforcing cross-brace assembly of wooden planks snapping and splintering.

Kane peered out through the windscreen at the narrow passageway. It was cut beneath the very wall of the ville itself, shored up here and there by heavy timbers. He saw no light ahead of them, and since the walls were approximately ten feet thick, the Sandcat didn't have far to travel.

The wag jounced roughly, its suspension creaking as its front end plowed into a barrier. Gray light suddenly showed, appearing in irregularly shaped patches and cracks. Then sunlight flooded the passage.

The Sandcat pushed inexorably through a false front, chunks of clay, squares of turf and masonry collapsing onto the hood, pattering across the metal. Kane couldn't help but laugh. Guana Teague had managed to burrow an escape tunnel right under the wall of Cobaltville. God only knew how many hours of labor it had taken him to dig it, and then construct the camouflaged exit. Bribery had to have played a large role in the project, as well.

As if reading his thoughts, Grant said, "He was a corrupt bastard, but a clever one."

Domi hissed, but not in reaction to the remark about Teague. She wrestled with the wheel as the wag tilted sharply forward, rolling fast down the face of the bluff. Though the windshield was still partially obscured by sliding sheets of grit and dirt, Kane recognized the area outside the east wall.

Teague had chosen well, since it was the least tactically important piece of real estate around the Ville. It was also something of a blind spot, positioned between a pair of Vulcan-Phalanx turrets. Before the sentries on the wall caught sight of the vehicle and brought the big guns to bear, they would be almost out of range.

The Sandcat picked up speed, and Domi made no allowance for the slippery bank sloping down to the river. It was a shallow ford, and as the front end nosed through the water, it caused an upsurging splash that washed away the dirt and masonry from the windshield. The wag churned across the ford, the river swirling almost to the doors. When it reached the opposite bank, one of the tracks began to spin, squirting mud and water in a high rooster tail behind them.

Domi cursed, worked the shift lever, and the treads found traction again, pulling them up the riverbank and onto dry land. Kane didn't make any comments. He pretended to have faith in the albino girl's expertise.

Hitching around in his seat, he asked, "What's your assessment of the kind of pursuit we can expect?"

Grant considered the question thoughtfully for a moment. "Not overland, even though we're cutting a trail a blind jolt-brain could follow. By air is the most likely. Three Deathbirds are flight ready, but the division is down to only two experienced sky jockeys, since me and Carthew are out of the loop. That leaves Pollard and Salvo, since you couldn't break your habit of not chilling Mags."

"I may not have chilled him, but the condition he's in, he couldn't jockey himself to the can. What about that new guy, Zack?"

Grant shrugged. "Zack's only in pilot's training, but they might press him into service."

"So, worst case is a pair of Birds, one piloted by a novice. Time factor?"

"Let's cut ourselves a break and hope it takes a minimum of an hour before Salvo and others are found and taken back to the division. Factor in another forty-five minutes before the Birds can be crewed and launched."

"Leaving us approximately two hours before we have to worry. But only half a minute to agree on a destination and a route."

Grant said, "Guana had a plan to hit the hellzone in Mesa Verde. He figured no one would want to look for him there."

"Not for him, maybe," replied Kane. "They'll be looking for us no matter where we go. Besides, there are no roads into Mesa Verde."

"Don't need no roads if you know the way," declared Domi.

The wag hit the base of a bluff and jarred everyone, dragging a pained curse out of Grant. "At the speed we're traveling," he commented, "two hours is barely enough time to reach the Outlands, much less the zone."

Kane tapped the side of his helmet. "I'll be able to pick up the comm link transmissions when they're three miles away, assuming they don't rescramble the frequency. We'll have a few minutes' warning, at least."

"What good will going into a hellzone do?" Brigid demanded. "You didn't save me from a quick death just so I can contract rad cancer and die slow, did you?"

"No, I didn't." Kane looked at her. Brigid's hair was tangled and disarrayed, and her lips were compressed and white with fear. He grinned.

"What's so funny?" she asked irritably.

"Remember what I said about surprising you?"

"So?"

"So, Baptiste—prepare yourself for a very big surprise. Maybe the biggest one of your life."

"After what I've just been through," she retorted, "it'll have to be gargantuan to impress me."

Chapter 24

The Sandcat was a miserable conveyance, especially traveling over rough terrain. Domi completely circumvented the single road from the ville, opting to drive along gullies and coulees. The old vehicle groaned a perpetual protest from every joint, seam and rivet. Many of the wag's metal tread sections were worn to thin wafers, and the racket made by the return rollers was incessant, as was the clatter from the diesel engine.

Brigid treated Grant's wound as best she could from materials in the medical kit stowed under the driver's seat. His pain was evident as she swabbed the shallow gouge with antiseptic and sprinkled sulfa powder into it. There were ampoules of morphine in the kit, but Grant refused them, saying he needed to keep a clear head.

While Brigid bandaged his leg, Grant told Kane how Salvo had triangulated his position over the trans-comm in his coat. "Seemed to make sense to wait for him instead of running, since I expected you there at any time. Domi hid inside the wag, and when Salvo arrived, I fed him the same story I gave you, about Uno and Guana chilling each other."

"He told you I'd fused?"

Grant nodded. "Said Baptiste here had seduced you, tried to get you to join the Preservationists. Said he had vid proof of you two in the nasty." Responding to a sharp glare from Brigid, he added hastily, "No offense."

Kane shook his head in disgust, wishing he could remove his helmet, but it was critical to their escape that the Magistrate trans-link frequencies be monitored. "Salvo is the one who fused out. Or maybe not."

"What do you mean?"

"And what about this big surprise?" inquired Brigid as she finished tying the bandage.

"That will have to wait until we're out of sight of the ville."

Domi chose to do that by driving through thickets, squeezing through copses of trees and jouncing along the bottoms of coulees. She expertly maneuvered the Sandcat up, then down, treacherous slopes. She appeared to know not only what she was doing, but where she was going, so Kane didn't question her.

Official Cobaltville territory extended in a fifty-mile radius, using the Administrative Monolith as the hub of a wheel. Beyond the rim of that invisible wheel lay the Outlands. Ville law was enforced in the Outlands, of course, but only when deemed necessary by the whim of the baron.

Kane was only vaguely familiar with the topography of the area immediately surrounding Cobaltville, but Domi knew where the checkpoints were. As an outlander, she would have their locations imprinted in her memory. One of the few redeeming characteristics of outrunners was their unerring sense of direction—

He caught that thought and glumly tried to chase it out of his head. All of them now were Outlanders, and a slip of an albino girl held seniority, outranking them by dint of her birth and years of experience. In the kingdom of the disenfranchised, she was pretender to a throne.

Checking his wrist chron, Kane saw that half an hour had passed since they'd forded the river. Mesa Verde was an hour's flight time by Deathbird, so he calculated an overland trek, especially one not following roads and side trails, would take about three hours, traveling at an average speed of thirty miles per hour. Unless Domi knew a shorter route.

He asked, "Do you know a shortcut?"

She gave him a quick, annoyed glance. "What you think this is?"

"The scenic route?" Kane muttered.

Brigid leaned forward, stretching her cramped legs. Gripping the back of the front seat, she said, "We're out of sight of the ville. Time for your big surprise."

Kane turned back, and she self-consciously averted her face. He realized she wasn't used to enduring such physical hardship and was ashamed of her sweat, grime and the state of her clothing.

"All right," he said loudly. "Listen up, because I only want to tell this once."

He should have known better. Because of the noise of the wag, he had to repeat himself several times, half shouting to be heard at all. By the time he had related everything about the Trust, the Totality Concept, the gateway in Mesa Verde canyon, the Archon Directorate, his theories on the attempted assassination of Grant and Brigid's frame-up, he was hoarse and his throat was dirt dry.

Brigid handed him a bottle of water. As he drank from it, he caught Grant's eye and saw how stunned and angry he was.

"Bullshit," Grant announced doggedly. "Bullshit, bullshit. *Bull*shit. How much of that crap did Salvo expect you to believe? How much of it *do* you believe?"

"To both questions, the answer is... I don't know. The Totality Concept stuff can be verified, at least as far as a mat-trans unit is concerned, so I guess I have to believe that part of it."

Brigid's eyes shone with suspicious contemplation. "Why would there be a gateway unit in a smuggler's slaghole?"

"To transport the merchandise, remember? Quick and easy."

"And you figure," challenged Grant, "that if we get ourselves there, we'll use it to beam ourselves to this Dulce place?"

Kane nodded to Brigid. "She claims she's memorized all the gateway codes. Presumably we can transmit ourselves anywhere."

"In theory," Brigid responded doubtfully. "It stands to reason that only the active-destination gateways can be accessed. Even if the unit is there, and it's operable, there may be a lockout on the controls."

Grant was shaking his head side to side, his expression set. "Listen, Kane. I'll go along with you on some of this, because there's a certain amount of proof. Salvo wanted me dead for some reason, then tried to con me that you'd gone over the edge. Okay, fine. He's following some sort of secret agenda, maybe sanctioned by the baron or these Trust groupies. Maybe not. But I don't see anything about Archons or aliens or anything else. All I know is I sacrificed everything for you. I owe you my life, and I trust you. But don't ask me to swallow the rest of this crap."

"You saw the gateway chamber in Reeth's slaghole, just like I did. He even called it a gateway, right?"

Grant nodded grimly. "I saw a funny room, which for all you and I know, could have been a fancy clothes closet. And even if it is one of those trans-mat things, Salvo ordered the place flash-blasted."

"He wouldn't touch the gateway."

"You don't know that. Listen, Mesa Verde is a box canyon. We can maybe hole up and hide and hold off a few Mags for a few hours. But all we'll be doing is making a last stand."

"What's your alternative?" Brigid inquired.

"Guana told me he was heading for the Western Islands or the Darks. He was only hitting the zone long enough to throw off pursuit."

"We've had this conversation," snapped Kane, growing angry in spite of himself. "That was Guana, not a pair of turncoat Mags and a condemned insurrectionist. For now, they'll chase us to the Western Islands, across the Cific and to fucking Mongolia before they give up on us. Later, they'll forget a bit and get busy with other things. Then we'll be able to slip back in, with the heat turned off.''

Grant opened his mouth to respond, then he considered the words he'd just heard and bowed his head. Dejected, he murmured, "God help us."

Kane said reasonably, "The gateway is our only chance. It's a long shot, I admit. A one-percenter. But we've got to play out the hand those bastards dealt us."

Grant blinked, angry tears shining in his eyes. "I've lost everything. *Everything.*"

Brigid ran a sympathetic hand over the back of his head. "We all have. Except our souls. We get to keep those."

Kane turned back around, gazing through the windshield. Domi cast him a single, dispassionate glance, then returned her attention to driving.

He felt wretched about everything. Now that there was a respite from the action, for the first time in nearly twenty-four hours, guilt filled him like a cup. His dislike of Salvo and his suspicion about the Mesa Verde penetration had resulted in the destruction of two innocent lives. He could deal with the consequences if they had landed solely on his shoulders, but when he pulled his own personal plug, he'd dragged two good people down with him. There was no way he could ever make it up to them. The sudden taste of self-loathing was so bitter, he nearly gagged. He busied himself with reloading his Sin Eater from the ammo clips taken from Salvo in the warehouse.

The Sandcat clanked and shuddered onward, entering the Outlands. Gently rolling hills bordering unbroken flatlands stretched before it. Here grew thorny shrubs and squat, scrubby trees so short they were more like overgrown bushes. In the distance were stands of cedars and ever-greens. The ground bore green traces of spring, but harsh rocks and boulders pushed up everywhere. Kane had heard it said Colorado had been spared much of the devastation that overtook the rest of the country, but he couldn't really tell it by the land they were traversing.

Every so often, Kane consulted the jury-rigged rad counter on the instrument panel. It was one of the ways to tell when they entered the hellzone.

The ride became rougher as the Sandcat began to maneuver hills and slopes. Domi took every hillock and every bluff in stride, maintaining a steady pace under forty miles per hour. She eased off on the accelerator only when she urged the vehicle to climb a particularly high slope. As the angle of ascent steepened, Grant and Brigid had to lean against the boxes of supplies in the back. Rocks were crushed beneath the rolling tracks, and Domi was forced to continually downshift until their speed was little better than a fast walk. The engine and moving parts strained and whined.

Finally the vehicle topped the brow of the slope. They had a panoramic view across the countryside. In the distance, cliffs, outcroppings and hills swelled, but they lacked trees and grass. The Sandcat was approaching the borders of the hellzone, where frequent showers of acid rains and chem storms defoliated the once lush countryside, allowing only the most hardy vegetation to survive.

The needle of the rad counter wavered, edging between yellow and orange. The level of contamination around them was still tolerable, if not exactly safe, at least if they didn't expose themselves to it for very long. He assumed Teague would have taken standard shielding precautions if he intended to drive the Sandcat into a hellzone.

Domi guided the vehicle up and over another bluff and onto fairly level ground once more. She increased the speed to forty miles per hour. After six miles, the rad counter slowly crept over to the orange band. The few trees they saw were leached of all color, a monochromatic shade of gray. It was like looking at the world through the night-vision visor, only not quite as stark. The sun overhead was bright, but the countryside was various shades of gray. A few dead branches crunched under the treads, falling apart like sculptures made of ash.

Ahead of them appeared a collection of improvised shelters made of rotting wood, cloth and canvas. A cluster of a dozen or so raggedy people stood around the structures. When they saw the Sandcat coming, they shuffled this way and that, fanning out to make room for its passage. Domi downshifted, easing off on the accelerator as they passed by. Kane looked at them, and they looked at him. The hairs at the nape of his neck tingled.

He'd seen more than his fair share of Dregs, but even so, he was repulsed by the disfigured faces. The rad count wasn't even midpoint orange, but generations of exposure had thoroughly tainted the people's gene pool. Blood and pus and serum dripped from clusters of boils all over their bodies, their afflicted faces grotesque parodies of a human being's.

As the vehicle rolled past, he noticed that a few of them reacted to his Mag armor, and they called out words in thick, beseeching tones.

"What do they want?" Kane asked. "Food, medicine?"

"No," said Domi. "They see a sec man. They want sec man to chill them." She bared her teeth briefly in a mirthless grin. "They want Mag's mercy."

Half to himself, Kane muttered, "What possible use did Reeth have for them?"

He didn't expect an answer, but Domi provided one. "They expendable. They as good as dead," she said stolidly. "Fewer born every year. Fewer live long enough to have children."

Anger burned redly in her eyes. "Heard term once. 'Planned extinction.' Thanks to fucking villes, thanks to fucking Mags. Thanks to fucking barons."

Domi stopped talking as she upshifted, pressed on the gas pedal and swung the Sandcat down into a dry streambed that twisted and turned among low hills. Everyone was jounced, bounced, tossed and thoroughly pummeled. It occurred to Kane that if the Mags didn't kill them, the escape route might. During the nukecaust, "earthshaker" bombs had not only completely resculpted the Cific coast, but had triggered month-long earthquakes that had shaken thousands of square miles with cataclysmic shocks and tremors.

The wag's suspension creaked and groaned so loudly, Kane was actually glad he still wore his helmet. The polystyrene foam lining helped a little to mute the sounds. The narrow streambed swerved around rock formations, and Grant swore as the vehicle yawed and tossed him against Brigid. Pebbles rattled noisily beneath the rolling treads and chassis.

The path swung up out of the dry arroyo with a lazy serpentine motion, and Domi steered the wag along a narrow trail overlooking a wide, shallow gully. Shouldering the sky in the near distance were the ancient eroded crags surrounding Mesa Verde canyon. Kane started to turn to tell the others in the back, then static hissed thinly in his ear. Ice coursed through his veins.

A faint crackly voice said ''...track...''

Kane tilted his head to the right, trying to focus on the voices filtering through his comm link.

''West by northwest...track...get...fix.''

Pollard's voice. Kane checked his chron. The Deathbirds were nearly half an hour behind schedule.

Chapter 25

"The Birds are just now coming into comm range," Kane warned. "We've got a three-mile lead."

Grant didn't conceal his anger. "Three miles or three hundred, what the hell difference does it make? Once they've fixed our position, they'll catch us in no time flat."

Domi said cheerfully, "Mebbe so, but I can make it hard for them." She yanked the wheel sharply to the right, down into the gully.

The Sandcat nosed up beside the rambling wall of a depression, so close that the far edges of the right tread assembly sheared off rock knobs and projections. Domi narrowly missed colliding with a jutting finger of stone, but she kept rolling the wag beneath overhanging stone shelves, and Kane understood her strategy, even though it was doomed to fail.

Hugging the sides of the gully and keeping under the rock overhangs might temporarily hide them from aerial eyes, but the tactic wouldn't conceal the engine-heat signature from the infrared scanners on the Deathbirds.

Kane didn't tell her that. He kept listening to the commlink transmissions. The hash of static faded with every passing second. A check of his chron and a simple calculation told him that the helicopters would be within visual range very shortly, probably within a minute.

"Point Bird to Bird Two, registering an infratrace. Do you copy?" Pollard's voice was flat, almost bored.

The answering voice sounded young, but very crisp and professional. Probably Zack. "Acknowledged, Point Bird.

Reading the same trace. Vector six-six-zero-niner. Adjusting course and altitude.''

There was more comm chatter, mainly about craft altitude and terrain features. Kane kept listening, kept gazing out of the windshield. It would be close, uncomfortably close, but it was very possible they would reach the mouth of Mesa Verde before a visual fix was acquired. With a prolonged, nerve-stinging screech, the roof of the Sandcat shaved an eighth of an inch from the underside of a rock overhang.

Ahead of them, the gully wall bulged outward several feet, and Domi was forced to swerve to prevent a collision. They were out in the open again, and a moment later, Pollard's triumphant tones crowed into Kane's ear. ''A fix! Got 'em in sight, Bird Two. Just like the wall sentry said, an old all-terrain wag, looks like a roamer junk-trap.''

''Coordinates,'' came Zack's unruffled response.

''Twelve-two-niner-twelve. Copy?''

''Copy, Point Bird. Lock and load.''

Covering his helmet transceiver with a finger, Kane said to Domi, ''Give me your blaster.''

Domi pulled the mini-Uzi from beneath her thigh and handed it to him without so much as a questioning look. Grant demanded, ''What are you going to do?''

Kane kept his finger over the transceiver so the voice-activated carrier frequency wouldn't be picked up by the crew of the Deathbirds. ''Somebody has to make a recce. I'm the only one in armor, so I guess I'm elected.''

Anxiety glinted in Brigid's emerald eyes. ''What if they see you?''

''They've already spotted the Sandcat, so they know I'm on board.''

Reaching up over his head, he undid the latches on the roof hatch. To Domi, he said, ''Try to keep this beast steady.''

''Will try, but no promises.''

The mini-Uzi felt strange in Kane's hand, almost like a

toy. He kept his Sin Eater leathered as he pushed the square
of metal up and over, then he cautiously stood up in the
seat. The fresh air was a relief after the stifling atmosphere
inside. Above the banks of the gully, the sky was a clear,
clean azure, not a cloud anywhere. The noon sun was so
bright, it stung his eyes despite the tinted visor.

He scanned the sky in every direction, having a hard time
keeping his balance as the Sandcat bumped and jumped
along its course. Over the clanking and rattling of the diesel
engine and the treads came another sound. It was a faint
swishing whisper for a handful of seconds, followed by a
violent downdraft that scoured the unprotected part of his
face with an abrasive combination of sand and gravel. His
visor was temporarily clouded by the wind-borne debris,
and he cleared it with a swipe of his left hand.

A Deathbird had made a low, high-speed pass, diving
out of the sun so rapidly and unexpectedly he didn't see it
until the black craft had completed its flyover. In his ear,
Pollard said jovially, "Kane, me old cock of the walk.
Good to see you. I guess Grant and your personal piece of
history are with you."

"You're late, Polly," Kane replied, swiveling his head
to watch the Deathbird perform a figure eight from east to
west. From the east, a dark speck chopped its way through
the sea of limitless blue.

"Better than never. Besides, it couldn't be helped. Took
Salvo a little while to come around and issue orders. He
said you might come back here."

"He give any reason?"

"Guess he figures jolt-brains don't need reasons."

"That what he told you?" Kane asked mildly.

"Among many other things. A jolt-walker is the least of
it."

"What were his orders?"

"Oh, the usual, you know." Pollard sounded cheery.
"Chill your ass, flash-blast you and everybody with you to
cinders. Garden-variety stuff."

The chopper described a wide, high circle above the gully. The second Deathbird fast approached its position.

"Hey, Kane?"

"Yeah?"

"Remember what you said to me just last night? You said, 'We're both heeled, right?' Remember?"

"I remember. It was right after I called you an overstuffed dipshit. But I was just teasing."

"Good. So am I."

Rotors spinning, both Deathbirds dived from the sky, zooming in from the rear. Automatic fire spit from the miniguns in the chin turrets. Twin streams of .50-caliber slugs slashed long trenches on the gully floor, dirt gouting up in high fountains. Kane loosed a short burst with the mini-Uzi just as the choppers ascended, correcting for the decreasing range. One of the bullets twisted the struts of a landing skid out of shape.

The Deathbirds swooped overhead, and he dropped down, back into his seat. A spray of bullets banged loudly on the Sandcat's hull. The choppers roared past, a bare ten feet above the roof of the wag. Domi instinctively ducked as the rotor wash drove a strong puff of grit-laden air down into the wag. Hugging the steering wheel, she threw him a frightened, questioning glance.

"Keep going," he ordered.

He popped back up through the hatch, transferring the mini-Uzi to his left hand and filling his right with the Sin Eater. The choppers climbed several hundred feet and hovered, hanging in the sky, their foreports facing each other, listing slightly from side to side. Kane heard nothing more over the comm link. Pollard had probably blocked the frequency and was communicating with Zack with hand signals.

Kane had known Pollard for years and had never really liked him. He was a simple, brutal, uncompromising man. In Pollard's mind, he made the ideal Magistrate, and more than once he had evinced jealousy of his and Grant's reputations. Therefore, he figured Pollard wouldn't want to end this too quickly. He would make another pass or two with the machine gun, and if that had no effect, he would deploy the rockets. He was no doubt relying on Zack to follow his lead.

The Deathbirds slowly revolved in the sky, then dropped. Kane bent his knees so only his head, shoulders and arms were out of the hatch. The Birds descended quickly, and one leaped ahead of the other. Zack and his gunner were too anxious, too excited. His chopper's rate and angle of descent were a bit too sharp, his airspeed a bit too high. Pollard's craft fell behind.

Zack's gunner opened fire before the proper range and trajectory were established. The stream of bullets flayed rock and soil, but none came within twenty yards of the onrushing Sandcat.

Kane fixed the foreport of the Deathbird in the sights of both of his blasters, held his breath and pressed the triggers. The two streams of subsonic rounds ripped across the gully at 375 meters per second. Spent shell casings fell down the hatchway, bounced across the hull. Over his helmet comm link, he heard a garbled, screaming voice.

The Deathbird met the double streams of steel-jacketed lead halfway. A series of starred holes appeared in the curving port, and the craft lurched as Zack tried to bank. A few bullets from the chin turret skimmed the Sandcat's hull, gouging shiny smears in the armor. Kane felt their impacts, but he didn't relax his fingers on the triggers. The chopper heeled to starboard and struggled to rise out of range of the blasterfire.

The whirling blades sliced into the bank of the gully, digging out pounds of rock and dirt in dust-filled eruptions. Sparks showered as steel struck stone, and the main rotors snapped with a painfully high-pitched, musical chime.

In a lurching sideslip, the Deathbird flung itself away from the bank, and its blades pinwheeled across the gully, chopping into and embedding in the soil. The main rotor assembly continued to spin with broken, jagged stems. The craft cannonaded port first against the gully floor.

A roaring ball of red-yellow flame mushroomed up from the ruptured fuel tank. Kane recoiled as the wall of hot air, pushed forward by the thundering explosion, slapped his face.

"Oops," he said mildly.

The Deathbird piloted by Pollard veered away, banking sharply, climbing above the cloud of black smoke and the column of fire. His enraged voice crashed over Kane's comm link: "Another pair of Mags for you! You traitor! They're the last ones! You hear? The *last ones!*"

The Deathbird dropped straight down, catching itself only a few feet above the gully, as if its plummet had been checked by an invisible string. It plunged forward in a roaring rush. A rocket burst from the port stub wing and soared, flaming, directly toward the Sandcat. It skidded past its right side and exploded a dozen yards ahead. Metal and rock fragments smashed into the vehicle's frontal armor, and smaller pieces put new cracks in the windshield. A lump of stone bounced off the back of Kane's helmet, jarring him off his feet. He fell clumsily into his seat. Terrified, Brigid asked him if he was all right. He waved her off with a gesture and shouted to Domi, "Evasive!"

She swung the wheel from left to right, swerving back and forth. The heavy machine responded sluggishly, wallowing laboriously. He knew it was already too late for such maneuvers to be effective.

The Sandcat shook with a bone-numbing shock as a missile detonated almost directly beneath it. The rear end jumped some three feet, and slewed around in a one-eighty at thirty miles per hour, all direction and control gone. The right back fender smashed broadside against the gully bank.

Kane had braced himself so the sudden jolting stop didn't fling him into the instrument panel or through the windshield. Before his stunned eardrums recovered from the concussion, he heard the jack-hammer clanging of treads shearing away from the rollers, the entire left track thrashing in a long flapping strip. Sparks showered and metal screamed as the roller rims slashed deep furrows into the rocky ground.

The air inside the wag grew stifling hot as the incendiary compounds of the warhead interacted with the armor. Smoke and the cloying smell of metal turning molten filled the cramped interior. Grant coughed rackingly, pushing Brigid ahead of him. "We've got to bail!"

The driver's door was jammed shut inside its warped frame. Kane shouldered the passenger door open and dragged Domi across the seats, then helped Grant and Brigid to climb out. From the undercarriage and from every seam of the Sandcat boiled a mixture of white, gray and black smoke. Blobs of burning napalm jelly clung to the armor, sending up spirals of flame.

Their backs against the gully wall, the four people crept away from the smoke-spewing Sandcat, all of them craning their necks, scanning the sky. The black chopper was nowhere in sight.

Her voice raspy from inhaling smoke, Brigid asked, "How far are we from this canyon?"

Domi jerked a thumb up over her head. "Up and over that way. We're there already."

"So is Pollard," Kane muttered.

"Maybe he thinks we're dead," Grant added, not sounding as though he believed it.

"Salvo ordered him to make sure we were flash-blasted," Kane replied. "So he'll make sure."

"Hell, at least we'll be right on course when he burns us down," Grant said. Though he wasn't limping, his right leg was stiff. "Let's get on with this."

Under the cover of the pall of smoke, scaling the side of the gully was fairly easy, the work of only a couple of minutes. But Kane noticed fresh blood seeping through the bandage around Grant's thigh when he climbed the slope.

Sheer walls rose to nearly a hundred feet on either side,

grooved with deep horizontal lines, here and there forming ledges where the softer layers of strata had eroded away.

The canyon floor was less than two hundred feet wide in some places, and it wended off to the right. Boulders and outcroppings were strewed all around, except for an unnaturally flat clearing a score of yards ahead of them. From it protruded the split-open stump of the Vulcan-Phalanx gun housing.

They moved toward it quickly and all of them heard the high-pitched whine from the sky. No one looked up; they just started running for a house-size rock formation. Domi, loping easily and gracefully, took Grant's arm to help him along. He shook her loose angrily.

"I don't need help!"

"Suit self." Her long white legs pumped, and she pulled ahead.

The four of them dived behind the outcropping just as three missiles impacted all around it. The explosions were deafening, and dust, smoke and chips of stone blew over them.

The Deathbird screamed on by overhead, lifting above the canyon rim, already starting to curve around for another strafing pass. They watched as it turned its nose downward and dipped into a sharp dive. Two missiles burst from the port and starboard stub wings.

They had managed to scramble around to the other side of the rock formation just as it took a direct hit. The double impact knocked pieces out of it, seemingly heaved it momentarily out of the ground, as though it were about to topple from its moorings. Fragments pattered all around them, and the concussion slammed all of them off their feet. They picked themselves up just as the sleek black craft screamed on past.

"Screw this," mumbled Grant, brushing powdery dust from his coat.

"I concur," said Brigid. A small spot of blood showed

high on her forehead where a sliver of missile casing or stone had nicked her. "I vote we run until we can't."

No one argued, and they raced through the canyon, bounding over tumbles of rock, dashing past the remains of the gun tower. Kane brought up the rear. Domi was far ahead, Brigid trailing her by only a few yards. Grant ran in a stiff-legged gait, grimacing with every step.

They were barely a score of yards past the Vulcan-Phalanx housing when Kane, glancing upward again, saw the chopper break off its circling and come plunging down toward them.

Yelling a warning, he skipped into a fissure in the canyon wall. He raised his Sin Eater and let loose with a 3-round burst, but not before the gunner loosed a missile. It struck very close to him. The explosion filled the canyon with rolling, thunderous echoes. A sheet of flame erupted, and shrapnel and rock fragments clattered against his arms and legs, rebounding from the armor.

Peering through the thick smoke, Kane couldn't see the others. Turning his head, he saw the Deathbird climb skyward, trying to keep to the center of the canyon to avoid the irregularities in the walls. A notion occurred to him, and he immediately acted on it, not giving himself the chance to think it through.

Before the breeze had cleared the smoke, Kane scrambled out of the fissure and lay down on the ground, very close to the smoldering crater. He carefully arranged his limbs, lying as he had seen corpses lie, arms and legs bent unnaturally and stiffly, head slightly to one side.

So far, it appeared as if the gunner was primarily targeting him, which made sense for a couple of reasons. First, Pollard hated him. Second, he seemed to be the only member of the party who was armed. Finally, his black armor made him stand out, not only among his comrades but against the buff-colored surroundings.

As he lay there on his right side, he heard feet pounding

on the ground, and Grant kneeled over him, grabbing at his shoulders. His face glistened with sweat.

"Kane—"

"Just get away from me," he hissed. "Pretend I'm dead, then work your way toward the ruins. Act upset."

Grant's face twisted in annoyance, but his tone was relieved. "If I found you dead, I'd *skip* my way toward the ruins."

Then he was up and gone, running back the way he had come. The wind thinned the veil of smoke, and Kane watched the Deathbird hover a hundred or so feet overhead, just above the uppermost canyon ramparts. It dropped slowly, below the rim, swinging out carefully. Pollard was very cautious, not just because he was checking out Kane's demise, but because of the unpredictable geothermals present in the canyon.

The chopper continued to descend. He imagined Pollard gazing down at his motionless body with the hope that he'd made the kill but knowing he had to make sure before he continued the pursuit. Slowly the Deathbird moved forward, at an altitude of thirty feet, airspeed at bare minimum.

Kane waited, made himself hold off, even after every cell in his body demanded action. Then he gathered himself, coiling his body like a spring. With all the speed his years of training and honed reflexes had given him, he sprang into a squat, then to a crouch. The Sin Eater roared with a prolonged burst.

Pollard reacted almost instantaneously, pulling back on the yoke for a fast, frantic ascent, but Plexiglass pieces of the cockpit canopy flying away in flinders showed he absorbed some damage. As the chopper gained altitude, it revolved, turning the port away from the bullets. Kane kept on blasting, and flame flared from the tail boom as an exhaust cowl was smashed away.

The overstressed engine whined, missed and cut out altogether. The Deathbird's sudden rise halted, as though it had bumped into a transparent roof over the canyon. Listing from side to side, it sank from view behind the ramparts. Kane waited for the sound of the crash.

When, after a few seconds, it still hadn't come, he bit back a curse, turned and ran up the canyon to rejoin his companions. They didn't have much farther to go, but they still had a lot to do.

Chapter 26

Kane and Grant led the two women on a circuitous route through the Cliff Palace ruins. Brigid kept slowing to examine the shapes of the doorways, the layouts of the kivas.

"Starborn, that's what the Anasazi tribe who built this place called themselves," she remarked, apropos of nothing. "They disappeared without a trace nearly eight hundred years ago."

Partly because of the stabbing pain in his leg, partly because he was exhausted and stressed out, Grant whirled on her, raging, "This isn't a field trip! Pollard and his gunman could be right behind us!"

"So what?" she demanded. "Don't we outnumber them?"

"We don't outgun them! They've got Sin Eaters and Copperheads, both with full loads. Compared to that firepower, we've got shit!"

Brigid glowered at him, but she didn't pause to examine anything more.

They reached the bottom of the palace itself, and Kane nimbly scaled the stone niches, waited for the others to climb up through the embrasure, then moved to the stairwell cut into the cliffside. It was very dark, and Grant put on his treated glasses, pulling his flashlight from a pocket, as well. Kane's image-enhancer sensor lit his way adequately, if not satisfactorily.

The metal door was open, and he pushed through it into the tunnel. The neon light strips stretching along the ceiling were dark. As he had only two nights before, Kane stalked along the tunnel. He went just a few feet before he stopped, listening and sniffing. He heard something but didn't smell anything. By all rights, he shouldn't have heard anything and should have smelled something very unpleasant. The tunnel should have been redolent with the stench of decomposing bodies. As a general rule, Magistrates didn't clean up after themselves, so somebody must have removed the bodies.

The sound he heard was very faint and innocuous, like papers ruffling. Turning, he used hand signals to inform the others to hang back. Kane walked down the tunnel on the balls of his feet. When the passageway opened onto the scaffold assembly, he dropped flat and belly-crawled forward. The bruises made by Salvo's bullets twinged. His elbows and knees made near inaudible scrapes against the wood.

He peered down into the square room below. At first the light-intensifying polymer of his visor showed him nothing but bullet-riddled equipment and boxes. The corpses of Reeth and his crew, including his stickie strong-arm, were nowhere in view. Then a figure shifted in the shadows, at the extreme limit of his helmet's image enhancer.

The figure was slight of build and very slim. Above the narrow shoulders rose a smooth, domed cranium, jet black and bald. The skull tapered down to a sharp chin, so the impression of the head was of an inverted teardrop.

The eyes were protuberant, completely round like an insect's, and between the large eyes was a pair of insectlike antennae spread in a "V." Kane caught his breath as the figure moved closer, deeper into the range of his enhancer. He got a better look at it.

After the first striking impression, Kane realized that the figure was wearing a black skullcap. Attached to it were night-vision goggles, a slightly modified version of the Mag-issue glasses. The antennae were a pair of infrared projectors.

Still, there was something about the figure's movements, something a bit too mannered, too sharp, too graceful. It was wearing a tight bodysuit that looked as though it was made of gray foil. Because he saw no secondary feminine characteristics, he assumed the figure was male, although it could as easily have no particular sex at all. A plastic tube-shaped holster was strapped to his right thigh.

Kane watched the man examine sheaves of paper resting in an open crate, then drop them with a gesture that almost seemed like disgust. The pale hands were long, slender, with very delicate fingers.

As he gazed down, he realized the figure's danceresque movements and general body shape were somewhat familiar. A chill went through him. They reminded him of Baron Cobalt's. For an instant, he wondered insanely if the man below was indeed the baron, but he dismissed the notion immediately. The baron was slightly taller, a bit shorter in the leg.

A scutter and scuffle of fast-moving feet echoed up from the tunnel. When the man heard it, he gave a great leap back, his huge, goggled eyes staring upward. Then he whirled and darted toward the dark doorway. His fleetness of foot was astonishing.

Kane swore, swinging his body over the edge of the scaffold, hanging on to the planks and pipes. Grant, Domi and Brigid rushed up. Breathlessly Grant said, "Pollard's on his way up."

"Follow me." Kane dropped down from the makeshift platform into the room. He stumbled when he landed, but he recovered his footing quickly and sprinted for the doorway on the far side of the room. Behind him, he heard his companions thumping down the staircase made of two-by-fours. Then Domi's voice rose in a short, shrill cry.

Kane heeled to a halt, turning to see her careen down the steps. Because of the wavering light of Grant's flashlight, the girl had made a misstep. Kane ran toward her, but before he reached her, she levered herself into a sitting position, probing at her rib cage.

Brigid stooped over her. "She's all right," she said tightly. "May've ruptured some intercostal cartilage."

"Get her up," Kane snapped, spinning around and running again. As soon as he entered the corridor, turning right at the T, he caught the whiff of death. The wooden door to the holding cell was ajar, and as he drew up to it he glanced in. All the bodies of the Dregs were riddled with circular punctures, obviously the result of automatic fire. Though flies had not gotten to them yet, putrefaction was well under way. He shoved the door shut, still in motion. He didn't waste time trying to reason out why these bodies had been left but the others removed.

From the end of the corridor, he heard a sound, like the distant howling of a gale-force wind, overlaid with the faintest of mechanical hums. He caught a flash of silvery light and he increased his pace.

The gateway chamber door was sealed, but he grasped the metal handle, turned and pulled. A tingling discharge of static electricity rushed through him, from the top of his head to the tips of his toes. He heard his hair bristling against the lining of his helmet.

The six-sided chamber was empty except for the vaguest curling wisp of white mist. The metal hexagons on the floor and ceiling shimmered faintly, a shimmer that faded away even as he looked at it.

He was still looking at it when the others caught up to him. He didn't have to say anything. Brigid made a wordless utterance of surprise and wonder, then grabbed the flashlight from Grant and played the beam over the armaglass exterior and the interior.

"Why'd you take off like that?" Grant demanded.

"Someone was in here."

"Who?"

"Maybe more like a what. He was wearing a night-vision headset and going through Reeth's hard-copy records. I chased him into here."

Grant looked around suspiciously. "Where is he, then?"

Kane gestured to the chamber. "He ran in there, transported himself somewhere else."

"You can't be sure of that."

"This thing was winding down when I got here," Kane declared. "Where else could he have gone?"

Brigid studied the keypad affixed to the armaglass next to the door. "This is pretty much like the schematic I saw. I think we can activate it."

"There's no power in here," said Grant. "Salvo shot up the generator."

"It has an independent power source, a nuke engine below it."

"We get in it, and it takes us away?" Domi asked skeptically.

"No!" Grant's tone was harsh. "We're not getting in that thing. We don't know for sure what it is."

Down the corridor, stealthy footfalls echoed.

"Pollard and his gunner," murmured Kane, and edged past Brigid into the passageway. He took position at the T junction. He waited as the steps got louder.

Then Pollard called out. "You're trapped, all of you. It's time to die, and it's time for you to accept the inevitable. You've got no food, no water. You'll perish anyway, but it'll be a long and lingering and painful passing. I promise to make it quick. The choice is yours."

"Have we tired you out?" Kane called. "We haven't accepted anything as inevitable except your next fuckup."

Pollard's reply was the characteristic *dut-dut-dut* of a Copperhead slamming dully down the corridor. Kane pulled back as a storm of slugs chiseled chips out of the angle of the junction.

He returned the fire with the Sin Eater, ricochets screeching and striking sparks from the metal girders and stonework. Grant shouldered up beside him, and for a long minute they exchanged fire with the two Mags at the end of the passageway.

"I don't care for our options," Grant said tightly.

"They're better armed and have more ammo, and more Mags are probably on their way."

"Unless you want to accept the inevitable, then you better reevaluate your fear of the gateway."

"I'm not afraid of it!" replied Grant vehemently. Then he shrugged and added, "I just don't like the whole idea."

The firing tapered off to a sporadic crackle. Kane signaled for Grant to stay while he returned to the mat-trans unit. Brigid had the flashlight on the keypad, and her fingers hovered tentatively over the buttons.

She said, "According to what I read, a fallback program can be accessed by this button." She pointed to a square key at the bottom of the pad. It glowed with two letters: "LD."

"What's it mean?"

"Last Destination. If pressed within five minutes of a successful jump, it'll reactivate the gateway and transport us to the last reception point."

Kane replied uneasily, "I don't know that's such a good strategy. We might end up in the baron's harem or something."

Brigid nodded distractedly. "Five minutes have passed anyway. I'll punch in the codes as I remember them. There were three in New Mexico alone."

Lips moving as she extracted the numbers from her memory, she tapped in a sequence of keys. A glass-fronted liquid-crystal display at the top of the pad flashed the word "Inactive."

She made a sound of dismay. "I was afraid of that. If the receiving units aren't powered up, we can't achieve a destination lock. Or maybe there is a security lockout to prevent what we're attempting—unauthorized transmission—and if that's the case, none of us are going anywhere."

"Try another code."

She did, and again "Inactive" glowed on the display. The process was too stressful for Kane to simply stand and watch, and he sensed he wasn't helping by anxiously hovering over her. He left her to rejoin Grant at the junction.

There came another flurry of cracks from the Copperheads. The bullets hammered ineffectually against the walls. Grant fired a single shot, and then a triburst, but Pollard and his gunner were safely out of range in the adjacent room.

"What's going on back there?" Grant whispered.

"She's working on it."

Kane went to one knee, bracing the Sin Eater on his left forearm. He took careful aim. He waited until he saw the snout of a Copperhead ease into the passageway and he pressed the trigger once.

His blaster roared, and a spark flew from the barrel of the Copperhead. There was a sharp clang, followed by a cry of pain and astonishment. The Copperhead, torn from Pollard's grasp, clattered end over end across the stone floor.

"You son of a bitch!" Pollard yelled, his voice thick with hatred, wild with fury. "You're dead, Kane! *Dead!*"

"Now we're not quite as outgunned," Kane murmured, straightening up.

Pollard cursed in a frenzy, and they heard his companion's murmured rejoinders for him to calm down. Kane chuckled, but Grant didn't find it very funny.

"That did it," he said dolefully. "You pissed him off so bad, they'll make a suicide charge. Since you're the only one in armor, you might last thirty seconds longer than the rest of us."

Brigid called out, "Hey! I've got something!"

They left the junction and went to the unit. The first thing Kane saw was the light from the readout display flashing "Active." He wasn't sure if he was relieved or not. "Where is it?"

"A place coded as Redoubt Bravo, somewhere in Montana. It was the fourth one listed in the records, and the fourth one I tried. We've got a transit line now."

Grant, Kane and Domi eyed the armaglass chamber hesitantly. Now that the possibility of matter transmission was no longer an abstract concept, Kane found his enthusiasm ebbing. He covered his uncertainty by consulting his wrist chron.

"Well?" asked Brigid impatiently.

"How does this work exactly?" Grant asked.

"I don't know," she said irritably. "I don't know if it works at all. According to the *Wyeth Codex,* the principle is based on hyperdimensional physics, phasing transport subjects from the relativistic here, through a quantum path, to arrive at a relativistic *there.*"

"That's not what I meant," replied Grant gruffly.

"Oh. Well, when you shut the door, the jump mechanism is automatically triggered, and *pfft!* you're on your way. To someplace."

Domi fingered her ribs. "Will it hurt?"

"The *Wyeth Codex* indicated there were occasional side effects, what she referred to as 'jump sickness.' Nothing too unpleasant."

"Assuming we get in there," Kane said, "what's to keep Pollard from just opening the door and blasting us while we're penned up?"

Brigid rapped the keypad with a crooked finger. "Simple. Before we shut the door, I'll enter a security-lock code, 108J. They can't get in until after we've transported unless they know the unlocking code."

Grant shifted his weight from foot to foot. "But can we get out?"

"Yes, we can get out," snapped Brigid in exasperation. "You wanted me to find an active-destination unit. I did. Now, are we going to stand around and discuss it some more or are we going to get jumping?"

Kane opened his mouth to voice an objection to her tone, then shut it again as swift, rattling roars came from the passageway. The sudden crash of noise was stunning. Bullets howled down the corridor, and fragments of splintered rock whined into the junction. Ricochets twanged like plucked guitar strings. Sparks blazed from the metal girders. Behind it all was the steady hammering of three blasters on full-auto. Howling like blood-mad berserkers, Pollard and his gunner charged down the corridor, weapons blazing.

Kane, Grant and Domi lunged into the chamber. Slugs splattered against the armaglass walls, flattening into gray blobs. Brigid frantically punched in the lock code, then she dived inside, trying to pull the heavy door shut by its inner handle. Grant gave her a hand. The door closed with a frighteningly final *chock*.

Immediately the hexagonal disks in the floor and ceiling exuded a glow, and a low, almost subsonic hum began, quickly rising in pitch to a whine. The noise changed, sounding like the distant howling of a cyclone.

Outside the room, they heard Pollard shouting in angry confusion, and the guns continued to blast. The bullets bounced off the armaglass.

The glow brightened. A mist, shot through with tiny flashing sparks, formed below the ceiling disks and rose from the floor. The mist thickened to a fog and swirled down and up to engulf them. Brigid moved toward Kane, and he put an arm around her. She tried a jittery, reassuring smile on him. Across the chamber, Grant had enfolded Domi in his arms. His face was an expressionless ebony mask.

Kane closed his eyes, and eternity hit him in the face.

Chapter 27

The universe exploded in a blaze of unidentifiable colors and images. Kane had the sensation of falling forever into a bottomless abyss. A nightmare vision of distorted space, of tangled geometrical shapes so crazed and complex, it was impossible for his mind to absorb them.

A never-ending stream of brilliant spheres passed by him. He retained a measure of consciousness, and for some reason he knew each sphere was a separate universe, a separate reality. Universes upon universes, realities upon realities bobbing in the cosmic quantum stream like bubbles. He hurtled between them, following a complicated, twisting, curving course, yet at the same time it seemed as if he were flying in a straight line.

He had felt frightened and trapped before, but never had he felt so crushed and helpless and impotent as now, and his mind recoiled from the effort to comprehend this welter of insanity, this streaming rush of extradimensional space. He knew he was hurtling headlong into a cluster of madness. One of the bright spheres loomed up ahead of him, and he tried to swerve away from it, around it—

Kane opened his eyes.

He struggled against dizziness and nausea, and his vision was clouded. A pain throbbed in his temples, like his hangover after his wine binge. His stomach quivered. Slowly his vision cleared, and he found himself slumped in a half-prone position against a wall. Below and above him, the glow faded from the hexagonal metal disks. He heard a moan.

Kane pushed himself up, looking around, seeing his companions stirring dazedly on the floor. Next to him, Brigid raked her hair out of her eyes, staring around unfocusedly. He asked, "You feel all right?"

She opened her mouth as if to answer, then bowed her head and dry-heaved violently for a moment. Nothing was ejected except a few strings of bile-laced saliva. Kane would have felt more sympathy for her if he himself felt better and if, at the moment, he didn't hold her irrationally responsible for his physical condition. Then, dragging in a harsh breath, she said, "I feel awful."

Grant said a little hoarsely, "Didn't work, did it? Still in the same place."

Domi knuckled her eyes, climbing to her knees. "No. Color is different. See?"

Kane hoisted himself unsteadily to his feet, putting a hand on the armaglass wall. It was tinted brown, not the silvery smoky hue of the walls in Mesa Verde. "Good God," he muttered. "We made it. We're someplace else."

Awe fell upon the people, mingled with incredulity. There was a spell of silence that Grant broke.

"You mean we've been transported—to where?" His tone was hushed.

Brigid got to her feet. It was obvious she was struggling against her own feeling of unreality. "Montana was the destination lock. Redoubt Bravo. We traveled through fourth-dimensional space on a carrier wave, shortcutting the other three."

Kane consulted his chron. It still worked, but showed that barely a minute had elapsed since he had last checked it. That didn't seem reasonable, but he didn't feel up to arguing about temporal anomalies. He moved to the door handle. "Let's see where we are."

The handle moved up easily, and the solenoid clicked open. Blaster in hand, he toed the door open and slowly eased out into an small anteroom. It was bare and unfurnished, holding only a polished table. On the other side of the table was a door. As his companions joined him, Kane examined the gateway chamber. It was a duplicate of the one they had entered, except for the color of the armaglass. The only other difference was a notice imprinted on the chamber wall, right above the keypad panel. In faded, maroon lettering, it read Entry Absolutely Forbidden To All But B12 Cleared Personnel. Mat-Trans.

Grant, Domi and Brigid followed Kane through the anteroom to the door. It was unlocked and he turned the knob, stepping through it into a room that stopped him in his tracks. It made the Intel section of the Magistrate Division look like a part-time hobbyist's cellar.

The room was long, with high, vaulted ceilings. Consoles of dials, switches, buttons and lights flickering red, green and amber ran the length of the walls. Circuits hummed, needles twitched and monitor screens displayed changing columns of numbers.

"How can everything still work?" Grant demanded, shifting the muzzle of his blaster to cover every corner, including the computer terminals.

"Nuclear engines," replied Brigid. "Atomic power is nearly eternal."

She examined several of the machines, finding they responded to experimental touches of the keys. "Fully functional. No dust, either. Surely this place hasn't been sealed since the nukecaust."

"Doesn't seem likely," Kane remarked. He met Brigid's suddenly frightened gaze and nodded toward the far wall. There was no door, but a man-size cavity was punched through it. "Let's see what's out there."

No debris lay around the base of the wall. Although the jagged edges of the hole had been worn and ground down in the past, old scorch marks indicated that the cavity had been made with high explosive, probably a long time ago.

As always, Kane took the point, his companions following closely behind. As he clambered through the cavity, he tripped a photoelectric beam, and overhead lights flashed to yellow life. Before them stretched a long tunnel. It was made of softly gleaming metal and shaped like a square with an arch on top. It was at least twenty feet across. Great curving ribs of metal and massive girders supported the high rock roof.

Brigid bent over and touched the floor. "Vanadium alloy, like the sec doors in the Enclaves and the monolith."

They moved forward, their footfalls making ghostly echoes so that their ears were confused. Grant stopped and turned twice, under the impression they were being followed. Even with the echoes, the silence was brooding and sepulchral.

They followed Kane for two hundred feet, then the tunnel reached a T. After a moment's consideration, Kane led them to the right. The corridor narrowed, and the walls here were lined on either side with doors. It was a temptation to open them as they passed by, but it was more important to find an exit. Nobody spoke as they walked. Ahead, the passageway seemed to debouch into a dimly lit space. Kane realized he was having trouble walking in a straight line. He was almost ill from fatigue and lack of sleep.

Kane slowed his pace, finger on the Sin Eater's trigger, aware he had maybe six rounds in the magazine. The tunnel abruptly ended against a massive sec door, obviously made of vanadium alloy. Connected to the frame at shoulder level was a small square panel, covered with a padlocked lid.

Just inside the door, emblazoned on one wall was a large, luridly colored image of a froth-mouthed black hound. Three stylized heads grew out of a single, exaggeratedly muscled neck, their jaws spewing flame and blood between great fangs. Underneath the image, rendered in ornate Gothic script was the word Cerberus.

Domi read the sign aloud, stumbling over the pronunciation. "Don't get it."

In a low whisper, Brigid announced, "Cerberus, the guardian of the gateway to Hades. Also the code name for the project devoted to the Quantum Interphase Mat-Trans Inducer experiments. This redoubt was the headquarters for

Project Cerberus. A major component of the Totality Concept itself.''

Kane repressed a shudder. The oppressive atmosphere of the redoubt was insidious. "Let's try to get that door open."

The voice speaking from behind them was pleasant. "But you've only just arrived."

Before the echoes of the first word faded in the passage, both Grant and Kane spun around, blaster barrels lifting, fingers crooked over triggers. Kane and Brigid recognized the erect but insubstantial-looking man standing in the vague light, but they were too stunned to speak his name.

Lakesh held out his hands, palms upward, in a gesture of welcome and to show he was unarmed. "Kane, you and Brigid gave us a rather difficult time." His tone was gently reproving. "You moved too fast for us to implement our removal plan."

His bespectacled eyes flicked appreciatively over Domi's form. "Nor did we make allowances for a fourth member of your party."

Harshly Grant demanded, "Who is this old crock?"

"A senior archivist," answered Brigid in a high, thin voice.

"And a member of the Trust," Kane added, his voice grim and cold.

"And Brigid's Preservationist contact," put in Lakesh. "Not to mention one of the original architects of the Totality Concept. Welcome to Redoubt Bravo. Welcome to Cerberus."

His eyes behind the thick lenses sparkled. "Welcome to your exile. We may as well begin the indoctrination."

He took a sideways step, and a half-dozen figures in white bodysuits emerged from the mouth of the corridor. They held pristine-condition SA80 subguns across their chests. The three men and three women were different as to skin color, height and build, but they were all sleek, fast and very efficient. They immediately took up position in a half circle facing the four people. They didn't level their blasters, but they handled them so deftly, Kane knew they were experts in their use.

"You will turn over your weapons," Lakesh said, "and accompany them to decam. Afterward, we will talk."

Brigid swept her green eyes over the six armed people. "Will we be allowed to leave?"

Lakesh gave her a sad, cryptic smile. "Of course, Brigid. But you have nothing to leave for and no place to go. I, unfortunately, contributed to that."

Grant and Kane exchanged a brief glance, then both of them handed over their side arms. Kane unsnapped his helmet's jaw guard and tugged it off of his head with an audible sigh of relief. Brigid glanced at him, did a double take and said in an undertone, "You look terrible."

"Good. First article of the Magistrate's oath. Mind and body should always be in sync."

Three of the people in white flanked them, and the other three closed up behind them. They walked back into the corridor and turned into the first door on the right. It opened up onto a wide, white-tiled shower room. Each stall was enclosed by shoulder-high partitions. Rad-counter gauges were affixed to the walls beneath the shower heads.

"Undress in there," one of the women said. She was stocky of build, her skin a deep bronze, her eyes dark brown, her ash blond hair braided at the back of her head. "Your clothing will have to be decontaminated, too."

Kane stepped into the cubicle, and the rad sensor read him. Though the needle stayed in the orange area, it wavered dangerously close to red. He shed his armor, piling it beneath the showerhead. A mixture of warm liquid disinfectant and cleansing fluid sprayed from the nozzle. He worked the decam stream into a lather and massaged it into his scalp and all over his body. He kept one eye on the rad counter. When the needle leaned over into the yellow zone, a jet of cold, clear water gushed down and rinsed him off.

After he stepped out of the stall, he felt much better. A

man handed him a white bodysuit, and he pulled it on. It fit well, except for the boot socks, which were a tad too small.

Grant's bullet wound was rebandaged and Domi's ribs bound after she was diagnosed as having a cracked third rib. When everyone was similarly showered and attired, they were escorted back into the corridor, then into a room near the T-junction. Lakesh sat waiting behind a desk in a small, sparsely furnished office. Besides the desk and four chairs, the only other piece of furniture was a small computer console.

He waved them to the chairs, then extended a hand, offering Grant and Kane a pair of slim cigars. They looked at them suspiciously.

"Tobacco cleanses the heart and calms the spirit, or so the Native Americans believe," Lakesh said. "Besides, I understand you two have developed a fondness for cigars. They're real, not that homegrown domestic stuff you get in Tartarus."

Kane and Grant took them and the big lighter Lakesh handed over. After they had set the cigars alight and sent gray wreaths curling ceilingward, Lakesh said, "I wish I could indulge myself, but at my age and condition, it's tempting fate. I'm on my second set of lungs as it is."

Brigid's hand, poised to fan smoke away from her face, halted in midmotion. "Sir?"

Lakesh interlaced his fingers on the desktop. "I have a great deal to tell you now that you're outlanders. Does it bother you that I employ that term?"

"No," stated Domi, matter-of-factly.

Lakesh smiled. "The mat-trans unit in this facility is the only one with no transit-feed connection to the others. Its jump lines are untraceable. This is a forgotten redoubt, considered long inactive by the barons and the Directorate. No one will ever find you."

"Is that an assurance," Brigid inquired, "or a threat?"

"Neither. It's simply the truth. Neither you, Kane nor

Grant can ever again appear as yourselves in the villes. Your former lives no longer exist. I am hoping you will find a place for yourselves here.''

Kane tapped ash onto the floor, affecting not to notice Lakesh's raised eyebrow. ''Where is 'here'? Is this the secret headquarters of the Preservationists?''

''Yes and no. The Preservationists as an organization does not exist. It's a convenient categorization applied to anyone who opposes the barons and the Directorate. Essentially it's a front, a diversion to conceal the real work that goes on here.''

''Real work?'' Grant echoed.

''I represent, and belong to, the underground resistance who oppose the agenda to make humans an endangered species. I saw that you were worthy, Brigid, of contributing to that work. If Kane hadn't involved you in his own personal crusade, you would have been brought here eventually. I fed you bits and pieces of information over the past year to see what you would do with them. A test, so to speak, and you passed. Your case was already decided. You arrived here by a different method than I envisioned, but you're here where you belong, nevertheless.''

His gaze shifted to Kane. ''Your case was already decided, too. However, the role you were selected to play was written to be very different. I had no idea you would break your conditioning so quickly, motivated by purely emotional impulses. You flew completely in the face of all my extrapolations. In fact, your actions may bring about an alternate event horizon, and I cannot describe how deeply that possibility intrigues me.''

Exhaling twin jets of smoke from his nostrils, Grant said, ''I cannot describe how deeply you are irritating me. All right, you say you know about us. Who the flash-blasted hell are *you*?''

''My full name is Mohandas Lakesh Singh. I was born in Kashmir, in the nation once known as India. Due to my extraordinarily high IQ, I came to America on a scholarship at age sixteen. When I was nineteen, I received my doctorate in cybernetics and quantum mechanics from the Massachusetts Institute of Technology. I worked as a consultant for NASA for a year before being wooed away by a government-contract electronics company. I found myself working at a military base in Dulce, New Mexico."

Kane made a spitting sound, as though trying to rid his lip of a shred of tobacco. It sounded disdainful. "You're old, but you're not that old."

The corners of Lakesh's eyes crinkled. "I was born in 1952, so yes, I *am* that old if you consider nearly two and a half centuries to be old. Of course, a century of that span was spent in cryonic stasis."

Dead silence fell over the office. Kane stared speechless, first at him, then one by one at his companions. Swiftly he stood up.

"Thank you for the shower and the smoke," he said crisply. "If you'll return our property, I think we'll be on our way."

The mild humor vanished from Lakesh's voice, and it rose in a reedy rasp. "Sit *down*, Kane! You have no 'way' to be on! Do you think you can leave this place, this room, unless I allow it?"

The old man's lips worked, and he drew in a breath. "You're so much like your father, and your grandfather. Brave and talented, but overconfident, reckless fools, and it takes so very little to knock your equilibrium out from under you. A few new concepts, new ideas, and you're reeling around in shock. Don't you understand that what you learned from the baron is but the merest tip of a vast iceberg?" He pointed a bony finger at him.

"You know just enough to get yourself and these others killed. The hidden mass of the iceberg is so huge, so thick, it stretches back many thousands of years. You can barely comprehend the events of the last two days, and you think you can strap on your gun, swagger out of here and blast your way to the truth? Rein in your inbred Magistrate's arrogance. You've smashed your brains out against the iceberg, but you're too ignorant to know it. You're treading black water, waiting to drown. And you'll sink straight to the bottom, straight to a fool's hell, an exile's hell, never knowing the *whyness* of it.''

As Lakesh spoke, Kane's expression grew remote, then his face was twisted into something dark and implacable. Tendons and veins stood out on his neck. His eyes blazed, and the atmosphere in the office grew electric with tension. His right hand tensed reflexively, the finger crooking to receive the trigger of a Sin Eater that was no longer there.

Brigid came to her feet, holding out a restraining hand toward him. "Kane, listen and wait."

He flung her hand away, not averting his icy gray blue gaze from the old man.

She cried out, "Don't waste that strength now! We'll need that energy, that anger yet—when we have to fight for our lives. Give him a chance and hear him out at least."

He slowly turned his eyes to hers, glaring at her, lips drawn back from clenched teeth. His left arm came up, fist knotted. Brigid stared back, no fear in her eyes or stance.

Then the furious fires in his eyes faded. He dropped his fist. Gutturally he said, "I've been threatened one too many times today."

"He wasn't threatening you." She gently touched his face as though to test that he wouldn't explode. "Unless it's the truth that threatens you."

"Truth," he repeated, his voice hollow. "Everybody I've run into lately claims to have a monopoly on it, yet it's always different. Nobody can back up anything with proof. Archons, the Trust, the Totality Concept. Truth, my ass. It's nothing but a bunch of fiction or self-serving lies that I'm supposed to buy into."

Lakesh, unperturbed by his near brush with violent death, remarked, "A predark Russian novelist, Solzhenitsyn by name, wrote, 'The simple step of a courageous individual is not to take part in the lie. One word of truth outweighs the world.' Are you brave enough to take that step?''

"I want proof."

"I'll talk first and you will listen. Then you shall have your proof."

I'LL TRY TO DRAW A MAP of events from the beginning,'' Lakesh said, "or at least the beginning as I understand it.

"Human history is intertwined with the activities of the entities we call Archons. They were called many things over many centuries—angels, demons, visitors, E.T.'s, saucer people, grays. Whatever they actually are, whatever they are called and even where they come from is unimportant at this juncture. Enough to know that they have been around long enough—on and off—on the planet that they consider themselves Terrans proper.

"Beginning at the dawn of human history, the Archons influenced human affairs. The concept of humanity as a slave race, owned by some mysterious power, was expressed thousands of years ago in many of the earliest recorded texts.

"The sinister thread linking all of humankind's darkest hours leads back to a nonhuman presence that has conspired to control us through political chaos, staged wars, famines, plagues and 'natural' disasters. It is a conspiracy that continues to this day, aided and abetted by willing human allies.

"The Archons have a standard operating procedure, which they have employed since time immemorial—they establish a privileged ruling class dependent upon them, which in turn controls the masses. The Archons' manipulation of governments and many religions was all-pervasive.

"I'm sure most of you have heard of World War II and its horrific excesses. What you haven't heard about are the secret societies that flourished in Germany prior to the rise of the Nazi Party. From information that I received, these societies, such as the Thule and the Vril, were in contact with the Archons, whom they referred to as their 'secret chiefs.' With the help of their chiefs, the Nazis enjoyed great technical advances, including the prototype of the aircraft known in predark times as a flying saucer. You may not be aware that the Nazis came very, very close to conquering the world, spreading the Archons' fascist views and racist ideas into the international population.

"Despite their superior technology and intellects, the Archons are not invincible or omniscient, as Hitler found out. World War II was not just the defeat of the Third Reich, but a defeat of the Archons, as well. Unfortunately they took measures to make sure they would never be beaten again. If the Archon Directorate had a written constitution, that would be its first article.

"Now, we reach my own personal experience. I must compress thirty years of my professional life, in order to make it coherent. My first introduction to the Archon Directive, though I didn't realize it at the time, came in early 1972. As part of my government employment, I was assigned to Dulce, a sleepy little town in northern New Mexico, then populated by only nine hundred people, many of them Jicarilla Apaches.

"Just outside of town is Archuleta Mesa, and buried below that a six-level research complex, connected to Los Alamos by a tube shuttle. The entire installation was devoted to a pair of the Totality Concept's overprojects, Whisper and Excalibur. The Overproject Whisper subdivisions were Operation Chronos and Project Cerberus. My work was conducted primarily on Level Four, and Chronos occupied Level Five. I knew Overproject Excalibur and its subdivisions occupied biogenetics laboratories on Level Six, and perhaps even a secret Level Seven, but inasmuch as I was a cyberneticist and physicist, my interest in genetics was limited.

"At any rate, my work focused on Cerberus, the mattrans units, on how to reconcile quantum theory with rela-

tivistic Einsteinian physics. The technology in Dulce was
not theoretical. The hardware worked, though no one really
knew *how* it worked, and no one wanted to admit where
the principles to build the first experimental gateway unit
originated. After a couple of years, after a few promotions,
after a few security-clearance upgrades, I finally did learn.

"The Totality Concept researches dated back to World
War II, when German scientists were laboring to build what
turned out to be purely theoretical secret weapons for the
Third Reich. The Allied powers adopted the researches, as
well as many of the scientists, and constructed underground
bases, primarily in the western U.S., to further the experiments. Dulce, of course, was a main nexus point.

"I was enthralled and delighted with the place, at least
for the first few years. The center was filled with meticulously chosen technicians, and it was a source of great pride
to be one of them. Dulce, for all its secrets, its stringent
security procedures, was devoted to pure research. We had
limitless support and funds. Since I was young and naive,
and my one passion was science, I was obsessed with my
work, especially since the Totality Concept was classified
'Above Top Secret.' It was known only to a few very high
ranking military officers and politicians. I doubt even the
Presidents who held office during my tenure there were
aware of the full ramifications. Obviously I felt very special.

"As the years wore on, I became Project Cerberus overseer. During my rise, I heard a number of whispers, rumors
about Dulce and about the other research on different levels. When my security classification was upgraded to
MAJIC status, I asked to visit the other divisions, which
hitherto had been off limits to me. Instead, an Air Force
general handed me a briefing paper and waited for me to
read it, hovering nearby with his hand on his side arm and
never leaving the room.

"The document was issued from an ultrasecret think tank
known as MJ-12. This was the name of a governmental

control group, more or less the people who oversaw and approved our work. Rather than answering my request, the document essentially outlined where the source of our technology originated. I learned it was not built on German research at all, but was the result of an alliance between the U.S. government and the Archons.

"Although I spent most of my time in the Dulce installation, I didn't live in a complete vacuum. Urban legends and conspiracy theories had filtered into the public consciousness to such a point that even I, in my vanadium-alloy tower, had heard the tales of aliens, of grays, of mysterious animal mutilations and of Area 51, where captured extraterrestrial spacecraft were allegedly undergoing back-engineering. As a scientist, I discounted just about everything I had heard or read or seen on television. You can imagine my shock when the briefing document confirmed nearly all I had been sneering at for years.

"That revelation was stunning enough, but when the general asked me for my opinion of the paper, my reaction was much the same as yours, Kane. I said, 'Prove it.'

"Unfortunately he did. I wish now, in many ways, he had simply shot me dead on the spot. I was escorted up to Level Three, which I had always assumed to be a maintenance area. There, the general allowed me to peer through a window into a room that held a visiting Archon, or as they officially designated them, 'Pan-Terrestrial Biological Entities.'

"I was terrified in its presence, even though it could not see me. At first, I told myself it was a cunningly crafted animatronic model, such as those built for amusement parks. But I saw it walk, move, breathe, blink and interact with another human being.

"I was only allowed to observe it for a minute. The general led me away. He seemed sympathetic to my stunned state, and was patient with my babbled questions. He explained that although the Archons had never allowed a physical examination of themselves, the military had in their possession several bodies taken from 'saucer' crashes that had occurred shortly after the war. Evidently these accidents precipitated modern contact with the entities. Autopsies had been performed on the corpses, and the consensus was that the Archons were descended from an unknown reptilian species that had cross-bred with sapient humans several millennia ago.

"Furthermore, the general told me that certain branches of the government had entered into a pact with the Archons, and in 1953, agreed on an exchange with them for high-tech knowledge, and to allow them the use of underground military bases. He refused to tell me what our side of the trade agreement was to be. He added that if I ever mentioned to anyone what I had just seen and heard, 'buzzards would be picking my bones out of the desert.'

"Though it was difficult, I focused on my work, trying to forget everything about Archons and trade pacts. My focus bore fruit, and in 1989, we had the first successful long-distance matter transfer of a living subject. That success was reproduced many times, improving and modifying the gateways. Then within a year of our victory, things began to change in a sinister fashion.

"By the early 1990s, the Project Cerberus staff were suddenly under the impositions of a timetable. We had strict schedules to keep, results we had to achieve, non-negotiable deadlines. We were ordered to basically mass-produce the units, to design them in modular form so they could be shipped and assembled elsewhere. Such a task was arduous, to say the least. The problems with the self-contained nuclear power packs were almost insurmountable. It all seemed very odd, very insidious.

"At this point, you must understand that while the Totality Concept scientists as a whole were working on some remarkable projects, the projects were rarely coordinated. Now, all of them were linked, even those in other bases in other states. For example, the technicians of Operation

Chronos used our mat-trans breakthroughs to spin off their own innovations and achieve their own successes.

"You may not be aware that Operation Chronos dealt in the mechanics of time travel, forcing temporal breaches in the chronon structure. Without getting too technical or metaphysical, because I really don't understand all of it myself, the purpose of Chronos was to find a way to enter 'probability gaps' between one interval of time and another. Inasmuch as Cerberus utilized quantum events to reduce organic and inorganic material to digital information and transmit it through hyperdimensional space, Chronos built on that same principle to peep into other time lines and even 'trawl' living matter from the past and the future.

"Then something very strange happened. A series of sweeping policy changes came into play, which created something far beyond the scientific ambitions of the Totality Concept staff. I learned much later that the changes came about as an edict from the Archon Directive.

"Other government agencies became involved, as well as other countries. In a short time, it appeared as if the Totality Concept was a deep-cover international cooperative. In 1998 a massive, almost frantic redoubt-construction program began. Keep in mind that for many years, especially at the height of the Cold War, underground complexes had been constructed under the Continuity of Government program, as an insurance policy in case of a nuclear war. Many subterranean command posts had been built in the fifties and sixties, located in different regions of the country.

"With the advent of the Cerberus success, the new installations—the redoubts—were built, linked to each other by gateway units. Though the COG facilities and the redoubt scientific enclaves were not part of the same program, there was a suspicious trade-off of design specifications, technology and personnel. Many of the Totality Concept's subdivisions and spin-off researches were relocated to these redoubts. Cerberus, obviously, was moved here, to Montana.

"The most ambitious COG facility was code-named 'the Anthill' because of its resemblance in layout to an ant colony. It was a vast complex, with underground sewage plants, stores, theaters and even a sports arena. Supplies of foodstuffs, weapons and anything of value were stockpiled, oftentimes in triplicate.

"Because of its size, the Anthill was built inside of Mount Rushmore, using tunneling and digging machines. The entire mountain was honeycombed with interconnected levels, passageways and chambers. I was told that once construction on the Anthill was completed, the entire Totality Concept program would be moved into it. I was expected to move there, too.

"I was very confused, very disoriented by all of these abrupt, almost overnight changes. A severe case of bunker mentality possessed everyone. It was as if they knew something truly terrible was in the offing, and they were grimly determined to weather it by any means necessary. It was a crazed time, a blizzard of sound and fury and near panic that signified very little to me—except a deep dissatisfaction.

"Morale was exceptionally low among the staff of the projects, and though we were forbidden to ever fraternize, because of all the confusion, we took advantage of the holes in security.

"One day, I met with a colleague from Operation Chronos, a man named Burr. Like myself, he was dispirited, demoralized. He told me that after many, many failures, his division had successfully retrieved—trawled—a living human subject from a past time line. Rather than acting exuberant, he was terrified. He dismissed his success, saying that the trawled subject proved so very troublesome he had been removed from Dulce. What he wanted to talk about was a practice he referred to as 'temporal peeping.'

"He said that his staff had peeped through a gap in the

chronon structure into a future date, January of 2001. They discovered that a nuclear holocaust had, for all intents and purposes, obliterated the world. That news was horrifying enough, but he had more. The discovery had been reported to MJ-12, and rather than take the measures necessary to prevent the destruction, they opted to survive it instead. He assumed that the construction of the redoubts and the frenzied activity of the last few months were due to that report.

"Burr said that further peeping experiments had set up a horrified suspicion in his mind that not only was the holocaust preventable, but it was not *supposed* to happen. Operation Chronos had disrupted the chronon structure and triggered a probability wave dysfunction. In layman's terms, we had created an alternate future scenario for ourselves.

"Assuming Burr could be believed, I realized if the alliance had not been initiated with the Archons, if the Totality Concept researches had been left to molder in old military-intelligence files at the end of the war, the apocalypse would not then, and would never happen.

"I know how insane it sounds now, especially with all these years of hindsight. Imagine living through it, being informed that doomsday was only a few years away, and that the very people who could prevent it actually *welcomed* it.

"Why? It took me a while to come up with an answer, at the risk of my position and my life. But I found it below Level Six of the complex, the staging area of Overproject Excalibur.

"It held the genetic labs, where experiments were performed on fish, seals, birds and mice, all altered from their original forms. The Archons had taught the human scientists a lot about genetics, things both useful and dangerous.

"It was when I encountered the humans in cages I realized I had entered a place privately referred to as 'Nightmare Alley.' I saw row after row of altered humans, human-Archon gene-blends and embryos kept in cold storage.

That's where I first saw mutants, the ghastly prototypes of the creatures later known as stickies and scalies. They were drugged, dazed, some of them cried and begged for help. I was at a complete loss. I couldn't understand the purpose of such horrific experiments.

"On paper, Overproject Excalibur's function was to map human genomes to the specific chromosomal locations. It was an ambitious project, and should have taken many years. It was obvious that it was either completed or near completion.

"In a stunning revelation, I understood that Overproject Excalibur was creating life-forms to survive in a world devastated by atomic war. It is a field called Pantropic science. Designer mutants, courtesy of the Archon Directive.

"I finally realized why the elite power group and their allies did not fear a coming nuclear holocaust. It was all part of the drive toward a one-world government, brought about by the culling of society's 'useless eaters,' and aided by a technology turned over to a humanity not prepared to handle the consequences.

"When the first warhead detonated on the twentieth of January, 2001, the Anthill facility had been in operation for some two months, inhabited only by a group of scientists, myself among them, and a few paranoid politicians and their families.

"Despite all of the precautions, the effects of the conflagration caused extensive damage to the Anthill. The consequences were far greater than any of the MJ-12 or military tacticians had foreseen. Rather than emerging in ten or so years into a world mercifully free of its parasitical humans, the timetable looked to be closer to a hundred.

"However, even if they managed to outlast the nuclear winter, they couldn't cure radiation sickness, nor could the provisions be stretched to support all the people for a century. Cryogenic facilities existed in the Anthill, and many people either volunteered or were forced into suspended animation. Others were the subjects of radical surgery, and over a period of decades, they received organ transplants, artificial hearts, prosthetic limbs, and some became true cyborgs, a hybridization of human and machine.

"I volunteered for the freezing process. I desperately hoped that I would revive in a brave new world, different but much better than the one which had been destroyed. It was a foolishly vain hope.

"I was resurrected fifty years ago. Much had changed over the course of a century and a half, but much was still the same. The Archons were now in charge, their Directive now a Directorate. Oh, they still operate behind the scenes, but now they enjoy hands-on control of their willing human marionettes, so they no longer have to deal through several layers of intermediaries. For some reason, though, they don't seem to be here on a permanent basis and come and go, but their power apparatus is fully in place.

"The barons are the most obvious example of puppet and puppet master. They are hybrids of Archons and humans, bred to survive, even thrive in the postholocaust world. The baronial hierarchy is composed of these hybrids, the mixture of genetic material. The last two generations of barons are of hybrid stock. It is a return to the ancient god-king system, where the subjects believed their rulers to be semidivine.

"Through them, the Archons implemented the so-called Program of Unification, which keeps a boot forevermore pressed on the necks of what is left of humankind. The world they tried to build using the Nazis as pawns has finally come to pass. The mass of humanity is guided, controlled, channeled—and they don't even know it.

"This is not our world any longer, and I pity those of you who were born into it."

Chapter 28

Dead silence reigned in the room. What they heard was too much to grasp and absorb in one sitting. They all stared at Lakesh in stunned silence, eyes wide with a pain hovering near disbelief. But by now they knew better.

Lakesh smiled sadly and leaned back in his chair. "Any questions?"

"Only a thousand or two," Grant said in a gruff, clipped tone. "I'll work from the end to the beginning."

Kane repressed a smile. Grant was in interrogation mode. He almost expected to hear "slagger" tacked on at the end of every query.

"Why were you thawed out?"

"The Program of Unification had reached a certain level of progression," Lakesh responded smoothly. "I and a number of others were resurrected to aid in the final shaping of ville governments. We were consultants, more or less. At the moment, there is one freezie, as we are called today, serving in at least one division of every ville."

"On the night of my initiation into the Trust, I was told the Archons supplied the barons with the necessary tech and firepower to make the unification program successful," said Kane. "Is that true?"

"Yes. The Archons observed humanity's adaptation to the postskydark world. They contacted the most-powerful barons, offered them near absolute power if they agreed to their terms. Most of the ordnance came from the Anthill complex and from a few still-hidden COG Stockpiles. The temptation was overwhelming for such avaricious egotists.

As you know from your own experiences, absolute power corrupted absolutely.''

''And the Magistrate Division was simply the old international police force idea, dusted off and updated?'' Brigid asked.

Lakesh nodded. ''Exactly.''

''And our division, the archivists? Why was that important?''

''The function of the Historical Division was to keep all information of any sensitive nature, especially any texts that hinted at the Archons' involvement in our collective past, completely secured. Aside from that, it was solid source material to reinforce the sense of shame and the guilt complex among the people. As you remember, historical precedent was always cited to keep the citizens in line, to keep them in their place. Like the Magistrates, the Historical Division was consciously designed as another control mechanism.''

''If you had so many reservations about it,'' Grant said, ''why didn't you oppose the plan?''

''Outright opposition was impossible. The slightest indication would have classified me as a security risk. Then I would have turned up as a suicide, as did so many of my colleagues who were foolish enough to express their objections. Buzzards would have indeed picked my bones out in the desert.''

Domi shook her head in bewilderment. ''This all *so* crazy. Why?''

Lakesh sighed. ''It's hard to offer a cogent explanation, my dear, especially so many years after the fact. Even before the war, the world seemed to be on the verge of some sort of catastrophe. Political systems were collapsing, socioeconomic inequities led to strife and crime. Madness was rampant, entire nations ran out of control. The world felt like it was coming apart at the seams. Something needed to be done to contain the insanity, the growing an-

archy. To my everlasting shame, I admit that I agreed with
that sentiment. At least hypothetically.''

"No," rumbled Grant. "She meant what is the Archon
agenda."

"Isn't it obvious? They now have a world pretty much
free of social strife, of crime. And once the planet repairs
itself, free of choking pollution. Of course, there is no liberty, no free will, but the Archons and their human allies
never liked that about us in the first place."

"What do they want?" Brigid demanded raggedly,
clenching her fists on the arms of her chair.

"What they already have. The planet is back in their
possession, as it was millennia ago when certain religious
cults worshiped them as gods. They have unrestricted access to Earth's natural resources, and a manageable population to supply them with everything from slave labor to
biological material. I also suspect that the geomagnetic
changes brought about by the nukecaust are more suited to
their metabolisms."

"If they're so superior, rather than trying to beat us down
and conquer us, why didn't they try negotiating with us to
share our planet with them?"

Lakesh took a deep breath. "They have no empathy for
us, don't value us. We're objects to be used or destroyed.
Trying to negotiate with the Archon Directorate would be
as futile as concentration-camp inmates bargaining with the
commandant for their freedom."

Angrily Kane said, "If it's so goddamn hopeless, what's
the point of your so-called underground resistance? Why
did you turn against them when it was too late?"

Lakesh steepled his fingers. He did not answer for a long
moment. When he did, his voice was a soft, sad rustle. "I
am old. I devoted my life to a single passion, and this world
is what came of it. I never married, never had children,
never contributed anything of value to my world, to our
shared reality. As history clearly shows, if you do not create
your own reality, someone else is going to create it for you.

I allowed that to happen, and I do not like the reality I got. Now, as the end of my life approaches, all I want is to enter the house of my deity justified. Besides, I feel that something is still holding them back. They are not here full-time yet.''

Kane uttered a short, bitter laugh. His hand trembled, and the glowing end of the cigar between his fingers shook ashes all over it. He stubbed it out on the floor. ''One last thing, then, before you change addresses. The proof.''

Abruptly Lakesh stood up. ''Follow me.''

They filed out of the office into the corridor. Grant, his voice subdued, said to Kane, ''This may be our chance.''

''For what?''

''To get our blasters and get the hell out of this jolthole.''

Brigid overheard and whispered impatiently, ''We're not prisoners.''

At that moment, a man carrying an SA80 fell into step behind them. Grant muttered darkly, ''You could have fooled me.''

Kane couldn't deny Grant had a point. He lengthened his stride until he was abreast of Lakesh. ''How many people are in this redoubt?''

''Counting you four, a baker's dozen.''

Seeing the confusion in Kane's eyes, he added, ''Thirteen. Of course, only twelve of them are human.''

''What?''

Lakesh stopped before a door. Unlike the others, it bore no knob or handle. Instead, a square keypad device was affixed where they should have been. He punched in six digits. There was a buzz, and the lock clicked open. The door was pulled inward by a tall, skinny black man. He looked very young, very earnest and sincere.

Lakesh said, ''How is he today, Banks?''

Banks shrugged, eyeing the four people behind Lakesh curiously. ''About how he's been for the last three years. Maybe he'll enjoy seeing some new faces.''

He stepped aside. With an ironic smile, Lakesh turned to Kane. "You should always be careful what you wish for, friend. Now you've got it."

He stepped through the doorway and indicated the others should follow him. They walked into a large, low-ceilinged room with several desks, most of them covered with computer terminals and keyboards. A control console ran the length of the right-hand wall, consisting primarily of plastic-encased readouts and gauges. Kane's eyes took in at a glance the heavy tables loaded down with a complicated network of glass tubes, beakers, retorts and bunsen burners. The smell of chemicals cut into his nostrils.

The left wall was constructed of panes of glass, beaded with condensation. Behind them was a room, deeply recessed and dimly lit by an overhead neon strip that cast a reddish glow. Banks moved to the wall, rapping on a sheet of glass. "We call him Balam."

"Call who Balam?" asked Brigid.

On the other side of the pane, shadows slid beneath the ruddy luminance. "Him," said Banks.

A shape shifted in the red-tinged gloom, like a swirl of seething mist, a deep dark against the very dark. Then the mist became even more dense before Kane was aware of a pair of eyes flaming out of the blood-hued murk. The eyes were overpowering, large and tilted like a cat's, completely black with no pupil or iris. Reflected light glinted from them in burning pinpoints.

Kane stared, transfixed, into those eyes. He heard a faint, agonized groan, and distantly he knew it had been torn from his own lips. A long, tormented moment passed before he recognized the emotion flooding through him as terror—an unreasoning, undiluted fear such as he had never known. He felt frozen to the spot, as if he stood in the icy blast of an arctic wind gusting from some nightmarish cosmic gulf between the stars.

The black, fathomless eyes held his captive, peering

deep, deep through them into the roots of his soul. In those obsidian depths blazed intelligence, cold and remote.

We are old, came the words into his mind. *When your race was wild and bloody and young, we were already ancient. Your tribe has passed, and we are invincible. All of the achievements of man are dust—they are forgotten.*

We stand, we know, we are. We stalked above man ere we raised him from the ape. Long was the earth ours, and now we have reclaimed it. We shall still reign when man is reduced to the ape again. We stand, we know, we are.

Suddenly Lakesh was there, standing in front of the glass, blocking his view of that narrow face and those black, depthless eyes. He raised a hand and snapped his fingers twice.

Kane mentally shook himself, feeling cold perspiration trickling down his face. His entire body was clammy with it. Around him, his three friends stirred, as if awakening from a nap.

He tasted bile in his throat and he wiped his face with a shaking hand. "What happened?"

"I apologize for not warning you," Lakesh said, "but you needed to experience Balam's patented telepathic speech for yourself. The creature has it on continuous loop for newcomers. The rest of us are immune to it, so we can tune it out. Even though we've had him in here for three years, he's still remote and superior. Balam simply can't adjust to his situation. He's incapable of accepting that we apes can and do hold him prisoner. The fellow suffers from a nearly terminal case of denial."

"Why is he in the dark?" Grant asked.

"He's uncomfortable in higher light levels," answered Lakesh. "His optic nerves operate differently than ours. We don't deliberately want to cause him pain."

"What does it—he—eat?" Domi's voice was a quavery whisper.

"Balam doesn't eat exactly," replied Banks. "He absorbs a mixture of cattle blood and peroxide through his skin. We synthesize the stuff here, and he more or less bathes in it.''

''A form of osmosis,'' put in Lakesh. ''He does ingest food normally on occasion. He's very fond of ice cream.''

Kane only half heard the old man. He sensed the words were directed more toward Balam, anyway. He turned away, breathing with difficulty. He desperately wanted to run out of the room, out of the redoubt, into the fresh clean air and wholesome sunlight, into a world where even the horrors of muties and Dregs could not compare to this.

Kane and Grant's glances met. A savage light shone in his friend's eyes, and he knew the same primal light gleamed in his own. It was as if the two men were primordial hunters, deciding to make common cause against an inhuman enemy.

''Chill that little fucker,'' Grant rasped. ''He's worse than a stickie.''

''That's everyone's initial reaction,'' Lakesh explained. ''A very visceral, xenophobic response. Quite primal and natural. But executing Balam will not solve anything.''

Voice high and strained, Brigid demanded, ''How can getting rid of that...*thing* possibly make things worse?''

''Balam is our only link with the Directorate. Even after all these years, we still don't know much about them. We do know this much, though—each Archon is anchored to another through some hyperspatial filaments of their mind energy, akin to the hive mind of certain insect species. Balam cannot communicate to his brethren his plight, but if he is killed, the absence of his mind filament would be instantly sensed by all Archons everywhere.''

Kane turned around carefully, looking slowly toward the recessed room. This time all he saw was a shapeless mass of thickening red shadows.

''You get used to his mind games,'' said Banks with a grin. ''You know what the oddest thing about him is? He smells like wet cardboard.''

The young man's remark helped dispel a bit of the fear and tension. Everyone managed a short, uneasy laugh.

"How many Archons are there?" Grant asked.

Lakesh pursed his lips and shook his head. "We don't really know, but we calculate there are only a few. Perhaps less than a thousand. Evidently they were a race on the verge of extinction long before the nukecaust. The hybrids are a different matter. Their numbers are growing exponentially."

"How did you get your hands on Balam?" inquired Kane.

Lakesh peered at him over the rims of his spectacles. "Appropriate that you should be the one to ask that question, friend Kane. Balam was brought to us by your father."

Kane felt his mouth falling open. Before any words came out, Lakesh moved quickly to the door. "Let me give you a tour of our retreat. You'll find it edifying."

Back out in the corridor, Kane moved in a daze, grappling with everything he had seen, done, smelled and heard over the past three days. It seemed like ages ago since he had palmed the computer disk in Reeth's slaghole. It was almost incomprehensible that the entire chain of sanity-staggering events had been triggered by that single impulsive act.

As they walked the corridors, Lakesh explained that the Cerberus redoubt was built into the side of a mountain peak and could be reached from the outside only by a single treacherous road. The sec door was usually closed, so the gateway brought people and materials in, and occasionally out. The thirty-acre facility had come through the nukecaust in fairly good shape. It, and most of the other redoubts, had been built according to specifications for maximum impenetrability, short of a direct hit. Its radiation shielding was still intact. Cerberus was powered by nuclear generators, and probably would continue to be for at least another five hundred years.

Lakesh showed them the armory, a room that was

stacked nearly to the ceiling with wooden crates and boxes. Many of the crates were stenciled with the legend Property U.S. Army, and others bore words in Russian Cyrillic script.

They moved along the walls, inspecting the contents of glass-fronted cases. M-16 A-1 assault rifles were neatly stacked in one, and an open crate beside it was filled with hundreds of rounds of 5.56 mm ammunition. There were SA80 subguns and 9 mm Heckler & Koch VP-70 semiautomatic pistols complete with holsters and belts. Farther on they found bazookas, tripod-mounted M-249 machine guns and several crates of grenades. Mounted in a corner was a full suit of Magistrate body armor. Every piece of ordnance and hardware, from the smallest-caliber handblaster to the biggest-bore M-79 grenade launcher, was in perfect condition.

Even Kane, in his mind-befogged state, was impressed. If he had doubted Lakesh before, he didn't now. To possess this kind of arsenal, only a step or two below the one in Cobaltville, the old man had to be tapped into a very special, very exclusive pipeline.

"Compliments of the Anthill," said Lakesh grimly. He added, as an afterthought, "I hate guns."

"Couldn't tell it by this room," observed Domi.

Gesturing to the Mag armor, Grant asked, "Where'd you come by that?"

"It belonged to a disaffected member of your former fraternity," Lakesh said quietly. "Anson, by name. For a time, he was part of our little group here."

"What happened to him?"

"He killed himself with his own side arm. He had seen too much, and the truth was far more than he could bear."

Lakesh doddered out of the armory, his face seamed with grief. "Come on, children."

Another big chamber held a pair of all-terrain vehicles, a modified and armored Hussar Hotspur Land Rover and a current version of the Sandcat. Its armor was rust free, the treads solid and sturdy, and a USMG-73 heavy machine gun was enclosed within a small turret. A diesel fuel pump stood in the corner.

Out in the corridor again, they approached the gateway chamber. Nodding toward the cavity in the wall, Lakesh said, "This redoubt has a historic significance other than its use as a base for Cerberus. Before the barons consolidated their rule, Ryan Cawdor and his band of warriors blew that hole in the wall. Redoubt Bravo was their first jumping-off point to many other installations, including those overseas."

"How do you know that?" Brigid asked.

Before Lakesh answered, he stepped to a section of vanadium-alloy wall. From the pocket of his bodysuit, he produced a small object molded of black plastic. He pointed it, pressed a stud and very slowly, a slab of alloy tilted inward at the top. It was precisely balanced on hidden pivots.

"If Cawdor and friends had a sonic key, they wouldn't have been forced to deface the redoubt."

They filed into the control room for the gateway, and Lakesh gestured to the rows of computers. "To answer your question, Brigid, all mat-trans units contain molecular-imaging scanners. Every pattern of every atom of transmitted matter is stored in the scanners' memory banks. They can be replayed and reviewed, if you know how."

"Cawdor, Wyeth and the others didn't know how?"

"No. They knew very little. Their destinations were chosen by the target-destination computers on a strictly random logarithm. Catch-as-catch-can. A damn dangerous undertaking, but I suppose it was better than traveling across the Deathlands on foot or by vehicle. Of course, all access to any functioning redoubt ended with the advent of the unification program."

"How are you able to operate this one under the noses of the barons and the Archons?" Grant asked.

"Very easily, friend Grant. As the former overseer of

Cerberus, the responsibility fell to me to determine which
redoubts were still operable or repairable. Having retained
a certain fondness for this one, I listed it as condemned.
Since it is in such an extraordinarily isolated area, not to
mention buried within a mountain, no one cared to challenge my decision.

"Nor can the gateway's energies be traced back here. I
altered the modulation frequencies of the matter-stream carrier wave, so they are slightly out of phase with the other
units in other places."

Lakesh regarded Kane keenly. "You are unusually solemn. I assumed most of the inquiries would spring from
you."

Kane cleared his throat. "Maybe I'm afraid to learn
more."

Lakesh said nothing. He only smiled encouragingly.

Kane blurted, "You knew my father?"

"Yes. You might say I selected him."

"Selected him for what? To join the Trust or join you?"

Lakesh sighed very, very heavily. He dropped into a
chair in front of one of the consoles. "Haven't you ever
wondered on what basis ville society is divided? Who de-
termines who lives in the Enclaves and who lives in the
Pits? Who chooses the elite, like you, Grant and Brigid,
and who chooses those relegated to live in the Outlands,
like Domi?"

"We were taught it was because of our parentage," answered Brigid. "Our grandparents and great-grandparents
were citizens of the original baronies."

"That is part of it. A very minuscule part. The class
distinctions are based primarily on eugenics, and this was
determined by the Directorate. They had in their hands the
findings of the Human Genome Project, you see. Everyone
selected to live in the villes, to serve in the divisions, had
to meet a strict set of criteria, one established generations
ago. The purer the quality of individual genetic character-

istics, the purer the quality of the hybrid. Purity control. Now do you begin to understand me?''

Kane, Brigid, Domi and Grant all exchanged baffled glances.

At length, Kane said, ''No. You're still talking in enigmas. It's past time for final answers, old man. No more riddles wrapped in cryptic bullshit.''

''Dulce,'' declared Lakesh firmly. ''All your answers can be found in Dulce.''

Chapter 29

Lakesh refused to speak any more about Dulce or what could be found there. "If you want to find your truth," he said ominously, "you must go there. However, if you go and are discovered, a protracted, painful death is the best you may hope for. Anson sought the truth in Dulce. The day after he returned, he put his weapon to his head. So think it over carefully. Sleep on it. When you've made your decision, we'll talk again."

The remainder of the day passed, and they ate, drank and rested. Kane, Domi, Grant and Brigid were assigned individual suites. According to one of the women in white, two dozen self-contained apartments were within the redoubt, as well as a dormitory and a small dining hall.

That evening, in his quarters, Kane shaved and had another shower. When he came out of the bathroom, his armor and Sin Eater rested neatly on a chair. Rather than feeling relieved, he sat on the bed and lost himself in gloomy reflections.

Though he had known Anson only by name, he easily understood why the man had pulled the trigger on himself. Under the circumstances, most people would feel overwhelmed and hopeless, and suicide didn't seem like such a cowardly option—but it did seem like an incredible waste, considering all he had gone through to be able to sit on this bed and contemplate it.

He recognized the symptoms of shock and tension. His aching muscles and outraged nerve ends screamed at him to be allowed to relax, to go to sleep. But every time he closed his eyes, Balam's black orbs crowded into his mind, pushing aside all other thoughts.

Kane felt like a boy who had lifted a rock and then, paralyzed with horror, watched as nightmarish monstrosities with pincers and stingers scuttled out in a never-ending stream.

He had a sudden yearning for ignorance, not to know what he had learned and to be back in his little flat in the Enclaves or the drab dayroom with its bad coffee sub. He longed for all the times when he walked like a tiger, muscles gliding under his black armor, all the less privileged scrambling out of his path.

But beyond the loss of a life path, something else weighed so heavily on him that he wondered if it were possible for a Magistrate to weep. That was a strange concept, for he had never thought of shedding tears since he entered the division as a child.

A deep ache came over him for all the terrible things mankind had endured and for the darkness or extinction even yet to come.

He was sick in every cell of his being. He lay down on the bed and allowed the waves of sleep to crash over him.

He slept, deeply and dreamlessly.

When he woke, he was fit, rested and grimly determined. His wrist chron told him he had slept for over fourteen hours.

In the bathroom, he showered. Next he crossed the suite to his armor and inspected every piece of it, then fieldstripped the Sin Eater, meticulously cleaned it and reassembled it.

He donned the ebony exoskeleton with deliberation, taking great care to firmly snap together the joints and secure all the seals. Since this could very well be the last time he would ever put it on, he paid strict attention to every nuance of the procedure. Each snap, click and clack of the pieces joining together held a new, special significance.

When he was armored up, the Sin Eater holstered in

place, the helmet under his arm, he did something he hadn't done in years, not since the first couple of months after receiving his duty badge. He examined his reflection in the mirror.

He liked everything he saw, except for the eyes staring back at him. They looked strange, different, almost unfamiliar. Slowly it dawned on him they were the eyes of a man who fully expected to die that day.

He turned smartly on his heel and left the suite. Out in the corridor, he looked straight ahead as he marched, wishing distantly that the alloyed floor didn't possess such sound-absorbing properties. The echo of his measured boot treads would have made a nice accompaniment during his walk to the armory.

Once inside, he took a Copperhead from its case, made sure all its moving parts were oiled and attached it to his belt. He slid half a dozen clips of ammo into his belt compartments, three for his Sin Eater, three for the subgun. Lifting the lid of a crate full of grens, he examined them in their foam cushions. He was eyeballing an incendiary, like a shopper studying an egg at market, when Grant stalked in.

"What are you armored up for?"

"I'm out of here," Kane replied brusquely. "No talking, no hand-wringing. I'm out of here."

"To where?"

"Dulce."

"I'm with you."

"No. I'm going alone. I've ruined your life, Grant. I don't want to be the one responsible for you losing it altogether."

"That no longer applies, knowing what I do now. How could I want it back? Besides, if I'm not going," Grant said, "then you're not going."

"Don't screw around with me on this. Please. If you were ever my friend, you won't interfere with me and you won't go with me."

Grant jabbed an accusatory finger at him. "You've gone simple on me, Kane. There are protocols here, and it's got nothing to do with friendship or sentiment. Hell, half the time, I don't even *like* you. But it so happens that we're partners, and partners walk the hellfire trail together."

Kane turned his back on him, still going through the grens. "We're not Mags anymore. The partnership is dissolved."

Grant stared at him speechless. Then he swore, whirled and stalked toward the door.

Kane didn't look at him or try to call him back. Grant stopped before he went through the doorway. His faked anger hadn't fooled either of them.

"All right," said Grant in an uninflected, unemotional voice. "No games. No horseshit. You can run off, looking for the truth, wanting to die in a blaze of glory when you find it. I don't blame you. I want to try to even up the score just as much as you do. But as long as you still wear that badge, we're partners. So here's how the stick's gonna float—we'll both go or neither of us will go."

Kane threw him a bemused glance. "How do you propose to stop me?"

Grant folded his arms over his broad chest. "I'll stop you." His voice held no heat, no anger, only an intractable belief in his own words. Kane believed him, too.

"Okay." Kane returned his attention to the explosives.

"Okay what?"

"Okay, we'll both go." He gestured to Anson's Mag armor in the corner. "Armor up."

Grant's brow furrowed, his heavy jaw jutting out. "You could've argued with me some more, you know."

"There's no time, and I don't have the inclination."

"Good," announced Brigid, sweeping into the room. "Neither do I." She was followed by Lakesh and Domi.

"Why don't we bring the whole redoubt in on this?" Kane asked. "Let's ask Balam if he'd like to go."

"No need," replied Lakesh. "Since he was dragged here

from Dulce, I'm pretty sure what his response would be. However, he can't provide you with the layout of the place. I can."

Brigid nodded. "Fine. Put it in a form I can study, either hard copy or digital. I'll take a look and commit it to memory."

Kane said wearily, "Let's not have any more volunteers. This is a penetration, not a tour group."

Brigid's eyes glinted fiercely. "Grant's going with you and so am I."

"He's my partner."

"And so am I. You saw to that, Kane, whether you intended to or not."

Kane didn't respond in words. From a gun case, he removed an H&K VP-70 handblaster, holster and belt. He tossed it across the room toward her, and Brigid snatched it effortlessly out of the air.

"Good muscle tone," he said. "But that's not enough. This may be a one-way trip."

"No," she stated firmly. "You do what you have to do, what you do best. I'll see to it that we come back."

Grant glanced over at Domi. "Don't you want to tag along, too?"

She shook her white, close-cropped head vehemently. "Hell, no! Not this time. Been through enough. Bed's soft and food's good here. Don't want to give 'em up so soon."

Lakesh patted her arm fondly. "Flawless logic, child. Besides, your bound ribs will slow you up."

"Won't you be missed at Cobaltville?" Kane asked. "After what's happened, won't the baron call an emergency meeting of the Trust?"

"He won't convene it over your flight. That's a problem he'll leave to Salvo to solve. Besides, Baron Cobalt is not in the ville at present. As for me being missed, Brigid can attest that my hours were unpredictable at best. One of the few privileges of my station and age."

"There's got to be a gateway in the ville, then," Grant said.

"Of course. On Alpha Level, known and accessible only to the baron, his personal staff and certain senior members of the Trust. I'd intended to use it to spirit Brigid here. It would have been a far smoother and faster trip than the one you endured."

"When were you planning to 'spirit' her away?" Kane asked. "She was about ten seconds away from execution."

Lakesh shook his head dolefully. "Yes, and you spoiled a perfect hairbreadth rescue. Enough recriminations. Domi, help Brigid prepare. All of you meet me in the control center in ten minutes."

Brigid left the room with Domi and Lakesh. Grant donned Anson's armor, relieved to discover they were approximately of the same physique and weight. The helmet was a shade too large, but he adjusted the locking guard to snug the fit.

"We must be operating on half a load," Grant said. "We don't even know if there's a functioning gateway unit there."

"There is," replied Kane.

They reviewed and supplemented their ordnance with gren-filled war bags, extra ammo clips and two flares apiece. After ten minutes, they walked to the control center. The door was open. Lakesh was seated before a computer console, busy working on the keyboard. He grunted in acknowledgment of their arrival.

From the redoubt's stores, Brigid had dressed herself for speed and stealth rather than protection. She wore black, skintight pants and soft-soled half boots. Her sleeveless shirt was also black, and her hair was tied and braided back so it wouldn't get in her way. A dark strip of cloth encircling her head kept her hair out of her eyes. The gun belt rode low on her hips. Domi was still applying stripes of combat cosmetics to her arms and face.

Lakesh hit another few keys and spun his chair around. "You look prepared, Brigid. Come here, please."

Brigid leaned over the console, and Lakesh pointed with a gnarled finger to a floor plan on the screen. "Levels Four and Five. You'll materialize here, on Level Four, in the mat-trans unit. It was the prototype, and it's still fully functional, though rather primitive in comparison to the later models."

She read aloud, "Redoubt Alpha. So that's Dulce's designation."

"Yes. From there, you can make your way down through the maintenance stairwell past Level Five, and then onto Six. There are elevators, but it's far too risky to use them."

Grant asked, "How much opposition can we expect?"

Lakesh shrugged. "None until you reach Level Six. The only time Four is staffed is when a prearranged transmission takes place. This one, obviously, is unscheduled."

"When I tried to verify the jump line for Redoubt Alpha before," Brigid said, " I received an inactive signal."

"Of course you did."

Lakesh adjusted a toggle on the console, and a section of vanadium spanning almost the entire wall slid aside, revealing a Mercator-projection map of the world. Spots of light flickered in almost every continent, and thin, glowing lines networked across the countries, like a web spun by a radioactive spider. Kane was a bit surprised to see that the map delineated all the geophysical alterations caused by the nukecaust. As far as he had been told, very little was known regarding the topographical or sociological conditions overseas.

"Here are the locations of known functioning gateway units, though not all of them are active all of the time. In Dulce, the matter-transit pathway is not open unless prior arrangements are made. What I will do from here is reroute and circumvent the target autosequence initiator and activate the unit's wave-guide conduits via an annular confinement matter stream."

Kane and Grant exchanged a glum glance, then Kane shrugged as if the matter were of little importance. As long as Lakesh understood his techno-babble, then he wasn't going to worry about his own poverty of comprehension.

"Now," continued Lakesh, "after you materialize, the unit will shut down automatically. I will reactivate it in two hours to the second from your arrival. The power will be on just long enough to initiate transmission. If you're not in the gateway, then there is nothing I can do. No rescue or search parties will be dispatched. Understood?"

Kane put on his helmet. "Understood."

Lakesh handed Brigid a small metal device, an instrument Kane recognized as a Mnemosyne. "The connecting doors to the levels are electronically locked. You'll need this to override them."

Brigid tossed the Syne uneasily from hand to hand. "Can you give us any idea of what we'll run into there?"

Lakesh sighed, shook his head. "I haven't visited there since my resurrection. As I understand it, the place was pressed back into service only in the last thirty or forty years. So my ideas of what you might encounter in Dulce are based only on my recollections from two centuries ago. In my opinion, the three of you will face the truth of humanity's ultimate destiny. And if you face it and can live with it, perhaps you will decide that destiny is not an absolute, but only a variable."

The old man wet his lips nervously. "Are you ready?"

Kane, Grant and Brigid exchanged long, silent glances, then they walked through the control center. They paused briefly at the door leading to the anteroom to look back. Domi called after them, very confidently, "You be back."

Grant smiled at her, and she smiled back, very widely. The three people went through the anteroom and entered the gateway chamber. Kane closed the door behind them. They all took deep, calming breaths. Even though they had experienced it before, the concept of having their bodies, their minds, everything that they were, converted to digital information, transmitted to a distant receiver and reassembled, was still a fearsome one.

The now-familiar vibrating hum arose, climbing to a high-pitched whine. The hexagonal metal disks above and below exuded a shimmering glow that slowly intensified. The fine mist gathered and climbed from the floor and wafted down from the ceiling. Tiny crackling static discharges flared in the vapor.

Kane closed his eyes and rushed headlong into the abyss of infinity, filled with spheres of brilliant light and swarms of stars.

Chapter 30

The first thing Kane saw when he opened his eyes was a square wall made of thick, mortared concrete blocks, not the translucent armaglass.

The door was a rectangle of steel set in the wall facing him, a wheel projecting from the riveted mass.

From overhead, a thread of light shone from a single fixture. By its feeble illumination, he saw Brigid and Grant groan, stir and sit up.

Brigid brushed back a loose strand of hair from her black-striped face. "Everybody feel all right?"

They did, none of them suffering from the nausea, dizziness and headaches that had afflicted them after their first jump. Grant climbed to his feet. The ceiling was low, and he couldn't stand at his full height.

"They must've tested this thing on midgets," he muttered.

Kane stood up and went to the door. He had to stoop slightly, too. He put his hands on the wheel-lock, giving it a clockwise twist. It didn't budge. Taking and holding a deep breath, he threw all of his weight against it.

Slowly, resistantly the wheel turned. With Grant's help, he was able to get a hand-over-hand spin going. The solenoids creaked aside, and Grant pushed against the steel door. Flexible rubber seals made a sucking noise as the thick portal swung open on squealing hinges. He stepped out first, Sin Eater in hand. Kane and Brigid followed, watchful and cautious.

They were in a medium-size room with a dozen desks, most of them covered with computer terminals and keyboards. A control console ran the length of one wall, consisting primarily of liquid-crystal displays and gauges, though a few indicator lights blinked and flashed purposefully. On the other side of the wall, behind the console, the electronic whine slowly wound down and faded altogether. As the sound disappeared, the lights on the console went out, plunging the room into darkness.

Grant handed Brigid a flashlight, and she swept the beam around. She murmured, "This is where Lakesh devoted thirty years of his life. So much stolen from him. Sad."

"What's sad about it?" asked Grant gruffly. "That devotion bought him survival when most of the world's 'useless eaters' were vaporized. His life wasn't stolen—it was bought and paid for."

"Quiet," Kane whispered.

The door at the far end of the room was wood paneled. It bore a knob rather than a lever or a sec-code keypad affixed to the frame. Kane walked to the door and slowly turned the knob. Brigid and Grant fanned out behind him, taking cover behind desks and drawing their weapons.

The door was unlocked, and he moved out into a wide, wood-paneled corridor. It stretched to his left and his right. Even with his image intensifier at full output, the hallway was shadowed and dim.

Brigid moved up beside him and said, "To the left here."

He started down it, moving rapidly and silently on the nap of the carpet.

They passed two doors, which were unlocked. Nothing lay in the rooms beyond them but empty spaces and a few pieces of dusty furniture. They came to an intersecting corridor and peered around the corner. To the right, a few yards away, a sign hung above a varnished wooden door. The faded lettering read Not An Exit. No Unauthorized Personnel. A red triangle bisected by three black vertical lines was stamped at the bottom of the sign.

Gripping their blasters tightly, they eased around the corner, careful to keep their bodies to one side. The door had a keypad instead of a knob. Brigid placed the Syne against it and initialized the decryption mechanism. They crouched on either side of the door, Grant covering the way they came, tensely waiting for the Syne to do its work. A few moments later, the computer-controlled lock slid aside.

Kane gingerly pushed the door open, then moved in, the other two sliding in after him, to his left and right. It was an empty, bare-walled landing. Painted on the wall was a red down-pointing arrow, and the words To Levels Five And Six. Carefully they soft-footed down the wide concrete steps, careful not to touch the metal banisters.

They reached another landing, another door, another inverted arrow on the wall, but they kept walking down. At the next landing, the door wasn't made of wood, but of steel. It was a heavy bulkhead framed within a recessed niche in a double-baffled wall. The door bore the emblazoned warning: Only Overproject Excalibur Personnel Beyond This Point! Must Have MAJIC-A Clearance To Proceed! Deadly Force Is Authorized! And imprinted below that, was the ubiquitous red triangle with black vertical lines.

"I'm sick of seeing that," murmured Kane.

Brigid put the Syne over the keypad and initialized it. The device overrode the lock's microprocessors, and with a squeak of rust and a hiss of pneumatics, the bulkhead slid into its slots between the double frame.

Semidarkness met their eyes, though there wasn't much to see. They faced a narrow, uncarpeted passageway, long and low ceilinged. A dim glow filtered from its far end. Cool air fanned their faces, and they heard a rhythmic drone of turbines and generators. A faint chemical odor hung in the air.

They moved on toward the light. Brigid turned out her flashlight. Kane's and Grant's combat senses were on full alert. The mechanical throb grew louder. The end of the passageway was blocked by a turnstile device, obviously meant as a checkpoint nearly two centuries ago. The metal prongs were rusted into position, so they were forced to clamber over the time-frozen barrier.

The passageway took on a downward slope, and was lighted by dim red bulbs strung from a cable on the low ceiling. The floor changed from bare concrete to metal plates ridged and flaking with rust. Here and there, the walls were smeared with illegible graffiti. The only phrases Kane was able to decipher were painted in swirls of orange paint. One read They're He-re! and the other was simply E.T. Go Home!

The passage ended abruptly at a door made of glass. It bore a sign stating, Biohazard Beyond This Point! Entry Forbidden To Personnel Not Wearing Anticontaminant Clothing!

Beyond the door was a small booth. From hooks on the wall hung a dozen one-piece coveralls. Hoods with transparent Plexiglas faceplates were attached to them. Kane pushed open the door, and the generator throb grew considerably louder.

Grant touched one of the coveralls with the barrel of his blaster. "Should we put 'em on?"

Kane shook his head. "We'd have to take off the armor. Besides, if we can't get back to the gateway in the next hour and thirty-two minutes, it doesn't much matter what kind of bugs we catch. And if we do get back, more than likely Lakesh can shoot us up with boosters and bug chasers."

"That's one way of approaching the problem," Brigid said skeptically.

"You can put one on if you'd like."

"Thanks, anyway. I'll share the risk with my partners."

Kane wasn't sure if she was being sarcastic, and he didn't request elaboration. He crossed the booth, pushed open the opposite door and stepped out onto a steel-railed balcony. Thirty feet below was a broad mezzanine, illuminated by crackling red light that played along the lines and ceramic pylons of a voltage-converter system.

In the center of the mezzanine, thick power cables sprouted from sockets in the concrete floor and snaked toward a strangely shaped generator. It was at least twelve feet tall, and looked like a pair of solid black cubes, the smaller balanced atop the larger. The top cube rotated slowly, producing a rhythmic drone of sound. An odd smell, like ozone blended with antiseptic, pervaded the air.

"That doesn't look like a nuclear engine to me," said Brigid.

"How many have you seen?" Kane asked.

"Dozens—schematics, at least. There's no mention of that monstrosity in Lakesh's floor plan."

Surveying the structures below, Grant commented, "Nobody around. Their security is for shit."

"I'd rather not have blastermen to contend with," Kane remarked. "Not if I can help it."

Suddenly he held up his hand in warning. Far below, two figures emerged from behind the base of the generator. Both of them carried toolboxes. Despite the shapeless coveralls they wore, there was no mistaking their slender, compact physiques.

Kane drew in a sharp breath and took a backward step, then stood and watched motionless as they walked away out of the mezzanine. He was struck by their lithe, graceful motions. Like the intruder in the Mesa Verde slaghole, there was something bizarrely beautiful in the way they moved.

Kane strode along the catwalk, trying to keep his eyes on the two people below, following them at a distance of a hundred feet. The noise from the generator smothered the sound of his footfalls.

The catwalk abruptly became a stairway, and by the time he, with the others trailing him, reached the bottom step, the figures were nowhere in sight.

The vast, dim room was strangely bare. Scars and gouges

in the gray concrete floor indicated heavy objects had been dragged and moved about some time in the not too remote past.

Kane looked toward Brigid. "Now where?"

"The floor plan wasn't like this. There's been a lot of changes." She looked around, turning her head very slowly, trying to reconcile their surroundings with the layout she had memorized.

Brigid stepped carefully forward, putting out her hand as though feeling her way along an invisible wall, reaching out for a vanished doorway. Kane and Grant followed her. She turned left after so many steps and again moved in a straight line. Finally she halted in a broad area surrounded only by shadows. Round holes in the floor showed that some large piece of heavy equipment had once been bolted there.

Craning her neck, she looked straight up. The men followed her gaze. Attached to a length of frayed cable, a photoelectric-eye device dangled overhead. Extending an arm, Brigid passed her hand in front of her in a right-to-left arc.

Inches from her feet, a square section of flooring began to turn over with a grating of stone and creak of metal pivots. It rolled up and stopped on edge, revealing a dim passageway leading below. The air wafting up from it was dank and laden with the acrid odor of chemicals.

Brigid said, "A disguised entrance, so the uninitiates of Overproject Excalibur wouldn't stumble over the real fruits of their labors."

Grant eased to one knee, studying the yawning opening. "What do you mean?"

Brigid's lips moved in a half smile, and she gestured theatrically to the square hole in the floor. "Welcome to Nightmare Alley."

Chapter 31

A short flight of stairs brought them down into a low-ceilinged anteroom. Another photoelectric sensor registered their presence, fed the signal to the portal and the square of concrete overhead rolled back into place with a crunch. Kane tensed, waiting for the brief wave of claustrophobia to pass.

"You okay?" Grant's voice was an anxious whisper.

"I'm grand," Kane responded in the same low tone.

Brigid shushed them into silence. She eyed the door at the far end of the room. It was of simple, innocuous wood. A push button was screwed into the frame with a small plastic sign above it.

"'Ring For Attendant,'" she read aloud. "Should we?"

"I hope you're joking," Grant snapped.

"I am. I don't think the people—or whatever—who took over this place still observe the predark security procedures."

"Let's go, then," said Kane, the Sin Eater filling his hand.

The door opened easily at the turn of the knob. They gazed down a tile-floored corridor, lined on either side by machines shrouded in plastic dust covers. Some were very large and bulky. As they walked between them, Brigid was able to identify much of the equipment—fluoroscope, an oscilloscope, centrifuge, evaporator, distillation tanks, a chromatograph.

"Old medical machines," she said softly. "Must have been moved down here when the facility was reactivated. Guess there wasn't much use for them anymore."

At the word "reactivate," Kane mechanically consulted his chron. "We've got one hour and seven minutes left."

"I'll track the time," Grant offered, "or we'll get stuck here."

Kane gave him an okay sign, then grimaced. The tart scent of chemicals was very strong, almost cloying, but they smelled and could almost taste a worse odor, the taint of death.

A set of sheet-metal double doors divided the corridor. Kane toed aside the one on the right, and Grant pushed open the left. Another corridor lay beyond, very long and nearly twenty feet wide. The ceiling was still low, lit by an arrangement of red bulbs, though the wattage seemed higher. The walls were composed of sheets of glass, all canted at forty-five-degree angles. The chromium frames glinted dully in the muted illumination.

"What's with this red light?" Grant demanded. "You could go blind in here."

Kane didn't offer a reply, though one part of his mind pounced on the most-likely answer. The eyes of Balam were huge and black, and therefore extremely sensitive to light levels above a certain brightness and spectrum. If this level of the Dulce complex housed Balam's brethren or his spawn, then it would have been converted for their comfort.

Brigid stepped forward. Kane reached for her, but she was too quick. She walked only a dozen feet before halting suddenly in front of a glass wall. Kane nearly trod on her heels.

Angrily he said, "Where are you—?"

His words caught in his throat. On the other side of the glass barrier, spread-eagled on a metal framework, was a flayed corpse.

It was a mass of yellow-white adipose tissue, ropy blood vessels and red-blue entrails. The body was all muscle, tendon and ligament—but the soft organs were pulsing wetly. It was covered, held together, by a clinging sac of transparent plastic.

Kane felt his belly fill up with something. Brigid lurched

away, making a strangling, gasping sound. He was only dimly aware of Grant stepping up beside him. Both of them stared in horrid fascination at the face, at the stripped head covered with a cohineal pattern of black-blue veins. Then an eye opened and stared back at them. It was a brown eye, and it held no particular expression.

Grant stumbled back a few paces, Sin Eater coming up reflexively. "It's still alive! Chill it!" he snarled.

"No!" Brigid whirled, securing a grip on his forearm. "We'll be discovered!"

Grant struggled for a second, then the tension went out of his arm. Brigid released him, struggling to regain a bit of her poise. The look she cast Kane was so filled with soul-wrenching horror and disgust, he could say nothing but "We're running out of time."

They walked along, and the sights they saw inside the glass-fronted cubicles didn't become any less nauseating but they didn't get worse, either. Perhaps the clinical atmosphere and the red lights contributed a sense of unreality, so even though they were on the edge of it, they didn't panic.

Kane's mind distanced itself from the externals, as though his eyes were vid cameras transmitting the images to the real him at some distant, safely removed location. He glanced past the glass walls, each one of them holding an artifact of horror, each one of them threatening his tenuous grip on sanity.

They passed glass cases and fluid-filled jars with floating human internal organs.

In one cubicle, they saw the naked body of a man. His complexion was ruddy, and his hair hung down his back in three thick strands. Parts of him were missing, but there was enough left of the face that they could see the snake tattoo imprinted across it.

Grant muttered, "Milt. At least he's dead."

"Now we know what happened to the bodies in the Cliff Palace," Kane said matter-of-factly, and continued on his way.

He clawed frantically for a grip on the real world, but the world around him *was* real. Everything outside of Dulce, this nightmare spot, seemed like a dim, half-remembered fragment of a dream.

Brigid moved ahead, obviously desperate to reach the end of the corridor. She glanced to her right, then slowed to a halt. Her "Oh, God" was hushed. Grant and Kane stopped on either side of her.

Beyond the glass, hanging from a ceiling rack, was a long row of transparent sacs filled with an amber gel. Small figures, curled in fetal positions, floated within the gelid contents.

"What are we looking at?" Even to his own ears, Kane's voice sounded creaky and old.

"An incubation chamber," Brigid whispered. "Artificial wombs, filled with synthetic amniotic fluid. This is where the hybrids are grown."

Kane stared hard at the creatures inside the wombs. He could see the vestigial noses and the small, thin mouths, almost reptilian in their neatness of tight lips and compressed cheeks. "That's why the bodies of the Dregs were left behind," he said half to himself. "They were genetically ruined. Reeth wasn't aware of the use his merchandise was being put to here, so he tried to slip in damaged goods. Salvo chilled him for it."

Kane felt the repulsion and snarling animal-fear rise within him. The hybrids were alien, more alien than human. Arrogance lay in their peaceful faces and relaxed bodies, which were bent almost in attitudes of prayer. They represented the future of the earth.

He whirled and walked away, feeling as though he were swimming through a tidal wave of fear. After a moment, Grant and Brigid fell into step behind him. A few paces past the nursery, they reached the crypt—or at least that was the first word that popped into Kane's mind upon seeing it.

Behind frost-streaked glass, naked men and women of all races were entombed, frozen in time. There were dozens of them. They stood in orderly rows, each one upright inside a transparent cryonic tube, arms crossed sedately over their chests. Their bodies had the appearance of pale blue ice, not only in color but composition. Their eyes were closed and they seemed to be slumbering.

"Cold storage," said Brigid with a shiver of repulsion. "Probably where the best of the best are kept."

"What do you mean?" Grant asked.

"What Lakesh said...purity control. The purest bloodlines, the highest sperm counts, the most perfect ovum. Everything to be cloned and spliced."

"Are they dead or just preserved?"

Brigid shook her head. "It doesn't matter to them anymore."

Kane scanned the bodies dispassionately, started to turn away, then focused his vision on the body of one man. He had seen that face before, though it was now carved in ice and relaxed in a forever sleep. He was looking at his father.

The realization entered Kane's soul, it clawed at his heart, it sent tentacles of torment into his brain. His spirit was shriveling, all conscious thought blotted out. Shock held him rigid. He opened his mouth, but at first nothing came out.

"Dad?" he asked, very quietly.

"You say something?" Grant inquired. He and Brigid looked at Kane questioningly.

Kane shook his head and walked blindly past his companions. His numb shock slowly gave way to a deep, visceral ache. He tried to collect his thoughts as he walked. He sought frantically for an anchor. A vision of his father, his mother and himself as a child hovered in his dimming mind. He began to run, his breath scraping in his throat, eyes burning with tears. He had wondered just last night if a Magistrate could weep. Now he knew.

The baron had said, "Kane, as your father before, you are now offered the opportunity to serve a greater cause." And later added, "You possess an admirable facility for seeking out answers. A facility shared by your father."

Salvo had said, "You know already. You just don't know that you know."

A glass-fronted, metal-framed double door loomed ahead of him. It was the only way out of the area, and it was locked. He kicked it open and lurched through it, panting. Sweat crawled between his armor and his skin.

He found himself in a maze of cool white corridors. Static-dust-collector screens and ventilator ducts were everywhere. Small-bore pipelines ran along the right wall, and he followed them, knowing they had to lead to a pumping station and a way back to the surface.

He kept running, not able to differentiate between the sound of his own rapid footfalls or those of Brigid and Grant racing behind him. In his ear, he heard Grant's breathless call.

He said, or thought he said, "Go back. Don't follow me."

"Kane! Use your head. We're short on time and you're short on brains! Stop and think. You don't know what's down there!"

Kane slowed down, but only because he was winded. There was nothing ahead of him he could possibly dread more than what lay behind.

He stopped in an alcove where cold, vinegary-smelling air dried the sweat on his face. The corridor terminated a few feet away at a door made of heavy-gauge wire mesh. A vague brightness lay beyond it.

Kane crouched there, gasping for air, ready to kill or to die or both. He heard voices on the other side of the door, and shadows flitted past the mesh. One voice he immediately recognized. He tensed, relaxed, then walked to the door. The voices had receded.

He was standing with his face pressed up against the wire screen, peering through the gaps, when Grant and Brigid appeared next to him. They turned to him, ready to ask the meaning of his actions.

Kane turned and savagely gestured them into silence. Then he calmly kicked the door open. The lock made a sound like a wet stick snapping. Still following the pipes, he walked into a high-ceilinged chamber, or series of chambers adjoined by partitions. Ahead of him he saw a cylindrical filter tank about twenty feet high. Its white surface glistened with moisture, beaded with condensation. Four of the pipes fed directly into steel-collared sockets at its base, and the other four bent away at a ninety-degree angle. He sidled silently around the curving wall of the tank.

Kane heard the familiar voice again. The musical, fluted tones were unmistakable. Slowly he eased his head around the cylinder for a view. He saw three men in gray bodysuits, and he recognized them from the night of his initiation into the Trust. The small man with the beginnings of a paunch was named Guende. The balding Asian was Ojaka. The tall one with the weather-beaten face and gray crew cut was Abrams. They were members of Baron Cobalt's inner circle.

They stood in a semicircle around a man whose excessively slender figure was draped in a golden robe. He wore a tall, crested headdress that exaggerated the elongated contours of his skull. His pale golden skin was stretched tight over facial bones that seemed all brow, cheeks and chin. The eyes were large, slanted and a yellowish brown in color.

Baron Cobalt faced a man that could have been his exact duplicate except for his bright blue eyes and shorter stature. He wore a tight-fitting silvery gray bodysuit that seemed of a metallic weave. Kane spotted the plastic tubular holster strapped to his upper thigh. Both men moved with a swaying motion, like reeds before a breeze. The movements were very precise, very ritualistic, and Kane knew it was a form of ceremonial greeting.

The man was saying in a high, lilting voice, "I regret not locating the document in question, Lord Baron, but I was interrupted by an intruder."

"An intruder?" Suspicion colored the baron's voice.

"Yes. Though I caught only a glimpse, I believe he was in the attire of one of your Magistrates."

The baron's swaying motion paused, then began again. "I was not informed of this by my subordinates. Abrams, what do you know of this?"

Abrams answered brusquely, "Nothing, Lord Baron. Salvo is the officer in charge, though at last report, he is still incapacitated."

Baron Cobalt brought a narrow hand to his chin. "When we return to the ville, I want him brought before me. On a stretcher if necessary."

One more of their group bustled into view, wearing a suit of baggy coveralls. When it spoke, the voice possessed a definite feminine timbre. "We are behind schedule, Lord Baron. Your bath loses its potency."

"Matters of my office must be addressed."

"Not here." The female swayed to and fro in agitation. "The Directorate is very exact on these matters. Nine days to bathe nine barons. The schedule cannot be adjusted for one without adjusting it for all."

Baron Cobalt's reply was polite, and cold. "I regret the delay. However, inasmuch as I serve the Directorate and you serve me, not only am I aware of my responsibilities, but you are dangerously close to exceeding yours."

The female fell silent and stepped back. Baron Cobalt and his staff followed her out of the range of Kane's vision.

Brigid tapped his shoulder from behind. "What's going on?"

"Get back to the gateway," he whispered. He leaned forward.

Her hand landed on his arm, but Kane shook free and turned to face her. "Damn it, I said get back to the gateway!"

"No," she whispered fiercely. "The way you're acting, you're going to get us all chilled."

"Not if you and Grant do as I say."

"We came here together," Grant whispered. "We leave the same way."

There was no time and no point in arguing. "The baron

is here. Lakesh probably knew he would be, and he probably knew we'd encounter him. Or he hoped we would.''

"Encounter him and do what?'' Grant demanded. "Chill him?'' He seemed very uncomfortable with the concept.

"Or to learn the final bit of *truth*.'' Kane said the last word venomously. "It's personal now, between him and me. You two stay here. Grant, when you hear me talking, depending on what I say, I want you to either get the hell out or come to me. Agreed?''

Neither Brigid nor Grant made a sound or a move. Kane rolled his eyes and circled the filtration tank. He found the maintenance ladder and scaled it quickly. Standing on the rounded top, he stretched up both arms, hooking his hands around a bound collection of pipes, and he chinned himself up onto them. By sheer force of will he managed to squirm his armored body into the small space between the pipes and the ceiling. He belly-crawled forward, feeling the pipe beneath him quiver with the strain of supporting his weight.

He didn't think about what might happen if the ceiling struts tore loose from their moorings and dumped down on the floor. Habit and training took over now. His Magistrate consciousness was at work, and it drove away his fears, his anxieties and his horrors. He pulled himself forward by his arms, worming his body along as fast as he could, as fast as he dared.

He heard Baron Cobalt's voice below him and he stopped his forward progress, peering down between a pair of pipes.

The female attendant's voice announced, "Your bath is drawn, Lord Baron.''

Chapter 32

Kane had seen pictures of ancient Egyptian sarcophagi. The object propped up against a crossbarred brace contrivance looked very similar, like a coffin following the body contours, only this one was molded from some transparent polymer. A pair of flexible hoses was connected to it at opposing midway points. The hoses, in turn, were connected to a metal tank with two valve wheels projecting from the top.

Though Kane was above the baron and his party, their backs were turned to him. Kane could see only the face of the female creature.

Abrams removed the baron's tall headpiece, and Guende and Ojaka helped him step out of his robe. Naked, Baron Cobalt backed into the transparent sarcophagus, and the little attendant swung the lid over and latched it, sealing it tight. She stepped over to the tank, turned a valve wheel and with a gurgling hiss, a thin, whitish fluid—like milk diluted with water—spurted from the nozzle of one hose. She twisted the second wheel. From the opposite hose spurted a thick red fluid. It dripped down the inner surface of the container, blending with the white liquid and becoming a brown-hued mixture.

The sarcophagus filled quickly. The liquid level rose above the baron's knees, lapped at his thighs and crept up above his waist. His head was tilted slightly back and up, his large eyes closed, and he breathed deeply and regularly through his open mouth.

When the fluid touched the base of his neck, the attendant turned the wheel valves simultaneously, cutting off the twin liquid flows.

She said to the men, "I will return in ten minutes to add the next compound. Remain here with the baron."

She moved away with a peculiarly graceful mincing gait. Guende, Abrams and Ojaka huddled together, speaking in low, grim tones. Kane couldn't hear much of what they said, but he was positive his and Salvo's names figured prominently.

Fingers curled tightly around a pipe, Kane twisted himself until he hung from his hands almost above their heads. They were so intent on their whispered conference, they didn't notice the pair of black legs dangling only a few feet behind and twelve or so feet above them.

Kane released his grip and dropped, bending his knees slightly to cushion his fall. At the sound of his boots hitting the floor, all of them turned in unison, their expressions of astonishment so similar that they could have been triplets.

Abrams was the biggest of the three, the most physically capable despite his advanced years. Kane took him out first. Abrams made gestures of negation, as if waving his arms would drive his attacker back.

Kane quickly stepped inside the man's out-flung arms and kicked his right kneecap. The pop of the patella being forcefully removed from the femur was clearly audible, even through the lining of his helmet.

Abrams went down on the floor, plucking at his maimed leg and howling in agony. He gaped up at Kane in incredulous horror.

Kane planted the steel-reinforced toe of his boot against the point of Abrams's chin, snapping his head back and down. His skull struck the concrete with a crack.

Kane pivoted on one heel and drove a roundhouse kick into Ojaka's lower belly. The man folded over Kane's leg, and while he was suspended there, Kane brought his left fist in a snapping arc against the bridge of Ojaka's nose. The man uttered a grunt, then flopped down on the floor.

Guende was paralyzed, merely staring, and breathing

wetly through his open mouth. He gaped at Kane and didn't move. Kane's right leg arced upward and around in a spinning crescent kick. The sole of his boot caught Guende on the left side of his head. Consciousness went out of his eyes with the suddenness of a candle being extinguished. He went down heavily on his face and made no movement afterward.

All three men lay helpless, and Kane walked over to the sarcophagus. The baron hadn't been aware of the brief struggle. He was still luxuriating in his bath, eyes closed as if in serene meditation.

Kane rapped on the transparent cover. Baron Cobalt's eyelids twitched. Kane knocked again. The eyelids fluttered, then lifted. The annoyance in them changed instantly when they took in the black helmet, the red visor and the cold, bare-toothed grin beneath it.

The baron's body convulsed, sloshing the fluid around, splashing it up onto his face. He opened his mouth to call for help, but only a shriek of fear and frustration emerged. Kane was a little surprised that he was able to hear it so clearly through the walls of the sarcophagus.

Baron Cobalt was still screaming when Kane flipped open the latches and heaved the lid aside. A torrent of liquid cascaded out. Kane smelled peroxide, alcohol and the faint coppery stink of diluted blood.

The sudden release of pent-up pressures washed the baron out. His feet scrabbled on the slick floor, trying to gain some sort of purchase. He sat down heavily with an undignified *whoof* of forcefully expelled air.

Setting his feet firmly as the liquid swirled around them, Kane bent down, closed his left hand around the short, delicate column of Baron Cobalt's neck and hauled him upright. He was remarkably light. Kane swung him around, slamming his back against the filtration tank, pinning him there with his hand around his throat. He raised the Sin Eater until its bore was on a direct line to a spot between the baron's eyes. His struggles ceased.

Despite the residue of the noxious fluid still clinging to

his body, Kane saw the baron was completely hairless; even his pubic area was smooth. His sex organ was a tiny bud, no larger or thicker than the tip of Kane's little finger.

"So, Kane," said Baron Cobalt in a sibilant hiss. "Traitor, criminal. Murderer. You will surrender yourself to me and confess your crimes."

"That doesn't work anymore, Baron. You're not a god-king, you're not divine. You're not even a good employer. You're a laboratory monstrosity with an attitude—a vampire living off the genetic material of human beings. You have to take baths in chemicals and gore. You're *disgusting* is what you are."

Baron Cobalt's eyes blazed in golden rage, a golden haughtiness. "How dare you presume to pass judgment, you filthy apeling. Are you truly so deluded that you believe you can defy the baronies and the Directorate?"

"You're a puppet whose strings are pulled by a bunch of little gray bastards, and you think *I'm* deluded?"

A cruel smile lifted the corners of Baron Cobalt's mouth. "You think the Archons are responsible for what happened to the world? We did it to ourselves."

"*We?*" Kane said mockingly. "Don't put yourself on the same footing as humans."

"I stand corrected. I occupy a much higher position. Yes, I am a hybrid of human and Archon, and I am ashamed of the human element within me. I take a bit of solace in the fact that at least my human genes spring from the very best, carefully selected stock."

Kane didn't respond. In anticipation of the baron's next words, his limbs began to tremble. Baron Cobalt noticed, because his smile widened.

"You face an interesting problem. Much of that superior genetic human material derives from your father. If you kill me, you'll be committing fratricide, after a fashion. A sin that, I recall from old religious teachings, immediately consigned souls to eternal damnation. Do you want to be damned?"

Kane gritted his teeth, battling the soul-destroying sickness threatening to overwhelm him.

"Why are you here, Kane?"

"To find the truth about you, about humanity. I had to find out if you and your kind actually existed or if you were some strain of mutant."

"I am human, Kane. The new human."

Kane studied Baron Cobalt's face, the golden eyes bright with intelligence, the too smooth skin, the high forehead, the small ears set too low on the head.

"No," he said. "You're outside of humanity."

"The humanity you know is dead. The new humanity is taking its place. All a matter of natural selection. Nature taking its course."

"Nature didn't create you."

"Sometimes nature must be prodded. Believe me, Kane," Baron Cobalt continued, his musical voice sounding notes of kindness, of compassion, "I sympathize with your shock, your disorientation. You would have been indoctrinated eventually into these secrets. Not even Salvo has been to this part of the installation. Return with me to the ville, and you will take his place in the Trust. You will occupy an exalted position. You will not be serving me or the Archon Directorate, but the *new humanity*. We are a highly evolved breed, and our numbers are growing. We find rewards in life that our forbears were incapable of appreciating. This is our world now, and nothing can be done to arrest the tide. Stop opposing us. It will do you no good. Accept our kind as we have accepted *your* kind."

A strange heat made Kane's voice thick, his tongue feeling clumsy. "My father and all those others did not volunteer to serve or to help create a new humanity. You enslaved them, stole their lives and their identities. No matter how highly evolved you claim your breed is, you still need lowly humans to survive. You need lousy humans like Reeth to supply you with fresh meat. So, explain to me, Lord Baron, how does all that scheming and stealing and double-crossing make you superior to us apelings? You're no different than the lowliest Pit boss in the worst slaghole of Tartarus.''

Baron Cobalt's hands came up, his long fingers clutching at Kane's wrist, trying to tear his hand away from his throat. In a rage, he barked, "You'll die, I'll have you dismembered while you're still alive—"

Kane chuckled. "Look at you. You're puny, your body is fragile. You have to be sustained by artificial means. You and the Archons are so terrified of us, you trick us into living down to our basest impulses, then condition us to be ashamed of the very positions you forced us into. No, you're not superior. What you are is a race of jealous, dick-less cowards.''

The fury in the golden eyes burned hot and molten. The baron struggled wildly, kicking at Kane's legs, long fingers flailing at his face. He fought like a trapped animal, crushing his knuckles on Kane's armored chest, mashing toes into his shin guards. Kane held him easily and laughed.

"I rest my case, Lord Baron. You can't beat us. You may have won a battle, may have won a lot of battles throughout history, but this is a war that's been waged for thousands of years. But humanity always manages to get back up one more time after the Archons have knocked us down. No matter how blasphemous it sounds to you, we'll get up again and we'll kick your genetically superior asses out of our lives, our futures, once and for all.''

To emphasize his words, Kane slowly squeezed the baron's throat. Baron Cobalt's face grew dark with congested blood. His pale tongue protruded past his thin lips. Kane maintained the pressure until the baron's slim frame shuddered and sagged.

Kane opened his hand, and the baron dropped limply to the floor, on his right side, splashing into the standing puddle of blood and chemicals. Kane gazed down at him, not sure if he'd choked the life out of him or not, and at the moment, not giving much of a damn.

"New humanity," Kane muttered, looking down at the

soiled, scrawny figure at his feet. He spoke into the helmet comm link. "Grant?"

"Right here."

"You heard?"

"Your side of it." His voice was strained.

"Where are you?"

"Where you left us."

"Stay there. I'm—"

A pulse of sound drove into Kane's head, penetrating his helmet and eardrums like a white-hot nail. He reeled in a sudden blaze of pain, his scuffling feet unsteady and seeking purchase in the puddle around him. A bass humming sound, almost physical, tightened around his brain like a steel vise.

He managed to keep from falling, shambling around in a half turn to see a quartet of hybrids approaching. The one occupying a center position wore the gray metallic suit and he held a slender silver wand in his right hand. The wand was about three feet long, and it hummed and shivered, its gleaming length somehow blurred.

The man with the wand said calmly, "I've seen him before, in the Cliff Palace."

The one beside said, "Subdue him or kill him."

Kane raised his blaster. The tip of the wand dipped toward him. Shrieking violence filled his head, and he collapsed, hammered to the floor by the storm of pain.

He caught himself on his elbows, steadying the Sin Eater in a double-handed grip. His first target was the man with the wand. He worked the trigger.

The gleaming rod swept out, fanning in a hazy semicircle. It hummed, popped and Kane heard the sharp clang of impact, then the whine of a ricochet. The slender man stood unharmed and smiling a gentle, patronizing smile.

Kane fired again, a 3-round burst, aiming for the middle of the high, unlined forehead. Again the wand inscribed a humming arc, its tip dancing from left to right. Three pops concussed the air, and bullets buzzed and screamed in all directions, crashing against and bouncing away from metal.

Somehow the rod produced an invisible field that deflected the bullets, yet at the same time directed energies that made his head feel as if it were about to burst. Kane couldn't understand the dynamic at work, and he doubted his questions would be answered if he asked them. He shifted the barrel of the Sin Eater a fraction to the right and squeezed the trigger.

The little hybrid standing beside the man with the wand catapulted backward, his torso squirting out blood like a squeezed sponge. The creatures on either side of him yelped in terror and reacted by trying to run blindly away, without even attempting to watch where they were going. Kane fired again, the blaster's roar painfully loud.

The heavy-caliber round took another hybrid in the chest and spun him around in a grotesque pirouette. Banners of blood streamed from the wound, draping his companions and the walls with red liquid ribbons. The man holding the wand stumbled aside, his face crimson bedaubed, trying to clear his vision with frantic swipes from his left hand.

Kane gathered his legs beneath him, sprang to his feet and began a dizzy, shambling run. He tasted blood sliding warmly over his lips, streaming from ruptured capillaries in his nose. He had no idea what kind of weapon the hybrid employed, but he was fairly certain his helmet had saved him from exploded eardrums or worse.

The floor pitched and yawed beneath him, and he had trouble running in a straight line. He fixed his gaze on the top of the filtration tank as a landmark and he raced toward it. Pale figures flitted near him, on either side in the red-tinged gloom, lithe and swift, seeking to draw ahead and cut off his escape.

He reached the base of the tank and was running around it when he heard Brigid yell, followed by the door-slamming bang of her handblaster. A fraction of a second later came the deep, stuttering roar of the Sin Eater. Piping voices, squealing in rage and fear, fluted all around.

He saw Brigid coming toward him, holding her H&K in

a double grip, backed by Grant sweeping the perimeter with his Sin Eater. A faint twist of smoke curled from the barrel.

Kane tried to stop, but he skidded and stumbled and would have fallen if Grant hadn't steadied him.

"They're on to us now," Kane gasped, wiping blood from his mouth with the back of his hand. "They've got some kind of weapon. I don't know what it is, but it's pretty nasty. They almost got me."

"Yeah," replied Grant, looking around warily, "they were trying to outflank you. Guess they thought you were alone, didn't expect to see us. The little fuckers are sure light on their feet."

The air suddenly shivered with a hum, and Kane jerked reflexively. The surface of the tank near his head suddenly acquired a deep dent, accompanied by a *whang* of sound. Wiry slivers of metal and scraps of paint burst up all around the impact point.

The three of them started to run. Brigid said briskly, "Ultrasonics, I imagine. Infrasound. Electric current converted to sonic waves by a little gadget called a maser. Something the military fooled around with as part of their nonlethal-weapons experiments."

Still battling waves of vertigo, Kane said, "Nonlethal, my ass."

Brigid saw how he swayed unsteadily on his feet, how he had to clutch at the pipelines on the wall for support. "You took a hit?"

"Yeah," he wheezed. "More than one."

"If it's any consolation, all you probably suffered was a little inner-ear damage. Nothing permanent."

The three of them reached the wire-mesh door and plunged into the tiled corridor. Grant stopped to look behind, digging into his war bag. "Keep going!"

He held the DM5 frag gren in his left hand, pulled away the pin with his teeth and tossed it underhanded. It landed where the wall joined with the floor, directly beneath the pipelines. He turned and sprinted down the corridor, counting backward beneath his breath. When he reached *Three*, the passage reverberated to a sharp explosion and rattling of steel balls. They punctured the pipes, and clouds of steam mixed with the billowing smoke. Even through his armor, Grant felt the puff of heat.

He caught up with Kane and Brigid. "Don't know if that slowed 'em up any."

"Let's assume it didn't," Kane said.

Foul-smelling vapor drifted toward them, and they jogged away from it. When they reached the glass door leading to the alley, they slowed to a trot. Kane didn't want to walk through it again, unless the circumstances were dire. He was on the verge of suggesting they seek an alternate route when he heard a humming buzz, like an angry insect. Grant cried out and fell forward, back arched, arms outstretched as if he had received a blow between his shoulder blades. As he toppled, Kane saw the fist-sized dent in his armor.

Simultaneously the door exploded inward in a shower of glass.

Chapter 33

Brigid's reaction was the fastest. Finger already on the trigger of the H&K, she swiveled from the hips and fired a whole magazine down the steam- and smoke-filled corridor, the reports coming so fast they sounded like a single, prolonged *bam*.

Grant pushed himself to his knees, wagging his head from side to side. Brigid stepped beside him, her eyes probing the mist. "You caught an overspill of the ultrasonics. You'll be okay."

Kane dragged him to his feet.

Grant kept shaking his head. "Something's wrong with my eyes. Everything's out of focus—"

"We're in wonderful shape," Kane observed dryly, hustling him toward the doorway. "The motion impaired leading the blind."

Brigid ejected the spent clip from her handblaster, thumbed in a fresh one and said, "Get going. I'll cover your backsides."

Kane and Grant kicked through the shattered ruin of the door and entered the alley. Grant said, "I'm better. Things aren't as blurry."

Releasing him, Kane turned to see Brigid backing through the scattering of broken glass, blaster trained on the corridor. "Don't see them," she said. "Maybe the going got too rough."

"It's apt to get rougher," Kane replied. "They probably have another way topside and they'll be waiting to cut us off."

He glanced at his chron. "We've got twenty-one

minutes. That's not enough time for all of us to get back to Level Four.''

"It's more than enough," she said grimly, "if you stop making gloomy predictions and get moving.''

Grant shook his head and declared, "This situation is the classic one-percenter.''

"We'll improve the odds as we go," Brigid responded.

They went back into the nightmare lab area. Kane saw no use in ordering a standard deployment of personnel and firepower. He was still suffering from bouts of vertigo and reeling drunkenly from time to time, Grant's vision was still foggy and Brigid was untrained. So they ran in a blundering rush, Kane occasionally veering from side to side, bumping into Grant, who was feeling his way along the glass-fronted wall.

When they approached the section where the bodies lay in cryonic stasis, Kane called a halt. He reached into his war bag and produced a pair of grenades.

"Incends," he said, hefting them in either hand. "How many do you have, Grant?''

He pawed through his pouch and pulled out a metal egg. "One.''

"What do you want those for?" Brigid asked anxiously.

"I want to blow this place.''

"Why? Diversion, revenge or what?''

"A little of all three. Also mercy. If those people are still alive, at least we can make sure they won't be used as biological material for the new humanity.''

"It might not do any good, Kane. Their cryonic canisters might be well shielded.''

"It might not do any good, it might not stop their program, but at least we can screw up their timetable a little.''

"What difference would it make?" asked Grant sourly.

"A great deal. To me.''

Using his thumbs, Kane flipped away the firing levers, tossed them behind him and started running. Grant cursed, pulled the lever of his gren, hurled it and ran after him. Brigid outdistanced them both.

Behind them, the lab disintegrated in a roaring white flash.

The glass-fronted cubicles shattered as if giant fists smashed into them. The entire passageway shuddered brutally. Shards of glass rained down on the floor behind them, and the scorching heat of the thermite charges buffeted their bodies.

Grant's incendiary detonated, and the rolling balls of flame overlapped, instantly building to a roaring inferno. The thundering shock waves felt like a storm-driven surf.

A hurricane of superheated air converged from all sides, slapping their breaths back into their nostrils. An intolerable white glare lit their way, casting their elongated, distorted shadows on the floor ahead of them. Their eyes, adjusted to the red-tinted dimness of the installation, stung and watered. Behind them they heard the screeching rasp of ripping metal and the splintering of glass. The floors and walls shook and trembled, and a cloud of smoke billowed after them, bringing with it a faint scent, like overcooked pork.

Long before they thought to have reached them, the set of double doors came in sight. The three people slammed them aside, rushed down the aisle between the old medical machines, kicked open the adjoining door and stumbled to the foot of the stairs, tripping the photoelectric sensor in the process. Overhead, the concrete slab pivoted up on its side, and they scrambled through it before it was fully ajar.

They ran across the bare floor and empty spaces toward the metal staircase. Kane, his eyes recovering from the glare, was aware of pale, graceful shapes flashing swiftly out of the shadows, but he and his companions reached the stairs and hauled themselves up them without being molested.

When they pounded onto the walkway, they saw why. The catwalk was blocked by a clot of hybrids, making mewing, giggling sounds. Several of them swished silver wands through the air, like fencers warming up for a duel.

Brigid took a step back, cast a glance over her shoulder and swore. "Hell night!"

Clustered around the base of the stairway glittered dozens of eyes. From the cluster rose a tittering murmur, abhorrent to the ear.

From the group blocking their forward progress, the hybrid Kane recognized stepped forward, the metal rod rocking back and forth in his hand, like the needle of a metronome. A smile creased his thin mouth.

He said, "It is our practice to subdue and contain intruders. Killing is sometimes a necessity, but oftentimes useful tissues are damaged. Will you accept the inevitable?"

Kane shared a brief look with Grant and Brigid. They gave quick nods, and he turned to face the hybrid. He slid the Sin Eater back into its holster. Grant followed suit.

Kane spread his arms wide, hands held at shoulder level. He approached the group slowly. "We accept your terms."

An expression bordering on disappointment crossed the hybrid's smooth, angular face. "A logical choice for an apeling."

Kane stopped a few feet away. "What are your orders?"

The deferential note in his voice inspired the hybrid to take a step forward, an arrogant tilt to his head. "First you will disarm, and then disrobe. You will be—"

Kane swung his left arm in a vicious sweep. His forearm took the hybrid across the throat with a crunching of bone and cartilage. He flailed backward, over the rail. In falling, he dropped the wand and clutched at one of his comrades, which cost the standing hybrid his balance. He stumbled and fell against those behind him.

The Sin Eater slid into Kane's hand and he fired it into the group of hybrids. Behind him, he heard the snapping of Brigid's H&K and a drumming roar from Grant's Copperhead.

The first trio of rounds from the Sin Eater reamed a path through the heart of the group at head level. Flame wreathed the stuttering muzzle of his blaster, and bodies reeled backward in a surge of exploding flesh and bones. Then a giant's blow struck his right arm, and he heard the

wrist bone break. He caught only a jagged afterimage of a
vibrating silver wand before he went down on the catwalk.
Agony lanced up his arm into his shoulder as he tried to
maintain pressure on the trigger. His hand didn't seem to
be there anymore.

His ears filled with hideous mewling sounds, and deli-
cately fingered hands clawed for him. Some of the fingers
had sharp little nails that slashed bloody furrows in his face.

Grant shouted, "Kane!"

Kane drove his right leg forward, and his boot sole collapsed and broke a narrow face bobbing above him. Rather
than try to unlimber his Copperhead from his belt, he
reached down and withdrew his combat knife from its boot
sheath. Gripping it in his left hand, he swung the blade
down again and again at the bodies remaining before him.

He thrust upward as a hybrid tried to bring a wand to
bear. The blade parried the humming rod, the knife vibrated
violently, stung Kane's fingers and flew from his hand, over
the side. He drove his fist square between the big eyes and
dropped him, senseless and bleeding on top of him. He
reached for the wand, but a hybrid's foot kicked it away.
He heaved the doll-like body up, carrying it with him as
he sprang to his feet. He flung the limp form into a pair of
hybrids, bowling them off their feet.

With a cold fury, Kane struck blow after blow with his
fist and feet, punching, kicking, stomping. Hybrids stam-
peded away from him, leaving the bodies of their brethren
lying with ribs and limbs broken, scalps split open and
leaking.

He fumbled with his Copperhead, bringing it to bear with
his left hand. The burst he fired toward the retreating hybrids was poorly aimed, but the storm of slugs picked up
several and hurled them forward, tumbling them limply
head over heels.

"See?" he roared hoarsely. "*See?* You little parasites
can die just as easily as us apelings!"

The sounds from the hybrids were chaotic, mingled cries
of outrage, fury and terror. Kane turned to see Brigid and

Grant, pale bodies and arms hauling at them from all sides. Grant was applying the butt of his Copperhead, trying to fend them off. Brigid's blaster was out of ammo, and hands gripped her ankles. She bent to beat them off with the barrel of her H&K, then other hands caught at her and brought her down. More of the hybrids pulled themselves up on the walkway and leaped upon her.

Brigid managed to break free, but a long hand clawed for her face. She sank her teeth into it, biting until she felt the delicate bones break. The hybrid snatched his hand away, shrieking. Kane moved over to her, clearing a path by kicking and stamping.

She managed to stagger erect, blood streaming from a dozen nail-inflicted scratches on her arms. More hybrids slithered up onto the catwalk. Here and there gleamed the wands.

Taking a firm grip on Brigid's arm, Kane raced along the walkway, followed in close formation by Grant, firing the Copperhead ahead of him. The howling hybrids in their path were driven to the rails, and they slipped over, preferring the thirty-foot drop to facing the crazed humans in the narrow confines of the catwalk. The floor plates were slippery with blood and viscera, and Kane booted several corpses out of his way.

When they sprinted past the two-tiered generator, Kane briefly considered planting the rest of his grens around it, but since he had no idea if the explosive loads would have any effect or an apocalyptic one, he discounted the notion.

A group of hybrids danced after them at a discreet distance, a hurried babble of hate-filled words rising from their tongues. They heard a few faint hums, and once the walkway under their feet vibrated strangely, but the range for the ultrasound weapons was too great to have any meaningful effect.

When they reached the booth, Grant paused inside of it while Kane and Brigid made their way out into the hallway. From his bag, he took a pair of flares, shut his eyes and snapped the rods in half. A blinding violet-white light splashed the room with an eerie luminescence. The blaze of light was so intense that even through Grant's visor and closed eyelids, it registered.

He tossed them against the hanging decam coveralls, and the old material ignited immediately. Before Grant rushed through the opposite door, flame flashed throughout the booth. He had reached the same conclusion about the creatures' sensitivity to high light levels, and he prayed the fire and the near-blinding incandescence of the flares would discourage further pursuit.

He rejoined his companions halfway up the ramp. Because of his broken wrist, Kane had trouble clambering over the turnstile. His feet caught in the prongs and dumped him unceremoniously to the floor, but he shook off Brigid's helping hands and started running again. All three were gasping and aching when they reached the landing. Fortunately the bulkhead was still open.

They staggered up the stairwell and, forgetting their earlier caution, clung to and hauled themselves up by the handrails. The door was unlocked as they left it, and as they entered the dim corridor on Level Four, Kane heard the distant whine and hydraulic hiss of an elevator.

"On their way by the elevator," he gasped out. He checked his chron. "Let's hope they don't arrive in the next two minutes."

They turned the corner and saw the open door of the control room. Approaching the door from the opposite direction was a group of small, pale figures. The two groups saw each other at the same time.

The three of them surged forward in a wild rush. Grant snapped off a couple of shots, aiming into the press of bodies, hoping to knock down his targets and trip up others. The hybrids kept coming, voicing sobbing laughs.

One of the hybrids outpaced the others and waved a silver wand over his head like a saber, racing bravely forward. Suddenly, with a spurt of speed, Brigid bounded ahead, head back, leg pumping. The pair met in the corridor when they were abreast of the open door.

The hybrid slashed down with the wand, its point aiming at her. She left her feet in a long dive, her shoulders catching the smallish hybrid at ankle level, smashing him sideways, bouncing him off the doorjamb and sending him careening into the room. She pounced atop him, wrestling with him for the rod.

She got the heel of one hand under the hybrid's pointed chin and threw all her weight into a sharp push. There came a snapping sound, and the hybrid's grip on the wand weakened. Brigid wrenched it from his hand, turned it and touched the left side of his head with the humming, vibrating tip.

His skull collapsed where the point touched. A small, perfectly round hole was punched through the epidermal layers, splintering the bones, liquefying and blowing most of his brains through his tiny right ear.

Kane and Grant shouldered their way into the room, sending covering fire down the corridor. Kane back-kicked the door shut behind them, and Grant wrestled a heavy chair across the floor, jamming the back beneath the knob.

Brigid got to her feet, tapping her palm with the wand. "That won't hold against an ultrasound assault," she gasped. "They may even be able to breach the gateway, since it's not made of armaglass."

"They've got less than one minute to prove it to us," Kane said.

They got inside the chamber, Grant pulling the heavy steel door closed and spinning the wheel-lock until he heard the click of solenoids catching and holding. The single overhead light came on.

Kane, cradling his broken wrist, sat down with a loud exhalation of air. Brigid eased down beside him. Both breathed heavily. Sweat had cut runnels in her combat cosmetics.

He asked, "Why did you take that chance out there, Baptiste?"

She raised the rod to eye level and sighted down its

length. "An artifact, a souvenir. It might tell us something about their technology."

Grant, hunched over beside the door, hushed them into silence. "I think they got in."

As soon as he said it, they heard the familiar buzzing whine, somewhat muffled by the heavy metal door and the thick concrete blocks of the gateway unit. The door shuddered as it took the terrible impact of focused infrasound. The paint split and blistered and peeled away in long strips. The cross braces vibrated violently, and rivets and bolts rattled and clattered. Bits of concrete around the door frame flaked, showered down and fell away in chunks.

Kane looked at his chron. Tightly he said, "He's behind schedule—"

The floor and ceiling disks sprang to glowing life. Mist gathered and thickened above and below. Tiny flashing sparks floated through the air.

Brigid sighed with relief. Grant sat down, putting his back against the wall, hands resting on his knees. "A one-percenter to remember," he said wryly.

As the mist curled down and entwined with the tendrils spiraling upward, Kane closed his eyes and leaned his head back. "Dad," he whispered. "Goodbye."

Chapter 34

It was an old road Kane walked, but since it was his first time, it was new to him. He had the impression of following the track of a giant broken-backed snake, whipping to and fro. The asphalt was cracked and deeply rutted.

The last crimson glory of the setting sun cast red shadows on the snow-covered mountain peaks above him. He breathed the fragrance of the wind that rolled up from the forests far, far below. Though craggy cliffs rose gray and gaunt before and around him, the foothills behind were rich with grassy meadows and green groves of trees.

On his right, the road wound and twisted and looped across the sheer face of a cliff, and to his left a deep abyss plummeted straight down a thousand feet or more. At one time, steel guardrails had bordered the lip of the road, but only a few rusted metal stanchions remained. Past the edge of the road, at the bottom of the abyss, were the metal skeletons of several vehicles. More than likely, they had lain there since the time of the nukecaust, weathering all the seasons that came after.

Now, in late Montana summer, they looked like tombstones. He picked up a rock from the roadbed and tossed it over the abyss, trying but knowing he couldn't bounce it from one of the metal carcasses. There wasn't the slightest complaint from the area where, just two days before, a burst of ultrasound had shattered his wrist. It was still encased by a lightweight cast halfway to his elbow, but none of the nerves had been damaged and the bones should knit quickly—at least that was the prognosis of DeFore, the resident medic.

He walked carefully, alertly along the curving road, keeping close to the cliff face. Lakesh had told him that when the Cerberus Redoubt was built, the road had been protected by a force field powered by atomic generators. Sometime during the past century, the energy screen had been permanently deactivated, when many survivors were scavenging off the land.

Kane went around a pair of bends in the road, and the split tarmac broadened onto a huge plateau. The scraps of a chain-link fence clinked in the breeze.

Inside the fenced perimeter was the base of a mountain peak, and nestled against the rock face was a high gate, corrugated metal gleaming beneath peeling paint. The gate opened like an accordion, folding to one side, operated by a punched-in code and a hidden lever control. It was open now, and Brigid, Grant, Domi and Lakesh emerged from it. Lakesh was leaning on Domi, as though he had lost his strength, but Kane was pretty certain he simply enjoyed leaning against a shapely young woman.

At least Lakesh had given him the whole story when they returned from Dulce. As Kane had already figured, Anson had accompanied his father to Dulce to bring back Balam. Only Anson and Balam made it. Having seen what went on there, knowing what would be the fate of the elder Kane, and not allowed to mount a rescue mission, Anson was consumed with guilt and horror. The knowledge was too much for him to bear and live.

Lakesh had tried to tell Kane how sorry he was for not warning him that his father was there, but the apology was unnecessary.

According to Lakesh, Dulce was not the only installation where the cloning of human DNA and the splicing of it with Archon genetic material was occurring. Furthermore, the hybrids they encountered in Dulce were only of a certain type. There were others.

Kane stopped and admired the sunset. It was difficult not to envision it setting behind the Administrative Monolith, but the glow around the mountain peaks was certainly more picturesque.

The others joined him. Without preamble, Lakesh said, "Friend Kane, I had hoped that affairs would take a slower pace after your return. They have not. I've just come back from Cobaltville—and from an emergency meeting of the Trust."

"Minus a few, I imagine."

"There are always more where Abrams, Ojaka and Guende came from. Besides, they're not dead. Just discouraged. Unfortunately the baron lives, as well."

Kane shrugged. "More where he came from, too."

Grant said, "They're looking for us, Kane. In dead earnest. They've convened a council of the nine barons."

Kane stepped closer to the edge, kicking a loose stone into the chasm. The wind tugged at his hair, and a smile tugged at the corners of his mouth. He saw the forests below, then raised his gaze to the mountains, the sun and sky. Beyond that lay the vast web of the universe. He had the feeling that his father was out there, gliding among the stars, watching what he did next. Hoping and aspiring and having faith in his son.

He turned and looked at Brigid, letting their eyes meet in a wordless exchange. He liked her strength and flexibility, though at times she irked him with her cool logic. There was something else about her that spoke to a part of him that was hidden, unpracticed, unacknowledged. As if in approval, he nodded at her, then scanned the faces of the others. They were good faces, strong faces, all different, showing age and wisdom, pain and determination, the courage of youth, and a kind of beauty and endurance. Human faces. Exiles from the world of their birth.

"Well," he said at length. "So the Council of the Nine are after us. All that means is we have our work cut out for us. Not just to save our skins—but to find the weapons to reclaim our blue planet."

Once again he turned toward the abyss. "Like it or not—" he stabbed his hand toward the purplish haze of the Outlands "—we're in this together."

DESTINY RUN, the next Outlanders saga from James Axler, is available in bookstores in September 1997.

Destiny Run

The harsh blast on a horn silenced the howling throng. The abrupt silence was broken by the clopping of unshod hooves and the squeak of saddle leather. Two mounted men approached the bonfire, through a path flanked by warriors and their women standing at respectful attention.

Flames played off the burnished iron scales of armor, winked from polished helmets. Though the two men rode abreast, Brigid didn't need Sverdlovsk to point out which figure was the Tushe Gun.

He was a head taller than his saddlemate, though the fanged bear skull mounted on top of his fur-trimmed helmet probably added a few inches to his height. A molded breast-plate of leather encased his torso and was reinforced by an interlocking pattern of metal scales. The long sword at his side, its scabbard set with gems, swung in rhythm to his dappled horse's prancing gait.

His face was strangely shaped, strangely shadowed, and it wasn't until he reined his mount to halt that Brigid realized he wore a mask. It was crafted of a thin layer of exquisitely carven jade—at least, it looked like jade because of its creamy green hue.

The mask covered his face from his hairline to just above his mouth, leaving only the lower lip and chin exposed. The mask held no particular expression, but from behind the curving eyelets glinted an imperious, hawklike gaze.

Sverdlovsk dropped to one knee and stuck out his tongue in the traditional Mongolian greeting and act of submission. The intent, expressionless scrutiny of the masked face was bent not upon the Russian but on Brigid. She tried to return the gaze with the same unblinking intensity.

The Tushe Gun spoke one word, a whisper she didn't understand. Sverdlovosk instantly sprang to his feet and whirled on her. "Grovel before the Avenging Lama," he snapped, and pounded a fist into the pit of her stomach.

Brigid bent double, hanging between the spear hafts, tears of pain clouding her vision but helping to dissolve more of the dried blood. She dragged in raspy lungfuls of air.

When she raised her head again, Bautu stood beside the Tushe Gun's horse, holding up the bundle of ordnance like an offering. The Tushe Gun poked and picked at the blasters with only a mild interest. He held up the transcom unit and spoke. His voice was resonant, but not particularly deep. It had a peculiar timbre, as if metal was grinding at the back of his throat. The language he used was Russian. "Does this function?"

When Brigid didn't respond, Sverdlovosk side-mouthed to her, "Answer the Avenging Lama."

"I don't know," she said, in Russian, despising the catch in her voice. "It may have been damaged when we were set upon."

The Tushe Gun dropped the transcom to the ground as if it were contaminated. He pricked his horse's flanks with his spurs and the animal lurched forward, hooves stamping on it. The casing broke with a crunch and a crack.

He took the blasters from the bundle, handed one to his companion and kept the other two, looping the gun belts over his saddle horn. Leaning forward, he said, "Tell me at once, woman. Why do you come here?"

"To explore, to trade. We meant no harm."

"How did you get here?"

"By ship."

"From America?"

"No, from China."

The Tushe Gun grunted softly. The blank mask stared.

"You did not come from the great Yurt. I would have heard about three travelers. I see falsehoods in your eyes, woman."

"I see nothing in yours," Brigid replied. "Take off your mask so I may look into your eyes, and perhaps we will talk."

Sverdlovosk's startled intake of breath made a high hissing sound between his teeth. The masked figure slowly stiffened in the saddle. When he spoke, his voice was hollow, toneless. "A thing is not hidden without reason, woman. Nor is it found without reason."

The Tushe Gun turned his horse's head away. "You are here to sap the flame within the Black City. Who sent you?"

"No one."

"I wish only to know that. A fox knows a great many things, a badger knows only one great thing. Who sent you?"

"Are you the badger?" she asked, "or the fox?"

The masked man did not reply to her question. To Sverdlovosk, he said, "Bautu will torture her until she speaks the truth. If she does not, she will feel the kiss of the dragon. You will watch and listen and report anything she says to me."

"Wait!" Brigid called. "You haven't heard everything. We sought only to make trading treaties—"

"I have heard enough." The Tushe Gun spoke over his shoulder. "Your people will come and your treaties will sap our strength and that of the Black City. I swore an oath to Shamos to fulfill our destiny."

Sverdlovosk said loudly, "Great Tushe, I have brought what you requested. Would you not care to inspect it?"

The jade face shifted toward the crates resting on the bed of the wag. "Unload them. Bring them to my yurt." His right hand jabbed toward the far end of the valley, and light glinted briefly from a ring on his gloved index finger. It was a massive ornament, made of thick, hammered silver, designed like a dragon coiled in four loops. The horned head was baleful and demonic of expression. The firelight made tiny, iridescent sparks dance within the eyes of yellow gemstones.

With a slight start of surprise, Brigid realized the configuration of the snarling dragon head corresponded to the mark on Bautu's forehead. It was almost as if the ring had been exposed to a flame and the superheated metal pressed into Bautu's flesh.

The Tushe Gun and his companion rode away, toward the scattering of yurts. Bautu grinned at Brigid, uncoiling his lash. As the Tushe Gun rode past, he directed a few garbled words at Bautu and the grin vanished from his face. The warrior hooked the whip onto his belt. He shouted and gestured to a pair of men at the bonfire and they joined him at the rear of the truck.

Sverdlovosk tucked his hands back into his pockets, watching the men untying the rope binders around the crates. Without looking at her, he said. "A respite, Baptiste. Not a reprieve."

She didn't answer.

Quietly he said, "Speak to me, Baptiste. Anything in Russian. Sound angry."

Brigid's mind raced. She groped for a phrase and she blurted, in a loud, sharp tone, "Russian vodka tastes like stump water."

Sverdlovosk wheeled on her, face contorted in anger. He took his right hand out of his pocket and closed it over her bound left wrist, shaking the spear haft. In a threatening whisper he asked, "Can you make it back to the Gateway?"

For a moment she was too startled to reply. Then, defiantly, she answered, "If I had transportation."

"The keys are in the wag." He spat contemptuously. "God help you if you're recaptured. I'll be howling for your blood just like the rest of these Tartar bastards."

Sverdlovosk removed his hand from her wrist, cuffed her

across the face and spun on his heel, marching toward the
men laboring to unload the crates. Brigid watched him go,
shouting and gesticulating imperiously with his arms. She
carefully folded her fingers over the small, open penknife
he had slipped into her palm.

Take
4 explosive books
plus a
mystery bonus
FREE

Mail to: Gold Eagle Reader Service
3010 Walden Ave.
P.O. Box 1394
Buffalo, NY 14240-1394

YEAH! Rush me 4 FREE Gold Eagle novels and my FREE mystery gift.
Then send me 4 brand-new novels every other month as they come off
the presses. Bill me at the low price of just $15.80* for each shipment—
a saving of 15% off the cover prices for all four books! There is NO extra
charge for postage and handling! There is no minimum number of books I
must buy. I can always cancel at any time simply by returning a shipment
at your cost or by returning any shipping statement marked "cancel." Even
if I never buy another book from Gold Eagle, the 4 free books and surprise
gift are mine to keep forever.

164 BPM A3U3

Name	(PLEASE PRINT)	
Address		Apt. No.
City	State	Zip

Signature (if under 18, parent or guardian must sign)

* Terms and prices subject to change without notice. Sales tax applicable in
NY. This offer is limited to one order per household and not valid to
present subscribers. Offer not available in Canada.

AC-96

James Axler

OUTLANDERS™

Trained by the ruling elite of post-holocaust America as a pureheart warrior, Kane is an enemy of the order he once served. He knows of his father's fate, he's seen firsthand the penalties, and yet a deep-rooted instinct drives him on to search for the truth. An exile to the hellzones, an outcast, Kane is the focus of a deadly hunt. But with brother-in-arms Grant, and Brigid Baptiste, keeper of the archives, he's sworn to light the dark past…and the world's fate. New clues hint that a terrifying piece of the puzzle is buried in the heart of Asia, where a descendant of the Great Khan wields awesome powers….

Available September 1997,
wherever Gold Eagle books are sold.

OUT-2